GALLERY WHISPERS

GALLERY WHISPERS

Quintin Jardine

HEADLINE

First published in 1999
by HEADLINE BOOK PUBLISHING

10 9 8 7 6 5 4 3 2 1

British Library Cataloguing in Publication Data

Jardine, Quintin
  Gallery whispers – (A Bob Skinner mystery)
  1. Skinner, Bob (Fictitious character) – Fiction
  2. Police – Fiction 3. Detective and mystery stories
  I. Title
  823.9'14[F]

ISBN 0 7472 1946 X (hardback)
ISBN 0 7472 6442 2 (trade paperback)

Typeset by Avon Dataset Ltd, Bidford-on-Avon, Warks

Printed and bound in Great Britain by
Clays Ltd, St Ives plc

HEADLINE BOOK PUBLISHING
A division of Hodder Headline PLC
338 Euston Road
London NW1 3BH

www.headline.co.uk
www.hodderheadline.com

This is for Eileen, who shines her light into dark places.

1

'How many feminists does it take to change a light bulb?'

She looked at him across the dinner table, with a light, indulgent smile. 'Okay,' she said, quietly. 'Let's have it.'

He beamed, in his small triumph. 'One.' He barked the word out, and in that instant his heavy eyebrows seemed to slam together in a frown. '. . . and that's not funny!'

Olive shook her head. 'You're not wrong there.'

Lauren, seated on his right, looked up at her father. 'I don't get that, Dad.'

He grinned. 'No, I suppose you're still a couple of years short of getting it.'

'Oh,' said the child. 'Do you have to be twelve before you can be a feminist?'

Neil gazed down at her, bland innocence written on her small round face, and realised yet again that if ever there was a mother's daughter it was Lauren Barbara McIlhenney.

A small hand tugged at his shirt-sleeve. 'Daddy, Daddy!' Spencer shouted, eagerly. 'Did you hear the one about the Hearts supporter who went into a pub with an alligator?'

He laughed as he ruffled his son's thick fair hair. 'Aye, I did, Spence, often. The first time I heard it, it was a Celtic supporter that had the alligator. Don't you go telling that sort of joke outside, though. You could get into real trouble if the wrong lad heard you.'

'And you could get into real trouble if the wrong woman heard you tell that other one,' Olive countered. 'Wherever did you pick it up anyway?'

'From Karen Neville.'

'Neville? Isn't she the new DS in Andy Martin's office?'

'That's the one. Not so new now, though. She's been there a right few weeks now.'

'Mum, can Spence and me leave the table? It's nearly time for the Holiday programme.'

She turned to her daughter and raised an eyebrow. It was enough.

'Sorry. May Spence and I leave the table?'

1

'That's better. Have both of you finished all your homework?'

Lauren and Spencer nodded in tandem.

'Very well; you may.'

Neil McIlhenney gazed at his children as they ran from the small dining room and across the hall. 'A gentleman's family,' his father-in-law, Joe Baxter, had pronounced after Spencer's birth. Son and daughter. One of each.

'I'll get the coffee,' he said, rising from his carver chair. 'You want milk in yours, or just black?'

'Have we any of that Bailey's left?' she asked him. 'If so, I'll take some of that in it.' He nodded.

Olive, in her turn, watched her husband as he left the room. Neil wasn't exactly fat, but over the thirteen years of their marriage, he had gained over two stone. Sure, he had a massive frame to carry it, but still, every time she thought of Chic, his father, and remembered the sudden awfulness of his death at the party for Spencer's christening, she felt a pang of fear for him. Chic had been fifty-four, a big, bulky man like his son. And he was only two years short of forty.

Without warning she felt another type of pang as the cough reflex kicked in.

Neil, in the kitchen, heard the paroxysm, then the quick puff of the inhaler as the fit settled down. This wasn't right; it wasn't bloody right. Anybody who knew them well would have realised that, simply by the fact that he was there making the coffee. Everyone in their circle knew that Olive couldn't stand his bloody coffee. Christ, she'd told them often enough. He either used too much or not enough, or ruined it by putting in too much milk, or made it straight from a boiling kettle and damn near scalded her. Now here she was letting him make the Kenco without a murmur. Indeed it was not bloody right.

'D'you not think you should go back to the doctor?' he asked, as he set a mug, its contents heavily laced with the last of the Irish cream liqueur, on the coaster which lay before her on the table.

She shot him the stare; the full, high-intensity spine-chiller that he knew so well, the laser look she could snap on in an instant. 'Olive's Silencer', her colleagues called it in the staff-room, in their awe at her ability to bring order to the rowdiest class without ever raising her voice.

'No I do not,' she retorted. 'I have asthma. The doctor's told me that, and she's given me my inhaler. She warned me that the cough would come and go.'

'It's the "go" part that I'm concerned about, love. Surely she could give you something that would settle it a bit quicker.'

'I'll be all right,' she snapped. 'Now pack it in. Change the subject. What sort of a day did you have? What's the news on the Chief?'

Neil backed off, for that moment at least. 'He's coming on,' he said. 'The boss says that he has another appointment with the heart specialist in Spain next Tuesday. If that goes okay they'll let him come home, provided that they take at least three days for the journey and that Lady Proud does most of the driving.'

'When will he be back at work?'

'There's no news on that yet. I understand from the boss that one of the force examiners will have to pass him fit before he can come back. The moment can't come soon enough for Big Bob, I can tell you. He hates every day he spends in that office.'

Olive smiled. 'I'm sure he's just saying that, in case anyone thinks he's trying to undermine the Chief. He's probably loving it, really.'

Her husband shook his head. 'DCC Skinner is many things, but he ain't that subtle. He doesn't like being tied to a desk, and he never will. I'm his executive assistant. I know this.'

'What if the Chief doesn't come back?' she asked. 'What would he do then?'

'Ah, but the Chief will be back. It was only a mild heart attack. They've put him on light medication and given him a diet.'

He paused, and she seized her chance. 'Speaking of diets, Neil McIlhenney; you could do with losing some weight.'

Elbows on the table, shoulders hunched, head bowed, he looked across at her; his look this time, out from under his heavy, beetling eyebrows with a secret smile that went right into her soul, and told her, far more eloquently than the words which now they used to each other only occasionally, how much he loved her.

'Christ,' he rumbled in his slow, deep voice. 'She sits there with bloody Bailey's in her coffee, and tells me to lose weight!'

2

He watched her as she slept. She lay on her right side, and although he could not see her face, he knew that her hand would be on the pillow, the thumb gently brushing her lips in an unconscious gesture which he had always guessed was a relic of a childhood habit. Her dark hair, thick and wavy, tousled at the ends from their energetic love-making, clung to her neck and shoulders.

Her back was to him as he looked at her, admiring the curve of her hip in profile against the street light which shone outside their curtained window. He had lain like this often before, sometimes unable to keep from touching her, from running a finger-tip softly down her spine, knowing what it did to her and that within a few minutes she would be awake and they would be locked together again.

Yet on this night her turned back seemed to him to be a rejection, for all her commitment in their coupling only a few hours before. It had been satisfying for each of them, yet there had been none of the sense of spiritual union which they had known at the beginning of their partnership. That was one of the things which had set her apart from the other women who had lain in his bed, before he had found her and she had tamed him. Yet now it was, at best misplaced, or worse, he feared, lost.

'What's the matter?'

She did not stir as she spoke her question, but her voice was clear, and wide-awake.

'Nothing,' he answered, softly. 'I'm just thinking, that's all.'

'About what?'

'Och, just the job. You know.'

'But the job's been quiet for the last wee while.' She paused. 'Are you still having flashbacks to that man with the gun?'

He shook his head at once. 'No. Absolutely not. That's only happened to me that one time, a couple of days after it happened.'

'Something else then?' She rolled on to her back and looked up at him, frowning. 'Not Ariel, surely.'

He smiled at her concern: a small, sad smile. 'No, no; not her. That

4

was a long time ago, and she's dead. She never really existed, in fact.'

'Ah but she did. And so did her brother. Once or twice . . . no, more than that . . . I've wakened in the night thinking of him, and had to hang on to you, to drive the fright away.'

'Nonetheless, they're in the past.'

'So?' she demanded. 'What's bugging you?'

'Nothing,' he insisted. 'I just can't sleep.'

No one could snort like Alex. 'Andy Martin,' she exclaimed, as she propped herself up on both elbows. 'You are one of the world's great sleepers. If you are lying awake in the dark, there is some reason for it. Come on, out with it.'

He reached out his left hand to cup her breast, but she shied away from him. 'That won't work. Tell me, what's the problem?'

He looked into her eyes. 'I think we might be.'

She frowned, quickly. 'Rubbish,' she said at once, but there was a defensiveness in her voice which proved she didn't believe her own denial.

He reached out his hand again, touching her forehead as if to rub away the frown lines. 'Alexis Skinner,' he whispered. 'You can tell me all night that there's nothing wrong, but you still won't make either of us believe it. I'm afraid . . . and I mean that literally, because it does scare me . . . that you and I are losing our way.

'When we got together, we had a shared vision of what we wanted: each other, above all else. I still feel that way. If I had to I'd give up everything I have, and walk away from everything I've achieved, just to be with you.

'But you've changed.'

'I haven't,' she protested. 'I love you just as much as I always did. I want you just as much.'

'Then why do you keep changing your mind about marrying me?'

'I haven't. Anyway, that's not the issue.'

He grunted. 'No, it's not, is it. It's the issue that's the issue.'

'Ah, now we're getting to it.' She fired back at him, suddenly. 'You're still on about the baby thing. I thought we'd agreed that we'd start thinking about a family in five years.'

'Aye,' he said, 'but there's a basic principle wrapped up in there, isn't there, about levels of commitment to each other.'

Her frown was back. 'Ah,' she countered. 'Andy says that he'd walk away from everything for Alex, so she must say the same thing. Is that it?' It was his turn to look defensive. 'That's sentimental, emotional, hypothetical crap, and not worthy of you. You've had achievements; you've got a successful career that you say you'd give up for love; well, good for you, boy. But surely I'm entitled to some professional

5

fulfilment of my own? Or are you really and truly saying that you expect me to put aside all my ambitions to satisfy your need to extend your line?'

'Hey, hey,' he soothed her. 'I'm not saying that at all. Apart from your dad, there's no one who thinks more of your ability and your potential than I do. I'm sorry about going back to the baby thing. That was a cheap shot. Listen, if you want to become the managing partner of Curle Anthony and Jarvis, I'll back you all the way. If you want to become a QC, I'm all for that too.

'I don't begrudge you your ambitions, my darling. But I'm coming to believe that as you pursue them, you'll leave me behind; you'll outgrow me. I'm afraid that's starting to happen already. When we got together you were a student. Now you've been marked out for stardom within your firm. And I can see the effect it's having on you.

'For the last few days, there have been times when I've had the feeling that you've been trying to distance yourself from me in some way. Deny it if you will, but that's how I see it. and I can only blame it on one thing; Curle Anthony and bloody Jarvis.'

He shifted his weight on his elbow. 'Listen, I do my job damn well, I think, and I'm completely committed to it, but I'm not in love with it. You are with yours. One day you may feel that you have to choose between it and me, and maybe that day's coming close. That's what keeps me awake at night.'

She leaned over and kissed him. 'Would it help if we got married next month?' she asked.

He looked sadder than ever. 'No, love, it wouldn't. If my fears are real, it wouldn't change a damn thing. You have to be all you can be, with, or if it has to be, without me. You're your father's daughter, and I can't change that.'

'So what are you saying?'

He gave a sigh so deep that her hair moved on its breeze. 'I suppose I'm asking myself whether it will hurt even more later than it would if we split now . . . if I backed off to let you concentrate full time on your career.

'I know how I would feel about it. But maybe for both our sakes, you should ask yourself the same question.' He looked at her solemn face, at her averted eyes. 'Yes, maybe you—'

As if it had been waiting for the perfect moment to intervene, the bedside phone burst into life. 'Fucking thing has a mind of its own,' Martin snarled, but still he turned to pick it up. 'Yes!' he snapped.

'Sorry Andy,' said Brian Mackie, on the other end of the line, 'but I've just had a call out to a suspicious death, in a steading development out near Whitekirk. From what I've been told it's a murder for sure. I'm just leaving for the scene. Do you want to turn out?'

The Head of CID looked at his fiancée, hating what he saw in her eyes. 'Aye,' he answered. 'I think that would be a good idea.'

3

James Andrew Skinner had always been, by any reasonable measurement, a considerate child. But cutting back teeth can upset the calmest temperament, so Sarah and Bob had shared floor-walking duties until finally, at around five am, their younger son had settled down.

They had been asleep themselves for little more than an hour when Brian Mackie had called, to ask Sarah if she could attend the scene of the Whitekirk death.

Bob sat at the kitchen table, nursing his first coffee of the day, watching his wife as she fed frozen bread into the four-slice toaster. He grinned at her. 'I never fail to be impressed by the way you can eat breakfast before you go out to look at a body.'

She turned towards him, returning his smile. 'Ah, but it doesn't always stay down,' she countered. 'Remember that one in Advocates' Close, before we were married?'

Skinner shuddered as the vision of that wet November morning reprinted itself in his mind's eye, for the thousandth time. 'How could I ever forget it? I was perfectly okay at murder scenes up until then, but from that moment on I haven't looked at a victim without feeling queasy.'

'Think yourself lucky then. Now you're Deputy Chief Constable . . . acting Chief, even . . . you don't have to do that any more.'

He knew that her remark was bait, but he rose to it nonetheless. 'Not so. I'll always lead from the front as long as I'm in this job, you know that. I might be past my sell-by date when it comes to looking at people who've been burned to a crisp or had their brains blown all over the walls, but it doesn't mean I'll run away from the duty if I think that it's required of me.

'It doesn't matter what office I'm in, if I think it'll help the effort or if I feel that it's expected of me, I'll be there.'

Her eyes narrowed, very slightly. 'What? "It doesn't matter what office I'm in",' she threw back at him. 'Hey, what happened to all that stuff about you not wanting to be a Chief Constable? Are you getting to enjoy sitting in Jimmy's chair?'

He smiled again, this time at her sharpness in leading him onto her hook. He accepted the slice of buttered toast which she offered him, and took a bite. 'I'll never enjoy sitting in Jimmy's chair,' he said finally. 'Precisely because it is his chair. I want to see him make a full recovery from this heart scare, and come back to work. Then I want him to stay in post . . . health permitting .·. . right up to retirement age.

'When it is time for him to go, I'll think seriously about my own ambitions; and my obligations even, to my force and my family. But just between you and me, over the last couple of weeks, I've been asking myself how I'd feel about someone else doing the job.'

'And how would you?' Sarah asked.

'Well,' he answered. 'I've been thinking through the likely candidates. There's not one of them couldn't get both feet into one of Sir James's shoes, far from filling them both. It would be very difficult for me to work with anyone else, apart maybe, from Willie Haggerty in Strathclyde . . . and there isn't a cat's chance of him getting it.'

'So you will go for the job when Jimmy retires?'

'Unless I decide to quit at the same time as him.'

She was rarely surprised by him, not any more, but as she looked at him astonishment shone in her big hazel eyes. 'You wouldn't do that. You're wedded to the force.'

He stood up, laughing lightly and took her in his arms. 'Wrong, Doctor Sarah Grace Skinner. I am wedded to you and no one else, and from now on I will do what's best for us and not me. For all I might chunter on to big Neil about being tied to a desk, I have never been as happy with my life as I am right now. That's because of the rock it's built on, namely you and the kids.'

'McIlhenney, eh,' she mused. 'I'll bet you're giving him a hard time just now. How's he doing? I haven't seen him for a few weeks.'

'I'm not giving him a hard time at all. Mind you, he has been a bit quiet lately; probably feeling as desk-bound as me. I'll cure that, though; I've got a job lined up for him.'

'What, out of your office?'

'No. Representing my office. It'll mean guaranteed nine-to-five working for a while so Olive will like it too.'

'Sounds like a departure for Neil. You'll have him carrying a briefcase next. What is it?'

'Just something I've cooked up with the other chiefs. It's a national problem but it's been agreed that we'll co-ordinate it. I'm going to talk to him and Andy about it today.' He squeezed her bottom, then turned her towards the door. 'That's all I can tell you about it: it's cloak and dagger stuff. So now, you'd better take your wee bag and get off to certify Mackie's stiff.

9

'If Andy turns up at the scene, tell him I want to see him this morning; ask him to tie up a time for a meeting with Gerry.'

'I'll do that,' she said, nodding as she spoke. 'Are you sure you're okay to stay here until the nanny arrives?'

'Yeah, that's fine.'

'Good, because if the guys want a quick postmortem, I might just go straight on into Edinburgh and do it myself.'

4

Even in the dark of the late autumn morning, Sarah reached Oldbarns, finding her way along the twisting country roads which she knew so well, in only fifteen minutes. Nestling on the edge of a wood a mile south of the hamlet of Whitekirk, it was one of a number of previously abandoned steadings throughout East Lothian which had been rescued by private developers and returned to use as homes.

In its transformed existence, the occupants were no longer farm workers; instead they tended to be city dwellers who had developed a middle-aged hankering for country life.

She could see the blue lights of the ambulance and the police vehicles ahead of her as she steered her Freelander carefully along the narrow, tree-lined approach way from the A198. She came to a halt next to a patrol car, its Day-glo flashes shining in her headlights until she switched them off.

The death house was at the end of one of three rows of terraced cottages, built of red stone blocks, with black slate roofs. Lights shone in all but one of the dwellings, which formed three sides of a rectangle, around an open green space. The fourth was a long barn, which had been adapted to provide covered parking. As she glanced around the small community, faces looked back at her from several windows.

Detective Superintendent Brian Mackie stood in the doorway as she walked up the path. 'Hello Sarah,' he said, nodding his bald, domed head in greeting. 'They always seem to happen at night, don't they. Your client's through in the back.'

She stepped inside, following him across the entrance hall and through a door at the other side, into a big farmhouse style kitchen. There a figure sat, slumped in a varnished captain's chair, drawn up to a heavy oak table.

The woman had her back to Sarah. Her head, which lolled on her right shoulder, was covered by a clear plastic bag. Like the hood of a hanged man, it was tight around the neck; secured not by a rope, but by heavy black adhesive tape.

'When was she found?'

11

Mackie glanced at his watch. 'Just over two hours ago. They have a milk round out here, believe it or not. The guy was putting the pinta on the front doorstep, and looked through the window.' He nodded towards closed double doors behind him. 'Those lead through to the dining room. They were open, and he could look right through. There was enough light from that table lamp over there to let him see what had happened.

'Milkmen have mobile phones these days, so he called us right away. The two officers from the car outside broke in through the back door and found her.'

'So what made you ring the bell for a full-scale murder investigation?' Taken by surprise, Sarah and the superintendent looked back towards the kitchen door, through which Andy Martin had come silently into the room. 'I've seen suicides that looked like this, plastic bag and all.'

'The black tape, sir,' said Mackie. formal in the presence of the uniformed woman constable who stood behind the Head of CID. 'Bright young PC Cowan here reckoned that if the woman had fastened the tape round her own neck, there would have been a roll of the stuff and scissors, lying on the table in front of her.

'As you can see, there isn't. PC Cowan even put on her gloves and had a look in all the drawers and cupboards. It's not there either.'

'Fair enough.' The chief superintendent nodded. 'Good work, constable,' he said to the girl at his side. 'Mr Mackie will make sure that your divisional commander hears of this.' He turned back to the other detective. 'Are Arthur Dorward's lot on the way?'

'Yes.'

'In that case we'd all better get our big feet out of here and avoid contaminating this scene any further. Doctor, can you certify death without disturbing the plastic bag? I want to leave her until she's been photographed.'

'Sure.' Sarah laid her small case on the table, opened it and took out a pen-light. *What's wrong with Andy?* she thought as she crouched down beside the body. *He hasn't called me 'Doctor' in years.*

The dead woman's eyes were open. There was no flicker of reaction when she shone the torch on her pupils. 'There's no fear in her expression,' she said, quietly, to the two detectives as she worked. 'She looks perfectly calm.' She held her wrist for a few moments, confirming the absence of pulse, then looked closely at it, and at the other. 'No marks on her either; at least none that I can see. Nothing to indicate that she's been restrained while this was done, then untied afterwards.'

Sarah looked into the woman's face once more. In life she had been attractive, in her early middle age, with dark hair showing only a few strands of grey. Then something caught her eye; something so incongruous that she kicked herself mentally for not noticing it right away.

'Andy. Brian. She's wearing make-up.' She lifted one of the dead wrists and sniffed at it. 'And perfume too. If you look in her bedroom, you'll probably find a bottle or a spray of a fragrance called Joy.

'Whatever happened to this lady, she got herself dolled up for it.' She leaned forward and peered closely at the plastic bag. 'Oh yes,' she whispered, 'that tells me a lot.'

She stood up and closed her bag. 'Okay,' she pronounced, her voice sharp and professional once more. 'You have formal certification of death. About four hours ago, I'd say; subject to autopsy confirmation.'

'The cause of death will turn out to be asphyxiation, I assume,' said Martin, as Mackie ushered them from out of the kitchen, to await the arrival of Detective Inspector Arthur Dorward and his squad of crime scene technicians.

'Don't assume,' Sarah replied. 'I could see no marks on the plastic bag. If she'd suffocated, I'd expect to find lipstick smears, from where she'd tried to suck in air.'

'Maybe she didn't try,' the Head of CID suggested.

'She didn't: but not because she had willed herself to stop breathing. You can't do that; it's a reflex. There's something else here. I'd say that this woman died, or at least became deeply unconscious, before she had a chance to suffocate.

'I'll tell you the whole story after the autopsy. D'you want me to do it, or do you want Joe Hutchison in on this one?'

'You do it, Sarah,' said Martin. 'If you feel you need a second opinion, call him in, but you handle it in the first instance. You've picked up the ball, so run with it as far as you can.' He turned to Mackie. 'Who was she, Brian?'

'The owner of the cottage is a Mrs Gaynor Weston. I'm assuming that's her in there. But that's all I have for now. Maggie Rose should be here soon, with some CID reinforcements. She'll direct the interviews with the neighbours and so on. Once Arthur's people have dusted the place fully, I'll look for personal papers, and see what they tell me.

'The first thing we'll need to do is locate a next of kin.'

'Too right,' the Head of CID agreed. 'When we do we'll need to be careful how much information we give. From the way this looks, the next of kin, or another close relative, could be the prime suspect.

'This woman was killed by someone close to her; someone she trusted.'

'And . . .' said Sarah, quietly, 'she was a willing victim.'

'So that means . . .'

She cut Mackie short. 'Yes, it means that this looks like an assisted suicide.'

'I agree.' Andy Martin frowned. 'But that's not what the Procurator Fiscal will call it. There's no such thing in the eyes of the law. The charge here will be murder, and the penalty will be life imprisonment.'

5

'How did it look out at Oldbarns, Andy?' Skinner asked, as his Head of CID settled into a low chair around the coffee table in the Chief Constable's office, just after midday.

'Very neat and orderly, boss,' Martin replied. 'The victim is a forty-three year old woman, Gaynor Weston. She was a training consultant, self-employed. Lived alone; divorced from her husband, Professor Nolan Weston, seven years ago. Next of kin is Raymond Weston, her only son, aged eighteen, just started his first term at Aberdeen University.

'Mrs Weston was seated at her kitchen table with a bag over her head, secured tightly by black tape.

'There was no sign of forced entry to the house, and nothing appeared to have been disturbed. Dorward's people found two plates, cups, saucers and cutlery in the dishwasher. It had been run, though; every damn thing in it was fingerprint-free. There were two long-stemmed wine glasses on the draining board, and an empty bottle of Mouton Cadet on the table. Each of the glasses still had traces of wine in them, and one had lipstick on the rim, the same shade as Mrs Weston's. The team tried to lift prints from them, but they were too badly smeared.'

'What about the bag?' Skinner grunted.

'It was strong, clear polythene, unmarked. No brand name on it, no store name; nothing at all. There were no others like it in the house or in the garden shed, nor was there any sign of the black tape. We've looked everywhere now; someone took it away, for sure.'

'Probably brought it too. The ex: what do we know about him? What does he Profess? Do we know yet?'

Martin nodded. 'Brian Mackie had all that before ten o'clock this morning. He's a surgeon. He has a chair at Edinburgh University, and works mostly at the Western General Hospital.'

'Mmm. Divorced for seven years, you say. Did Mrs Weston have any man friends?'

'Apparently so. Maggie found a neighbour, a Ms Joan Ball, another single woman, who claims to have been a close pal. According to her,

Mrs Weston was having a relationship with one of her clients, a guy called Terry Futcher. He runs an advertising agency, and he's married.

'The husband was still around, as well. They stayed friends after the split . . .'

'Do we know why they were divorced?' the DCC asked.

'It seems to have been her idea. She told Joan Ball that she just wanted her own space. She wanted the freedom to be herself, she said. After they parted, the boy stayed with his father during the school term and with her during the holidays. The Prof has a cottage up in the Highlands and occasionally the three of them went up there together.

'He'd visit her at the steading on occasion too. Joan Ball knew not to call on her when she saw his car there . . . or Futcher's for that matter.'

'And did these cars stay all night?'

'Of course.'

'Did she see any cars there last night?'

'No, she didn't,' Martin replied. 'She was out herself, and got home well after midnight. She said that Gaynor's lights were on, but other than her own, there was no car at the door. She'd have noticed if either of the blokes were there.'

'Did the Prof know about Futcher?'

'Yes. But Ms Ball didn't think that the boyfriend knew about him.'

Skinner shook his steel-grey head. 'Shit. Two-timing the married boyfriend with the single ex-husband. That's a nice twist.'

Martin smiled, suddenly and wickedly. 'Who said the ex is single?' he asked. 'Professor Weston married his secretary five years ago.'

'Jesus!' The acting Chief Constable laughed out loud. 'Two cheated wives, a cuckolded lover, and an ex-husband with a guilty secret. There seems to have been a whole queue of people with a reason to top this woman.'

'Except,' countered the Head of CID, 'that Sarah's thinking, and mine, is that Gaynor Weston topped herself, with assistance. Now why would she want to do that? According to Joan Ball's account, she was living the life of Reilly.'

'Could you and Sarah be wrong?'

The DCS frowned at his friend. 'The postmortem may show that, but I don't think so.'

'Then I hate the sound of this one,' Skinner said. 'Unless we get a clear DNA link to the helper . . . suppose they made love before they did it . . . it could be a bastard to prove. Christ, I almost wish this person had been just a wee bit cleverer; hadn't left the second glass, and most of all that the bugger had left that roll of black tape

16

. . . stuck, preferably, to Mrs Weston's fingers.

'If he . . . or she . . . had done that simple thing, we'd be reporting this one as a suicide, and saving ourselves a lot of work; and probably grief.'

He frowned. 'Did she leave a note?'

'No. We turned the place inside out; even looked in her computer. Nothing at all.'

'Apart from her gentlemen callers, did Mrs Weston have a big circle of friends?'

Yes. Her diary was chock-full.'

'In that event, all those people will have to be checked out . . . as indeed will the very helpful Ms Ball, if she's as close a pal as she told Brian. At the moment she's our only witness. I wonder if she has a roll of black tape in her toolbox?'

'Let's wait for good Doctor Sarah's postmortem report, said Martin. 'Once we have that we'll have a better idea of the basis of our investigation. If we do find ourselves with a lot of interviewing to do, I'll give Brian extra resources to handle it, if he needs them.'

The Head of CID looked across to the far end of the big room, as Gerry Crossley, the Chief Constable's secretary, came in carrying a tray with two mugs and a plate of biscuits. 'Apart from all that, though, sir,' he said, as the young man placed the tray on the coffee table, 'why did you want to see me?'

'I want to brief you on something that's developed. And to ask your view on what I intend to do about it.' He paused, as the door closed behind the secretary. 'I've called a meeting of heads of Special Branch from all eight Scottish police forces; two o'clock this afternoon, in this building.

'But before I get round to that, let's deal with the really important stuff. Sarah called me from Edinburgh Royal, while she was waiting for the body to arrive from Oldbarns. She said that she was worried about you; that you weren't yourself this morning.

'I can tell just from looking at you that she's right. What's up, son?'

Martin picked up his mug, took a sip to test the temperature, then a mouthful. He held it, cradled in both hands, for several seconds, staring across the room and out of the long window. Finally his gaze swung round to Skinner.

'It's Alex and me,' he said, at last. 'We're in bother. I think we might be breaking up.'

There was an edge to the silence which filled the room. Andy looked at his friend, trying to gauge his reaction.

'Anybody else involved?' Bob asked quietly.

'Yes,' Martin replied. 'But not in the sense you mean. Mitchell

Laidlaw's the problem; Laidlaw, and the mighty firm of Curle Anthony and Jarvis. With every day she spends there, Alex's ambitions are becoming more clear. Before she graduated, they were vague, and involved going to the Bar.

'Under Mitch's influence she's become hooked on litigation. That's the specialist area she wants to follow, and being Alex, she's only interested in becoming the best there is.'

'Do you begrudge her that?'

'No, I don't. But her ambition and my hopes for the two of us don't fit together any more. We've been dancing around this for a while now. This morning I brought it to a head. I asked her whether she wants to break off our engagement to concentrate on her career.'

Skinner gasped. 'That's a bit heavy, Andy, isn't it?'

'Maybe it is. But she didn't say "no".'

The silence returned, ever more palpable. Bob stood up, walked over to the window and looked out. 'Is this purely about Alex?' he asked, quietly. 'Or does her mother come into it too?'

'What d'you mean?'

'You know bloody well what I mean. You tell me you see her career as a rival; but are you coloured in that by what you know about Myra? Let's not piss about: Alex's mother was a serial adulteress. Are you asking yourself whether this new-found ambition of hers, this lusting after something other than you, might be some sort of genetic inheritance setting itself free?'

Martin threw back his head. 'Jesus, Bob!' The words burst out in a great gasp.

'Alex isn't a bit like her mother. It's you she takes after, and that's what really worries me. I'm sorry to be so blunt, but all that time that Myra was screwing around, you hadn't the faintest idea of it, because you were so wrapped up in the job. If she hadn't been killed, your marriage would probably have gone on.'

Skinner snorted. 'You think it would have survived her being pregnant by another man?'

'Sure. She'd either have had the kid aborted without your know-ledge, or she'd just have told you that it was yours. You'd never have doubted that for a second.'

The big man's eyes narrowed. 'So my family's subordinate to my job is it?' he whispered.

'No it's not,' Martin snapped. 'Not any more. You've sorted out your priorities. But you've done it from a position at the top of the tree. Alex hasn't, and she's only just started to climb. I hadn't thought of it this way before, but if I think of you and Myra, then look at Alex and me, the roles are reversed.

'I'm not saying for one moment that I'm afraid Alex will start sleeping around: but sometimes I'm not so sure about me.'

'Ahh Christ,' said Skinner wearily, shaking his head. 'Life's never easy, pal, is it. Look take it from me, my daughter loves you. Do you love her?'

'Of course.'

'Well? Isn't that enough?'

'That's what I'm asking Alex. So far, I've had no answer, just silence. And to me, that's speaking volumes.'

6

There is nothing especially mysterious about Special Branch. Every police force has such a unit within its organisation, and they link loosely together into a network which is responsible for protecting the public against subversion, terrorism and other threats outside the bounds of run-of-the-mill criminal activity.

Nevertheless, looking at the eight officers, seven men and one woman, who were seated at the conference table as he came into the room, Bob Skinner experienced an unusual sense of personal power, and pride. He was Chief Constable only on a temporary basis, during the absence of Sir James Proud, struck down by a mild heart attack while on holiday in Spain. Sir John Govan, the outgoing Strathclyde Chief, and new security adviser to the Secretary of State, could easily have assumed command of the operation he was about to outline, and yet it was Govan himself who had proposed Skinner for the task.

'Bob has a track record in this type of situation,' he had said. 'The rest of us are pen-pushers by comparison, so let's all of us agree to put our people under his command until this crisis is resolved.'

Skinner and the two men who had accompanied him into the room took their places at the head of the table. As they did so, the eight others looked at them in complete surprise. The DCC scanned their faces. Detective Inspector Mario McGuire, his own Special Branch chief, Superintendent Harry McGuigan from Strathclyde, then Lorraine Morrison, from Tayside, Walter Paton, from Central, Joe Impey from Dumfries and Galloway, Brian Burns from Fife, Andrew Macintosh, from Grampian and Ian Evans from Northern, detective inspectors all.

'Good afternoon, people,' he said briskly. 'Welcome to Fettes, and thank you all for getting here promptly.

'I know that in your roles as heads of Special Branch, you maintain regular contact with each other, so wholesale introductions aren't necessary. However, for those of you who don't know my companions, the officer on my right is Detective Chief Superintendent Andy Martin, my Head of CID, and on my left is Detective Sergeant Neil McIlhenney, my Executive Assistant.

20

'Mr Martin is here as my deputy in these matters. I'll explain DS McIlhenney's role later. Now, to business. All of you, even Mario McGuire, my own head of Special Branch, thought that this was going to be an ordinary liaison meeting. It isn't, and for that small deception, I apologise.

'So why the hell are you here? Don't worry, I'm going to tell you, but first, I want to say this. You all work on a confidential basis, and know the importance of keeping your mouths shut. This meeting isn't just confidential, it's Top Secret. Neither its existence nor its subject are to be discussed with anyone, other than members of this group, or with your own Chief Constables. In this instance, all of you are working directly under my command, so that's an order.'

He picked up McGuire's glance. 'Yes, Mario, that applies to you too. I know your wife's a Detective Chief Inspector, but she doesn't need to know about this.'

Skinner looked round the table. 'You'll all remember a couple of years ago, when we had major problems here in Edinburgh with a gang of terrorists at the Festival.' There was a general murmur of confirmation round the table, and a few nods.

'Well this time, we may have something similar on our hands.

'Like all of you,' he continued, 'I'm part of a secret network. Mr Martin, Neil and Mario are aware of this, and now you should be too, if only so that you understand the strength of what we're dealing with here. Sir John Govan may have taken over from me as the Secretary of State's security adviser and good luck to him . . .' Only Martin and McIlhenney caught the edge of bitterness in Skinner's tone. '. . . but that doesn't affect my links with, or my position within, M15.'

He paused, to let his words sink in. 'Last weekend, the Director General had a call from his opposite number in the Secret Intelligence Service. The Cold War may be long behind us, but as we've seen all too often, that doesn't make the world a less dangerous place, or take away the need to gather knowledge of potential threats to our national interests.

'There are some people out there who are potential threats to everyone. They're for hire, and the skill they sell is violence. The media call them international terrorists, but that's too broad a description. Very few of them are motivated by creed or belief; their driving force is large lumps of cash paid into Swiss bank accounts. They are not street criminals. You won't find them behind any gang murders, not in the States, not here, not in Russia, not anywhere.

'They are what the boys in the CIA really do call wet workers; assassins for hire to take out political and other targets. There are no formal qualifications required, but in fact most of them are ex-special forces.

'All of the major intelligence services have a list of these people. They know who they are, where they're based, the identities they use, the type of job they handle. There's a database in Langley which lists them all, and which even shows their operational records. We have partial access to it.' He smiled, softly. 'Partial, because the CIA is understandably shy about even us getting to know which projects they've sponsored themselves.

'As far as possible, these subjects are kept under constant observation by the Western Intelligence services, who in this instance at least pool resources and information. But they're good, these folk; they're aware of that, and whenever they've got something cooking, they simply drop out of sight, to reappear, maybe somewhere else, maybe under another name once the job's done. These patterns of movement actually give a good picture of who was behind what. They also give the intelligence community a clear idea when a project is under way.'

Skinner looked round the table. 'That's what's happened here,' he said. 'The message which M16 passed to Five a few days ago, concerned the disappearance of one Michael Hawkins from surveillance in Cape Town.' He looked around the table once more.

'Michael Hawkins is the current identity of a man formerly known, during his service with the South African army, as Hencke van Roost. Using a variety of names, other than those, he has completed projects for the intelligence services of five different countries, and for at least six political or fundamentalist organisations.

'His credits include the assassination by bomb, a few years back, of an Asian Head of State, a shooting in Dublin which was thought to be gang-related but which in fact was carried out for political reasons, and the elimination of a very high-profile international public figure . . . Guess who? . . . in which the official verdict was accidental death.

'When one of these people goes to ground, then naturally enough the intelligence services want to know why . . . unless one of them already knows, in which case the word is passed discreetly to the sponsor's friends.

'When Hawkins slipped his surveillance it took everyone by surprise. The first thought was that he had a role in the recent US Embassy bombings in Africa, and was running for his life, or indeed that he might already have lost it. But the US scotched that one. The Osama bin Laden terror group did have a specialist adviser in those incidents, but he was taken out in the initial missile strike on Afghanistan.

'The Americans, however, did volunteer information from one of their people, a woman who they had infiltrated into Hawkins' close circle . . . that's their description; you work out what it means. This was quite a gesture on their part, since they've had to pull that agent out of South Africa altogether, now that she's been exposed.

'She gave them one clue, that was all. The only thing Hawkins said when she asked him where he was going.

'He told her "I'm flying north for the winter".' Skinner paused. 'For the winter, he said. That could be significant.'

'I appreciate, lady and gentlemen, that it could also mean anything, and as I speak the search for Hawkins is going on all over Europe, and in the US. However there is a strong possibility that he might be coming here. I'll explain that later. For now . . .' He turned to McIlhenney. 'Neil, if you would.'

The big sergeant stood and walked to the far end of the table, where a slide projector stood. 'Old-fashioned technology,' Skinner apologised, as his assistant flicked off the conference room lights and switched on the projector. On the portable screen opposite a face appeared; a young man, in his early twenties, with reddish blond hair, staring seriously at the camera.

'This is Hencke van Roost,' said the DCC, 'as he looked when he enlisted in the South African Army at the age of twenty-three. Before he signed on he completed an engineering degree at Massachusetts Institute of Technology. He comes from a wealthy family, does our man. His father, who died a few years back, was a rancher and wine producer.'

McIlhenney pressed the button of the remote changer and the carousel turned, revealing a second photograph. 'He's still van Roost in this one,' Skinner continued, 'four years into his army service. By now he's a captain in Special Forces. This was taken on an operation in Namibia. The CIA agent copied it.' The man was bare chested, wearing only green shorts, socks, and heavy boots. His hair was bleached even more fair than it had been in the earlier image and he was smiling. A sub-machine gun was slung over his shoulder and three black men lay, sprawled awkwardly in death, at his feet.

He nodded to his assistant, who moved on to the next slide. 'She copied this one too,' he said, as the watchers gasped. The South African's grin was even wider. Again he was bare-chested, his muscles standing out impressively in the sunlight as he stood, flanked by his fellow soldiers. There was a machete stuck in his belt, and in each hand he held, by the hair, a glassy-eyed, mouth agape, severed white human head.

'The CIA managed to identify those two, believe it or not. They were Americans, hired by the Namibian insurgents. Every time van

Roost's unit captured a mercenary, that was how they dealt with them. They were known in every southern African battle zone as the Head-hunters.'

Skinner paused. 'The platoon didn't only work abroad. The Government used them to foment tribal violence in the townships. It was even suggested that van Roost invented the necklace.' Lorraine Morrison shot him a puzzled look.

'You don't know about that fashion accessory, Inspector? It involves filling a car tyre with petrol, hanging it round some poor bugger's neck and setting it alight. It was common practice in the townships for a while, and some say our man Hencke came up with the idea.'

He nodded to McIlhenney once more, and a fourth photograph appeared on the screen. It could have been a different person. This time the smile was gentle, perfectly civilised and framed by a thin moustache, while the well-groomed hair was darker, more noticeably red. The man wore an expensively cut blazer, and his gold-rimmed glasses made him look studious.

'During his eventful army career,' continued Skinner, 'van Roost, not unnaturally, made many enemies. So, after five years, when his tour was almost completed, the top brass did him a favour. They reported him killed in action in Namibia, brought back an unrecognisable body, and had a funeral. A few months later, Mr Michael Hawkins, whom you see there, returned from an extensive spell in the US, and set up in practice in Cape Town as a consultant civil engineer.

'His firm has done pretty well in the twelve years since then. Initially it was given a leg-up with a few Government contracts, but it built up pretty quickly a list of significant private sector clients, in South Africa and abroad. Today it has a staff of twenty . . . although there's a vacancy since the CIA pulled their woman out.'

The DCC paused as McIlhenney turned off the projector, switched on the lights and resumed his seat. 'He did other things for the former South African regime too,' he went on. 'Ten years ago he paid a business visit to the US, to advise the government on an office purchase in Chicago. While he was there, Samuel Tshabala, the leader in exile of a radical black faction, was killed; shot by a sniper as he got into his car in San Francisco.

'This was very embarrassing for the Americans; the guy had been under their protection, and more than a few people in Africa accused them of setting him up. So the FBI and the CIA, in a rare show of co-operation, threw everything at it. Eventually, the Bureau discovered that Mr Michael Hawkins had entered the country ten days before the hit, but had never left. They also discovered that one Peter Veivers, South African national, had left the country through Los Angeles

Airport on the day after, although when they checked, they found no record of his ever having entered.

'They placed Veivers in a hotel in San Francisco, where he had stayed for seven days, checking out on the morning of the shooting. By sheer chance, the Drug Enforcement Agency had been staking out the same hotel during Veivers' time there, waiting for a crowd of Colombians, and were able to give the Bureau a piece of good quality video footage of their man, far better than they had taken from the house security cameras.

'They handed over to the CIA at that point. Now as it happened, the Agency had been very interested in the late Hencke van Roost. He had killed a couple of their people in Namibia . . . the very two you saw a few minutes ago, in fact . . . so they were very pleased when they heard he was dead. They had his picture on file from his MIT days, and from South African press coverage of his alleged death, so they made the connection quickly. Then they had a look at Mr Michael Hawkins, back at work in Cape Town, and put the whole story together.

'There was some talk of terminating him, there and then, but in the end they did something much more sensible. They recruited him. Michael Hawkins was blackmailed into handling sticky jobs for the Agency, and that really was the start of it.'

Skinner leaned back. 'Okay,' he said, 'I've been talking for long enough. Any questions so far?'

DI Morrison raised a hand. 'If he worked for the CIA, why did they have to plant someone in his office?'

'Because he doesn't work for them alone; he works for virtually anyone, and he doesn't ask Agency approval before he takes on a job.' The DCC grinned. 'They might think they do, but the CIA don't actually run the world. The Tshabala affair left them with egg on their faces, and so did the Asian assassination I mentioned earlier; that man was a client too. So they put their spy in Hawkins' camp as a sort of early warning system.'

Mario McGuire raised a hand. 'How many aliases does the guy use, sir?'

'Every time he goes under,' Skinner replied, 'he does it under a new name, and he switches to another after the job's done.'

McIlhenney shifted his massive frame in his seat. 'Can I ask a question, boss?'

'Of course. You're not just here to work the projector.'

'Why does the present South African government tolerate someone like this?

'Because chances are he's worked for them too, in the past. No one knows for sure who set up Tshabala, but the CIA were fairly certain that the ANC were involved. That suspicion, was more or less confirmed when the murder was taken off the agenda of the Truth and Reconciliation Commission.

'The awful truth is that people like Hawkins are useful, very useful, for a time at least. They're very good at what they do, and they don't have links to anyone.'

'So what are we to do with this guy if we catch him? Stick him on a plane to South Africa and let him carry on in business?'

Skinner glanced at Andy Martin, looked around the room, then back at McIlhenney. 'Not this time, Neil. No one ties my hands, not in my own country or anywhere else. If Mr Hawkins is coming here on a project, then if we can, we will stop him . . . with whatever force is appropriate. If, by ill luck, he succeeds in his objective, we'll do our damnedest to make sure he doesn't leave Scotland. But if he does, he'll be hunted down.

'I have a free hand in this. As I said, people like Hawkins are useful, for a time. This man's time is up. Wherever else he goes after this, it won't be back to Cape Town.'

'The big question, though, Mr Skinner,' said Superintendent Harry McGuigan. 'Why would he come to Scotland?'

'If we knew that for sure, we could plan very specifically. But we can make some pretty decent guesses, and one that's really informed.'

'Political?' asked McGuigan.

'Almost certainly. This guy only works for governments and their opponents.' The DCC leaned back in his chair, stretching his long lean body. 'What political target in Scotland would be important enough to justify the hiring of a very expensive international assassin to take him out?

'Let's begin with the obvious: there are currently five members of the British Cabinet from Scottish constituencies. As of now they're all on round-the-clock protection, but realistically, only two stand out as potential targets . . . the Defence Secretary and the Foreign Secretary.

'Ministry of Defence security have been given overall responsibility for protecting those two. That makes me happy, since my friend Adam Arrow will be in command of that end, and he's a bit special. I'm pretty confident that if either of those two men is Hawkins' target, his chances of success are poor.

'Other possibilities? A member of the Royal Family?' He shook his head. 'I don't believe that one for a minute. Okay, maybe a splinter Irish nationalist group might like to kill a British Royal; but those boys would want to do the job themselves. I can't see them hiring in outside talent. Nevertheless, that angle isn't being ruled out. All Royal visits in Scotland have been quietly cancelled, until the threat is eliminated.

'No, the intelligent guess has to be that if Hawkins is coming to Scotland on a contract, in line with his cryptic remark to his CIA girlfriend, then his target is a VIP visitor, rather than a Scot. And that's where this gets really worrying; because here's where I get round to the informed supposition I mentioned earlier.

'It hasn't been announced yet, but in a couple of months' time, in December, there will be a special meeting of world Heads of Government and Finance Ministers, to consider the effect of the international response to the continuing global economic crisis. It's an initiative by our own Prime Minister, who as you'll have noticed, likes to cultivate his image on the international stage.

'Where?' He looked around the table at eight frowning faces. 'You've guessed it, people. Right here in Bonnie Scotland, in the Edinburgh International Conference Centre, to be precise. The USA, Germany, France, Russia, the People's Republic of China, Japan, Canada, Italy, Singapore, Malaysia, Indonesia, and many others, have been invited to attend.

'Until now, the only people who have known about this meeting have been the people involved, and their immediate advisers. The main players agreed the timing and venue at the last G8 meeting. EICC don't even know yet that they're hosting it. So if Michael Hawkins' trip to Scotland is related to that, it points to someone on the invitation list having ordered a hit on someone else.

'Now that might be a bad omen for international relations, but it's a secondary issue for me. I don't need to remind you that a few years back a visiting Head of State was assassinated right here in Edinburgh. The argument that he was better off dead cuts no ice with me: he was done on my patch. I swore then that such a thing would never happen again. It won't.

'I've been told that we don't need to worry about protection in this case; that will be the job of the military, advised by Sir John Govan. I don't envy Jock his task. The army's security approach is usually based on deterrence. Hawkins won't be scared off by any number of soldiers. He's clever, he's resourceful and as far as anyone knows he has never failed. All he needs is one opening and the President of the United States, or Russia, or our Prime Minister . . . Christ, maybe more than one of them . . . can kiss their arse goodbye.'

The DCC smiled, calmly. 'Lady and gentlemen,' he said, 'we are going to prevent that. If Michael van Roost Hawkins is in Scotland, we are going to find him. If he has yet to arrive we are going to try to nab him at his port of entry. You and your officers all have no other task but this. Each of you will report progress to me, through Detective Sergeant McIlhenney, on a daily basis. Any instructions Neil may give you, will be with my full authority.

'Watch the airports, of course, but let's proceed on the assumption that he's here already. Your starting point will be to check all landing cards completed by non-EU nationals on entry to the UK. You will receive full co-operation, if necessary, from your opposite numbers in police forces in England and Wales. Remember that they do not need to know what this is all about, nor should they.

'It's quite possible that Hawkins will be travelling on a false EU passport, and in that case there will be no landing card. So hotel checks are important too. He may have rented accommodation; speak to all the letting agencies in your areas. Of course, when you go to check the properties, indeed whenever there's a chance you could come face to face with this bloke, you will be armed. That's not a suggestion; it's an order.'

Skinner picked up a number of sealed envelopes which he had brought with him into the room and handed them round. 'These are some photofit treatments of Hawkins prepared by the people in MI5. They're based on the last photograph you saw and they show how he might look in a variety of disguises.

'One thing he can't hide though. Van Roost took a bullet in the right leg towards the end of his army days, and he's walked with a limp ever since.

'As well as the prints you'll also find in those envelopes, DS McIlhenney's office and home phone numbers, plus my own and Mr Martin's.'

'Why would he come here so far ahead of the meeting, sir?' asked DI Burns, from Fife.

'Planning, Inspector. Planning. This man is meticulous in everything he does. If someone attending this conference is his target then his track record says that he'll come here weeks in advance, to check out the cityscape, to work out the best positions for an attempt and to prepare his means of escape. This man is not a martyr; his aim will be to complete his contract and fade into the background.'

'What do we do if we find him, boss?' McGuire spoke quietly, but his voice was loaded with meaning.

'Keep him under observation if you can,' said Skinner, 'and send for me. Try not to confront him, but if you have to, and he as much as looks at you the wrong way, put a bullet in him.'

'What, you mean in his good leg, sir?' said DI Impey, from Dumfries and Galloway, smiling along the table.

Poker-faced, the DCC turned and looked at the man, freezing his grin. 'No, Inspector.' He ground the words out, slowly. 'I mean right between the bloody eyes. If he has to, this man will kill you stone dead, then take your head as a trophy.' With a nod around the table, and a final glare at Impey, he stood up, bringing the briefing to a close, and strode out of the room, followed by McIlhenney, leaving Martin to see the visitors on their way.

'I don't fancy that Dumfries bloke, boss,' said the sergeant as they walked along the Command Corridor.

'Me neither, Neil. Give him a hard time when he makes his daily reports. Question him; keep him on his toes. Make sure he's checking the ferry terminals on his patch. Hawkins could come in from Ireland.'

'I'll do that, sir.' As the two men stepped into the Chief Constable's office, Skinner looked at his assistant.

'Neil,' he asked, abruptly, 'what's up?'

'What do you mean, sir?'

'You know bloody well what I mean. First Andy, now you. You've got something on your mind. I know this job can be boring at times. Do you want a move back to the action?'

McIlhenney's great shoulders sagged, and he seemed to slump into himself. 'I'm sorry if I've been letting anything show, boss,' he said. 'That's not my way.

'Aye,' he admitted, 'something's up. But it's got nothing to do with the job. It's Olive. She's ill and she knows it, yet she won't do anything about it. She's scared, boss, and oh by Christ, so am I.'

'I see,' said Skinner quietly. 'Sit down man, and tell me about it. Maybe there's something I can do to help.'

7

Although Brian Mackie's patch took in a big rural area, the divisional CID Commander's office was in the St Leonard's Police Station, on the east of Edinburgh. The detective superintendent did not care for the modern brick building, and would have preferred to have been based in Haddington, beside his deputy, Detective Chief Inspector Maggie Rose, but he kept these feelings to himself, understanding the thinking behind Andy Martin's deployment of his CID resources.

He was at his desk, in mid-afternoon, reading his way through faxed witness statements taken from the neighbours of Gaynor Weston in Oldbarns, when there was a light knock on the door.

'Come in,' called Mackie. He had expected a uniformed officer with more statements from Maggie Rose, and so he looked up in surprise as Dr Sarah Grace Skinner stepped into the room.

'Hello, Doc,' the thin, bald detective exclaimed, standing, with his unfailing courtesy. 'An office consultation; this is an honour.'

Sarah grinned at him. Suddenly it struck him that the drab, wet day outside was just a little brighter. 'All part of the service in this new era of forensic pathology,' she said, as the took a seat at Mackie's conference table.

'Coffee?' he offered.

'No thanks, and you shouldn't either. I'm trying to cut down Bob's consumption just now too. You desk jockeys drink far too much of that damn stuff.'

'Desk jockeys indeed,' Mackie grunted, but with a smile. 'You'll wind the boss up if you call him that to his face. 'S not true anyway; where was I at six o'clock this morning?'

'Yeah, I know. I was only kidding with you . . . not about the coffee, though. To be serious, I've just finished the autopsy on Mrs Weston. My report is being produced right now and should be with you before five o'clock, but I thought I'd call in and talk it through with you in—Damn.' She broke off as her mobile telephone warbled its call signal, frowning slightly as she produced it from the pocket of her jacket.

'I'm sorry, Brian. I forgot to switch it off.' She took the call nonetheless, pressing the 'Receive' button.

'Bob, hi. Look I'm in a meeting right now. Yes. Okay.' Mackie watched her as she listened, for almost a minute. 'Yes,' she said eventually; she was hesitant, and wore worried frown on her face. 'I can do that. I'll need to be careful to avoid ethical problems, but . . . Yes, okay. I'll do it after this. Give me the address.' She switched the phone to her left hand, took a notebook and pen from her bag and scribbled a few words, quickly. 'Got that; I know where it is too. See you tonight. Bye.'

She ended the call, switched off the phone and put it away. 'Problem?' asked Mackie.

'I hope not,' Sarah replied, the worried look lingering on her face. 'Something that Bob volunteered me to do, that's all.' She snapped her gaze back on to the detective. 'Okay, once more: Mrs Weston.

'I've done a full postmortem examination and had most of the lab work rushed through. The plastic bag over the head was a precaution . . . or maybe it was meant to distract us, I don't know . . . but it was unnecessary. Gaynor Weston died from a massive overdose of diamorphine, injected into her left thigh. She would have lost consciousness in seconds and died within two minutes. There was no question of suffocation.

'There were no signs of violence on the body, and nothing at all to indicate that the subject had been restrained before the injection was administered. Shortly before her death, she ate a fillet steak – medium-rare – with courgettes and French fries. Also, over a longer period, she drank the best part of a bottle of red wine and followed it with black coffee.'

'Any sign of recent sexual activity?'

'No, Brian, none at all. I can't help you with a DNA trace, I'm afraid.' She shook her head.

'There were no romantic goodbyes here. When the meal was over, Gaynor sat in her kitchen chair – placed where it could be seen from outside, after the event – and allowed herself to be put to death.'

Mackie leaned forward. 'You could state on oath that there was no possibility of the injection being self-inflicted?'

'No. But what I will say is that, even if she fixed the bag over her own head first, there was no possibility of the victim injecting herself directly into an artery, then disposing of the hypodermic before she lost consciousness.

'You didn't find the tape at the scene, and if you didn't find a hypo, or a bottle with traces of diamorphine—'

'—which we didn't.'

'Then that will rule out the possibility of suicide. The minimum

31

any jury could possibly do would be return a verdict of culpable homicide, dependent on the mental state of the perpetrator, but this was so premeditated that you will have about a ninety-nine percent chance of a murder conviction in any trial, assuming that you can place the accused at the scene at the time.'

'Excellent,' said Mackie. 'But why? Why did Gaynor Weston let herself be switched off?'

Sarah looked at him, unblinking. 'About two weeks ago, Mrs Weston had an operation to remove a growth from her left leg. There was another growth on her foot, and the fact that it hadn't been excised indicates to me that it had developed since then. I removed it and had it analysed.

'The woman had a malignant melanoma, a form of cancer which offers little prospect of a cure, unless it is discovered at a very early stage. In this case, from the depth of the earlier excision, when I explored it, if that too was a melanoma – as I am quite certain it was from the nature of the procedure – I would say that the size of the tumour removed would have pointed to a prognosis of death within three to four months. The disease had already metastasised to the spine, liver and lungs. Any treatment would have been purely palliative: the most honest course of action would simply have been to keep the patient as comfortable as possible for the time she had left. That would have meant, in effect, limited chemical treatments supported by tranquillisers and increasing sedation. Diamorphine would have been used in increasing quantities to keep Mrs Weston out of pain. In the event, she took the lot at once.'

Brian Mackie let out a great sigh. 'Very neat and tidy for her,' he said. 'But a right bloody mess for us. Shit, why didn't she top herself down in Hawick, say, on John McGrigor's patch. Big John's a pragmatist. He'd probably have washed the glasses, planted a roll of tape and a syringe at the scene and closed the book on it.

'We'd better find out where she had this operation two weeks ago, then take a close look at her circle of friends.'

'I can help you with the first part of that,' Sarah offered. 'Normally, a procedure like this one would have been performed in the Department of Clinical Oncology at the Western General Hospital. I checked with them. It wasn't. The Royal Infirmary has no record of it either, nor has St John's in Livingston, nor Bangour, nor Roodlands. I asked at Murrayfield Hospital, and they said no. But then I checked with St Martha's, a little private clinic on the South Side of the city.

'The administrator there said that she was bound by confidentiality and wouldn't talk to me. I told her who I was, and what I was doing, but she still would not open her mouth. "Not without a Court order", she insisted. So if you want to search her records, you better go get a Sheriff's Warrant.'

'I'll talk to her myself before I go that far,' Mackie replied. 'But maybe Andy Martin and I should short-circuit all that and go to see the ex-husband. Given his profession, his has to be the main name in the frame.'

'Only if you can place him at the scene.'

'We can probably do that. According to witness accounts he was a regular caller at Oldbarns, so he'll have left traces of himself. The big problem is placing him, or anyone else for that matter, in the house at the time of Gaynor Weston's last supper.' He picked up the witness statements. 'None of the neighbours saw a bloody thing.

'Even if someone walked in this minute and confessed, we wouldn't have enough to go to trial. At the moment our only hope of that rests with the clever people in Arthur Dorward's forensics lab, but I can't see how even they're going to help this time.'

8

Andy Martin and Mario McGuire sat in the Head of CID's office, on the second floor of the Fettes headquarters building, half an hour after the visitors had departed. After Skinner and McIlhenney had withdrawn, the chief superintendent had continued the briefing for a few more minutes, until he was sure that each of the visiting officers had a complete grasp of the situation, and that everyone's priorities in the search for the assassin were the same.

All of Scotland's police forces have points of entry to the country within their territory, even Central, which although it has no ferry ports or air terminals, does have docking facilities at the BP oil installation at Grangemouth. Martin's concern was that every possible route into Scotland should be identified and covered as far as possible.

'If you were him, sir,' asked McGuire, 'what would you do?'

The DCS's vivid green eyes flashed as he smiled grimly at his colleague. 'What's the most obvious thing?' he said, throwing the question back.

'Fly into the busiest airport, I suppose, which has to be Heathrow, then catch the Shuttle, or hire a car and drive to Scotland.'

'And if you were Hawkins, where would you fly from?'

McGuire stroked his chin. His black beard grew fast; a dark shadow always showed by mid-afternoon, for all that he had a wet shave every morning. 'Anywhere but South Africa,' he answered eventually.

'Right. But if you were South African and your real name was van Roost, maybe your natural inclination might be to route through Holland. The Low Countries' airlines are making a real effort to pinch travellers from Scotland away from London. You can access just about anywhere in the world out of Glasgow, Edinburgh or Aberdeen, through Schiphol and Brussels. That works in the other direction too, so you'd better check out KLM and Sabena landings. Their computers should tell you the origin of each passenger's journey, even if they were onward travellers from outside Holland or Belgium.'

'Damn it,' Martin scolded himself. 'I should have come up with this clever thought that at the briefing. Mario, make sure that big Neil passes that on to McGuigan and Macintosh, so that Glasgow and Aberdeen landings are checked too.'

'Ach, I'll tell them myself.'

'No. The boss has set up the chain of communication through McIlhenney so that he can keep in touch with everything that's happening. Let's do it his way.'

'Very good, sir. I'll nip along and tell Neil now.'

'You do that.' The detective inspector started for the door. 'Hang on a minute,' the DCS called out. 'Are you happy that you've got enough manpower for this job?'

'Well,' McGuire answered, slowly, 'since you ask. Another set of legs with a sharp brain to drive them wouldn't do any harm.'

'Okay. I'll lend you Karen Neville or Sammy Pye from my personal staff. Take your pick.'

The DI frowned, considering his choice. 'Are either of them firearms trained?'

'Both. First class shots, the pair of them.'

'Then it's hard to choose between them. But I'll take Neville; Maggie's worked with her, and rates her pretty highly.'

'Okay, you've got her. Pick her up on your way out and brief her. Remember, though, she only needs to know that we're looking for this guy. She doesn't need to know why.'

McGuire nodded and turned towards the door once more, only to hear a knock, then see it open, as Brian Mackie stepped into the room.

Martin looked up, surprised. 'Hello, Thin Man,' he said. 'What brings you here?' He waved a hand in farewell as the Special Branch Commander left. 'Cheers, Mario. Good luck.'

'With what?' asked Mackie, casually, as the door closed.

'His Lottery ticket. So what's up?'

The tall detective looked up, glumly. 'This Oldbarns investigation, that's what.' He handed a folder to the Head of CID. 'That's Sarah's postmortem report. The woman was full of cancer: undoubtedly she'd have died within months. Someone helped her on the way with a great big dose of pharmaceutical heroin.'

'Any thoughts on who?'

'I don't want to jump to any conclusions here. I've sent Maggie and young Stevie Steele, from Dan Pringle's Division, out to interview the boyfriend, to see how he reacts. However, someone performed an operation on Mrs Weston two weeks ago. There's no record of it in any of the main hospitals, or at the Murrayfield, but Sarah found a wee private clinic on the South Side that's acting a bit shifty. They clammed up when she asked them about it.

'I'm wondering whether her ex-husband, who's a surgeon,

35

remember, did the exploratory op, and then—'

'—did her a favour when she asked.' Martin finished his colleague's supposition for him. 'He'd have had access to the drugs, I suppose. Ach, I'd be heart sorry for the poor bastard if he did that . . . even although it's against my principles.'

'Unless . . .' Mackie began, hesitated for a few second, then gathered his breath and went on. 'Unless we succumb to a rare burst of professional incompetence and close the book on this one: write it up for the Fiscal as a suicide.'

The Head of CID looked at his friend in silence for around thirty seconds, then he opened Sarah's report and read it, still without a word. Finally, he looked up.

'Brian, I'd hate to see this man lose his career and his liberty for doing something that he wasn't cruel enough to refuse. But we're only investigators, mate; not judge, not jury, not even prosecutors. Whatever our different private feelings, we have a public duty to establish facts and report them to the Fiscal, and we can't neglect it. Not ever.

'Let's you and I follow this for a bit, one step at a time. First, let's pay a joint visit to this clinic that obstructed Sarah and give them a hard time until they tell us whether Mrs Weston was a patient there, and if so who treated her.

'We'll see where we go from there.' Martin paused. 'What have you done about the press?'

'Royston's told them that we're waiting for the result of the PM before reporting to the Fiscal. Sarah's still waiting for a small piece of lab work, so technically that's still true.'

'Fine. It can stay like that overnight. Let's go and see this clinic. What's it called, by the way?'

'St Martha's.'

Andy Martin grunted, with a grim anger which surprised his colleague. 'She won't be much help to them if they get in my way.'

9

Olive McIlhenney was not an easy woman to take off guard. Her husband had been trying for many years to achieve this, but with very few successes. However when she opened her front door, and saw who was standing on the step, a green Barbour thrown over her shoulders to protect her from the rain, her normally imperturbable expression changed to one of complete surprise.

'Dr Skinner,' she exclaimed. 'Come in, quick, out of the rain.'

'You remember me then,' said Sarah, as she stepped into the narrow hall way of the semidetached villa. The two women had met only once, at a social event more than a year earlier.

'Of course I do. Here, give me your coat. What brings you here, anyway?'

As well as being unshakeable, Olive was quick witted. Even as she was hanging the waxed cotton rain-coat on one of a row of hooks behind the front door, she answered her own question.

'Has that husband of mine been talking to you?' she asked, quickly: too quickly, for the cough took her unawares, racking her body, sending colour to her cheeks, making her visitor realise how pale they had been before, and highlighting the contrast of the dark circles under her eyes. She produced an inhaler from the pocket of her cardigan and took two quick puffs.

'No,' Sarah replied, truthfully, as the fit subsided. 'Neil hasn't said a word to me. But my husband has been worrying about him, and this afternoon, finally, he made him tell him what was wrong. So if you want to blame anyone for this visit, blame Bob.' As she spoke, she followed her hostess into the living room, where Lauren and Spencer were watching *Grange Hill*, intently. Neither turned as the two women passed through into the kitchen, although the chocolate-point Siamese cat which lay on the floor between them did flick an ear in their direction.

Olive's complexion had paled once more, after the paroxysm. 'Maybe I shouldn't say this to you, but Neil never has trusted doctors,' she said, as she closed the door on the children. 'He's just being silly. My GP says I have a touch of asthma; that's why she gave me the inhaler.'

'And does it help?' asked Sarah, very quietly, catching her eye as she did so, not allowing her to look away.

'No, it doesn't,' she answered, in a whisper.

'No, I didn't think it had. Olive, I'm here as a friend, and the last thing I want to do is to undermine your confidence in your relationship with your family doctor, but I have to ask you; have you had a chest X-ray recently?'

The other woman shook her head. 'Not in the last seven years. My last one was clear, though,' she added, quickly.

'Has your doctor suggested an X-ray?'

'No.'

'How long have you had this cough?'

Olive frowned, leaning back against a work-surface and looking at the ceiling. 'I suppose it would have been around the end of June when it started. I had a bit of bother when we were on holiday just after that. Neil and I like to walk, but I found that I was getting short of breath if we went too far. We gave up on the walks, and the problem went away. I put it down to a chest infection at the time.

'Then at the end of September, it came back. I went to see Dr Jones then. She said it was probably asthma and gave me the inhaler.'

'I see.' Sarah paused. 'Listen Olive, I have to be honest here. If you were my patient I'd have sent you for an X-ray straight away, to eliminate certain possibilities if nothing else.' She glanced at her watch. 'I have a friend who works in the chest clinic at the Western. I checked with her earlier; she's on duty now, and she'll fit you in.

'If you like, I could take you along there. Best have this cleared up, yes?'

Olive McIlhenney looked at her shrewdly. She knew exactly what was being said; what her visitor meant by 'certain possibilities'. She had smoked too many cigarettes in the years between ages fifteen and thirty-four not to have been aware of them. Still, those were possibilities for others, not for her.

'Well,' she said at last. 'If it'll reassure that big daft bugger of a husband of mine, why not. Hang on here a minute. I'll ask my neighbour to keep an eye on the kids and the cat, till Neil gets home, then I'll write a note for him, and we can be off.'

She moved towards the back door. 'That sure is a lovely cat,' Sarah remarked, casually.

'Samson? Yes. The kids spoil him rotten.' As she turned to answer, Sarah noticed, for the first time, a small lump on the right side of her neck.

10

'St Martha's.' Andy Martin read the name aloud. That was all there was, picked out in gold lettering on the small green board, fixed to the gate-post at the entrance to the big red sandstone villa, in one of the quietest streets in the Grange, one of the wealthiest of Edinburgh's southern suburbs.

'Doesn't tell you a lot, does it?'

'No,' said Mackie, 'as private clinics go this one seems almost secret.'

'Let's go and find out what secrets they are keeping.'

The Head of CID locked his silver Mondeo and led the way up the gravel path, holding a huge golf umbrella as shelter against the rain. The storm doors of the clinic were open as they reached them, revealing a big grey-glass-panelled door inside. As Martin folded the umbrella in the wide vestibule, Mackie tried the door handle. It turned and they stepped inside.

The entrance hall was a study in mahogany. The polished floor shone, a heavy balustrade ran up the wide stairway which led to the upper floor, and a huge piece of furniture, all coat hooks and mirrors, stood against one wall, facing a varnished door, on which the word 'Reception' was etched on a brass plate.

Mackie tried the second door, but it was locked. As he frowned at the Head of CID a woman appeared at the rear of the big hallway. 'I'm afraid our office is closed, gentlemen,' she said, sharply. 'In any event we do not receive representatives without appointment.'

'You will receive us, though, madam,' the detective chief superintendent barked back at her, producing his warrant card as he spoke. 'We are police officers.' Afterwards it occurred to Brian Mackie that Andy Martin normally would have seen the funny side of her remark.

'I see,' murmured the woman, examining his card, and Mackie's, closely. She looked to be in her early fifties, dressed in a severe grey skirt and pullover, which almost matched her hair. It was drawn back in a bun. 'I, in turn, am Miss Emma Pople,' she said, through thin lips. *This woman has all the warmth of a mackerel*, thought Mackie. 'I am the administrator here. What is the reason for your visit?'

'What services do you provide here?' Martin asked.

'We provide convalescent facilities for Roman Catholic ladies recovering from surgery, or other debilitating treatments. St Martha's is owned by an Order of nuns. Some of our patients are themselves sisters.'

'Who attends your patients?'

'Usually they are seen by the surgeons or physicians in whose care they have been.'

'Do you have surgical facilities here?'

'We have a small theatre, for emergencies. We don't have Health Board approval for everyday surgery.'

'Ah, I see. So is that why you obstructed our pathologist colleague when she called you earlier on today?'

For this first time, Emma Pople looked unsure of herself. 'You remember,' Martin went on. 'Her name's Dr Skinner. She called this clinic earlier today asking for information on a Mrs Gaynor Weston; more specifically whether she had ever been a patient here. You did speak to her, didn't you?'

The woman's mouth set even tighter. 'That is correct. I was unable to help her.'

'No, Miss Pople, you refused to help her. Told her to get a court order, I believe.'

'I may have done. I may tell you the same thing.'

'Just you do that, ma'am,' said the Head of CID, evenly. 'In that event, Mr Mackie and I will take you at your word. We'll go to the Sheriff, and he'll give us a warrant to search these premises. But we won't do it privately, or even quietly. We'll make a fuss about it in the media, and we'll make damn sure Lothian Health Board hears about it too.

'Is that what you want? Would the Holy Sisters appreciate the publicity? Would the Health Board like what we might find?'

Emma Pople looked at him, and realised that he would do exactly as he threatened. Her grey armour seemed to crack.

'Very well,' she muttered, defeated. 'Come through to my office.'

11

The television was still on when Olive McIlhenney showed Sarah into her living room. But this time Neil was watching, shirt-sleeved and alone, as the opening titles of *The Bill* showed on the screen.

'Looking for tips on policing?' Sarah ventured, with an awkward smile.

The big sergeant turned to look at her. He began to heave himself out of his chair, until she waved him to stay seated. 'I was mocking the afflicted, actually,' he answered. 'None of those buggers would last five minutes with the boss. That CID room of theirs is a joke; most of them seem to be sat on their backsides all day.'

'Kids upstairs?' Olive asked. He nodded in reply. 'I'll just go and see what they're up to. You have a chat with Sarah.' A quick look passed between husband and wife. Sarah saw it and thought that she had never seen so much said without words, in only a moment in time.

'You've got something to tell me,' he said quietly, as the door closed.

As she looked at him, she felt fear's cold hand clutch her stomach. This was not something she had ever done before; not to a friend at least. None of her training had covered this moment. 'Yes, Neil, I have. Olive asked me to explain things to you alone, while she's with Lauren and Spencer.

'She and I have just been to the Chest Clinic at the Western. We saw Dr Miller, one of the registrars there. She's a very fine doctor; we couldn't have seen anyone better. She sent Olive for an X-ray: when the print came back it showed a big patch covering most of the lower part of her right lung. The left one is clear.' She paused.

'What does that mean?' Neil asked, speaking slowly as if to keep his voice steady.

'It could have meant pneumonia, with other symptoms, or pleurisy. In the present circumstances the next stage of investigation would normally have been a bronchoscopy. That's a procedure in which an instrument is passed into the lung, and a piece of tissue is snipped out, for biopsy.

'However Dr Miller found a lump in one of the lymphatic glands at the base of the neck. She took tissue from that with a needle and sent that for analysis. I persuaded her to call in a favour from someone in the lab, and have it rushed through while we were there.'

She stopped, to gather herself and to fight back the tears which she knew were not far away. 'A biopsy tests for malignancy, Neil. I am afraid that Olive's was positive. She has what is known as a non-small cell carcinoma of the right lung. It's at a fairly advanced stage, since it has metastasised into the lymphatic system.'

She looked at the big detective, and he stared back at her. 'Are you telling me that Olive has lung cancer, Sarah? Is that what all that stuff means?'

'Yes.' Her answer was a whisper, yet it seemed to fill the room.

Neil sagged back into his chair, feeling the cold sweep through his body, feeling his heart hammering in his chest, feeling a panic akin to nausea rising in his throat. 'What are our chances?' he asked, his voice as quiet as hers.

'All the better with you at her side,' Sarah replied. 'This disease can't be cured, but there are treatments which can drive it into remission. Dr Miller has arranged an appointment with one of the consultants in the Department of Clinical Oncology at the Western General. His name's Derek Simmers: he's fitting Olive in at his Friday Clinic, tomorrow afternoon at two fifteen.'

'Would it help if we went private?'

She shook her head, brushing her auburn hair against her shoulders. 'Not at all. There is no finer centre for the treatment of cancer anywhere in the country than the Western General. It's a major research hub, and it exchanges information with other centres around the world, so whatever treatment is offered to Olive will be state-of-the-art.'

'He's good then, this Simmers?' asked Neil, struggling to control the shivers which were coursing through his body.

'The best.'

'Will he operate? Can he cut the thing out?'

'I can't say for sure, but as I understand it, surgical intervention at this stage of Olive's disease would be unlikely. Because of the metastasis it would have to be radical, and there would always be a danger that it would actually make the cancer spread faster.'

'Does Olive know all this?'

'I think she knew it before we went to the Clinic.'

Sudden fierce anger shone in his eyes. 'And that GP of hers told her she had asthma!' he snapped. 'I'll have the woman struck off.'

'Neil,' said Sarah, urgently. 'We all make clinical judgements based on what we see, and on what our patients tell us. Anyhow, you can't let yourself be side-tracked by anything right now. Dr Miller has written to Dr Jones telling her what's happened, and I'll speak to her myself tomorrow.

'You have to be completely focused on helping Olive fight this thing. Don't think about anything else. I'll speak to Bob, and I'm sure he'll give you compassionate leave as and when you need it.'

'I don't want that,' the detective replied, at once. 'I'll go with her to see Simmers tomorrow, of course, but we have to hold on to our normal life, as far as we can.'

'I understand that, and it's good.' She bit her bottom lip, an unconscious gesture. 'God, Neil, I can't advise you on this, because I can't really imagine being in your shoes.'

'Oh no?' he countered, quietly. 'What about that time the boss was stabbed?'

She smiled, sadly. 'No, that was different; that was only a forty-eight hour crisis. You and Olive have a longer fight on your hands to beat this thing.'

'But beat it we will,' Neil McIlhenney said, determinedly, as the door opened and Olive came into the room. She was smiling. Sarah thought it was the bravest thing she had ever seen.

She turned, patted her on the shoulder and, without a word, left them together. She was in her car, shoulders wet from the rain which was still falling heavily before, finally, the tears caught up with her.

12

'Couldn't you have visited me at my office tomorrow?' the man asked, as he showed Maggie Rose into his small study.

'I'd have called at your office this afternoon, Mr Futcher,' the red-haired detective replied, 'but you were out and your secretary didn't know when you'd be back.' She glanced around the study; the ornately papered walls were covered in photographs of its owner, mostly in evening dress, and all with other people in groups. As her gaze panned around the room, she recognised several sports and show business personalities, three Scottish business heroes, and a number of public figures, including, to her surprise, Deputy Chief Constable Bob Skinner.

'Did you tell my wife why you're here, when she answered the door? Not that it matters of course,' he added, too hastily.

'No, we simply introduced ourselves and asked to see you.'

Terry Futcher glanced at Detective Sergeant Stevie Steele. 'Why are there two of you anyway?'

'It's our normal practice in circumstances like these,' the detective chief inspector answered. 'I take it you know why we're here.'

Futcher nodded his head. He was a tall, well-built man in his early forties, sun-bronzed even in late autumn, with immaculately groomed brown hair and a tightly trimmed beard. 'Yes, I can guess. You've come about Gay.' He pointed to a green leather Chesterfield settee. 'Take a seat, please,' he offered, lowering himself into a matching armchair. 'Take a seat.'

'Thank you,' said Rose, settling against an arm of the comfortable sofa. 'How long have you known Mrs Weston, Mr Futcher? she asked.

'For just over four years.'

'How did you meet?'

'I hired her consultancy firm to train my people. She was a specialist in human resources; an inelegant term for what people used to call personnel management. She was very good on team-building and motivation, and I thought she could add a cutting edge to our new business presentations. I must admit that at first I thought her methods were a bit silly, but they worked very well. The Agency's billings have grown in each of the years she's been helping us.'

'Your relationship went beyond the office, though, didn't it?'

Futcher did not meet her gaze as he nodded.

'Since when?'

'That started a few months after she came to work for us, and it's been going on ever since.'

'How often did you see each other?'

'Hard to say, really,' the ad-man replied. 'We'd get together whenever we could arrange it.'

'Would you describe it as an intense relationship?'

'Hell, no! The opposite, in fact: it was a very relaxed thing. We liked each other a great deal, and we had sex on occasion, but we weren't in love with each other.' Futcher took a breath. 'Look, Inspector, I play around. Okay? I mean it's the sort of bloke I am. As for Gay, she came out of a marriage a few years back principally to make her own space and live her own life. Our arrangement didn't threaten that, and it didn't threaten my own marriage.'

'That's as frank as I can be with you.'

'You couldn't have put it more clearly,' said Rose. 'Tell me, did Mrs Weston have any other, er, arrangements, to use your term?'

'Was she seeing anyone else, you mean? Not that I know of; she certainly never gave me any hint of that. But to be honest I wouldn't have known if she was. I never visited Gay without checking that it was okay with her. That was the way she wanted it; all part of her having that space of hers . . .' Futcher broke off, sinking deeper into his chair, gazing at the ceiling.

'When did you find out about Mrs Weston's death, sir?' Steele asked him, quietly.

'This afternoon,' he replied, gathering himself. 'My secretary picked up a copy of the *Evening News* at lunch-time. There was a story about police being at the scene of the death of a single woman at Oldbarns steading. She showed it to me as soon as she saw it. As far as I know there are . . . were . . . only two single women living out there, Gay and Joan Ball. I switched on Radio Forth; their two o'clock news bulletin gave out the name.'

'Are you telling us that your secretary knew about Mrs Weston?'

Futcher glanced at the young detective. 'Katie knows everything about me, sergeant. She's been with me since I founded The Futcher Agency twelve years ago.'

'From your concern a few minutes ago, I guess your wife doesn't know about her though.'

Futcher looked at Steele again, uncomfortably and with a touch of anger showing. 'No, she bloody doesn't,' he snapped.

'What did you do when you heard that Mrs Weston was dead?' asked Rose.

'I went to Church, to the Cathedral at the end of York Place: to pray. I'm a practising Catholic.'

You should practise a bit harder; at least until you get to the bit about the Commandments. The response was on the tip of the detective chief inspector's tongue, but she fought it back. 'All afternoon?' she asked instead.

'Almost. I went back to the office just after five, and asked Katie to call a journalist friend of hers in the *Herald*'s Edinburgh office, to see what he knew. He told her that the police were being cagey about it.'

'Is that right? Is there a problem? How did she die?'

Rose ignored his questions. 'When was the last time you saw Mrs Weston?'

Futcher stroked his beard. 'Just over a fortnight ago,' he replied. 'Just before she went into hospital.'

'She went into hospital?'

'She told me she was going into a clinic for a minor operation. She didn't say what it was for, so I assumed it was some sort of women's thing.'

'Have you spoken to her since?'

'Several times, by telephone. She told me that the operation had been fine, that she was recuperating and that everything would be sorted out soon.'

'Is that your phrase or hers?' asked Rose.

The man looked at her, curiously, for a second. 'Hers, in fact. Her exact words; I remember her saying them; I remember it vividly.'

'What did you take her to mean by that?'

'I suppose I thought she meant that her plumbing would all be healed up, and we could . . .' His voice tailed off.

'. . . and you could resume a sexual relationship?' Steele offered.

'That's right.'

'Where were you in the early hours of this morning, Mr Futcher?' He looked round, eyes narrowing, at her sudden sharp question. Rose leaned forward on the leather settee, closer to him.

'In bed,' he answered, quietly.

'From when?'

'From about eleven o'clock.'

'You didn't go to Oldbarns last night did you?'

'No, I did not.'

'You didn't help Gaynor Weston end her own life?'

Futcher's face paled. 'Is that what happened?'

'You were nowhere near Oldbarns at two o'clock this morning? You were in bed?'

'No I wasn't,' he gasped. 'Yes I was.'

Maggie Rose settled back into the comfortable old Chesterfield, and smiled gently at him. 'That's okay, then. I'm sorry to have been so direct, Mr Futcher. We have to ask these questions, you understand.'

He sighed. 'Yes, of course.'

'Good, that's good.' She glanced round, at Steele. 'That's us almost finished, Stevie.'

'Yes Ma'am. Just one other thing to do, really.'

'That's right.' The chief inspector, still smiling, looked back across at Futcher. 'If you'd ask your wife to join us, sir. Just to confirm formally that you were here in bed at two o'clock this morning.'

The last vestige of the bronzed look vanished from the man's face. 'No!' he cried out. 'Leave Penny out of this.'

'I'm sorry, sir,' said Rose, trying to sound as if she really meant it. 'I know it's difficult for you, but we need corroboration of your story, for the Fiscal.'

Terry Futcher thrust himself out of his armchair, took a pace towards the room's small window, then turned abruptly, to face the two police officers once more. 'Then don't ask Penny,' he snarled at them. 'I was in bed all right, you bastards, but I never said I was here.

'I was with Katie, my secretary.'

13

'Here, take this. You look as though you need it.' Bob handed his wife a huge vodka and tonic, ice and lemon fighting to break the bubbling surface near the brim of the crystal tumbler.

'Oh I do, my love. How do I need it.' Barefoot, she leaned back against the kitchen work-surface, and took a mouthful of the strong mixture. 'Are the boys asleep?'

'Jazz is. Mark's reading.' He took a deep breath, reading her silence. 'Bad, is it?' he asked at last.

She nodded, and sipped again at her drink. 'It's bad, all right. Poor Olive. Poor Neil. Poor kids. Olive has lung cancer, with at least one secondary, in her lymph glands. They'll give her a scan at the Oncology Clinic to determine whether it's spread any further than that.

'Honey,' she said, bitterly, 'it's at times like this I feel thankful that I work in pathology. I don't think I could cope if I had to hand down death sentences on a daily basis.'

He threw back his head, exhaling a great gasp of air. 'Oh dear Christ,' he exclaimed, filling up with blind, helpless anger. 'Olive and Neil McIlhenney are as nice a couple as you'll meet in a day's march. They adore each other, and those kids of theirs are a pair of wee gems. What the fuck have they done to deserve this?

'Does she have any hope?' he asked.

'Depends on what the scan shows. If there are no other metastases, then clearly her chances will be better. I'm no expert on current treatments, but I do know the stats. They show that the great majority of people with this type of cancer, at this stage of development, die within a couple of years.

'However, being as positive as I can, the available figures only show the position as it was about five years ago. That's how long it takes for the statistical picture to emerge. Against that, the oncologists, the drug companies and the clinical researchers are re-writing the book on cancer every day. I dare say I could connect to the Internet right now and find a whole list of treatments for lung cancer that I've never heard of before.'

Bob turned down the heat on the rice and on the marinera sauce, crossed to the fridge and poured himself a drink as big as the one he had mixed for his wife. As an afterthought, he topped up her glass with vodka.

'Is there anything we can do to help them?' he asked.

'You can give Neil tomorrow afternoon off, for openers, so that he can go to the clinic.'

'Jesus, I'll send him on compassionate leave as of this minute.'

'No,' said Sarah quickly. 'He must be the judge of that. Olive's teaching career will be on hold for a long time, at the very best, but it's important for them both, from a morale point of view, that he continues to work as normally as he can. Neil picked that up right away.

'One thing did occur to me, though. Do you know what the grandparent situation is?'

His forehead furrowed, characteristically, as he thought. 'Neil's father's dead. His mother has pretty bad arthritis. She lives in a sheltered flat. Olive's mother isn't around any more. She went off to England with another bloke years ago. Her dad's a civil servant; works in the Benefits Agency up in Aberdeen.

'Brothers and sisters?'

'Olive has a brother; he's a soldier, based in Aldershot. Neil has a brother called Charlie and a sister called Mavis. He's in Australia and she's in Canada.'

'Right. In those circumstances, the most helpful thing that we could do for them is to look after Lauren and Spencer as the need arises. If this disease is treatable, it'll be done mostly on an out-patient basis, and Olive could be pretty sick for a day or two after each session. It'd be best if the kids didn't see that. So if there are no handy relatives, why don't we offer to put them up?'

'Absolutely.' He turned back towards the hob, and their supper.

'Life can be a bitch, Sarah, can it not,' he said quietly as she came to stand beside him. 'Until ten minutes ago, I was getting quietly worked up about my daughter putting her career before her relationship with Andy.

'Something like this puts that well in perspective. It makes me feel guilty, too, about how lucky I am. If everyone got what they deserve, then how would my life have panned out, and Neil's . . .'

14

He lay in the dark, staring at the ceiling, listening to his wife breathing beside him, waiting for his emotions to define themselves.

Since Sarah had broken the news, he had felt rage, pity and a terrible, terrible fear, all mixed together. He and Olive had eaten a quiet supper and then they had gone to bed. Her dignified, pale-faced silence had upset him more than anything else, but he had been afraid to break it, afraid that if he did he would say the wrong thing.

At last she turned to him, and he took her in his strong arms, beneath the duvet. Her tears came then; great, heaving, frightened sobs. 'Why me?' she asked him. 'Why me?'

'Because, my darling,' he said, softly, his deep voice quavering as she had never heard it before, 'there is in this world, no fairness, no justice and no righteousness. If there were, things like this just wouldn't happen.'

He pressed a hand to her breast. 'Love, if I could take this thing from out of you and put it into me, you know that I would. I can't do that, but I will be at your side as you fight it, every step of the way. This is a team game; we're in it together, for you are what my life is about.

'Let's agree two things. First, that whatever treatment they offer, we grab it, and second, that through it all the "D" word will never be mentioned. Okay?'

He felt, rather than saw her nod.

'I'm sorry to be so weak,' she whispered.

'You! Weak?' He chuckled in spite of himself. 'You are about as weak as a large whisky and Irn Bru. You are the strongest woman I've ever known. This bloody disease doesn't have a clue what it's letting itself in for, taking on Olive McIlhenney. Just keep giving it that look of yours, It'll get the message and bugger off, sharpish.'

'I wish it was that easy.'

'Aye, but it is in a way. I know next to nothing about these things, but I do know that determination has a big part to play.'

She kissed his chest. 'Okay, I'll do that. I'll give it The Silencer; and you can take it somewhere quiet and give it a kicking. We'll teach the bloody thing to try to come between us.'

15

'He gets around, then, this Mr Futcher,' said the Head of CID, as he and Brian Mackie turned the corner into Crewe Road South. The Western General Hospital lies only a quarter of a mile from the police headquarters building in Fettes Avenue, and so the two detectives had decided to walk to their appointment with Professor Nolan Weston.

The rain of the previous day had gone, but the afternoon was drab and cold. Martin seemed to wear its greyness like an overcoat, to match his mood. He and Alex had spent a silent night: the crisis between them remained unresolved.

'So it seems,' Mackie answered. 'Maggie and Steele saw Katie Mearns, the secretary bird, first thing this morning. She backed up his story, right enough. She told them that Futcher and she worked late the night before Mrs Weston died. When they were finished he took her for a steak, then ran her home. She invited him in for coffee and afters, as she sometimes does, she says, and he stayed until two in the morning.'

'Did Maggie believe her?'

'Yes, on balance she did. So did Stevie. They gave her a moderately hard time; made her go over the story time and again. She never varied at all. Eventually she got annoyed and went into some very graphic detail about the size of Futcher's tackle. Impressive, apparently. His line to the other ladies is that the wife can't take too much of it.'

The superintendent paused. 'I was thinking of asking Maggie to go along and take a look at the evidence,' he added, with a sidelong smile. 'Unless you wanted to lend me Karen Neville, that is.'

Martin chuckled, in spite of himself. 'Neville would love the job, I'm sure. But she's doing something else just now,' he said, as the two men turned into the hospital's entrance roadway.

The Department of Clinical Oncology is a complex which includes some of the newest buildings within the Western General's sprawling grounds. Mackie led the way through the automatic glass doors and into the yellow brick reception area. 'Professor Weston, please,' he said to the nursing assistant seated behind its high wooden counter.

'You're the gentlemen from the police?' she asked, quietly. Martin nodded. 'Yes, he's expecting you. If you go round the corner through the double doors and up the first flight of stairs, then through another set of doors, you'll find his office third on the right. I'll buzz him and let him know that you're coming.'

They followed her directions to the letter. As they pushed their way through the second set of doors, they found a tall man standing in the hall. He was shirt-sleeved in the warmth of the hospital, wearing the trousers of a brown suit. He was as bald as Brian Mackie, but his head seemed bigger and more pointed than the superintendent's gentle dome. 'Gentlemen,' he greeted them solemnly, 'I'm Nolan Weston.'

'Hello, Professor,' said Martin accepting the proffered handshake as he introduced himself and his colleague. 'Glad you could see us so quickly. We'll try not to take up too much of your time.'

Weston led them into a tiny room, so small that there was barely room for two chairs on the other side of his desk. 'This is about Gay, of course,' he began.

'Of course,' said the Head of CID. 'When did you last see your ex-wife, Professor?'

'Three weeks ago,' the tall man answered, as he folded himself awkwardly into his swivel chair. 'She and I took Raymond, our son, up to Aberdeen, for his first term at University.'

'That's just not true, Mr Weston,' Brian Mackie exclaimed. 'You've seen her since then.' He lifted his briefcase on to his lap, opened it and took out a folder. 'Two weeks ago you removed a growth from her leg at St Martha's Private Clinic in the Grange; a procedure for which those premises are not authorised, incidentally. These are your notes, and the biopsy report, which confirmed that your former wife was suffering from a malignant melanoma.'

'Where the hell did you get those?' Weston demanded angrily. 'Those are confidential.'

'Not in the context of an inquiry into a suspicious death, they ain't,' Martin retorted.

'Suspicious death?'

'Extremely,' Mackie went on. 'I have here also, a copy of our postmortem report, which comments on the procedure you performed, and says that secondary tumours were developing rapidly. If you read it, you'll see that your ex-wife's death was caused by a massive overdose of diamorphine. Does that surprise you?'

Nolan Weston looked at him impassively. 'It saddens me, Super-intendent, but no, to be frank it does not surprise me.'

Andy Martin held up a hand. 'Perhaps at this stage, sir, you would like to consider legal representation. It might be better if this interview continued on a more formal basis.'

'No, no, no,' exclaimed the surgeon. 'Let's carry on. I want to hear where this is going.'

'Let's go back to my first question, then,' said Mackie. 'When did you last see Mrs Weston alive?'

'The last time I saw her at all, officer, was when I discharged her from St Martha's. I had a very difficult conversation with her about the biopsy report, and I offered to refer her case at once to Mr Simmers, a consultant colleague of mine. She refused to let me do that. She said that she wanted to go home for a couple of weeks to think things through and put her affairs in order.

'I agreed to that on condition that if she experienced any growing discomfort she would contact me.'

'Have you spoken to her since?'

'I phoned her a couple of times of an evening, just to see that she was all right. I spoke to her last on Monday. She said that everything was as it had been, and she said that I would hear from her on Thursday.' His head dropped briefly. 'I understand what she meant now.'

'Where were you on Wednesday night, sir? Specifically, between midnight and two am?'

'I was at home, in bed, with my wife.'

'And she will confirm that?'

'If necessary. She is extremely pregnant. She kept me awake most of the night. But why do you ask me this?'

Martin shifted in his uncomfortable chair. 'Because someone helped Mrs Weston end her life, Professor. She was injected, and a plastic bag was secured over her head.'

'She couldn't have done it herself?'

'No way. Whoever did it took away the syringe and the roll of the black tape which was used to secure the bag. She had help; no doubt about it.'

'This man she saw from time to time? Futcher, the ad-man. Was it him?'

'No. We don't think so.' There was a pause, as Weston looked from one detective to the other.

'Why were you so secretive about treating your former wife, Professor?' asked Mackie.

'Because I didn't want my present wife to find out about it,' came the retort, sharply.

'Couldn't you have referred her to someone else from the very start?'

'Gay didn't want that. She asked me to do the procedure; and I always did what she asked.'

'Including divorcing her?'

Averting his eyes once more, Weston nodded.

'Tell us about your relationship with her, please,' said the Head of CID.

The man across the desk laughed, softly. 'How long do you have?' He leaned back in his seat, until his shoulders and the back of his head were touching the partition wall behind him. 'Gaynor and I were married for twelve years,' he began, 'and throughout that time we were extremely happy . . . or so I thought. Then, on our twelfth anniversary, she told me she was leaving me; just like that.

'She told me that there were things that she wanted to do with her life, and that she simply could not achieve them within the confines of marriage. There was no discussion; she just moved out, to a small flat in Barnton. A year later we were divorced by mutual consent. We had joint custody of Raymond, but it was agreed that he should live with me during the school term.

'During our separation and immediately after our divorce we didn't see much of each other; nothing at all, in fact, if Ray wasn't the reason. I heard about her, of course; heard how her consultancy career was going from strength to strength. Raymond would mention the odd name too; men's names, gentlemen callers, I suppose you'd say.

'Almost all of my life was work at that period; but not quite all. I formed a relationship with Avril, my second wife – at that time she was my secretary at the University – and five years ago, we married. To my surprise, Gaynor didn't like that at all. She didn't speak to me for a year. Then out of the blue, I had a call from her asking me to bring Ray out to Oldbarns, to which she had just moved, for supper.

'I did that, and we had a good time together; it was like being a family unit again, almost. This became a weekly event, until one time when Ray had flu. I called her to tell her this, but she asked me if I'd like to come anyway, on my own.'

Weston looked at the two detectives. 'You have to remember, I'd never stopped loving her. So I went out there, for dinner, on the excuse that we had to discuss Ray's schooling. Our relationship changed that night: I found myself having an affair with my ex-wife.'

'Did she regret the divorce?' asked Martin.

'No. Not for one minute. The thing about Gay, you see, was her craving for danger; yet conversely, she didn't like to feel threatened. Futcher, the ad-man, he was married too, like me. There was that element of risk of exposure, but safety too in that the involvement was purely physical.'

'What about you? You still loved her.'

'Yes, and she loved me. But we had defined our relationship long before.'

'So there was you, and there was Futcher,' Mackie intervened. 'Was there anyone else?'

A shadow seemed to pass across Nolan Weston's face. 'There may have been,' he replied. 'She told me once that Futcher and I weren't the only arrows in her quiver. Her phrase, not mine. But she never mentioned a name.'

'Might your son have known?' asked the superintendent.

'It's possible. I'll ask him, but not tonight. He's still in shock, poor lad; as are we all, to an extent.'

'It's important, sir. If you can't, we may have to interview him ourselves.'

'No, leave him to me, please. I'll have a talk with him tomorrow morning.'

'Fair enough,' Martin agreed, 'but no later. When did he get home?'

'Last night. He has a car up in Aberdeen, but I felt happier going up to collect him myself, rather than let him make such a long drive in an emotional state.'

'You must have been fairly emotional yourself, Professor.'

'I'm a surgeon, Mr Martin. I was emotional two weeks ago, when I realised that Gay was going to die. Yesterday I felt an element of relief that she, Ray and I had been spared the weeks and months of torment which we had all faced.'

'You didn't give her the diamorphine did you, Professor?' the Head of CID asked quietly.

'No sir, I did not. To be frank with you, had she asked me for it, I think I would have done. But she didn't.'

'Just as well, then,' said Martin rising slowly to his feet. 'Thank you, Professor, for your help. Brian, give Mr Weston your number, so that he can call you directly once he's spoken to his son.' The superintendent's hand had already left his breast pocket, a business card held between the first two fingers.

Nolan Weston walked his visitors to the top of the stairs. The two policemen made their way silently down to the ground floor, through the reception area, which was much busier than it had been earlier, and outside into the cold grey afternoon.

'What did you think of him?' said Mackie, as the glass doors closed behind them.

Martin stared at him, blankly, a shocked expression on his face. 'What is it, Andy?' the superintendent asked.

'You didn't see them then?'

'Who? Where?'

'In there just now, in the waiting area. They had their backs to us, but I'd know them anywhere: Neil and Olive McIlhenney.'

55

16

'So far, Inspector, there have been seventeen sightings of this man Hawkins across Europe.' Skinner glanced at the report on his desk. 'Every one of them has been checked out, and at the end of every one there's been a wild goose.

'Fake Hawkinses have been seen in Germany, France, Poland, Italy, Switzerland, England and Spain. Oh, sorry, I forgot Luxembourg. These have all been registered in the past twenty-four hours. The Polish contact turned out to be a tall blonde transsexual, who just happened to have a limp.' He smiled. 'I guess we'll hear about a right . . . few more before we fasten onto the right man – if we ever do.'

'It's not like you to sound pessimistic, sir,' McGuire remarked.

'Realistic, Mario; I'd rather you said realistic. This bloke is a professional, just like us. Let me ask you something. If you wanted to go undercover for any purpose, how easy d'you think it would be for us to find you? Yes, even us, your close colleagues?'

The swarthy detective laughed. 'You mean if I decided to do a runner from the wife? How scarce could I make myself?

'I suppose I'd do the obvious things. I'd dye my hair and eyebrows another colour, as far away from black as possible . . . maybe red like Maggie. I'd wear glasses, dark wherever I could, to cut down the chance of eye contact with someone who might know me or might have seen a picture. I'd try to do something with my teeth; dye them too, perhaps, to make them less white and sparkly.' He paused, thinking. 'Yes, and I'd try to do something about my mannerisms as well; to eliminate recognisable things like, for example, the way I smile.

'My ace card, though, would be to speak Italian everywhere I went.'

Skinner nodded. 'Right. Now I don't think that all of those things put together would fool Maggie, or me, or Mr Martin or Neil: not the people closest to you. But someone else, even in the force, they'd have trouble.'

'How many languages does Hawkins speak?' asked McGuire, suddenly.

'Hey,' the DCC responded, 'that's a good question. I'll get on to London and ask them. Maybe we're looking for a German, or an Italian.'

'Not an Italian, boss. Even if he dyed his hair black, like mine, it wouldn't work. His features are wrong.'

'I'll take your word for it. Anyway, it all leads into the point I was going to make. You and I, we're amateurs in the anonymity business. Hawkins is a pro. His life depends on it. If you can come up with a few simple dodges on the spur of the moment, he's going to pull something really special out of the hat. All that artwork in the envelopes I handed out yesterday, Mario; probably none of it's worth a damn.

'We're blind, my friend, stone blind. As coppers we're used to events and people we can come to grips with, and we've got all sorts of toys to help us look for them. But in this task we're an extension of the intelligence community; groping about in the dark trying to catch a puff of smoke in our hands.

'That's the way it is in their world. They deal in rumour and suggestion, not substance; they stand sightless in some damn great gallery, picking up each and every whisper, analysing them, giving them form and putting them together until the jigsaw picture is complete; or at least recognisable.'

Skinner leaned back in his chair. 'So, inspector, what murmurings have you been picking up around your patch?'

McGuire shook his head. 'So far, boss, the silence has been deafening.'

17

Neil McIlhenney stared out of the only window in the small consulting room. It looked on to a car park, in which every space seemed to be occupied. 'I never realised—' he whispered, to himself.

'What?' said Olive sharply, beside him.

'Sorry love,' he replied. 'I was thinking out loud. The car parks here; there are so many of them, and they're all full. I never realised that there were so many sick people.'

'You just concentrate on this one!' The strain in her voice tore at his heart; he reached across and took her hand, feeling the pressure as she squeezed his.

'Sure, love, sure.'

They had been in the clinic for just over two hours. In that time, Olive had been weighed, examined by a thin-faced girl who had introduced herself as Dr Berry, Mr Simmers' registrar, and sent for a scan. A few minutes before they had been called back into the consulting room.

They looked over their shoulders, simultaneously, as the door opened. A tall, well-built, fair-haired, round-faced man strode into the room, wearing a white coat and with the tool of his trade, a stethoscope, hanging from his neck. 'Good afternoon,' he said. 'I'm Mr Simmers, your consultant. Sorry to have kept you waiting; I'm afraid that the first consultation always seems to take for ever. That's because there are so many things we have to do.'

He sat, not behind his desk, but on it, and looked directly at Olive. At once Neil was struck by the gentleness of his eyes and by the calmness of his expression. From out of nowhere, an inexplicable feeling of relief swept over him.

'The first thing I have to ask you, Mrs McIlhenney, is this. Do you understand what is happening to you?'

'Yes,' she replied; the word was clipped, but controlled.

'That's good. In these situations we can't afford to prevaricate. You have an incurable disease, Mrs McIlhenney; we can't avoid that fact. You have a carcinoma of the right lung in the second stage of development. Now I use the word incurable because that in clinical

58

terms is what it is. However it is not untreatable; there are ways of attacking your tumour, and the secondary growth.

'Surgery isn't an option here, not with the metastasis in the lymphatic system. But we do have the options of chemotherapy or radiation therapy or a mixture of both. There is a chance that if you react favourably, your cancer can be driven into remission, possibly indefinitely. Looking at your X-Ray, and on the basis of Dr Berry's examination, I would propose that we start you on a course of chemotherapy. Radiation might have a part to play later, depending on the rate of progress, but not just yet.'

For the first time, the consultant looked at Neil, then back to Olive. His gentle blue eyes were unblinking. 'I'm not going to play anything down here. These treatments are aggressive, and the side-effects . . . at least initially . . . will be unpleasant. You'll experience a day or two of fairly violent sickness, but we'll do what we can to control that, using steroids.

'However . . .' He paused. 'However; there is a further alternative which I have to put to you, and that is that we simply give you palliative treatments and concentrate on keeping you as well and as comfortable as possible, for as long as possible. The choice has to be yours.'

To her complete surprise, she smiled at him. 'You mean I can give up?' she asked. Then, without waiting for a reply, she looked sideways at Neil, raising her eyebrows very slightly. He gave the briefest of nods.

Olive McIlhenney turned back to the consultant. 'As my husband would say, if I didn't have him so well trained,' she said, 'bugger that for a game of soldiers.

'When do we start the treatment?'

18

'Neil doesn't have the problem, Andy. It's Olive who's in bother.'

'Cancer?'

'Look, don't ask me about it, man. The big fella asked me for help and I got Sarah involved. If he wants to tell anyone about what's happening, he will. But until he does say something, you and Mackie forget about seeing them. Okay?'

Martin nodded, emphatically. 'Absolutely. I'll call Brian to let him know; not that he's an office gossip type, mind you. Christ,' he said, 'it's a cliché, I know, but something like this doesn't half put your own troubles into perspective.'

'Don't talk to me about them either. Sarah and I have decided that you and Alex can sort your own lives out. Selfish bastards we may be, but you two are adults. Only you know how you feel.'

He spun away from the window of his office. 'Let's change the subject. How's the Weston investigation coming along?'

'It's not going to be a quick fix,' the Head of CID replied. 'That much I do know. The husband looked like a good bet, but he claimed that he was at home in bed with his wife. Brian's gone to interview the lady, but I've no doubt he was telling the truth.'

'Anyone else in the frame?'

'Well, there's the son, Raymond. Professor Weston let slip that he has a car up in Aberdeen, so it's possible that he could have driven down to Oldbarns. He's only a kid, though; just eighteen. I don't think for a minute that his mother would have involved him in helping to end her life.'

'Still, he'll have to be interviewed,' said Skinner.

'Sure, I know, but it's not a priority. No, there's one other line of enquiry open to us. Mrs Weston was killed with a pharmaceutical quality drug. If we can trace the source . . .'

'You're sure it couldn't have been street heroin?'

'Bob, the stuff was absolutely pure. If anything like that was in circulation, we'd be finding bodies all over the city.'

'Aye, I suppose you're right. So what are you going to do about it?'

'We're doing it right now. Rose and Steele are contacting the

Chief Pharmacists in every hospital in the city, asking them to verify their stocks of diamorphine, and report any short-falls. The Drugs Squad maintains regular contact with the only manufacturer in the area, but their procedures and security are exemplary, so I don't believe for one moment that the stuff that killed Mrs Weston came from there.'

The big DCC sat on the edge of the Chief's desk. 'It's bloody difficult to nick heroin from a hospital pharmacy as well. The stuff's kept under lock and key, and only released on a doctor's signature.' He looked across at Martin. 'But maybe if you were a doctor . . . a consultant, even.'

'But Nolan Weston didn't do it.'

'According to his wife. Come on, Andy; if you had solid circumstantial evidence against some hooligan and he offered his wife as an alibi, would you accept it at face value? Bloody sure you wouldn't. Professor's wives don't tell porkies? Is that what you're saying to me?'

'Touché!' The chief superintendent laughed, gently. 'However if you were a juror – not a cynical bastard of a copper, but an ordinary, innocent, conscientious juror – and the nice, pregnant Prof's wife stood up in the witness box and swore on the Bible that when her predecessor was off-ed, she was making him a nice cup of hot chocolate, would you believe her? Almost certainly, you would.' It was Skinner's turn to smile.

'Anyway,' continued Martin. 'I believe Weston.'

The acting chief constable pushed himself off the desk and took two steps back to the window. 'Okay, I won't argue with that.' Suddenly his right hand shot up, index finger pointing at his colleague. 'So Weston didn't do it. But maybe he supplied the diamorphine.'

'He denies that too.'

'Nonetheless, let's see what your check with the hospitals shows us.' He turned once more to look out of the window, but stopped and looked back at the younger man.

'Oh aye, and make sure you check that St Martha's place as well. If I wanted to misappropriate some smack, I'd do it there rather than at the Western or the Royal.'

'Brian and I covered that when we were there,' the Head of CID countered. 'They store some prescription drugs there, but not diamorphine. They buy their supplies from the pharmacy at the Royal, on prescriptions signed by the doctors who consult there. The dragon Miss Pople signs personally for every issue.'

'Bugger. Are you trying to slam every door in my face, pal?'

'No.' Martin smiled. 'Look, just let us get on with it, Bob, eh.

There's nothing you would do if you were running this show that we won't cover, believe me.'

'Sure, I know that, my friend. Don't mind me; it's just this bloody office. It may be only a hundred yards from yours, but when the door's closed it seems like miles.

'You carry on, and I wish you the best of luck; for you're going to need it. Without evidence tying anyone to the scene, you're going to have to find the source of the diamorphine to have a chance of clearing this one up.'

'Don't I know it—' He broke off as the door opened and Gerry Crossley's head appeared.

'Sorry to butt in, Mr Skinner,' he said. 'Will you take a call from DI Impey of Dumfries and Galloway Special Branch. Neil's not available, so he's asked for you. He says it's really urgent.'

The DCC smiled. 'McIlhenney must have put the frighteners on him right enough,' he said to Martin. 'He's probably decided to report everything as of now, on an urgent basis.'

'Okay, Gerry, put him through.'

He crossed to his desk and sat behind it, picking up the phone on the first ring. 'Inspector,' he barked, 'What have you got?'

'A possible contact with our target, sir. We're following him right now, and he's heading your way.' Impey's voice sounded hollow; there was a rushing noise in the background.

'Tell me you're not calling on a car-phone, Inspector,' said Skinner, heavily. 'Please tell me that. Those things are about as secure as a politician's fly.'

'I'm sorry, sir,' said the detective, a shade plaintively. 'I'd no choice. It all happened so fast. I didna' even have time to pick up my sergeant.'

'Okay, just tell me where you are. Minimum details.'

'I'm on the road from Moffat to Edinburgh, up by the Devil's Beeftub. Our subject's in a red Vauxhall Vectra, Northern Ireland registration Delta Echo Whisky 4357.'

Skinner thought fast. 'Okay. If you're on that road you won't come off it before Leadburn, that's for sure. Is there a lot of traffic?'

'Aye, sir, there's a convoy of two tourist buses and three lorries up ahead. It'll be slow going, like.'

'Well just you be sure that your man doesn't get the jump on you as he clears it. Don't let him twig you either, though. When you get to the Leadburn junction you'll find Mario McGuire parked and waiting for you. Transfer into his car as quick as you can and continue surveillance.

'Brief Mario on the circumstances when you team up.'

'Very good, sir,' said Impey, his words crackling as his carphone lost its signal.

Martin, curious, was gazing at Skinner as he hung up.

'Hawkins?'

'Could be. If it is, I only hope he doesn't rumble our friend Impey, otherwise we'll find the poor bastard dead in a ditch up Tweedsmuir way.'

19

'As expected, Brian?' Martin sounded weary as he spoke into the telephone.

'Entirely,' Mackie replied. 'Avril Weston confirms that she and the Professor were at home together at the time of Gaynor's death. They were doing the *Telegraph* Crossword, as a matter of fact. The lady is indeed very pregnant, and she has difficulty sleeping, like he said.

'She knew about Gaynor's condition, apparently. Nolan told her about it after he did the operation at St Martha's; he was in a right state, as you could imagine.'

'Did she know what sort of a relationship her husband had with his ex-wife?'

'I don't believe so,' the superintendent answered. 'I did ask her – very gently, you understand – whether she approved of his seeing her. She told me that as far as she was concerned it was good for Raymond that his parents remained on friendly terms after their divorce. But she didn't give me the impression that she knew they were having it off.'

Martin heard a slurping sound come over the phone line, and guessed that Mackie must be drinking from a mug of coffee. 'The boy was up and about, by the way,' he continued. 'He seemed *compos mentis* to me so I asked him a few questions.

'He said that the first he knew of his mother's illness was when his father told him yesterday, when he picked him up from Aberdeen. The last time he spoke to her was on Wednesday night. She phoned him at his hall of residence; only just caught him, the boy said, before he went out to a Freshers do with his pals.

'She sounded okay, according to the lad, although it struck him at the time that she didn't really say why she was calling him. He knows now that she was saying goodbye.'

'Ahh, poor kid,' Martin murmured. 'Did you ask him about—'

'—his mother's sex-life? Yes. I was never happy with the idea of leaving that to the father. As far as he knew she didn't have any boyfriends. Obviously Futcher never went out to Oldbarns while the lad was there. He did say that his mother used to go to SNO concerts and to the Opera, and he was under the impression that she went with someone, although she never mentioned a name. It needn't have been a man.'

'Worth looking into, though.'

'I agree. I've asked Maggie and Stevie to go out to Oldbarns this evening to re-interview the Ball woman.'

'Christ, watch the overtime!'

'I didn't have any choice. She's off to the Canaries tomorrow morning, so we've got to catch her tonight.'

'You don't fancy her for it? Not even a wee bit?'

Mackie drew a breath. 'Nah, worse luck. There's something I never told you about Joan Ball. She has severe arthritis in both hands. She was given early retirement from the Civil Service three years ago on health grounds. No way could she have injected Gaynor; even fastening the plastic bag over her head would have been beyond her.'

'Jesus, this doesn't get any easier, Thin Man, does it.'

To Martin's surprise, a gentle laugh sounded down the line. 'Ah, but I haven't given you the good news yet,' said the superintendent. 'Arthur Dorward's clever people have managed to lift a saliva trace off one of the two wine glasses that were left in Mrs Weston's sink – the one without Mrs Weston's lipstick on it. Hopefully, it'll give us a DNA match; if only we can find the bugger who left it.'

20

'Is Special Branch always like this, Inspector?' asked Karen Neville.

'Nah,' Mario McGuire answered. As he spoke he kept his eyes firmly on the rear-view mirror, watching the road behind. The angled, four-way Leadburn junction lay two hundred yards beyond their parking place.

'Most of the time it's the sort of stuff you've been doing; checking on known or potential troublemakers, surveillance, VIP protection. We rarely get to do action things.'

'You don't sound very excited by the prospect.'

'That's because I'm not, sergeant. Five years ago, I might well have looked forward to a bundle with an international terrorist, but not any more.'

Neville frowned. 'What happened to change you?'

'I got married, for one thing. I like going home to the wife at night with all my bits in place.' His mouth twisted wryly. 'I suppose getting shot might have affected me too.'

'You were shot!? When?'

'A few years back; in a good old-fashioned gunfight.'

'Were you badly hurt?'

'Oh aye. When you're on the floor, feeling numb all over, listening to the blood bubbling out of your chest and someone says to you, "It's okay, son, take it easy . . ." you know you're badly hurt. The thing I remember best is Bob Skinner talking to me. He said all the right things, but I could see from the look in his eyes that he was just doing his best to reassure me.'

He laughed. 'Practical to the end, that's the boss. I remember him saying, "the Royal Infirmary's right next door". Funnily enough, that was the thing that made me feel better.'

'You went through that,' said Neville, 'yet here you are in SB, carrying a gun and waiting for a bad guy? Couldn't you have asked for a uniform job?'

'Sure I could. But if I had, then that bullet would have taken more out of me than blood and a bit of lung tissue. I have to do the job the

66

way I've always done it, for my sake; but that doesn't mean that I have to relish it.'

'Don't you worry about . . .' She hesitated. 'Should I worry—?'

McGuire read her thoughts. 'Should you be worried in case the action starts and I freeze up?' he asked. 'No way, Karen. One thing getting shot does for you; it makes you very keen not to get shot again. Freeze, and that's what's going to happen.'

'Have you ever shot anyone?' she asked, quietly.

'I don't know, to tell you the truth. We were all blazing away that night. I might have hit the guy, I suppose, but I don't think so.'

'Has anyone else on the team?'

'That's not a question you should ask. Those who have don't like to talk about it. But since you have asked it . . . Andy Martin and Brian Mackie have. They got the guy who shot me. The boss has too. He put another guy down that night in the hall. Andy had to do it another time as well . . . and don't, in your daftest moment, ever ask him about that. Oh aye, and so did Brian.'

'Brian Mackie?' Neville's surprise burst from her.

'Aye, the Thin Man; never batted an eyelid either. He's the best shot on—' His eyes narrowed as he looked in the mirror. 'Hold on. A red car just came round the bend in the distance.'

The sergeant turned to look out of the rear window. 'Yes. I see it. A silver car, then a green one, then red. It looks like a Vauxhall too.'

'Okay, look this way now. Don't give the driver any idea that we might be waiting for him. Eat your apple or something.' Quickly, from a pocket in the driver's door, he took two miniature football boots, joined by a white cord and slung them round the rear view mirror. 'Some of the lads take the piss out of me about my theory, but I can't think of a better way of disguising an unmarked car. Could you imagine a cop wagon with windscreen ornaments?'

'How about a nodding dog on the back shelf?' Karen suggested, dryly.

'Nah, nae use. The bad guys might think it was McIlhenney.'

'Don't you knock Neil. I think he's nice.'

'I'm allowed to knock him. He's my best pal.' He glanced in the side mirror, as he tugged the ring-pull to open a can of Pepsi and raised it to his lips. 'This is the guy all right.' He drank from the tin as the red car swept past. 'Delta Echo Whisky 4357,' he read, switching on the engine of his Nissan as he spoke. 'Get ready.'

Less than thirty seconds later, the rear off-side door of the car was jerked open and a man slid quickly into the back seat. 'Hello Joe,' said McGuire. 'This is Karen Neville.' He handed the can of Pepsi to the newcomer. 'Finish that for me.'

Slipping into first gear, he slid from his parking place on the verge and moved smoothly into traffic, behind a blue Volkswagen. Ahead of them, the red Vauxhall took a left turn at the junction. 'Heading for Penicuik,' the inspector muttered. 'Okay, Joe. Tell us all about it.'

'Haud on a minute, son,' the veteran, grizzled Detective Inspector Impey grunted, breathing heavily from his short sprint to McGuire's car. 'I need this.' He raised the Pepsi and threw his head back, emptying the can in a single swallow. 'Hah, that's better.

'Right, about our man.' He tapped his colleague on the shoulder. 'Don't get too close now, Mario.'

'Teach your Granny,' the other man growled.

'Dinna be so touchy. Here, son, I don't think your boss likes me.'

'Joe, there'll be someone else doesn't like you if you don't get to the bloody point!'

'Aye, okay, okay. This is the wey it happened. We were watching the Irish ferry coming into dock at Craigryan, lookin' at the folk through binoculars, like. All of a sudden, Ah sees this bloke. He's a dead ringer for one of those photofits that your boss gave us. Ginger hair, big thick moustache. You ken the one ah mean.

'Then, while I'm watching him, he gets up and walked across the deck, and he's got a limp. Ah'm really interested then.' He paused. 'Got ony mair Pepsi?' Neville reached into her bag and handed him a can. 'Thanks, hen,' said Impey as he opened it. The sergeant fought off an urge to make clucking noises.

'Normally we give a' the cars coming off the ferry a quick once over, looking for familiar faces from the circulation list. Things might be quieter in Ireland these days, but old habits die hard, like. My oppo was up the ramp, and I was at the exit with a uniformed polis. It was fine till we got tae this bloke. He takes a look at the uniform coming towards him, shouted something at him and put his foot down. Ah didnae have time to wait for my oppo. My car was handy, so I jumped in it and got after him.'

'Why would someone like Hawkins panic at a police ferry check?' Neville asked casually.

'How the bloody hell would I know, hen?' Impey snapped at her, then turned once more to look at the back of McGuire's head. 'I couldnae be sure where he was going until he turned off the A74 for Moffat. That was when I phoned McIlhenney, only he wisnae in, so I phoned your boss.'

'He told me,' muttered McGuire, as he drove into the centre of Penicuik. 'I don't suppose you called anyone to ask for a number trace.'

'Naw,' Impey replied. 'Ah was concentrating on the subject, wasn't Ah.'

'That's okay, for we did. Our man's driving a hired car. We're trying to dig up someone in Eurodollar to give us the hirer's details. Bugger.' He swore softly as the traffic lights in the middle of the small Midlothian town turned to amber. As he watched, helplessly trapped behind two other vehicles, their quarry hit the accelerator and shot across the junction.

'Pull out and go through,' Impey urged.

'Don't be daft, Joe. If he looked back and saw me do that, he'd rumble us for sure – if he hasn't already that is. Patience, man, he's got traffic in front of him; we'll catch him up.'

Like a watched kettle, the lights seemed to take forever to change, but eventually the three police officers resumed their pursuit. For a time it seemed that McGuire's confidence had been misplaced, as they found themselves trapped behind two articulated lorries which had pulled out of a small industrial estate just beyond the town centre. They had reached Glencorse Barracks before the road cleared far enough ahead to allow overtaking, but once they had passed the obstruction, the inspector was able to put his foot down.

They were nearing a stretch of dual carriageway, when Neville pointed to a coach less than two hundred yards in front of them. 'I think he's in front of that bus. I caught a flash of red just then.' As if to prove her right, the red Vauxhall pulled into the overtaking lane of the widened roadway and speeded up. McGuire accelerated steadily, keeping pace with it but being careful not to be drawn too close.

Their target led them down the straight road towards Edinburgh, reaching, after five minutes, the double roundabout of the Straiton junction with the city bypass. At the second of the huge islands, the suspected Hawkins indicated right and swung off the Edinburgh road, heading eastwards.

'Why are we going this way, I wonder?' McGuire mused aloud. 'He's heading away from the posh end of the city.'

'Maybe he's going south?' Impey suggested.

'Maybe, but I doubt it, Joe. If he was heading, say for Berwick, he'd have taken another route. Unless, of course, he spotted us way back and he's been pulling our chains ever since. We'll find out when we get to the end of the bypass.'

'How's that, like?'

'Because if he heads for Leith, he's probably close to his destination. If he heads down the A1, then he's taking the piss and I'm going to have him. You got your firearm handy?'

'Ah'm not carrying, Mario,' Impey confessed, sheepishly.

'Christ, are you going out of your way to wind up Bob Skinner? Did you not hear his instruction at that briefing?'

'Aye, but Ah just dinnae like guns. Ah had a mate once shot himself in the leg with his.'

'I hate to think where the boss'll shoot you if he finds out you've ignored his order. Okay, Karen's armed and able to back me up, and we're only going after one bloke, but if we'd been after a team, you could have put us all in danger.'

Impey growled. 'Ach you city polis. Yis are all fuckin' cowboys. Excuse my French, hen.'

'C'est rien,' Neville replied.

In a little under ten minutes they came to the junction which marked the end of the bypass. McGuire drew the Nissan a little closer to the red car, ready to cover his move, whether he headed north or south. Beside him, his sergeant shifted edgily in her seat.

Their quarry took neither option. Instead he headed straight through the junction and turned into the service area on the other side of the wide A1. 'Going for petrol,' McGuire guessed. He slipped quietly off the roundabout, hanging back as far as he dared, then turned into the narrow access road, slowing to check that the Vauxhall had not turned into the motor lodge car park, but had indeed carried on to the filling station beyond.

There were six pumps on the forecourt, all occupied. The red car stood a little back from them, waiting for one to clear. As he slid quietly behind him, McGuire could see the driver clearly for the first time, in profile as he looked at the pumps. He had lit a cigarette; his right arm was leaning on the open window. 'I can see the likeness right enough, Joe. And yet . . .' Something gnawed at the back of his mind.

'Mario.' Karen Neville touched his arm, interrupting his search of his memory. 'One of the pumps just cleared. Why isn't he moving up?'

'Maybe he needs diesel?' Impey suggested.

'Unlikely in a hire car. Maybe he's just finishing his fag before he goes to fill up. Whatever, he's off guard and I'm having him. Otherwise I'll have to buy bloody petrol or he'll twig us. Karen, you take the passenger side. Joe, you stay here.'

Mario McGuire was a big, easy-going man, until the action button was pressed. He opened his door and stepped out of the car, his gun in his hand in an instant. Swiftly and noiselessly, he closed the gap to the red car.

The man inside was drawing on his cigarette; he started in surprise as Karen Neville stepped into his line of vision. In the same moment the inspector reached through the Vectra's open side window and pressed the cold muzzle of his Walther to the back of the man's head.

'Good evening, sir,' he said, in a quiet, conversational tone. 'Just in case you're in any doubt, we are police officers and that thing you feel against your skull is not a piece of pipe, or a banana or anything like that. It's a real gun, and they make me nervous, so if you move the wrong muscle you won't move any others, ever again.

'Now, I want you to step out of the car, keeping your hands in the air; then I want you to lie face down on the ground.'

21

'Where is this man Impey now?' said Bob Skinner. He spoke quietly, but there was something in his tone which send a cold shiver running down Mario McGuire's spine.

'On his way back to Dumfries, boss. I told him to get the you-know-what out of Edinburgh before you got your hands on him.'

'Well the bugger can't run fast enough, or far enough. Wherever he surfaces again he's going to find out that my bite is a hell of a lot worse than my bark.'

'Don't be too hard on him, boss. He was showing initiative; he just made an honest mistake.'

'So did the captain of the *Titanic*. Thanks to that man and his monumental stupidity, I've had the commander of the Interpol task force on counterfeiting moaning down my phone for the last half hour. You were advised of this operation, as was every other Special Branch office in the country, including Dumfries and bloody Galloway. You were all told that they were watching a major software forgery centre in South Armagh and you were all given photographs of the agents involved.

'In spite of that, because of Impey's "honest mistake" we've ruined the culmination of the operation. The guy you lifted was following a courier; the purpose of that was to discover the bootleggers' main distribution route and from that to catch their customers with the stuff in their possession. The Interpol people even sent a fax to Impey's office warning him that the man was on the move. I've checked; it's in his in-tray and it was there when he left to check the ferry passengers.'

McGuire scratched his chin. 'Oh shit,' he groaned. 'Poor old Joe.'

'Don't waste your sympathy on the guy, Mario. He should have committed that information to memory, and he should have had that man's face imprinted in his brain. That's standard SB procedure as you know well. If Impey isn't up to following it, he isn't up to the job. But he won't be in it for much longer.

'He'll have a very embarrassed chief constable waiting for him when he gets back to his office tomorrow morning, and believe me, Archie Deas is not a man anyone wants to embarrass.'

'What'll he do to him?'

'Hang him up by his soft bits until they drop off, probably. Once they have, he'll stick him back in a uniform and post him to Auchencross, or some place like that, with a bike to get around on. At least that's what I've suggested to Archie that he should do.'

He swivelled in his chair. 'What about Mr Steyn, the agent? Have you calmed him down?'

'Just about. I've booked him into the George for the night, on our tab. He'll go back to Ireland in the morning.'

'Take him out to dinner, just to show real contrition. Take Mags along if you like.'

McGuire frowned. 'I can't do that, boss. I've promised to meet Neil tonight. He says he's got something to tell me.' The frown turned into his dazzling smile. 'From the way he sounded, I suspect that Olive's in the club again.'

22

It seemed to Stevie Steele that while Joan Ball couldn't have been more than fifty-five, her hands looked as if they could have been ninety. They hung from her wrists like two claws as she spoke to her visitors, knuckles hugely swollen, fingers twisted cruelly into her palms.

She caught the young detective's glance. 'What do you think of my talons, sergeant?' she asked, holding one up against the light from a table lamp beside her chair.

'I think it's a damn shame, Miss Ball. Don't they make it difficult for you to live out in the country? I mean, you can't drive, can you.'

'No, I can't. But I manage all right. The Social Services are very good; they provide all sorts of support. Home help; someone to do my shopping and so on. Then there are the disabled charity people; they helped me with adapting the house, and in other ways too. I have a brother in North Berwick who takes me about, and a sister in Edinburgh. And of course, Gaynor was a great help to me too, in all sorts of ways. For example she was good with a sewing machine, so she would alter clothes for me. I can't manage buttons or zips any more: too small and fiddly. She would replace them with Velcro fastenings. She was a very kind person, very thoughtful; I'll miss her a great deal.'

Her steady gaze moved from Steele to Rose. 'I take it that you want to ask me more questions about her.'

'You take it right,' the chief inspector replied. 'Did you see much of Mrs Weston in the two weeks before her death?' she asked.

'Quite a bit, really; she was off work all that time.'

'Did she tell you why?'

'She said that she had a little women's trouble, and that she had been ordered to stay at home for a couple of weeks. No gentleman callers.' Her eyes narrowed as she looked at Rose. 'Would I be correct in guessing that it was a little more serious than that?'

'Yes you would. Mrs Weston was very ill; without hope of recovery in fact.'

'I see. So she decided to end her life, and now you're looking for the person who helped her.'

'How do you work that one out?'

'Come on sergeant.' She threw him a withering look. 'Almost the first question I was asked when I was interviewed before was whether I had seen Nolan's car, or the man Futcher's, outside Gaynor's house that night.'

'And you still can't recall seeing either one?' asked Rose.

'No, because they weren't there. But that doesn't matter a damn. The covered parking at the far end of the square is never full. There's no car in my space, for example. If Gaynor had a visitor he could easily have put his car in there, or even left it on the approach road.'

'None of the other residents saw anything parked on that road. I don't suppose there's any way of checking the other possibility. In any event, we're pretty satisfied that neither Professor Weston nor Mr Futcher were there that night, so we have to look for alternatives.'

'We've been through Mrs Weston's address book; as far as we can tell most of the entries and telephone numbers in there relate to business associates.'

'Yes; that would be right. Gaynor's work was her life; her professional and social circles were pretty much interchangeable. However, I don't believe that there was anyone at work with whom she was particularly close.'

'No one at all?'

'I suppose you could talk to her secretary, and the other staff in her business.'

'We have,' said Steele. 'The secretary knew of her relationship with Futcher, but that was all. The other three employees didn't even know where she lived, other than that it was in East Lothian. Rosamund, the secretary, is the only one who's ever been out there.'

'However,' Rose continued, 'Mrs Weston once made a remark which suggested that there might have been a third man in her life. Do you know anything about that?'

Joan Ball frowned. 'Gaynor never mentioned anything to me about a third man.' Rose groaned inwardly, but even as she did, the woman drew in a deep breath, clasping her twisted hands together. 'Nevertheless,' she went on, 'I did have a suspicion that there might be. Whenever she had a visitor she would always mention it at some point. I always knew when Futcher was there, or Nolan such . . . a nice man, Nolan. I remember the times when Rosamund came to visit; if they had a rush job on, sometimes Gaynor would work at weekends.

'But there were, I think three occasions on which I saw a car there, at night, following which she didn't say anything.'

'Can you describe the car?'

'Four wheels and a roof, other than that I'm lost. I have no memory for colours, and I wouldn't know one make from another . . . other than Beetles; I used to have one of them. But this wasn't a Beetle.'

'You can't be sure the visitor was a man, though,' said the chief inspector.

'No, I can't, but the car was still there in the early hours of the morning on at least two of the occasions . . . I'm a poor sleeper . . . but gone by my breakfast-time. Read into that what you will. I can't help you any further I'm afraid.'

'Can you remember when these visits took place? That might help.'

'Over the last six or seven months. The most recent occasion was about a month ago.'

'Good. Even that gives us some extra help.' She stood, and Steele followed. 'Thank you very much, Miss Ball. We'll just go next door to Mrs Weston's now. I've brought the keys, and there's something inside I want to check.'

Their arthritic hostess showed them slowly to the door. 'Enjoy your holiday,' said Rose.

'I'll try. I'm going with a disabled group; they have people to help you pack and so on. I'd rather be on an ordinary tour, but it's for the best. The important thing is to get some warmth into these things.' She held up a ravaged hand to wave them goodbye.

'She's a game lady,' Steele remarked as they stood outside in the evening darkness. 'Listen, ma'am, what did you mean about checking next door? I'm expected home at some point tonight.'

'It won't take long. I want to take a look at Mrs Weston's laptop. She didn't keep personal appointments on her office machine. Maybe she had a computer diary out here. I looked at her Filofax myself, and if there had been anything in it about a night visit from a gentleman caller I'd have remembered.

'Let's just check while we're here.' She led the way across the grass to Gaynor Weston's front door, and opened it with a key from the labelled bunch in her pocket. Switching on the lights, she trotted up the short flight of stairs to the attic room which the dead woman had used as an office.

The laptop lay on a small desk, plugged into a wall socket. Quickly Rose opened it and looked at the small keyboard, until she found the start-up button in the top right-hand corner. The two detectives waited as the machine booted up. 'Do you know these machines?' asked the chief inspector.

'Yes. No problem.' Steele placed the cursor on the apple symbol in the menu bar and dragged it down until he found a folder headed 'recent applications'. He triggered it open and looked at the software list. 'Right,' he said briskly, 'Claris Organiser; that'll be it, if there's anything on here.' He opened the program, revealing a fresh, clean diary page for that day. Swinging the arrow up to the menu bar he selected Calendar, and a different page appeared showing four full days. Steele clicked on a tab at the side of the page. The display changed once more, setting out a full month. Several of the dates showed appointments.

'Look at the last one,' Rose whispered, pointing at the screen. 'It says; "Write to Ray", on the afternoon before her death.'

'But there was no note,' said Steele.

'No; yet I'll bet this was a woman who kept her appointments. Let's look at the rest.'

They went back over the month. In the two weeks before the reference to her son, there were no entries, none until two words: 'St Martha's', and a time: '10am'. Three days before that was a further entry, 'Terry Futcher; 8pm', and on the Saturday before, 'NW, Ray; Aberdeen.'

'This is all personal stuff, Steve. No business appointments at all.' Rose scanned quickly through the month. 'But I don't see anything here that helps. Can you go back?'

The Sergeant nodded, clicked on a minus symbol at the top of the page, and the previous month's listings appeared. He read through them, carefully. 'There,' he said, with a slight nod of his head towards the display. 'Look at the entry for the twenty-eighth; "Deacey, dinner, OB; 8pm" OB means Oldbarns, I guess, but who's Deacey? Surname or forename?'

'Who knows? Let's see if he features earlier. Run over the previous months.'

The sergeant scrolled back through six more months of entries: they revealed four more visits by 'Deacey', the first of them, as Joan Ball had said, seven months earlier. There were also three entries referring to theatre dates with the same person.

'Looks like Mrs Weston's third arrow,' Rose murmured. 'Our mystery man.'

'Let's see if the mystery's answered here,' replied Steele. He went back to the menu bar and selected 'Contact list'. A series of names and telephone numbers appeared, listed alphabetically. Nolan Weston's name was there, also Terry Futcher's; there was no Deacey, no listing beginning with the letter 'D'.

'Bugger,' the sergeant swore quietly.

'Never mind, Stevie,' said Rose. 'He might not be listed in here, but with a name as unusual as that, it shouldn't take us long to fit a face to it.'

23

'It's a step forward, Brian; but don't let the team get too carried away about it. Even if you identify and trace this Deacey character, you're still a bit away from placing him at Oldbarns on the night of Gaynor's death.'

'Not if his DNA matches the trace Dorward's lot found on that glass.'

'Straws on the wind, man, and you're clutching at them.'

'We'll see. There's another straw as well. There was an entry on Wednesday, reminding her to write to her son.'

'I wonder if she ever did?'

'You bet she did. She was thorough and methodical, this woman. That letter's kicking around somewhere. I'm going back to see the lad tomorrow morning; I'll take Maggie with me.'

'Just you do that, mate. But that's enough for today. Call me over the weekend if you have to, but otherwise, I'll see you next week.' Martin replaced the receiver.

'Are you a step nearer to tracing Doctor Death?' asked Alex, as he turned towards her.

'Don't use that term even in fun,' he replied, a little sharply. 'I've been dreading the tabloids picking it up. So far this has been a quiet low-key investigation into what most of them have decided is a suicide, thanks to the careful wording of Alan Royston's press release.'

'Maybe if you were a bit more forthcoming the person you're after might came forward.'

'Maybe if you buy a bikini, it'll be warm enough for you to go swimming in the sea tomorrow. People do not walk into police offices asking to be locked up for life; not as a matter of course, anyway.'

She beamed across the table at him as he resumed his seat, sipping at his coffee, which had cooled during Mackie's call. 'Surely this might be the sort of person who would do just that. Helping a friend to die must be an awful thing to do; I'll bet that whoever did it, it's preying on their mind right now. I'll bet they'd love to get it off their chest, whatever the consequences.

'Why don't you let Brian Mackie call a press conference and explain exactly what's happened? I'll bet it would work.'

He looked back at her, unsmiling. 'For a cautious lawyer, you're throwing a few bets around tonight. You're also forgetting basic legal principles. If Brian did that, he'd have the Fiscal down on his neck in an instant for compromising the whole investigation, and prejudicing a future trial.'

'Okay, he doesn't need to spell it all out, just enough to let the press draw conclusions.'

'Alex, I don't care whose daughter you are; just leave the police work to us, okay.'

Her gaze dropped as she sat back in her chair, hurt by his snub. Then tossing her napkin onto the table, she stood, picked up her mug and stepped silently into the kitchen. She was pouring herself more coffee when he appeared in the doorway.

'You can get your own!' she snapped.

'Alex, love, I'm sorry,' he said, 'I didn't mean to bite your head off.'

'Well, I meant to bite yours,' she fired back, unappeased.

'Sorry, sorry, sorry. Let's not shout at each other all night. We've got unfinished business, you and I, from a couple of nights ago. You know it as well as I do, but you've been dodging the subject ever since.'

Alex had never been able to sustain anger for any length of time; she had never been sure whether this was a strength or a weakness. 'Okay,' she said, quietly. 'Truce. Let's talk: I've been working myself up to have it all out with you tonight anyway. That's probably why I was so snippy.' She picked up her coffee, walked past him, back into the living room, and sat on the long sofa, staring across the room, without a hint of a smile.

'I don't want to break off our engagement, Andy,' she began. In spite of himself, he felt his heart take flight in his chest . . . and then she shot it down. 'Yet I think you're right: we need to stand back from each other and take a look at our future together and how it would be. For unless each of us gets what we have a right to expect out of life, it isn't a future I want to contemplate.

'From where I stand,' she looked at him for the first time, a light smile on her lips. 'or in this case, sit, I have as much right to a career as you have. You, on the other hand do not have the right to put pressure on me about having children; or to make me feel guilty about not having them – as you've done already.

'I want what my step-mother has; a successful professional life, built up to the point at which she can adapt her work to suit her circumstances. The age difference between my Dad and Sarah is about the same as it is between you and me, yet they've made it work. Yes, even after Pops' mid-life crisis – in spite of it – they've made it work. If you want to be jealous of anything, Andy, don't make it my job, be jealous of them, for they are what we should be aiming to be.

'We should be thinking long-term, but you don't seem capable of that.'

His green eyes seemed to lose their sparkle as he looked at her. 'You're getting it off your chest, all right. I wonder if you realise just how calculating you sound. Does love come into this at all?'

She turned on him. 'Of course it does, and do I love you. But taking for granted comes into it too, and that's what you do with me.' He opened his mouth in a retort, but she cut him off. 'Ask yourself this. Just lately have we been making love, or have we just been fucking? I know the difference. Do you?'

'Let's try not to wound each other any more than's necessary, eh,' he whispered.

She softened at once. 'Oh I'm sorry,' she exclaimed, taking his hand. 'You know what I mean though.'

He nodded his blond head. 'Yes, I know, I know. So what do you want to do about it?'

'I'm going to move out, Andy,' she said. 'I really don't want to break off our engagement, far from it: but please understand; I'm still learning to be me as an adult. I think I need room to finish the process.'

'Christ,' he chuckled, 'you're more grown up than me in some ways. Where will you live?'

'I'll buy a flat. I still have the money from selling my student flat in Glasgow; and my furniture's in store. It's a sensible thing to do; when you and I have ourselves sorted, and when eventually we do get married, maybe I can rent it out. In the short term, Gina, my pal in the office, has room to spare at her place in Comely Bank. I'm going to move in there with her.'

She paused. 'I want you to leave me for a week, till I get things sorted. Then maybe we could go out for dinner next Saturday, like we used to, and start again from there; try to build a more comfortable relationship.'

'Okay,' he agreed, still reluctantly. 'When will you go?'

'Tomorrow. Then I'm taking a couple of days off at the beginning of next week.'

'All planned, eh?'

She smiled at him, cautiously. 'It was time for someone to be decisive, wasn't it?'

'Yes, sweetheart, I suppose it was. Tonight though . . .'

'What?'

'Let's make love.'

24

'You're not serious,' gasped Mackie, with sudden, shocked incredulity. He pulled his car to a stop on the Greenway.

'How I wish I wasn't,' said Maggie Rose. 'Neil asked Mario to have a drink with him last night; he told him then.'

'Ahhh,' murmured the superintendent. 'I really was trying not to think about it. Andy and I saw them at the Western yesterday, when we went to see the Prof. Later on, we agreed that we hadn't if you know what I mean.

'I supposed there must be something, but still . . . Olive; lung cancer; poor lass, that's terrible. How's Neil handling it?'

'Mario knows him better than anyone. He says that inside he's scared stiff, but on the outside he's putting on the strongest face he can. He and Olive have decided that they're not going to treat it as some dark secret; they're going to tell all their friends what's happening, and how things are going, all the way along.'

'Are they going to operate?'

'They can't; it's too advanced. She goes into the Western next Wednesday to start chemotherapy.'

'How long will she have to stay there?'

'Just a couple of days once a month, with top-ups on a day-patient basis.'

'And what are her chances?'

Rose smiled. 'Neil says she's going to make it. He won't contemplate any other outcome, and neither should we.'

'Oh God,' muttered Mackie, still shaken. 'Let's just pray that he's right.'

'Brian,' said his deputy, grim-faced once more, 'if you believe in prayer, give it all you've got.'

They sat in silence for a few seconds, until it was broken by the insistent hooting of a bus, its driver furious to find a car blocking the lane which he regarded as his exclusive property. 'Ah, bugger off!' snarled the superintendent, with uncharacteristic ferocity, but he slipped into gear nonetheless, and moved off.

They drove on for a few more minutes, heading westward along the

Glasgow road, until they arrived at the junction with Murrayfield Avenue. Mackie took a right turn, drove for two hundred yards up the sloping street, then turned left. Nolan Weston's house was only a few yards from the corner.

It was Saturday, and so the detectives were not surprised when the surgeon opened the door; he on the other hand looked decidedly puzzled. 'Mr Mackie,' he said, 'I wasn't expecting you this morning; especially since you interrogated my son yesterday without my permission.'

'I'm sorry if that upset you, sir, but the opportunity arose so I took it. I don't think any harm was done, do you?'

Weston shook his head. 'No, I don't suppose it was.' He smiled. 'In any event, I keep forgetting that Ray is eighteen. You don't need my permission to talk to him, do you.' Maggie Rose had been on the verge of telling him that very thing.

'Come in, please,' the professor continued. 'I haven't met your colleague.' Mackie introduced his deputy as he led them through to a small sitting room which opened into a semi-circular conservatory. The garden beyond was lush and well-tended, and rich with the colours of autumn.

A heavily pregnant woman sat in a bamboo armchair on the left of the glass room. She smiled at Mackie, who nodded in acknowledgement. 'Ah yes, you met my wife yesterday,' said Weston. 'Avril, this is Chief Inspector Rose. Now, what can I do for you?'

'We need to speak with your son again, I'm afraid,' said the superintendent. 'Something else has come up, and it involves him.'

'Very well.' He took a pace towards a door in the right-hand corner of the room. Rose could see that it led to the kitchen. 'Ray,' Weston called. 'Come on in here.'

A few seconds later a young man ambled into the room. He was tall, at least six feet three inches, but fine-featured and rake-thin, his dark hair flying in all directions from his high forehead. There was a thick slice of buttered toast in his right hand, 'Wh' is it?' he mumbled, then saw the two detectives. 'Oh, hello.'

'Morning, Ray,' said Mackie. 'Sorry to bother you again. This is DCI Rose. She and I need to ask you a couple of things. First, have you had any mail in the last couple of days?'

The youth shrugged his shoulders. 'Not yesterday, that's for sure. Today, I don't know. Dad?'

'I haven't sorted the post yet,' the Professor answered. 'Let me have a look. It's still on the hall table.' He left the room; the others waited for him in silence, Raymond munching on his toast. When he returned he was waving a brown A5 envelope. 'This is for you. Aberdeen postmark.' He handed the letter to his son.

The detectives looked on as he tore it open and peered inside. 'There's a note,' he said, withdrawing a slip of paper and handing it to Mackie. It was a short message, a simple scrawl in a strong hand. The detective read it aloud. 'It says, "This arrived today" and it's signed "Beano". Who's he?'

'My room-mate.' Raymond peered into the brown manila once more. 'It's a letter.' He shook it free and held it up for the detectives to see, a simple, cream-coloured envelope. As he looked at the hand-written address, his face paled. 'Dad,' he whispered, plaintively. 'It's from Mum.'

'Then I think you should read it alone, Ray,' his father said.

'Yes,' Rose agreed, 'but first, do you have a letter opener, Professor? That envelope has to be handled carefully from now on. We don't want any more fingerprints on it.'

'Why?' asked Weston, puzzled.

Rose took the letter from his son, holding it by a corner, and looked at it. 'It's post-marked Thursday. The day *after* Mrs Weston died. We need to find the person who posted it, and chances are his prints are on this.'

'I see.' The surgeon went into the kitchen and returned with a thin-bladed knife, which he handed to Rose. Carefully the chief inspector slit the envelope along the top, shook out the letter within, and handed it to Raymond.

As the young man went into the kitchen, Avril Weston pushed herself from her chair and came over to join her husband. The four stood silently, watching the door. Eventually, the sobbing began, growing louder, heart-rending. Avril started for the kitchen; at first Nolan held her back, but eventually he released her hand and allowed her to go to her step-son.

She returned a minute later, maybe two, with the letter, which she handed to her husband. He held it up and began to read:

'My lovely Ray,

When you receive this, you'll know. Dad will have explained everything, and although he did not know that I was going to do what I've done, I know that he'll understand and that he'll support my decision.

I watched you grandmother die of cancer when I was your age. It all but destroyed me, and I will not put you through the same experience. I'm not afraid of what I would have faced, and I am not doing this thing for me, but for you and for your father, because I love you both so very much.'

Nolan Weston's voice faltered for a moment, but he gathered himself and read on.

'I want you to live the rest of your life for me, and to be all you can be for my sake. Of all the good things in my life, and there have been many, you and Dad have been absolutely the best.

Live well for me.

With all my love

Mum'

He looked up as he finished and saw that Ray had come back into the room. They embraced, father and son, as if they were welding their grief together. Mackie nodded towards the conservatory, and the two women followed him, leaving them together.

Eventually, the two tall Westons rejoined them. 'Do you need the letter as well?' asked Raymond.

'No,' said Mackie. 'Not just now anyway. I don't think for a moment that there'll be any prints on that other than your mum's. The envelope's all we need.'

'But,' the young man demanded, 'if Mum didn't post it herself, then who did? Did she give it to her secretary?'

The detectives looked at each other. Almost imperceptibly, Mackie nodded. 'No,' said Rose. 'We know that your mother wrote the letter only a few hours before she died. We believe that it was posted next day, by the person who helped her end her life.'

'That's what all this is about?' Raymond Weston exclaimed. 'Someone killed my mum?'

Rose replied simply. 'Yes.'

'But that's not right!' the young man shouted. 'It should have been me. Or Dad. Dad, why didn't you help her?'

'Believe me son,' said Nolan, quietly. 'If she had asked me to, I would have. But she loved both of us too much ever to have involved us.'

'Ray,' asked Mackie, briskly, 'does the name Deacey – that's D-E-A-C-E-Y – mean anything to you?'

'Deacey? Never heard of him? Why? Was it him?'

'We don't know that. We just need to find him, that's all. Professor, does the name mean anything to you?

Weston dropped his eyes and shook his head. 'The third arrow, I guess,' he murmured, sadly, Avril's presence forgotten completely.

25

'What the hell brought this on anyway?' Bob Skinner asked his daughter. 'You just turn up out of the blue. I can't remember the last time you wanted to go out for a run with your old man.'

'I can't remember the last time I wanted to go for a run with anyone,' Alex panted. They were jogging eastward along the shore of the Forth estuary, away from Gullane, in the direction of Fidra Island which stood guard, with its lighthouse, over Yellowcraigs beach. Bob was taking it easy, but still maintaining a respectable pace, making her work to keep up.

'I've let myself get really out of shape,' she gasped, 'since I started with the firm. From now on, I'm going to do more of this, and go to the gym twice a week instead of once a month. You're twice my age, and twice as fit.'

'Christ, you'll be joining the girls' rugby team next.'

'No fear, Pops. Bad for the boobs, I've always thought.'

He stopped abruptly, beneath the isolated house which was the only sign of civilisation along that stretch of coastline. 'Why is it,' he said, breathing only slightly hard, 'that people always seems to pussy-foot around these days when they want to tell me something? Am I that much of a bear? Come on, kid. Out with it.'

'What do you mean?' gasped Alex.

'I mean that you could have done three laps of Holyrood Park just to burn off energy. You didn't need to come down here. You're working up to telling me something. Let me guess: it's about you and Andy.'

She looked up at him, screwing up her eyes against the watery winter sun. 'Has he been talking?'

'We did have a chat, but it didn't amount to much. I told him that Sarah and I wouldn't get involved. So I'm right, then.'

Alex shifted her footing on the shingle on which they stood, and gazed across the calm water towards the Fidra light. 'Yes, you're right. I'm moving out this afternoon.'

'Bugger.' He frowned, his mouth tightening. 'What is it about our family these days, that we can never manage to all be happy at the same time?'

86

'Look, Pops,' she said, in an attempt at reassurance, 'it's not that bad. We're not breaking off the engagement; just stopping living together for a while. It'll do us good in the long run.'

'Maybe it will; and maybe I should even be pleased. I can still be old-fashioned from time to time; the concept of living together before marriage is not one I was brought up to believe in. Nonetheless, in my experience when you take one step back in a relationship, it's very difficult not to take another; before you know it there's a gap which can be very difficult to close.'

'We'll be all right,' Alex insisted. 'We just need some breathing space, that's all.'

'No, my lovely daughter,' he said firmly, 'that's not true. Andy doesn't need breathing space; you do. So don't go pinning the blame on him; not in that way anyway. Right now, you're finding this relationship stifling – okay, maybe that's his fault – but you're the one who's making all the decisions.'

'Do you think I'm right?'

'That's irrelevant, because I'd support you even if I thought you were wrong.'

'No it's not. It's important to me. Do you think I'm right?'

'As it happens, I do. Secretly, when you got engaged, then moved in with Andy, I thought that you were giving away too much of your life too soon. Now that you've decided to claim at least some of it back, I can only be pleased – not that I want you to tell Andy that, mind.'

'Why didn't you say?'

'I said plenty when your relationship began, remember, and caused mayhem. For a while, I lost my daughter and my best friend. I don't want that to happen again. Anyway, you're a big girl now; you've got the right to make your own mistakes. And, hopefully, to learn from them.'

He smiled, suddenly, his face lighting up. 'Now,' he said, giving her sweat-slicked pony-tail a quick tug, 'you're going to learn the folly of buggering up my Saturday morning. We're nowhere near half-way through this run, so let's get back to it . . . and at a decent pace too. You want to get fit, kid? Okay, just follow me and find out what it takes.'

26

'You want some time off, Andy?'

'You think I need it?'

'I don't know, pal. But if you feel you do, I'll accommodate you.'

Andy Martin smiled across the chief constable's low table. 'With all that we've got on our plate at the moment, you're offering me leave? Bob, what you're really doing is asking whether I can keep my eye on the ball, with Alex moving out and all. Given the example of Neil McIlhenney, I'd be no man at all if I couldn't. Anyway, I respect what she's doing, and our long-term plans haven't changed; she's still wearing the ring.

'Now, can we get on with our Monday briefing, as usual?'

Skinner nodded. He was in uniform, in preparation for a meeting of the police board, and shifted uncomfortably in his seat as he sipped his coffee. 'Okay, let's do that. What do I need to know?'

'The main item is the Weston investigation. The son received a letter from his mother on Saturday morning. It was posted in Edinburgh on the day after her death.'

'Was it indeed? Prints?'

'Covered in them: at least five different thumbs, for a start. Some of them will be Post Office staff, and one is Gaynor's.'

'Are you trying to trace the postmen, to eliminate them?'

Martin shook his head. 'No. Their union hates that; they'd probably strike if we suggested printing them all. Anyway, it's not necessary; when we find the person we're after, and his dabs match one on the envelope, that's fine, it'll be another piece of evidence. If they don't—'

'It could help the defence,' Skinner suggested.

'True, but I'm not going to start sweating about it till we catch the man.'

'Could Mrs Weston have given the letter to anyone else to post for her? Have we established whether she had any visitors during the day?'

'As far as we can. Joan Ball, her neighbour, looked in on her in the morning. Then, in the afternoon, she made a few phone calls to her office. With hindsight, it's clear she was putting her affairs in order.

However there's no evidence that she had any visitors other than Miss Ball, and the person who helped her die. So it's unlikely that she gave the letter to someone else to post.'

Martin paused. 'However, all that aside, we've got a new name to go on. Maggie and Steele found it on her computer diary. A man, called Deacey.'

'What are they doing to trace him?'

'The usual. Step one: check whether he's known to us. He isn't; according to our intelligence unit there are no Deaceys – first or second name – known to the police in Scotland. Step two: look up the telephone directory. They've done that already, and come up empty. No "Deacey" listed in Edinburgh, the Lothians, Greater Glasgow, Fife or Tayside. So this morning they'll check with the Department of Social Security, the Registrar General, the Passport Office and the Driving Licence Agency.'

'Is he a serious contender, d'you think?'

'Right now, Bob, he's our only contender.'

'Well, let's just find him and hope. I'd really like to get a clear-up on this one. Too many unresolved possibilities if we don't; too many whispers, too many fingers left pointing, at Professor Weston, or at his son.'

'Fine, but just how much of our resources do we commit to this?'

'As much as is necessary. We cannot be seen to have backed off from this investigation in any way, whatever our personal feelings might be.' Skinner paused. 'For what it's worth, my very private belief is that, given her circumstances, Mrs Weston had every moral right to do what she did, and if she needed someone to help her, so be it.'

'Would you apply that belief to Olive McIlhenney?' asked Martin, solemnly.

'You know about that?'

'Yes. Brian called me on Saturday. He had it from Maggie, via Mario.'

'Well, God forbid that it should come to that, but if it does, then yes, I believe that Olive should be able to choose her moment . . . and that Neil should be free to be part of it, should he choose. What about you?'

The Head of CID took a sip from his cup, and slowly replaced it in its saucer. 'I had this conversation last week with Mackie,' he began, 'in a roundabout way, but mostly I hid my views behind the law then. The fact is . . .

'Bob, as you know, I was brought up as a Catholic. As I've grown older, I've come to differ with my Church on a number of issues. For example, no bloody celibate is going to dictate to me about contraception or about interpersonal relationships. However the one thing that's ingrained in me is my belief in the sanctity of life.'

Skinner's eyebrows rose. 'Even after all these years, you surprise me, Andy,' he said, quietly. 'Especially given the things that you've had to do in this job. I don't have to remind you of them.'

'How could I forget? That once I had the choice between killing someone or letting you die. Afterwards, when I had done it, I discussed it with my confessor and I was absolved. The priest agreed with my choice. But that wasn't enough for me. I went to confession in four more churches, and in three of those I was absolved again. The fourth priest, an Irishman and old by the sound of him, told me that what had been about to happen was God's will and that I had committed a mortal sin. He refused me absolution.

'Right there in the box, through the grille, I told him to go and fuck himself. I haven't been to Church from that day; I suppose I have to recognise that I've withdrawn from it. And yet its teachings still will not allow me to accept that life is something that we can switch off as a matter of course. Look at it this way. If a state will not take the life of a murderer, how can it sanction the killing of the innocent?'

'I take that point,' Skinner conceded, 'and I'll think hard on it. But to come back to you. Given your belief, how can you bring yourself to carry a firearm on duty?'

'Because I accept that there are circumstances when a gun can be used to preserve life – yours, for example. But I can never be dispassionate about it, like you and Brian, say.'

The big DCC grunted. 'Huh. I can't speak for Mackie, but there's nothing dispassionate about me, Andy. When I've had to shoot people they've bloody deserved it, and I've been positive about it.

'Take this Hawkins man, for example. When he's traced, he'll be arrested if he doesn't offer resistance. Depending on who catches him, he might be delivered to the CIA, but somewhere along the line, someone will put a bullet behind his ear and the South African press will be told that a well-known local businessman has been killed in a car crash or whatever. That's the way this one will be played out, make no mistake. If that troubles your conscience, maybe you'd better have no more to do with the search for the man. If you'd prefer it I'll take you out of the chain of command altogether.'

Martin shifted in his seat once more and grunted. 'No, don't do that. This man's a fucking head-hunter, for God's sake, and he could be after our Head of Government. My responsibility is to the innocent, and I'll fulfil it. I've already made that choice, remember, even if that old Irish bastard did damn me to Hell for it!

'So what's the latest on the Hawkins front?' he asked.

90

Skinner glanced at his watch. 'McIlhenney should be ready to report by now. Let's call him in.' He reached across to the console on his desk and pressed a button. Less than a minute later the side door of the office opened and the bulky sergeant stepped into the room, carrying a thick folder. To Martin, he seemed tired and drawn. There was none of the usual joviality in his eyes; in its place, the chief superintendent saw a steely determination.

'Sit down, big fella,' said the DCC. 'Want a coffee?'

McIlhenney laid his folder on the low table. 'No thanks, boss. I've decided to cut that out. I went to the doctor on Saturday morning and had myself checked out. The last thing we need right now is for anything to be wrong with me.'

'There isn't, though?'

'Naw. He just told me to give up coffee and lose a few pounds. I've to get more exercise, he said, but the fact is I've lost five pounds in the last week without doing a bloody thing.'

'How's Olive doing?' asked Skinner.

'She's fantastic. She told the kids last night that she had a wee problem, and she'd be off work for a while, but that it was nothing to worry about. Incidentally, boss, I talked to her about your offer to look after Lauren and Spencer next weekend. It's very kind of you and Sarah, and we'd like to take you up on it.'

'That's good. When does the treatment begin?'

'She goes in on Wednesday afternoon for assessment, then they begin on Thursday. She gets out about five on Friday.'

Skinner nodded. 'Okay, Sarah'll collect the children after school on Friday afternoon.

'Right,' he continued. 'Hawkins: what's to report?'

'Absolutely nothing, I'm afraid. Since that bloody fiasco caused by the man from Dumfries—'

'—whose hide is even now drying on his office door.' Skinner interrupted with a growl.

'. . . there hasn't been a sniff of him in Scotland, not a single scent. There's been nothing else across Europe either. You know, boss, it's been a while since the original tip came out of South Africa; I'm beginning to wonder whether he's slipped the net altogether.'

'So am I,' said the DCC, heavily. 'But we maintain surveillance regardless, though. The preparations for the economic conference are going ahead too. ACC Elder's working on the general policing arrangements, and on traffic management, following the blueprint that was drawn up when we had the Commonwealth Heads of Government. We may make the vehicle restrictions even tighter than they were then.

91

'That's all background stuff, though. As far as our force is concerned, McGuire and Neville, and the rest of the SB people, are our front line.'

27

'How much longer will this operation run, Mario?' asked Karen Neville.

'Until the last head of government's plane takes off for home,' the inspector replied. 'Or until Mr Hawkins resurfaces in South Africa fresh from a winter holiday in Europe. Or until we catch the bugger.'

'You don't think there's a chance he really is on holiday do you?'

'Sure, there's a chance of that. He could be sliding down mountains in Switzerland while every secret policeman in Europe is combing the airports, the ferry terminals, aye, even the bloody streets, looking for him.

'This search is based on information from the spooks, you see, Karen: the MI6 crowd. They're all too clever by half, and most of them are panic merchants; the sort to have the world chasing its tail on the back of the faintest hint. I remember once, not so long ago, they started a panic hunt for a terrorist suspect who, as it turned out, was in fact in the south of Spain on holiday with his best friend's wife.'

He grimaced. 'However, there always is that five per cent chance that their information is accurate, so it has to be checked out. In this case, the boss seems convinced that it's a lot stronger than the usual twenty to one shot.

'So tell me, sergeant, what have you got planned for today?'

'Checking more male landing cards, Inspector, looking for a limping guy with a false beard and moustache.'

'Funny,' chuckled McGuire, 'that's exactly what I'm going to be doing. We've got a fair few to work our way through this week, though.' He picked up a pile of cards from a tray at the side of his desk. 'There's a conference of international economists up at the conference centre this week, sponsored by Edinburgh University.

'How about this for a title? "The development of sub-national economies within supra-national structures". The opening session is this afternoon; there's an address by Bruce Anderson.'

'The Secretary of State?'

'That's the boy.'

'Aren't you involved in the security?' asked Neville.

'Not on this one. I've been kept informed, and I've allocated our two SB colleagues to assist, but the Protection Squad are in charge. Anderson isn't regarded as a prime target, so the view is that you and I are better employed on Hawkins surveillance.' He tapped the pile of cards. 'This is where we're involved. This is an attractive event for economists; it's attracted over two hundred and forty delegates, two thirds of them from outside the European Union. They've been pouring into Edinburgh all weekend.

'So, after filtering out the female delegates, we're left with one hundred and fifty-two of these things to go through. When Sergeant Brown and DC McNee are finished with the Secretary of State, they can get on with checking the individual cards which come in on a daily basis, so for the purpose of this exercise, you and I are on our own.' He split the cards into two lots, then folded them. 'There you are,' he said, brightly. 'There's the best part of a week's work there.

'Henry Wills, the Secretary of the University, is our main contact at the conference. He'll tell us which people are in which hotels, so that we can give them the once-over.'

'You don't think for a minute that Hawkins would show up at an economists' conference do you?'

McGuire shook his head. 'No, I don't; but he could try to sneak in among them. Conceivably he could even register. Once we've checked all the delegates, if one of these cards isn't accounted for, or if one of the holders checked in but isn't actually taking part in the event, that could be interesting.'

28

'This can't be the man we're after,' the sergeant gasped. 'I mean, look at that place; it's a bloody rabbit warren. Gaynor Weston was a classy woman in her forties; she wouldn't have been interested in an unemployed twenty-seven year-old from a tip like this.'

'You never know, though,' mused Maggie Rose, with a light smile. 'Tell me, Stevie, are you familiar with the phrase: a wee bit of rough? Or maybe this stinking pile will reveal a dazzling urbanite damned by cruel fate to live under what's left of its roof.'

If Edinburgh's housing was divided into descending categories from one to ten, the property before which the two detective stood would have rated a marginal thirteen. It stood as a monument to ill-conceived public housing, the last remaining eyesore, the last rotting tooth, in a street on which all the other filthy tenements had been razed to the ground. More than half of its windows were boarded up, yet ironically, half a dozen satellite dishes were fixed to its wall.

'Christ knows what's in there,' Stevie Steele muttered, 'but they must have pissed off the housing people up at the City Council, every last one of them. Are you sure you want to go in there, ma'am? I could call up a couple of uniforms to huckle our man down to St Leonards.'

'The first time I come across a building that I won't go into,' the chief inspector replied, evenly, 'then I'm done for in CID. Come on; he's in number 23F3, or so the woman at the DSS said.' She led the way up the weed-infested path and through the open entrance to the tenement.

'Who's the listed tenant?' asked Steele. 'It's not him, I take it.'

'No. According to the Council, the tenant is a Mrs Hannah Mason.'

Once upon a time there might have been a door at the entrance to the building, but if there had it was long gone and its frame had been torn out. Beyond was a long narrow corridor, which stank of urine; they followed it until they came to a flight of stairs.

It was late on a Tuesday afternoon, and all of the bulbs had been stolen from the stairway lights, and so they made their way up to the third floor landing in almost pitch darkness. As their eyes became accustomed to the gloom they saw six doors, off a long corridor. Two had planks nailed cross them, two had glazed panels, and the remaining two had boards where originally the glass had been.

'They're really helpful in this part of town, aren't they,' said Rose. 'Not a single number on any door. Not a single name.'

'No. They take them off to confuse the debt-collectors.'

Behind one of the glass panels, a light shone; the only sign of life along the silent corridor. Steele walked up to the door and pressed a buzzer set in its jamb. There was no sound; guessing that the batteries were dead, he pounded on it three times, with the side of his closed fist.

Eventually, the sound of shuffling came from within the house, the dull green door swung open and a woman appeared, framed against the light. From within, a smell of almost indescribable staleness threatened to engulf them.

'Aye?' From the tired hostility of her tone, Rose guessed that there had not been a welcome caller at her door for years. She was perhaps forty-five, but looked ten years older; in her youth she might have been pretty, but now her features were worn and weary. She was short and dumpy, with lifeless grey hair that was sadly in need of a wash, as was the loose purple nylon dress which hung around her.

'Police,' Steele announced, flashing his warrant card quickly. 'Is this number twenty-three?'

'Ah dinna fuckin' ken,' She snapped back at him, a scowl disfiguring her still further.

'You live here, don't you.'

'Aye, but Ah wouldna ken whit number it wis. Naebody ever writes tae me. Only the Social, and Ah tear them up.'

'We're looking for a Mr Deacey,' said Rose.

'Well, he's no here,' the little woman replied emphatically. 'There's jist me. Me and ma budgie. There's nae point in yis talking to it, though. Wee bastard nivir says a fuckin' word.' She would have slammed the door, but Steele put a hand against it.

'Okay,' he growled, roughly. 'Who else lives on this floor?'

She pointed along the hallway, to a door opposite hers, one with unpainted wood in place of its glass panel. 'There's a hoor along there; an' a bloke wi' her, Ah think. Yis could try there. She'll no' have gone tae work yet.'

'Thanks,' said the sergeant, allowing her to return to her squalor.

'Poor budgie,' muttered Maggie Rose as she strode across the corridor, to rap briskly on the wooden panel.

There was no answer. She knocked again, without success. Stevie Steele's patience reached breaking point. 'Excuse me, ma'am,' he

96

said. Taking a heavy black leather glove from his overcoat pocket, he put it on his right hand, then punched the plywood panel. It split neatly down the middle, and the sundered pieces fell away into the flat.

'Police! Open up,' the sergeant shouted into the hall, in which the blue light of a television shone.

The woman who appeared in the doorway a few seconds later still had her looks, but the detectives knew that in not so many years she would be almost exactly like her neighbour across the way. There was a hardness in her eyes, a cold, resigned glare in which her future was written.

She fumbled with the catch of a short, red, imitation-leather skirt, her other hand smoothing her silver-blonde hair. She stood around five feet six, with the assistance of a pair of inordinately high heels.

'Who are you then?'

'CID, Mrs Mason,' Rose answered. 'We're involved in a murder investigation and we're looking for Malcolm Deacey.'

'Who?' Steele thought that her bewilderment was genuine, but the DCI refused to buy it.

'Let's find out who,' she said, stepping past the woman, rocking her back on her heels.

The sergeant followed her into the hall, and through a doorway at the end. Before them was a man, sitting in a low armchair, watching television. He looked up at them. He was black, with garish orange dreadlocks. 'Who you?' he asked, lazily, showing a studied insouciance which the detectives recognised from many interview rooms.

'Edinburgh CID,' Rose answered briskly. 'We want to ask you some questions about a woman, Mr Deacey; a dead woman.'

'Sho',' he grunted, pushing himself easily to his feet. 'Less go, den.'

Rose had begun to turn towards the door when he sprang at her. Instinctively she threw up her right arm, in a gesture which was literally face-saving. Like Steele she wore an overcoat and a jacket beneath, but neither was protection against the open razor which Deacey swung at her, savagely. She cried out, more with fear than pain, as it sliced into her forearm.

The man turned towards Steele; to be met by a heavy gloved fist which caught him square in the middle of the forehead. His knees buckled, his eyes glazed and he went down, sprawling limply on the floor as if he was something that had been shaken from a sack. The sergeant stamped down hard on his right hand, trapping the razor. He took it from the helpless fingers, folded it and slipped it into his pocket. Then, calmly, he rolled the dazed Deacey onto his face, drove a knee hard into his back, and hand-cuffed him.

'You try to get up, pal,' he whispered, 'and I'll cut your fucking ears off.'

Pushing himself quickly to his feet, he turned to Rose. Blood was pouring from her arm, down her hand, and dripping onto the carpet. 'You,' he snarled at Hannah Mason, who stood in the doorway, stunned by the sudden explosion of violence, 'get me clean towels, tissues, anything you have.'

He helped the DCI out of her bloody overcoat and jacket, and looked at the cut. It was bone-deep; it ran along the full length of her fore-arm. For a few seconds he felt nauseated, but he fought off the temptation to throw up. Then the woman was back, with a decently white towel, and a box of Kleenex tissues. He padded the wound with the paper handkerchiefs then took the towel and clamped it on top. 'Press that hard, Maggie,' he said. Rose nodded, pale-faced, but clear-eyed. She held the towel tight, watching him as he ripped the belt from his waistband and used it to fasten a tourniquet just above her elbow.

As he finished, Deacey began to stir on the floor. Steele put a foot on his neck as he took out his mobile phone and dialled the St Leonard's police office. Identifying himself to the telephonist, he barked out the address. 'I have an injured officer. Ambulance, pronto, and back-up to take a prisoner back to the nick.'

He glowered down at the man, who had given up all thoughts of struggling. 'You might think you're in trouble, mister,' he said, coldly and evenly. 'But believe me, you don't have the faintest idea of how deep in the shit you really are.'

29

'Let's promise each other something, eh?'

'What's that?' she whispered.

'That this is going to be the last time that either of us visits the other in this bloody place.' Mario McGuire had never been more sincere in his life.

As his wife looked up at him, the thought came to him that she had never looked more lovely. Her red hair had been brushed by a recovery room nurse, and was spread softly on the pillow, her eyes were still slightly hazy from the anaesthetic, and her appearance was one of gentle vulnerability. Her right arm lay above the covers, encased in a huge, thick bandage from just above the elbow to the wrist.

'Life is the scene of one continuous accident, my dear,' she mumbled, with a light half-stoned smile. 'But yes, let's both do our best to make sure we don't.'

'What the hell was that boy Steele thinking about,' McGuire growled, 'letting you get into a situation like that. When I see him, I'm going to—'

She squeezed his arm, lightly with her left hand. 'You're going to thank him from the bottom of your heart, and buy him a great big drink. You couldn't have kept me out of there any more than he could.' She grinned again. 'Who's the ranking officer here?

'When it came to the bit, Stevie was brilliant. He flattened the guy and secured him inside ten seconds, then took care of me like an expert. Deacey went for me because I was nearest. If he had got to Stevie first . . .' The smile left her face, and she shuddered.

'Shh,' he soothed her. 'Let's not talk about it any more. All things considered, let's just thank our lucky stars.' He looked at her, at her heavily bandaged right arm, and at the tube which ran from her left arm to a drip set up by the bedside. 'I've talked to the guy who operated on you,' he said. 'There was quite a bit of tendon and muscle damage, but they've been able to sew everything back together. They're confident that everything will sort itself in time and that you won't have any impaired movement in your hand. You lost a lot of blood, though. They're going to put a couple of pints into you.'

She frowned at him. 'You mean I'm not getting home tonight?'

'Nor tomorrow night, nor the night after that. They're going to keep you in until Friday at the very least.'

'Oh shit. It's only a cut.'

He sighed. 'Mags, love, it's one of the worst wounds of its type that your surgeon has ever treated. To guarantee a full recovery they have to keep your arm immobilised for a while. So do what they say, if you want to be able to button up your shirts with your right hand.'

Her grin returned. 'Or unbutton yours,' she chuckled, woozily.

He could tell that she was ready for sleep. 'I'm going to go now,' he said. 'They're going to move you to a ward in a minute. I'll look in tomorrow morning. We're working up here just now.' He leaned across the bed and kissed her. 'Sleep tight, – and watch that arm.'

'Mario,' she whispered as he made to stand. The heavy sedative was kicking in, with a vengeance.

'What?' He smiled at her, amused. He had never seen her as intoxicated.

'Wrong bloody Deacey,' she murmured. 'But he's the only one . . .' Her voice trailed off, as the drug drew her into sleep. He kissed her once more, on the forehead, stood, and turned to leave. The surgeon stood in the doorway. 'You sure she'll be all right, now?' McGuire asked. Something in his voice made it clear that there had better be only one answer to that question.

'Yes, if she does what she's told for the next few days.' He sighed. 'Rough job for a woman.' Suddenly Mario, felt a lump in his throat. He looked back over his shoulder, towards the bed, so that the man could not see his eyes.

'Some woman,' he said, lost in love and admiration.

He shook his head as if to clear it, zipped up his Barbour and headed out of Edinburgh Royal Infirmary, into the night. The clock in his car, which was parked near the A&E entrance, thanks to his Special Branch clout, told him that it was just after eight thirty. Instead of heading home, he swung right out of the hospital gate and drove off in the direction of the St Leonard's divisional headquarters.

The officer on duty at the entrance nodded an acknowledgement as he walked into the building. 'Mr Mackie still here?' he asked.

'Yes sir,' said the man. 'Up in his office. DS Steele's still here too.'

McGuire trotted upstairs, gave a brief knock on the divisional CID commander's door and walked in. Mackie and Steele were seated at a long conference table, shirt-sleeved. The superintendent held a mug of coffee while the sergeant was sipping from a can of Sprite. They stood anxiously as he closed the door behind him.

'How is she?' asked Mackie.

'Drugged up to the eyeballs, and having blood pumped into her; but she's going to be all right, thank Christ.'

'Mario, I'm sorry—' Steele began.

'What for? Saving her life? We owe you one, son. Thanks from both of us.'

'But I should have held her back,' the young sergeant protested. 'That place was a snake pit, I should have gone in first.'

'Stevie,' said McGuire steadily. 'If you had held her back, even now you'd have been shaking the mothballs out of your uniform.' He peeled off his Barbour and the jacket of his suit together, and threw them across the table. 'What's the Deacey story then, Brian?'

'He isn't one,' the superintendent answered sourly. 'We printed him, then ran a PNC check. The guy's real name is Winston Joseph; he's a pimp, from Birmingham. He's been wanted for four years, since one of his girls was murdered, cut to bits. He was the only suspect; witnesses saw them together at the scene. The other tarts in his string said that the dead girl had been doing freelance jobs and he'd found out. He hasn't been seen since; the CID down there assumed he'd gone back to the Caribbean, but now it turns out that he got himself fixed up with a new identity. We were put on to him by the DSS people. He was the only Deacey that their records showed up.

'It's obvious that when Maggie told him that she wanted to talk to him about the death of a woman, he jumped to the wrong conclusion, i.e. that he'd been rumbled, and that she and Stevie were there to lift him for killing the girl.

'We've charged him with attempted murder. But as soon has he's been up before the Sheriff tomorrow for a formal remand, we've got to send him down south for questioning there. Our Brummie colleagues are very grateful to us.'

'That's good. Mags'll be pleased too.'

'Yes, but he was our only Deacey, and no way was he Gaynor's boyfriend. We can be sure of that much. So the Weston investigation's at a dead stop. She won't be so chuffed about that.'

'I suppose not,' McGuire grunted.

'Coffee?' asked Mackie.

'Please.' He paused. 'I'll just go for a piss first.'

Still in shirt-sleeves, his warrant card hanging on a chain round his neck, he left the room. He walked straight past the male toilet, which was not far from Mackie's office, then downstairs and along the corridor to the station's holding cells.

'Hello Davie,' he said to the custody sergeant. The man looked at him for a long time, unsmiling.

'Remember that night in Muirhouse, when those three guys had you trapped?' McGuire asked, meaningfully.

The sergeant reached a decision. With a grim nod, he rose, and led him along the row of cells, until they came to the last door on the right. 'It's Tuesday, the night,' he said at last. 'Quiet. Naebody else in yet.' He turned his master key in the lock.

Winston Joseph was squatting on the bed against the far wall of the cell when the black-haired, shirt-sleeved, thick-necked figure stepped into his world. He jumped to his feet. 'I told y'all already. Ain't got nothin' to say, mon.'

'That's fine,' McGuire growled. 'I don't want you to say anything. I just want you to scream for a while.'

He stepped forward, reaching out with his left hand as if to clip the man on the side of the head. Instinctively Joseph leaned back; as he did so, the swarthy detective shifted his weight and smashed his right fist into the fleshy triangle just below his rib cage. The smacking sound seemed to bounce off the cell's tiled room.

For a moment, the bizarre orange dreadlocks stood out straight, as if their owner had been struck by lightning. Indescribable bolts of pain flooded through the bulky body of the former Malcolm Deacey, as his legs buckled beneath him and he slumped to the floor. He did his best to scream, but found that all the air seemed to have been driven from his lungs; they burned, adding to his agony, as he gasped for breath.

His smiling nightmare allowed him squirm on the floor for a few seconds, then hauled him upright, held him by the throat with his left hand, and hit him again, in the same spot, but even harder. This time, Joseph lost control of his bladder, as well as his legs.

'Just in case you were wondering,' said Mario McGuire, conversationally, as he dug his left thumb, agonisingly, into the bunched nerve endings at the base of the man's neck, 'that was my wife you cut this afternoon. I wish I had more time to get to know you, but still, I've got enough. You, my man, are in for the worst few minutes of your life.'

Somewhere in his befuddled brain, Winston Joseph knew that the smart thing to do would be to pass out. Unfortunately, he never had been very smart.

30

Every Special Branch commander for a decade had come to know Henry Wills well. Student politics were no longer seen as a major subject for surveillance, but even in relaxed times, those in charge of the security of the state thought it prudent to be aware of the broad spectrum of campus activity. Very few things happened in Edinburgh University of which its Registrar was ignorant.

Wills was a polite, urbane man. As he sat at his meeting table with Mario McGuire and Karen Neville, his reading glasses, perched on the end of his nose, made him look even more owlish than usual.

'Before we begin, Inspector, I must ask you. How is your wife? I read all about her mishap in this morning's *Scotsman*.' As he spoke he glanced through the window towards the sprawling buildings of the Royal Infirmary, of which the nearest was less than three hundred yards away.

McGuire smiled. 'She's doing fine thanks, Mr Wills. I looked in on her before I came here. She had a good night. God help them today, though, once the post-op sedation's all worn off. Maggie's a hellish patient.'

'And how are you, Mario?' the Registrar added, quietly.

'To tell you the truth, I still shake every time I think what might have happened. It'll be a while before I can put that thought out of my mind.'

'And the man who did it?'

The inspector looked at his watch. 'He's due in the Sheriff Court just about now; once he's been charged formally he'll be off to England to be questioned about a murder.'

'Does that mean that he won't be punished for attacking your wife?'

'No, not at all. When our courts want him, we'll get him back. They'll take a plea *in absentia*, I should think, and he'll be sent to the High Court for disposal. He'll get ten years at least. Hopefully the judge will make it consecutive, to be served after he's due for release from his life sentence for the Brum murder.' He glowered at Wills. 'If he makes it concurrent, then effectively the bastard will have got off with it.'

He placed his hands palms-down on the table, his way of indicating that the subject was closed. 'How many of your economists do we still have to check, Henry?' he asked.

Wills looked at the bundle of landing cards which lay on the desk before him, and at the registration sheets which lay beside them in matching order. 'Today should see it done,' the Registrar replied, looking from one detective to the other. 'Those are the details of the people in the last two discussion groups. Once you work through these, that'll be everyone accounted for. A pity, in a way. I've enjoyed your morning visits.'

Mario McGuire fought to suppress a chuckle. Most men enjoyed a visit from Karen Neville, but he was surprised to hear the bookish, middle-aged academic admit it. The sergeant was a rare combination of attractive features and spectacular physique; in addition she had a quick open smile, and a way of looking through her blue-grey eyes at most things male which made them feel as if there was no one else in the room. She was the second most desirable woman McGuire had ever seen. In the past, her own desires had been quick to surface; this had led her into trouble on more than one occasion.

Her smile widened a little as she ran a hand over her thick designer-blonde hair. 'I envy you your office, Mr Wills,' she responded, looking round the oak-panelled room. 'Ours is a steel-furnished box.'

'That's right,' said the inspector, intervening before their host could reach melt-down point. 'Special Branch isn't that special when it comes to accommodation.' He looked on as Wills divided the papers into two sets. 'Anything exceptional in this lot?' he asked.

'Well,' the other man began, 'there is one chap whose sheet struck me as slightly odd. The thing is, he doesn't appear to be an economist. His name is Wayne Ventnor. He does list a degree, but it's in Chemical Engineering, from the University of Western Australia. At first sight, it's not clear what he's doing here.

'My supposition is that he's a civil servant nominated by an Australian state government, although his registration sheet doesn't say that.'

'That sounds plausible, all the same,' McGuire agreed. 'The sheets still show the same information as the ones we've seen before, do they?'

'Yes. Name, nation or university of origin, qualifications, any special area of interest, conference number, discussion group allocation, and hotel or other accommodation.'

'Only one thing missing, isn't there.'

104

'What's that?' asked Neville, as Wills nodded, sheepishly.

'A photograph of each delegate,' said the inspector. 'If we'd had those, we could have done this check in a day.'

'Don't I know it,' the Registrar acknowledged. 'It's supposed to be standard practice for University events, but the people who organised this conference are a law unto themselves.'

You might tell them,' McGuire grumbled, 'that when it comes to security, I'm the law around here, and that I don't appreciate having to go round eyeballing two hundred plus people when we could have handled most of it at a desk, if they'd done a professional job.

'Come on, Karen,' he said. 'Say goodbye to Mr Wills, and let's get on down to the conference centre to get this lot looked over.'

31

'Maggie is going to make a full recovery, isn't she?' Bob Skinner asked, anxiously. The wounded chief inspector had served for a time as his executive assistant; she was one of the group of officers whom he regarded privately as his inner circle.

Brian Mackie, another of the select group, did his best to reassure him. 'The surgeon told Mario that he expects her to be fine. It was a brutal cut, and her arm is full of internal sutures as well as the clips on the outside, but if she behaves herself, everything will heal up fine.'

The DCC nodded. 'Good. But when she's ready to come back to work, it's down to you to make sure she does toe the line. Office duties only until the surgeon certifies that there's no further chance of long-term damage.'

Mackie frowned. 'You tell her that, please, boss; I don't think I've got the guts. You know what Maggie's like; she'll be desperate to get back into the front line as quick as she can.'

'I'll tell her this very morning. I'm going up to the Royal when I leave here.' He looked around Mackie's office. 'I came down here for a purpose, Brian. Allocation of CID resources is Andy's responsibility, but I don't want you to feel shy about asking him for a replacement for Mags while she's off. I know that overall, we're tight on manpower, but if he asks me for another senior body, I'll accommodate him. We have chief inspectors in uniform with CID experience; I can transfer one of them on a temporary basis.'

The superintendent nodded his appreciation. 'Thanks, sir. But let me try it on my own for a bit. I'll try and fill the gap myself, by getting out of the office more.'

Skinner laughed. 'Who does that remind me of, I wonder?'

'You,' Mackie replied, promptly. 'You've got a lot to answer for; this force is littered with reluctant delegators, made in your image.'

'I'm not just indulging myself though,' he continued. 'If I brought someone else in I'd just have to bring him – or her – up to speed on the Weston investigation. No, I've got a great regard for young Steele. I'm going to team up with him myself.'

Skinner nodded. 'I share your view of the lad. He'll get a

commendation for bravery for what he did yesterday; that'll be his second in a fairly short time.' The DCC paused. 'Is that bastard Joseph still downstairs?'

'No, boss. He's off to court. He'll be charged, released without bail so that we don't run into trouble with the hundred and ten day prosecution rule, then rearrested immediately on suspicion of the Birmingham murder. He won't be coming back to this nick, though. He'll be held in Saughton until escorting officers arrive from down south.'

'Just as well,' the DCC muttered. 'Every minute he spends here, Mario must feel like going down there and battering the shit out of him.' There was a sudden silence in the room; it lasted for one second too long, before Mackie broke it. 'Yes indeed.' Skinner looked at him, an eyebrow raised, opened his mouth as if to speak, then closed it again.

'Joseph's brief came up to see me before he went to court,' the superintendent continued, hastily. 'He said that his client was after a deal; he'd plead guilty to the Birmingham murder if we'd drop the attempt to murder charge, and if the DSS drop their fraud complaint over his false identity.'

'Eh? He'd plead to murder to avoid a serious assault charge, and a DSS fiddle?'

'He doesn't want to do time in Scotland, apparently.'

'So what did you tell the solicitor?'

'What the book tells me to say; that he should take it up with the Fiscal. But I added that personally I didn't give a shit about Birmingham, with one of our own wounded.'

'Quite right too. I'll have a word with Davie Pettigrew myself, just to keep his backbone stiff. Mr Joseph will do time in Scotland for cutting Mags, that's for bloody certain.'

Skinner rose to leave. 'How about the Weston investigation? With Joseph eliminated, it's dead in the water, is it not?'

Mackie smiled. 'Maybe not. I've had a report from that new orthopaedic hospital out in Dalkeith. The Head Pharmacist there wants to talk to me. And she wouldn't tell me why, over the phone. The boy Steele and I are going to see her this afternoon.'

32

The job was relatively simple; in most cases all that McGuire and Neville were required to do was to take one look at a subject, to confirm his presence at the event, and to eliminate him from the list.

However it had to be done discreetly, without anyone being aware that they were under surveillance. The two officers had learned very quickly that they could work most effectively by ignoring those parts of the conference which all delegates attended. The University organisers had split their guests into eight smaller groups, and given them a programme of detailed study and discussion of eight key topics.

It was a simple matter for the detectives to cover one seminar room each, and wait for their subjects to come to them.

Karen Neville sat at her desk at the entrance to Room G, as discussion group Seven began to file in. She wore a badge which identified her as a member of the conference staff, and had before her a list of the members of the group. Beside some of the names she had placed a tiny, innocuous blue dot.

Smiling, she checked each delegate's pass as they reached her, and put a tick against their name on the list. There were thirty-one people in group Seven, which, for a reason best known to the organisers, contained twenty of the female attendees. Neville was accustomed to women sticking together at police events, but somehow, she had not expected economists to behave in the same way. Nonetheless, she checked each lady's badge as carefully as the rest.

Looking at the line, she wondered, for the third time that week, whether there was an international uniform for academics. Not one of them was dressed in anything resembling a formal manner. Most of the women wore trousers, several with shapeless cardigans. Only a minority of the men wore ties, and one or two were unshaven.

Of the eleven men, six were from EU countries and therefore not on her landing card list. Every one was over fifty, and overweight. Of the other five, two were Sri Lankan, one was a dour-looking, bespectacled Australian in a wheelchair, another was a twenty-seven-year-old American from North Carolina, too young to be a disguised

Hawkins, and the last was . . . not there, she realised. She looked at her list: Wayne Ventnor, the incongruous chemical engineer, had not checked in for the discussion.

As the group settled down and the event chairperson stepped up to the podium, the sergeant counted heads once more; sure enough, there were only thirty delegates present.

As Neville slipped out of the room, she made a mental list of possible reasons for the man's absence; illness, alcohol and boredom were the top three. She walked along the curving corridor, heading clockwise towards Room E, where McGuire was stationed.

She had gone barely twenty yards when she reached, on her right, a makeshift refreshment buffet. It was staffed by two white-coated ladies, standing guard over a tall metal urn, a large tea-pot and a range of biscuits, but it had only one customer, a big, long-legged, brown-haired, bearded man. He was seated in a low chair, a coffee before him on a low table, and he was reading a copy of the *Independent*, through gold-framed glasses. Instinctively she checked her stride and turned into the café area; affecting diffidence, she shuffled up to the man and leaned over him, peering at the laminated badge which was clipped to the jacket of his navy-blue suit. It read, 'W Ventnor, Australia.'

The man blinked and looked up from his newspaper, not into her face, if that had been his intention, but at her bosom which was directly in his eyeline as she bent over towards him.

'I'm sorry,' she began, smiling. 'I was just checking that you are Mr Ventnor; I'm Karen, from the conference staff. It's my job to know where everyone is, and your name wasn't ticked off from my list.'

His eyes reached hers, at last; his sudden smile was dazzling. 'Secret police, eh?' he said, in a broad Aussie drawl.

She chuckled, covering her inward gulp. 'Hardly. Freelance conference organiser, in fact. The University hires my firm to help with the administration of events like this.'

'How have I missed you up to now?' he asked, turning up the grin one more notch.

'I've been around, I promise; it must just be that our paths haven't crossed.'

'Well, now that they have, Karen, can I buy you a coffee?' He nodded at the empty cup on the table. 'It's passable, I promise.'

'That would be nice,' she said.

As he pushed himself to his feet, and headed for the buffet table, a chill ran through her; he walked with a distinct limp on his right side.

One of the helpful ladies at the counter, pleased to have customers, insisted on bringing his purchases to the table on a tray. As she placed coffee and a KitKat before each of them, Neville smiled at him again, trying to keep a twinkle in her eyes, rather than the naked excitement she felt.

'So why are you playing hookey?' she asked. 'Have you crossed your boredom threshold as far as sub-national economies are concerned?'

'I crossed it as soon as I walked into this place,' the man replied. His hair was a very light brown, she noticed, with fair highlights, and his beard was very definitely not false. As he reached out to pick up his coffee, she was struck by the thickness of his wrists. 'I'm no economist.'

'I didn't think so.'

He looked back at her, a little too quickly for her comfort. *Careful, Karen*, she told herself.

'Why's that then?'

'Because you're wearing a suit,' she said. 'In fact, you're the only smartly dressed man in this building.'

He laughed, an easy, relaxed confident sound. 'They are a scruffy shower of bastards, aren't they.'

'So what are you doing here?' she made the question sound as light and inconsequential as she could.

'I'm a minder, of sorts.' For a second or two, she was puzzled, wondering whether their surveillance was being duplicated by another agency. 'Did you see Dennis? Dennis Crombie, the guy in the wheelchair?'

She nodded. 'Yes, I've just checked him in.'

'Well I'm looking after him. That's why I'm here. I work for Blaydon Oil on an offshore oil rig, and I'm on a long leave. Dennis is an old mate, so when he told me that he was planning to come to this conference, I offered to tag along as his helper.'

'But why are you registered as a delegate?' she asked, out of genuine curiosity, as she broke a finger from her KitKat.

'There's no other category of visitor. We were told that with the Minister being here, there would be security; Dennis reckoned that it would be easiest if I registered just like everyone else. He needs me close by him, most of the time, you see.'

'You must be quite a friend, to sit through this sort of event for him.'

Ventnor smiled again. 'I've never seen Scotland,' he said. 'I've always wanted to visit the original Perth.'

'You're hardly going to see much of it, given the conference programme.'

'Ah, but we're staying on for a couple of months, afterwards. Dennis wants to do some research here, after the conference. That'll give me the chance to spend the odd day sight-seeing.'

'Let me know if you need a guide,' she said. It burst from her unchecked; without a thought.

'Hey,' grinned Ventnor, 'that's damn white of you. I'll take you up on that.' he paused. 'Say, what are you doing tonight? Dennis turns in around nine. Maybe I could buy you a pizza and you could tell me about Edinburgh?'

'I shouldn't fraternise with the punters,' she began. 'But what the Hell! Where do you want to meet?'

'You tell me. It's your city.'

'Giuliano's, opposite the Playhouse theatre. Just take a taxi, if you don't know it. I'll book a table for nine fifteen.' She rose from the table. 'I'll see you there. Right now, though, I have to find my colleague.'

33

'He really does have perfect teeth,' she thought. 'Even after all the rough-houses he must have been in his time, they're still straight and shining.'

McGuire's mouth hung open as he stared at her across his desk. 'No,' he gasped. 'She didn't really say that, Mario. You just imagined it, son, with all the strain you've been under in the last twenty-four hours. She didn't tell you that she's found a Hawkins suspect and made a date with him.

'No, of course she bloody didn't.' His mouth came together in a grim line.

'Oh yes she bloody did,' said Karen Neville, quietly but defiantly.

'Then what the hell were you thinking about, sergeant? Or didn't thought come into it. Weren't you listening when I told you how dangerous Michael Hawkins is?'

'Yes! Now you listen to me, please, inspector. I said that I thought at first that this could have been Hawkins, especially when I saw the limp. But now I know that it isn't. I've run checks already with the University of Western Australia. Wayne Ventnor did graduate from there fifteen years ago. I've also checked with Blaydon Oil; they do have a senior production engineer named Wayne Ventnor, and he is on long leave just now. He's recovering from an on-board accident, in fact. He broke his right ankle in a fall.'

'Fine,' McGuire shot back. 'But you didn't know all that when you made the date with the guy? You could have been putting your lovely blonde head on the block. If this had been Hawkins, did it ever occur to you that he might have checked up on you too? Suppose he did, and found out that you weren't a freelance conference organiser?' He shook his head. 'Jesus,' he hissed. 'It doesn't bear thinking about.'

'I could have handled him. Hawkins likes the ladies. Remember the CIA plant? He didn't rumble her, did he?'

'Karen, when CIA operatives are placed it's done carefully, with cover stories that stand up to investigation. You've spun this Ventnor man a yarn: now you've got to stick to it. You can't turn around and tell him you're really a copper, or you've blown our operation.' He grunted. 'The best thing you can do is stand the guy up.'

She glared back at him. 'But I don't want to stand him up. Now I've checked him out there's no reason why I should.'

'I could order you.'

'Could you? Are you sure about that?'

Suddenly his eyes were like ice. 'Karen,' he whispered. 'This is Special Branch. I could have you locked up for twenty-four hours if I wanted.' And then his gaze softened again. 'But I won't. Just watch the pillow talk, that's all.'

'Pillow talk?' The retort burst from her, indignantly. 'What sort of a woman do you think I am?'

He leaned back in his chair as if he was recoiling from her attack. 'Okay, okay. I'm sorry. I didn't mean that literally. It's just that in this section you can never forget who, or what you are; and you can't forget the nature of your work. I can't even tell Maggie about the Hawkins operation. Andy Martin can't tell Alex.'

'I heard Alex had chucked him,' said Karen, quietly. 'A friend of mine lives in the same street at Haymarket. She told me she saw her moving out at the weekend.'

McGuire's eyes widened. 'Is that so? Well here's some more serious advice. If you bump into him, don't you go commiserating with him. Mr Martin doesn't like his business on the bulletin board.'

34

Legend has it that there is in Newcastle a hospital ward which is largely populated by drinkers of a famous local ale. By the same token it is said that Edinburgh's orthopaedic hospital provision exists mainly to patch together the victims of motorcycle accidents.

Neither fable stands up to close examination. In particular, the East of Scotland's reputation for excellence in reconstructive surgery is founded on decades of exceptional work with patients, many of them children, suffering from congenital or degenerative conditions.

Dalkeith Orthopaedic Centre had been open for less than a year, Detective Sergeant Steve Steele learned from the plaque on the wall of its main entrance. He vaguely remembered the wrangling which had preceded the decision of the previous government to commit funds to the project, public and surgical opinion having been at odds over the construction of a specialist unit in times of financial shortage.

Eventually, the Ministers of the day had given the nod to the electors, mollifying the medics by providing the new hospital through a private finance initiative.

'What exactly is a PFI, sir?' Steele asked Mackie as they stepped through the main entrance to the centre, passing into a welcoming reception hall, well appointed both with furniture and potted palms.

'The only thing I know about it is that someone makes a buck out of it, long-term,' the detective superintendent answered, dryly.

He stepped up to the reception point and introduced himself, and his colleague. 'We have an appointment with Miss Berry, the Head Pharmacist.'

The young man behind the desk gave him a cool, appraising look, then pointed towards the busy waiting area. 'If you'll take a seat, gentlemen; I'm sure she'll be with you when she can.' Something about his tone needled Mackie. He suspected that the receptionist had had other meetings with police officers.

'I don't want a seat,' he said, quietly. 'I've got plenty of seats. You just tell her we're here.'

The detectives stood by the desk, watching the youth as he pushed a button on his telephone console and spoke quietly into its microphone. 'Your two-thirty appointment, Miss Berry,' he said. They heard a bright voice answer. 'I'll be right there.'

'Do you think this bloke was going to jerk us about, sir?' Steele asked, loudly enough to be heard on the other side of the desk.

'It happens, Stevie,' said Mackie. 'It's an occupational hazard. Damn silly, though, for we coppers never forget.' He leaned towards the young man. 'Bloody elephants, we are.'

They had been waiting for less than two minutes when the chief pharmacist bustled round a corner. She was a pleasant round-faced woman in her late thirties, with close-cropped auburn tinted hair and big round spectacles. She looked at the two men, then settled on the older. 'Mr Mackie?' she asked, looking up at him with a hand outstretched. 'I'm Margie Berry.'

He shook it. 'That's right; this is DS Steele.' He smiled. 'You picked us out right away.'

The little woman grinned back at him, tugging the lapels of her white coat. 'Nothing odd about that. You two can stand unaided. Most people come in here on crutches.'

The superintendent looked across at the waiting area, and saw that the patients clutched an assortment of sticks, Zimmer frames and other supports.

'Come along to my department,' said the pharmacist, 'and I'll tell you why I asked to see you.' They followed her round the corner from which she had come, down a long corridor and through a door at the end. The hospital pharmacy was smaller than Mackie had expected. Margie Berry appeared to have two assistants: a man and a woman, each in their twenties, were working at desks, and a third was vacant. There was no room for anyone else.

'Bill, Jenny,' she called out as she swept into the room. 'Take your teabreaks now, please.'

'Okay Marge,' the man answered, with a grin. 'We'll get out so you can play your game.'

Mackie looked at the door as it closed on the two assistants. 'So they don't know what this is about either?'

'Hell, no. That wouldn't have been fair, either on them or on the person involved.'

'So,' said the superintendent, 'you've found a discrepancy in your stocks?'

Miss Berry shook her head. 'No, I didn't say that. I keep a running check on my supplies, Mr Mackie. If I had a discrepancy within the pharmacy, I would know about it in the week it happened. Everything that's gone out of here tallies exactly with the prescriptions submitted.'

She looked at Steele. 'A hospital pharmacy operates just like a high street chemist, sergeant,' she explained. 'Prescription drugs go out only on a doctor's signature. As for diamorphine and the like, that has to be signed for again, on receipt.'

'How about drugs held on wards?' asked the young detective.

'They're kept in a secure container and dispensed by a senior nurse. That's the responsibility of the ward sister.'

'I see; so if anything was taken, the chances are it would go from there?'

'No; the certainty is that it would. In this hospital at least.'

'And can you pin it down to a single ward?'

'Easily,' Margie Berry replied. 'A record is kept there of drugs administered to each patient. I can tell by looking at it, and at prescriptions issued, exactly how much should be in the drugs trolley at any given time. Every so often, I will visit a ward, unannounced, and verify the figures.

'When your department called asking me to check on diamorphine stocks, I did very discreet spot checks on all wards, going back several weeks, and found discrepancies on two of them. Not huge in themselves, but added together, we're talking about a significant dose of diamorphine.'

'Enough to kill?' Asked Mackie, intently.

'Enough to kill a pony, never mind a person.'

'In what form was the stuff taken?'

'In phials, for injection. Diamorphine is used here mainly in post-operative situations, so we shove it into the patient's arm or bum with a hypo, rather than administering it through a pump, as they often do on medical wards.'

'When did the stuff disappear?'

'Over a four-day period, around two weeks ago.'

'And is there a linking factor?'

The pharmacist looked at the superintendent. 'Only one that I can find. The drugs were all issued on the prescription of the same doctor. But what is really unusual is that he, rather than the ward sister or senior nurse, signed for them personally.' She paused.

'So gentlemen, it's in deepest confidence – and this is why I asked my assistants to vacate the premises – that I'm giving you the man's name. He's Doctor Surinder Gopal, a Registrar on the staff of Derrick Strang, the Clinical Director. But guess what . . . he's missing.'

35

'I'm afraid your informant was exaggerating, officer.' There was a patronising tone to the man's voice for which Stevie Steele did not care, but he let it pass. Derrick Strang had been in the operating theatre when the detectives had gone to seek him out, and so Mackie had called up a patrol car to take him back to St Leonards, leaving the sergeant to cool his heels in the Clinical Director's outer office for over an hour, drinking coffee and making small talk with his middle-aged secretary.

'Dr Gopal is not missing from his post,' said the surgeon, 'at least not in the sense you mean. He's on leave; to which, incidentally, he is more than entitled. There's not a doctor in this unit who works harder than Surinder does.' He stripped off his white coat and hung it on a hook behind the door, then leaned back, throwing his arms above his head, forearms together, stretching the muscles of his back and shoulders.

For the first time he smiled, and became less formal. 'Sorry about the exercises; I've just done a hip replacement on a very large man. Lay people don't appreciate it, but orthopaedic surgery is very demanding physically, on the surgeon as well as the patients. By the time we're ready to retire, most of us need new parts ourselves.' He touched the tip of his nose with his fingertips, then pulled his elbows back, sharply.

'What's all this about, anyway?' he asked

The detective shook his head. 'I'm sorry, Mr Strang; I can't tell you that, not until I've spoken to your colleague.'

'Is it a professional matter? Is it something I could help you with?'

'No, it isn't. We just need to talk to Dr Gopal, that's all. We believe that he may have information which is relevant to a current investigation. When did he go on leave?'

'Last Monday, or rather, Tuesday morning, if one wanted to be pedantic about it.'

'What do you mean?'

'I mean that he called in on Tuesday and asked me if it would be all right if he took three weeks' leave, with immediate effect. I told him that would be okay, that I would arrange cover for his list.'

Steele made no attempt to hide his surprise. 'Did you ask him why he couldn't give you notice?'

'Of course. He said that he was burned out, and I accepted that. It happens to hard-working young doctors, you know.'

'Policemen too,' the detective murmured. 'I must try that one on my superintendent some time.'

He looked up at Derrick Strang. 'Where does Dr Gopal live?'

'Edinburgh. That's all I know. Our personnel people will have his address on file. I'll ask my secretary to get it for you.' He opened the door, and leaned into the outer office for a few seconds.

'Are you close colleagues?' Steele asked. 'Do you know each other well?'

The Clinical Director shook his head. 'I wouldn't say that. We have a cordial relationship, but it's purely professional. Surinder is a member of my team, and he does very good work. He's a very conscientious young man, as I've said, and a pleasant person into the bargain, but we rarely socialise away from the hospital, other than at the Christmas lunch and the Burns Supper.

'Nothing racial about that, by the way,' he added, hurriedly. 'Golf is the main out-of-hours activity among the clinical staff, but young Dr Gopal doesn't play the game.'

'How long has he been with you?'

Strang eased himself into his chair, facing the detective. He scratched his chin. 'Let's see. He's been with me here since we opened; before that around eighteen months at the PMR: two and a half years, give or take a month. Before that he worked up at the Western, as a junior on Nolan Weston's staff.'

Steele managed to maintain a casual tone. 'Is that Professor Weston?'

'That's right; Chair of Surgical Oncology, at Edinburgh University. Surinder thought about specialising in that area, but he decided that the future lies in orthopaedics. He's right too; the trend in cancer is away from surgery, whereas in our field we have all sorts of new ground being broken.

'Ten years down the road, sergeant, we'll be transplanting a lot more than organs; that's a certainty.' He raised his right hand and extended the index finger. 'We can do these now, but that's only a start.'

As he spoke the door opened. Strang's secretary came into the room and handed him a note. The consultant took it and passed it to Steele.

'There you are, sergeant: Surinder's address. Maybe once you've spoken to him you can tell me what the mystery was all about.'

36

With every passing minute Karen Neville grew more uncomfortable as she sat in the centre of the restaurant, facing the door, watching each shadow cast on its glass panel by the street light outside. Giuliano's is at its quietest in the middle of the evening, since most of its trade comes from theatre-going diners before and after the nightly performances at the Playhouse.

She took yet another sip of her San Pellegrino, and glanced at her watch yet again: it showed nine thirty-three, and her *aqua minerale* was almost finished. She was sure that the young waiter was laughing at her as he sidled up to her table. 'Can I bring you a glass of wine, perhaps, madame?' he asked.

'No thanks,' she said, grimly. 'You can leave a menu though.'

'You are waiting for a gentleman, si?' She knew that his accent was authentic, since most of Edinburgh's Italian restaurants employ genuinely Italian waiters.

Karen fixed him with a look that would have frozen South Miami. The waiter simply shook his head. 'He mus' be a crazy man, to keep you waiting,' he grinned.

On another night she would have gone along with the joke, perhaps flirted with the olive-skinned youth . . . who was not bad looking, she admitted to herself. On another night, in fact, she might have called his bluff. But the beginnings of anger were stirring in her; at that moment he was simply a nuisance to be blown away.

'No,' she said. 'He has responsibilities at home. He has to put his partner to bed every night; Dennis is very fussy about that. I'm used to it.' At that moment, the door swung open, and Wayne Ventnor swept into the restaurant. As he approached, she noticed that his limp seemed more pronounced than it had at the conference centre.

'Karen, I am so sorry,' he burst out. 'I was afraid you'd have given up on me by now.' He smiled as he sat opposite her, and she felt her annoyance dissolve.

'Another ten minutes,' she replied, 'and you'd have found me eating. But it's okay. Did you have trouble with your friend?'

'No, that wasn't it. Edinburgh is a bloody awful place to find a taxi, that's all. No, Dennis is never a problem. He might look a bit grumpy, but he's a good bloke really.'

'Why's he in the wheelchair?'

Wayne frowned. 'He's got some sort of degenerative disease. Not MS, but something similar. I don't know. I'm ignorant when it comes to medicine.'

'How about you? Where did the limp come from?'

'From falling off a ladder on my rig.' He smiled at her. 'Hardly your stereotypical Aussies, are we? One in a chair, the other with a bent wing.'

'You're not limping just now,' she said, softly.

They concentrated on their menu cards for a few minutes; once the deflated waiter had departed for the kitchen with their orders, Karen turned to the Australian. 'So how did the rest of your day go?'

'Just like the part you saw. The sandwiches at lunchtime were okay, though. If it hadn't been for you, that would probably have been the highlight of the day. How about you?'

'Me? Oh, I just went back to base and got on with the preparation of our next event.' Inwardly she groaned. *Don't chuck in unnecessary detail*, she scolded herself.

'And what's that?' came the inevitable question.

'A group marketing seminar for a big insurance company,' she offered, hoping that it sounded sufficiently boring to end his interest.

'What's your company called?' he asked her. For a second, she wondered whether it might be a trick question.

'I thought I told you this morning, I'm freelance. I have an associate; we trade jointly as McGuire and Neville. We don't have an office, though; we work from home.'

She imagined that she saw a shadow cross his face. 'Ah,' he said. 'You live together.'

'No we don't. I'm sorry, I meant from each of our homes. He's married, and I . . .' She lowered her voice. 'I'm gay.'

In the silence that followed, she asked herself what had made her say that. Did she still suspect him? Or had she simply laid down a marker of her determination to follow McGuire's advice on pillow talk? Whatever the reasoning behind her instinctive remark, his reaction made it superfluous.

'That's all right then,' he said, taking her breath away as she had taken his. 'So am I.'

They laughed; spontaneously and simultaneously. 'I know a joke about a gay Australian,' Karen offered.

'Sure. He preferred women to beer.' Suddenly all her uncertainty was gone. She felt completely relaxed.

'Which one are you, by the way?' he asked. 'McGuire or Neville? You realise I don't even know your second name.'

'Didn't you read my badge at the conference centre? Or are you dyslexic on top of everything else? I'm Karen Neville.' She smiled as she offered her hand. 'Pleased to meet you.'

37

'You're certain that it's Dr Gopal who's been nicking the diamorphine?' asked Andy Martin.

As he nodded, Brian Mackie's dome gleamed under the fluorescent tubes which lit the Head of CID's office. 'As I see it, there's little doubt about it. He signed for the stuff; it was spread between two wards. We went back out there this morning and interviewed the sisters, and the nurses in charge of the drug trolleys.

'The only way the discrepancy could have arisen was if there had been collusion between at least two of them. But they all know that Margie Berry makes regular checks. Gopal didn't know that; he prescribed the diamorphine and signed for it. Everything points to having kept some for himself then delivered the rest to the wards.'

'How far back did the pharmacist check her records?'

'I asked her to look back over the past year, and to check who signed for drugs issued on prescriptions written by Gopal. There were no other discrepancies; this was a one-off event, a few days before Gaynor Weston died. And a couple of years ago, Gopal was on Nolan Weston's staff.'

'I see,' said Martin, leaning against his window-sill. 'That puts the Professor firmly back in the frame, doesn't it.'

'On the face of it,' Mackie agreed. 'At the very least, it means that we have reason to go and interview him again. Want to come?'

'Not a lot. I will, though, if you want. However I think you should find Dr Gopal before you do anything else. There's a *prima facie* case against him, so he should be our priority. Until you've talked to him, anything you say to Weston will be pure supposition. Incidentally, I know we initiated the check, but has the hospital made a formal complaint about the missing drugs?'

'Not as such. But we know about it, so we have a duty to investigate, whether they do or not.'

'Yes, I suppose so. There's no need to be a stickler for the book, but still, I think I'll have Sammy Pye draft a report to the Fiscal, just to cover our legal tails. After all, we are dealing with the theft of a significant quantity of a Class A drug. I take it that Dalkeith was the only hospital to report a discrepancy.'

'Yes, thank Christ,' the superintendent confirmed. 'Right. I'll head off to find Dr Gopal. He lives in the Old Town, apparently.' He paused. 'Before I go; I hope you don't mind my asking you this, Andy, but are you all right?'

Martin glowered at him. 'What makes you think I'm not?' he said, curtly.

'You seem a bit pre-occupied with something. And if that wasn't the case, the fact that you just bit my head off is a good indication.'

The Head of CID shrugged his shoulders. 'Sorry if I hurt your feelings, Brian, but the fact is I'm becoming a bit pissed off with well meaning friends asking me if I'm OK.

'Listen up: I'll tell you this, and then the subject's closed, because I don't like my problems being public property. Alex has moved out, okay. She's saying all the usual things about giving ourselves room to develop as a couple, and yes, maybe to save my own face I'm agreeing with her, making all the right noises and so on.

'She could probably argue that I pushed her into making that decision, but I didn't really think that she would. I don't like it, and privately, I don't agree with all that "growing space" crap, either.'

'Are you still engaged?'

'Oh, she's still wearing the ring, Brian; but only on her finger, if you know what I mean, not in her heart.'

'What's the Big Man saying about it?'

'Nothing: Bob's maintaining a determined neutrality. But I know him better than that. He wouldn't admit it under torture, but deep inside, I reckon he's pleased. He has ambitions, professional ambitions, for Alex, and I suspect he was worried that she might have been giving too low a priority to her career.'

He glanced at Mackie. 'How do you feel about Sheila's career, Brian?'

'It's a fact of our life; it doesn't bother me.'

'But longer term, d'you think it might?'

'Andy,' said the slim detective, 'she and I have only just started living together. Right now, I'd settle for knowing that we have a longer term. We might split up. I might come up against the wrong bloke in the job and get shot. Sheila might get cancer, like poor Olive.

'If you learn nothing else from the McIlhenneys, you should learn this. Fuck the longer term; concentrate on now, because that's all the certainty you've got, mate.'

Martin sat on the edge of his desk, with a wry smile. 'My trouble is that I'm not certain of anything any more where Alex is concerned.'

'But maybe you're just a selfish bastard where she's concerned. Think on that.'

123

38

Not all of Edinburgh's Old Town fits that description. The spine of the original city rests on a hogsback which runs from the Castle, invincible on its great volcanic rock, down through the High Street past St Giles and the Council Chambers, and through Canongate, to the Palace of Holyroodhouse, the seat of generations of Monarchs of Scotland and of the United Kingdoms.

Rather than having been preserved as a monument, it has evolved as a living community. Many of its buildings have stood for centuries: those which did not survive have been replaced under the critical eye of the powerful civic watchdogs; some elected, others self-appointed.

Dr Surinder Gopal's address was in the lower part of the Royal Mile, on the outer limits of a stone's throw from the Palace. It lay at the foot of a narrow close which ran beneath a modern tenement and connected the Canongate with Calton Road. Brian Mackie surveyed the grey stone building, trying to make sense of the numbering of the apartments.

'What do you think this was, sir, before it was turned into flats?' asked Steele.

'I believe it was a brewery.' The Superintendent pointed to double doors which opened out on to a small balcony at third floor level. 'I reckon they used to store the barley up there . . . you can still see the spar for the hoist, look. The brewing would have been done in this part.' He nodded towards a square two-storey block which looked as if it might be an entire house, rather than flats.

They found the name 'Gopal' alongside the first of a row of buttons, above a speaker grille. Mackie pressed it, leaning close to be sure that he caught the reply. He waited for thirty seconds but none came; he pressed again. Still there was no reply. He pushed the buzzer for a third time.

'Bugger it!' he hissed, at last. 'The so-and-so must have gone on holiday right enough.'

Suddenly there was a click from the grille, and a low buzz. 'Yess?' It was a female voice, nervous and tremulous.

'Detective Superintendent Mackie, DS Steele: St Leonard's Police Station. We'd like to speak to Dr Gopal.'

'That is my son, but he is not here,' the woman replied. Even through her accent, which was heavily Asian, she sounded frightened. 'What do you want with him?'

'It's something connected with his work, that's all. Routine. Can we come in for a minute?'

'I don't know; you really are the police?'

'Yes, we are. But before you let us in, call our office.' He recited the number of the Divisional headquarters. 'The names are Mr Mackie and Mr Steele, remember. They'll vouch for us.'

'Wait there,' said the woman. A few seconds later, through the hum of the intercom, they heard her voice faintly. Eventually she returned. 'It's all right, they say. You can come in. Come all the way up to the top floor.' There was a click as the lock on the heavy green door was released.

Inside, the building was a warren. Doors opened to no discernible pattern off the narrow winding stair; on one floor it divided, leading them on a brief wild goose chase. Eventually at the top of yet another flight, they turned, to find themselves facing a small, middle-aged, dark-skinned woman. She wore traditional Indian dress, bright cloths wound around her, embroidered with golden stars. Her oiled, greying hair was swept back from her forehead, upon which a caste mark was imprinted.

Mackie took out his warrant card at once and held it up, Steele following suit.

'Good morning, gentlemen,' she said in clipped proper tones, no longer apprehensive. 'Won't you come in.' She stood to the side and allowed them to walk past her into the flat.

Stevie Steele whistled softly as he looked around. 'Nice,' he whispered to Mackie. 'I fancy this.'

'Not on your wages,' the superintendent murmured. The apartment was virtually open plan, divided by sliding panels rather than doors. Short flights of steps at either end led to galleried areas; one was a bedroom, while the other seemed to be a study. The decoration of the rooms was fresh, and their pictures and ornaments displayed a mix of Western and Asian influences.

'As you can see, detectives,' said the woman, 'my son is not here.'

'We didn't doubt you, Mrs Gopal,' Mackie assured her. 'But we do need to find him. We hoped that you could tell us where he is.'

The surgeon's mother shook her head. 'No. I cannot tell you that. He is away.' She looked up suddenly, making eye contact for the first time. 'The kettle is just boiled. You will have tea?'

Both policemen nodded. 'Thank you,' said Steele. 'Darjeeling, of course.'

She smiled, 'What else, in this house?'

They watched her as she stepped into the small kitchen took a tea caddy from a shelf then picked up a big porcelain pot. 'No tea bags here,' she called out to them in a sing-song voice as she heaped in four measures.

'Do you live with your son?' Mackie asked her.

She looked over her shoulder. 'No, of course not. I live with my husband. Surinder is on holiday so I come here every morning, to get his mail, to clean and to feed his bird.' She pointed to one of the long room's two windows. There was a cage on the sill, and in it, a blue budgerigar sat on a swing, eyeing a piece of cuttlefish bone which was clipped to the bars.

'How long has he been gone?'

'About ten days, maybe; I don't know.' She put the pot on a tray, together with three china cups and saucers, and carried it out of the kitchen area to a carved wooden table in the centre of the room. 'Sit, gentlemen, please,' she insisted, as she began to pour the tea.

'What did he say to you when he left?' asked Steele.

'He told me that he was going away for two or three weeks, on holiday. He said that he had not decided on the places he would visit, but that he would take his car and tour around. Go to Europe, maybe, for the sunshine. He told me that he had been working too hard and that he was in terrible need of a rest. I said fine, son; you go rest, I take care of your house. I haven't heard from him since, but that doesn't worry me.'

'Does Dr Gopal ever talk to you about his work?' Mackie's question seemed to set the woman's dark eyes sparkling.

'Superintendent, that is all he ever talks about. Surinder loves his work. His only ambition is to be the best surgeon in the country.'

'Does he ever mention his colleagues?'

'He talks a lot about Mr Strang; he admires him very much. One day, Surinder will be Mr Gopal, like him. He tells me that the most important doctors are the ones who are called Mister.'

'What about the place where he worked before he went into orthopaedics? Does he ever mention that?'

'Not often. It's been a while since he left there.'

'Does he still have friends there?'

Mrs Gopal nodded. 'Professor Weston, he is still a friend. It was he who say to my son that he should go in for another sort of surgery, since there would be more opportunities there. The Professor still takes an interest in Surinder's career. He have them here for an Indian dinner once, Professor and Mrs Weston. Not so long ago.' Suddenly she looked around towards a low bookcase, which stood against the wall between the windows. She pushed herself to her feet, walked over to it and took a slim volume from the top shelf.

'They gave him this as a present,' she said, handing it to Mackie. He looked at the cover. It was a copy of *The Jungle Book*, by Kipling. Idly he opened it, at the title page. It had been signed; the words jumped out at him.

'For Surinder, in memory of a delicious evening, Nolan and Gaynor.' He handed the book to Steele, still open at the dedication. Neither detective said a word; they simply sipped their tea.

'Do you know if your son intended to go on holiday alone?' the young sergeant asked, eventually; to break the silence, more than anything. Mrs Gopal stared at him as if she did not understand his question. 'Might he have taken a girlfriend with him?'

'My son, he does not have girlfriends.' She spat the word out as if it was something distasteful. 'Our family is traditionalist; he is traditionalist. When he is ready to marry, he will tell his father and a marriage will be arranged for him. Until then, he works.'

'Does Dr Gopal keep a diary?' She frowned at Mackie's question. 'An engagement book.'

'No. If he did I would have found it when I dusted.'

'Does he have a telephone answering machine, or service?'

'No.'

'I see. He really is out of touch then.'

'As I told you.'

Mackie nodded. 'Yes indeed.' He took out a card. 'If Dr Gopal should phone you, would you please ask him to contact either Sergeant Steele or me, on this number. Tell him it's important.'

Mrs Gopal's forehead wrinkled. 'When detectives come looking for my doctor son, I know it is important.'

39

'I should have asked you before. How was the hot date, then?' Leaning against the wall of the small office, Karen Neville looked at McGuire. He wore a mischievous grin.

'Cool, actually. He was nearly half-an-hour late, then when we started to get to know each other, he turned out to be gay.'

The inspector gasped in surprise. 'What? Him and the bloke in the wheelchair, you mean?'

'I asked him that. No, they're just friends, apparently, from their younger days. I don't think Dennis is up to any sort of nookie these days, straight or bent, from what Wayne told me. He has to lift him in and out of bed, and on and off the toilet – unless it's disabled-friendly, that is. Plus he has to help him dress, bath and everything.'

'Where are they living? In one of the big hotels?'

'No. The University found them a serviced flat that's been specially fitted out for handicapped people.'

'Whereabouts?'

'Down in Canonmills, Wayne said. I think I know where it is. At least I hope I do. I'm picking him up from there tomorrow night.'

'What? But you just said he was . . .'

She smiled. 'In which case you don't have to worry about me giving away secrets in the heat of passion, will you, Mario. Anyway, he's a nice guy, good company and if he's only in the market for friendship . . . well, that makes a nice change from the usual.' She paused, and blushed slightly. 'Plus, I told him I was gay first. I thought if I did it might avoid complications.'

McGuire laughed out loud, drawing a stern look from the customs officer across the room. 'Jesus.' He shook his head.

'Inspector,' the customs man called out. 'The people from the Amsterdam flight should begin coming through in a minute. We'll check the non-EU passport holders at that desk there.' He pointed through a one-way window which looked out on to a narrow corridor. 'Apart from the four cards that were drawn to your attention by the Dutch people, there have been six more completed during this flight, five of them by males.'

McGuire and Neville crossed the room to stand beside him. 'We've seen a lot of your unit out here in the last few days,' the officer said, casually. 'Is there a major alert?'

'Just business as usual,' McGuire murmured, as the first passenger, a tiny Arab, wearing a headdress, made his way to the passport control point. He was swaying slightly, as if he had spent too long in the bar at Schiphol.

'Hmm,' the man grunted moodily. 'Meaning "mind your own business", I suppose.'

McGuire treated him to his most dazzling smile. 'Absolutely,' he said.

'That's nice. We are on the same team, after all.'

'No we're not,' the policeman murmured. 'You'd nick me in a minute if I was out there with a extra bottle of duty free . . .' He pointed through the glass at the Arab, who was almost weighed down to the ground by the polythene bag which he was carrying. '. . . just like that bloke there.'

'What?' exclaimed the customs officer. 'Excuse me for a moment, please.' He hurried from the room.

Left alone, McGuire and Neville looked on in silence as one by one, the passengers who had completed landing cards were checked through. Three were Asians, one had an arm missing: none bore the remotest resemblance to any of the Hawkins photofit treatments.

'You know, Karen,' said the inspector, as they made their way out of the Edinburgh Airport terminal building and headed for the car park, 'I am beginning to get just a wee bit bored by this surveillance. Just ever so slightly.'

'I know how you feel.'

'Huh,' he chuckled. 'At least you've got something out of it – even if he is bent.'

40

'The missing heroin, Brian,' asked Skinner, 'enough to do the job was it?'

'At least twice, sir, or so the hospital pharmacist told us.'

'And there's a definite link between Gopal and Gaynor and Nolan Weston?'

'He entertained them to a curry night up at his place. The mother showed Stevie and me the present they gave him. She assumed that the Prof had brought the current Mrs Weston.'

'Must have been her night off,' the DCC chuckled. 'So what do you propose to do now?' He looked at Mackie across the desk, then switched his gaze to Andy Martin.

'We're going to have to re-interview Weston,' said the Head of CID. 'Brian and I were contemplating picking him up and taking him to St Leonard's for a formal interview, under caution. If he was an ordinary Mr Joe Criminal, we'd do that without question.'

'But he isn't. Look, gentlemen, Professor Weston isn't going anywhere; he doesn't know that he's still under suspicion. Wouldn't it be better to get some answers out of Dr Gopal before you do anything to unsettle him?'

Mackie frowned. 'That could take another couple of weeks, unless we put out a Europe-wide alert for his car.'

'You know what he drives?'

'A silver Alfa Romeo 146,' the superintendent answered. 'Registration T197 VSG. But I wasn't serious about the alert: not at this stage anyway.'

'I should hope not. We can wait for the boy to get back from his holidays; I do not see him and Weston as potential fugitives.' Skinner shot a glance at Martin. 'How are the press on this one?'

'They haven't forgotten about it, if that's what you mean. Alan Royston's a bit worried that if we don't give them something concrete soon, the tabloids will start writing speculative stories. Joan Ball's had a couple of reporters at her door; Christ knows what she's told them.'

'We'd better quieten them down then,' said the DCC. 'Andy, have a word with the Fiscal's office. Ask Pettigrew to schedule a Fatal Accident Inquiry into Mrs Weston's death for some date in the future, and to let the media know. That'll get them off Royston's back, without him having to tell them any porkies.'

'What if we don't turn up anything before the FAI date?' asked Mackie. 'What if Gopal doesn't come back?'

Skinner shrugged his shoulders. 'In that case, it goes ahead. We put the facts before a Sheriff and jury and let them decide. If they bring in a suicide verdict – and you never know, they might: juries have done dafter things in the past – then that's what it is. If they call it unlawful killing, the investigation stays open.

'But Gopal will surface again, I'll bet. This pharmacist person isn't going to tell him about your visit, is she?'

'No, not a chance.'

'Then he doesn't know that he's got anything to run away from.'

'Not even if he injected Mrs Weston?'

Skinner shook his head, and pushed himself out of his chair as if he hated it: which in fact, he did. 'If he did that, and whether or not the Prof is involved . . .', he pointed a finger at Mackie, '. . . you must not necessarily assume one from the other. There could have been an entirely separate relationship between Gaynor and Gopal for all you know . . . the likelihood is that he's taken himself off for a while just to ensure that there's no aftermath.

'If that's the case, when he hears that an FAI's been scheduled, he'll assume that no one's connected him.'

The big man beamed at his colleagues. 'You came to me for counsel and advice, gentlemen. You might think I'm the last person who should be telling you this, but: be patient.

'For what it's worth, I don't believe that Professor Weston played any part in his wife's death. He's been interviewed twice by senior policemen – Brian, you've seen him both times – and from what I've heard, his story hasn't wavered. You guys are used to dealing with professional liars; this man's an amateur, yet you haven't seen a chink in him.

'As far as Gopal is concerned, who knows about him? If I wasn't still tied to this office, I might have a go at finding out myself. But since I am . . .

'Let this investigation simmer for a bit lads. It's a mystery now, but it won't be for ever.'

'Okay, boss,' Martin sighed, wearily. 'How much longer will you be on this side of the corridor, d'you think?'

'A few weeks yet, probably,' Skinner replied. 'I had some good news from Jimmy yesterday though. The Spanish consultant was pleased with the results of the tests they did last Tuesday. He's given him the all clear to drive, so he and Chrissie will be starting home on Monday.

'Once he's back home, we'll see what his own doctor, and our own ME, have to say about coming back to work.'

'What'll you do when he comes back, boss?' asked Mackie, with one of his rare smiles.

'Brian,' said the DCC earnestly, 'I think I'll spend a week just cruising the streets.'

41

Neil McIlhenney sat in the waiting area of the Department of Clinical Oncology becoming acquainted with a new companion. He had never known Fear before, not until Sarah had made the introduction after bringing Olive home from her first visit to the Western General.

Of course there had been the odd scary moment in his life, the occasional anxiety. He remembered . . . he must have been seven or eight at the time . . . waiting for his father to come home, having upset his mother, and suspecting that he might be in for a real leathering. Then there was the hour he had spent in the corridor of the Maternity Unit, waiting for Lauren to be born. On another night early in his police career he had found himself in a cul-de-sac, in uniform, with his back to the wall and four large, threatening youths blocking the exits.

Those had just been minor crises, mere butterflies in his expansive stomach, and each one had had a happy outcome. His father had decided that the wait had been punishment enough, and had lashed him with his tongue rather than his belt. There had been the indescribable miracle of Lauren's birth, the moment of holding his first child, for the first time. And on that third occasion, Constable Mario McGuire had appeared behind the four young thugs, a Satanic smile on his face as he contemplated the mess that he and McIlhenney would leave behind them in the alley.

This was different though; this was something which threatened to consume him, yet which he knew had to be conquered and contained within him, never allowed to show on the outside, least of all to Olive. Since the illness had been diagnosed, he had experienced a succession of horrors. Now, waiting for his wife to come down from the ward, he sat contemplating apprehensively the weekend to come.

They had been warned about the treatment, about the sickness that was the most common side-effect of the drugs. 'These are very powerful and toxic chemicals, Olive,' their supervising nurse had warned as she had talked them through what would happen. 'Their job is to seek out and kill the cancer cells, but they will have a hell of an effect on your entire system. We'll give you steroids to control it, but the chances are that you'll be very sick for a couple of days after your first treatment.'

At that moment, he was fearful of that imminent crisis more than anything else. His mind had simply locked away the long-term possibilities, refusing to contemplate them, but right there and then he dreaded the very thought of watching his wife's distress.

'Mr McIlhenney?' The calm voice broke into his fearful antici-pation. 'How are you getting on?' He looked up from his chair to see Derek Simmers standing over him.

'Okay,' he replied, trying to smile. 'Just waiting for Olive, as instructed.'

'I've just left her,' said the consultant. 'She'll be another twenty minutes or so. Don't wait here; come on through to my office. I'll tell reception where you are, so she can find you when she comes down.'

Neil nodded. He stood, picked up his coffee and followed the tall, fair-haired Simmers to the desk at the entrance, where he paused, then round a corner and into a small office opposite the room where their initial consultation had taken place. There was no desk, only a few chairs and a low coffee table.

'Sit, down, sit down,' the physician insisted. And then unexpectedly, he sighed. 'You know,' he began, 'I've lost count of the number of patients I've treated in this place. I've lost count of the number of husbands and wives that I've seen in your shoes; but still I can't really imagine how it must feel for either the patient or her partner.'

'I can try. I do, of course; but, not having experienced it for myself, not having sat on your side of the desk at the consultation, seeing with your eyes, listening with your ears; not even having sat out there being ministered to by the WRVS ladies in their canteen, I don't suppose I even get close to the reality.'

'No,' McIlhenney answered quietly. 'I don't suppose you do.'

'Maybe that's a good thing, though. Because it ensures that I remain objective, and as long as I do I have something to offer my patients beyond the mechanics of the treatment.' The gentle blue eyes settled on the policeman, and he felt the same wave of inexplicable relief which had swept over him at his first meeting with Simmers.

'I will never lie to Olive, or to you,' he said, earnestly. 'I will always tell it to you like it is; to a great extent the success or failure of her treatment will depend on the interpretation which both of you place on my words. I am dedicated to the preservation of life, Neil, for as long as that can be. I will prescribe and administer the most appropriate treatment for Olive's physical condition.

'But once I've done that, your job begins; you have to remain positive and you have to remain mentally strong. From what I've seen of you both, you will be able to do that.

'The next couple of days will be tough, for both of you; make no mistake about that. But in the course of this treatment, which will last for up to six months, they will probably be the worst you'll experience.

'My best advice to you is to set yourselves targets. For example, in a couple of weeks, maybe even next weekend, you might be able to contemplate an evening at the theatre. After two months' treatment, you might want to go on holiday. If you do, I'll make a gap in the schedule for you. Working towards and achieving objectives like these will be a tremendous psychological help to you both and will improve Olive's chances of keeping this thing at bay.'

Simmers paused, and McIlhenney saw pain written in his soft eyes. 'The hardest thing for me,' he continued, 'is to tell devoted partners like you and Olive that one of you has an incurable disease. I don't discuss survival rates or make prognoses; anyone can pick all that stuff off the Internet if they have a mind. I can tell you this though, from long experience: the people who believe from day one, without doubt, that they will wind up on the positive side of the ratio, whatever that might be, are the people who do best.

'You do believe that, Neil, don't you?'

The policeman felt his jaw tighten as he returned the consultant's gaze. 'Absolutely,' he said.

'That's good. Hold fast to that belief; it's the best advice I have for you.'

The physician rose to his feet. 'We'd better go back out there. Olive should be down from the ward any minute.'

McIlenney nodded. 'Thank you,' he said. 'Thank you very much, Mr Simmers.'

The man laid a hand on his shoulder. 'Listen Neil, over the coming months you and Olive and I are going to have to maintain a close, trusting relationship. So please, drop the Mr Simmers stuff. Don't call me Derek either; I've never cared much for that name. Call me by the name my friends use. Call me Deacey.'

42

She found the apartment without difficulty: a short taxi trip across the Bridges from her own small flat off Nicolson Street, down Broughton Street, through the traffic lights at Rodney Street and there it was, facing her as Wayne had described it.

He was ready to leave when he opened the door, tall and handsome in jeans and a red LaCoste waterproof. His beard looked as if it had been newly trimmed.

'Am I late?' she asked, untypically concerned that he might think she was evening the score for Giuliano's.

'Not at all,' he drawled. 'I saw your taxi arrive, that's all. Say, before we leave, come on in and say hello to Dennis. He's ready for bed but he's decent.'

Karen was not entirely certain that she wanted to meet Wayne's friend again, remembering his sourness when she had checked him in at the conference centre, but she followed him inside. The paraplegic was in his wheelchair, dressed in pyjamas and a silk dressing gown. His hair was damp at the edges, and his skin slightly pink, as if he had just come from a bath. He seemed to be concentrating hard on the *Scotsman* crossword.

'Say hello to Karen, mate,' the tall Australian commanded.

Dennis Crombie looked up, peered at her through his spectacles, and barked a quick, 'Hello.'

She grinned back at him, and pointed towards the newspaper on his lap. 'Friday's usually the hardest,' she said. 'That's what I find, anyway.'

'Eh?'

'The crossword.'

'Oh. Yes, it's tougher than yesterday's.' The faintest smile seemed to cross the economist's face, and a gold filling in one of his upper canines caught the light for an instant. 'Too many Scottish words, that's the problem for me.'

'Don't worry, if you're staying on for a few weeks you'll learn the language.'

The smile vanished. 'As long as I can stay warm, I don't give a

136

stuff about the language. I never thought Scotland would be so cold.'

'Hey, it's not that bad,' she protested.

'It is when you can't move about.'

She felt a mixture of guilt and sympathy. 'I'm sorry, Dennis, I didn't think.'

'No,' said Crombie. 'People don't. They can't imagine what it's like to look at the world from this angle.' He smiled again, but it looked forced. 'Hey, don't mind me. I'm just an embittered old cripple. You two get going. Wheel me though to bed first though, mate.'

Wayne nodded and took the guide handles of the chair. As Karen stepped back into the entrance hall she heard Dennis call out. 'Have a nice night now. Don't do anything I can't.'

Her escort joined her in a couple of minutes, breathing a heavy sigh as he closed the door behind him. 'You sound tired,' she said.

'Relieved, more like it. It was bath night for Dennis. That's always a performance.'

'Never mind,' Karen chuckled, 'the best is yet to come. Where are we going?'

'Well,' he answered slowly. 'I thought we might have a couple of pints in the pub on the next corner, the Northern Bar, and then go for a Chinese in the place a few doors down, the Loon Fung.'

'Absolutely,' she agreed. 'You couldn't have chosen better. That place does lemon chicken to die for.'

Three hours later, he had to agree with her. 'That was just magic,' he murmured, as the last forkful disappeared. An extra couple of pints and half a bottle of red wine had taken the rough edge from his accent in the course of the evening, most of which Wayne had spent talking about Australia, aboriginal rights, and life on board an oil rig. 'Do you know any more places like this?' he asked.

She nodded. 'A few. Maybe we'll get round to them, all in good time.'

'Maybe.'

'You're all right you know, Wayne,' she whispered, feeling as relaxed as she had in years. She smiled, broadly. 'For a poofter, that is.

'It's a pity,' she went on, 'that male-female relationships are usually so hopeless. Most of them just start and finish with that sticky business, all that pushing and shoving and sweating and shouting. It's nice to be able to enjoy an evening with a man, just as two sensible people.'

'Couldn't agree more.'

'What sort of a bloke are you, back home?' she asked. 'I mean are you an action man? D'you play rugby? Are you a Wallaby, or is it a Kiwi?'

137

He frowned. 'I ain't a Kiwi, that's for sure. I hate fucking Kiwis.'

She reached forward and tapped the back of his right hand lightly with one of her long finger-nails. 'So don't fuck any,' she said straight-faced.

The Chinese waiters looked across at them as they collapsed in laughter, heads touching across their table. Then they looked away: they were used to Friday night customers fresh from the local bars.

'Coffee?' she asked, eventually.

'Not here. My place. I've got some really fine Colombian grounds, and some decent Spanish brandy.'

'Sounds good.'

Karen insisted on taking her turn to pay for the meal. 'You come again,' the head waiter called as she stepped out into the night, which had gone from chilly to frosty.

'Christ,' she said. 'Dennis will be freezing his balls off.'

'Nah. That apartment's like an oven, plus, he's got an electric blanket.' He paused and she could see his smile under the street lights. 'They've been numb for years, anyway.'

They stumbled through the door of the flat, almost comic in their efforts to be quiet. She followed him into the dining kitchen and watched him as he made the coffee, admiring the care with which he measured the grounds into the filter and tamped them down. 'The brandy's in the cupboard behind you,' he told her, without turning from his task as he poured water into the cone-shaped filter.

In that moment, Karen realised that more alcohol was the last thing she wanted. Yet what she did have in mind was not, it seemed, on offer. 'I won't thanks, Wayne. I've had well enough.'

'I won't either then. I don't really need a bad head in the morning.'

He waited until he judged the coffee to be perfect, then poured two medium sized mugs.

'Let's sit through there,' he said, nodding toward the living room.

He placed the mugs on a glass-topped table and sat beside her on the comfortable sofa. 'How big is this place?' she asked, quietly.

'You've seen most of it. There's this, the kitchen diner, bathroom, toilet and one bedroom. Why d'you ask?'

'I just wondered,' she said. 'Like whether you have a room of your own.'

'This sofa is a convertible. I sleep on it.'

'Mmmm.'

She looked at him suddenly, catching him off-guard, catching him in a glance which told her all she needed to know. He told her, anyway. 'I'm not really gay, you know. I only said that to make you feel more comfortable.'

'I know,' she murmured. 'Neither am I. I only said it because I wanted to keep you at a distance for a while, until I could work out if I really fancied you as much as I thought at first.'

'And do you?'

'Oh yes.'

He leaned across kissed her, hearing her soft moan as she responded, feeling her tongue searching for his. His touch was light; even his beard felt smooth against her cheek.

As they embraced, his hand slipped under her sweater, fingers gently, sensually, counting off her vertebrae one by one until they reached the clasp of her bra.

It came unfastened with a single flick, and as it did he broke off the kiss, to draw the loose-fitting jumper up and over her head. 'Jesus,' he said softly, as she unfastened the buttons of his shirt. Her breasts never failed to impress at first sight; they were huge and firm, nipples hard, thrusting at him.

He stood, drawing her to her feet with him as she unbuckled his belt, reaching behind her once more for the zipper of her skirt.

Greedily, lustfully, they tore off the remainder of each other's clothing. Karen gasped with surprise, in her turn, as she saw the size of him. 'Gimme,' she said huskily, sinking back down on to the sofa-bed, throwing her legs wide apart, hands on his buttocks, nails digging in as she drew him, pulsing, deep into her moistness.

She gave a quiet little scream, but remembered even then the man next door, and muffled it almost at once by biting Wayne's shoulder. She drew up her thighs, and wrapped her legs around him, driving with her hips, her thrusts in time with his, feeling his velvet hardness, clasping it within her, all of it: and then, the sudden, delicious, pulsing heat as he climaxed, unstoppably. 'Oh damn, Karen,' he moaned in her ear. 'Too soon, too soon. I'm sorry; I'm sorry.'

'What for?' she laughed, in a throaty growl. 'There's more where that came from, surely. And we won't be interrupted.' She chuckled again, wickedly. 'The wheelchair's in here, remember.' Holding him inside her as she felt him subside, she began to move again.

43

However much Sarah would have liked it to be otherwise, Saturday breakfast in the Skinner household was usually an impatient affair. Mark was allowed two hours' surfing time on the Internet, and would be on the edge of his seat from the moment his cereal was put in front of him, until the last of his bacon, tomato and mushroom disappeared. James Andrew would eat determinedly in his toddler chair, knowing that a clean plate meant that he would be turned loose among his toys.

And Bob . . . Often Bob had gone off to an early teeing-off time on the golf course, a slice of toast clamped between his teeth as the door closed behind him.

This Saturday was different though. The family sat around the dining table in the conservatory, augmented by Lauren and Spencer, their weekend guests. There was toast in a rack, milk for the cereals and for the coffee in a jug, and scrambled eggs and bacon keeping warm in the hostess trolley.

Bob smiled as he looked at the children, from one to another. 'Isn't this just great,' he said. 'Civilisation comes to the Skinner household.'

Lauren frowned back at him, through her solemn, ageless eyes. 'Don't you do this every Saturday?' she asked. 'My mum does. She makes Spence and me use our napkins and everything. She makes my Dad say grace and then she makes him clear the table when we're finished.'

Spencer was staring at her as she spoke. 'No she doesn't,' he protested, loudly. 'She gives us our breakfast on trays while we watch *Live and Kicking*. It's only on our birthdays she does that.'

The little girl glowered back at her brother for a few seconds, until her head dropped, and until the first big tears fell into her lap.

'Hey Lauren,' said Sarah, gently, 'come on through here with me for a bit. Bob, you dish up the cereal.'

They were gone for around five minutes. When they returned, the child was pale but smiling, her eyes red, but dry. She took her place without a word, and began to tuck into her breakfast. Spencer reached across and gave his sister's arm a quick squeeze. 'Hey Lauren, look out there,' he spluttered, his mouth not quite empty. 'We've been watching an oil rig.' He pointed out of the conservatory, towards the estuary, where two tugs were hauling a great three-legged structure out towards the open sea.

'Sometimes they bring rigs in here for maintenance,' said Mark, in his matter-of-fact voice. He was younger than either of the McIlhenney children, but carried himself, automatically, as their equal, as often, he did with adults. Bob and Sarah's step-son, adopted after the death of both of his parents, was a remarkably assured and gifted little boy; if they had a concern about him it was that somehow, through all his experiences, part of his childhood had passed him by.

'Okay,' Sarah interrupted, briskly. 'What are we going to do this morning?'

'Internet,' Mark replied at once.

Jazz simply laughed and slammed his spoon down on the tray of his high chair. 'Stop splashing, young man,' his mother said. 'Mark, you can go on the Net any time during the weekend. I've got a better idea. Lauren, Spencer, I asked your dad to pack your swim stuff, so what say I take the three of you to the Commonwealth Pool, and we all go on the flumes?'

Spencer's eyes lit up. 'Phwoah! Yes please!'

'That would be nice,' Lauren added.

'As long as I don't have to go on the big one,' Mark whispered. Always, he made that proviso, Sarah knew, yet always, when it came to it, he plucked up his courage and made the vertical slide.

'Right,' she said. 'That's a done deal. As soon as breakfast is over you can go and get ready.'

'What about Jazz?' Spencer asked. 'Can't he come?'

'James Andrew is still a bit young for the flumes. His dad will look after him while we're swimming.'

'Hear that, Kid?' Bob laughed. 'It's just you and me. Maybe we'll go fishing: how about that?'

'You can do what you like, as long as you meet us afterwards at the Bar Roma. I'll book a table there for one thirty.'

The pace of breakfast picked up. Soon the three older children were excused from the table, to go and pack their swimming trunks and towels. 'How was Lauren?' Skinner asked, as soon as the little girl had gone.

'Scared,' his wife answered. 'She's a very perceptive kid. She doesn't really understand what's happening to her mother, but she knows it's not good.

'I told her that Olive had an illness and that she was having treatment that wouldn't hurt her but that would make her sick for a day or two, before it made her better. I told her that after that, she

141

would need Lauren to be very grown up, to help by doing things around the house that she might be too tired to manage.' Sarah smiled. 'Know what she said then?'

Bob shook his head.

'She asked if her daddy would be all right.'

'What did you say?'

'I told her that Neil needed her to be brave, just as much as Olive did.'

She broke off as the children reappeared. 'Okay,' she called out. 'Line up, let's count heads and let's go. Bob, I'll take your car, just so we don't have to swap over Jazz's safety seat.'

Skinner nodded, reached into the pocket of his jeans and tossed her the key. He walked them to the door, waving them off as the BMW pulled out of the drive, then returned to the conservatory, where his younger son was shifting impatiently in his feeding chair.

'So, young man,' he boomed. 'Here we are. The toys, is it? Or would you rather do something else?' A slow, wicked smile spread across his face. 'How would you like to come to work with your Old Man? No, you're never too young to learn about being a detective.'

44

There was an empty parking space at the back entrance to the veterans' nursing home in Calton Road, next to Dr Surinder Gopal's flat. Skinner lined up Sarah's 4×4 against the white wall, and looked up at the top floor of the old brewery store, where Brian Mackie had said that the missing doctor lived.

'She comes here every morning,' he said to his son, over the noise of the Spice Girls. They were Jazz's favourites; he was still short of his second birthday, but there was something about their music which could keep him happy for hours. 'She does the dusting, feeds the budgie and takes in his mail. The boy's Mammy's good to him, isn't she.

'Let's just check whether she's here just now. Back in a minute.' He jumped out of the car, paid the parking fee, grudgingly as always, then walked to the entrance door to the old building. He found the buzzer marked 'Gopal' and pressed, leaning on it for several seconds.

Eventually, a woman's voice answered 'Yess?'

'Is Mary in?' Skinner asked.

'Pardon?'

'Is Mary in?' He looked at the names beside the other buzzers. 'Mary Blake.'

'There no Mary here,' said Mrs Gopal, impatiently.

'Aw sorry, hen,' said the policeman. 'Must have pressed the wrang bell.'

He was still smiling as he climbed back behind the wheel of the Freelander. Sitting with his back turned to the door, he looked into the back seat, at his son, who was still listening to the Spices, and mangling a picture book in his strong hands. 'She's in, right enough. Let's just wait and see where she goes next.'

'This is what CID work is really about, Jazzer,' he murmured. 'Long hours spent sat on your bum . . .'

'Bum,' the child repeated.

'. . . or worse, stood out in the could freezing your chuckies off. But every so often . . .' He smiled, '. . . you get lucky, and that makes it all worthwhile.'

He sighed. 'I miss it, you know, Wee Man. Times like this; they're bonding experiences, the detective and his neebur – or neighbour, as we say in Edinburgh – his partner, sharing the hours of boredom, then sharing the buzz when they do get a result.

'I have to tell you, too, that I still get a perverse pleasure out of stealing a march on the lads.' He laughed, softly, as Jazz began to sing nonsense sounds along with *Stop*, making a passable effort at following the tune.

'I almost told Mackie yesterday that he should try this, but then I thought, "No. Keep it for yourself, Robert. Take the chance to get out of that bloody office." '

He was still smiling when he heard the soft knock from behind him, on the driver's window. He turned, annoyed by the interruption, to see Steve Steele looking through the glass, a shade anxiously.

He had to switch on the car's electrics before he could lower the window. 'What the hell are you doing, sergeant?' he asked.

'The same as you, I think, sir. Just being curious.'

'Do it in here then. Get in.'

The young sergeant nodded, walked round the back of the car and climbed into the passenger seat, being careful not to scrape the door against the wall. Skinner nodded towards the back seat. 'This is my oppo,' he said, 'my younger son, Jazz.' He looked over his shoulder. 'Wee man, this is Stevie. There's worse detectives than him on the force, believe you me.'

He paused. 'Did you tell Mr Mackie you were going to do this?' he asked.

Steele shook his head. 'No sir. I suppose I should have.'

'Aye,' said Skinner heavily, guilt setting in. 'So should I.'

He glanced at the entrance door as he spoke, and saw it open. 'That's her, sir,' Steele burst out, as the woman emerged, wearing Indian costume as before. She had a small handbag slung over her left shoulder and carried a handful of mail in her left hand. They watched her as she walked up to a blue Toyota Picnic parked nose-in to the building, opened the driver's door and climbed in.

'Okay,' the DCC murmured. 'On your way, Mrs. You're probably only going home, but let's just make sure.

'Do you know where she lives?' he asked Steele as the Picnic reversed back from the building and headed off up Calton Road. He started the Freelander and followed, a safe distance behind as Mrs Gopal turned into New Street.

'She and her husband have a shop up in Slateford, sir. They live not far from there, in Craiglockhart Avenue.'

'Indeed?' said Skinner slowly, watching the car indicate a right turn into Market Street. 'Why's she going that way then?'

'Probably going shopping in the town, sir.'

'I know the probabilities, Stevie. It's the improbabilities we're looking for.'

They followed her along Market Street, across Waverley Bridge and Princes Street, then left into Queen Street. 'So much for shopping,' Skinner muttered to himself as the Picnic turned right towards Howe Street. The midday traffic was heavy as they neared Stockbridge, and so Skinner was forced to close up on their quarry. 'Bets?' he asked.

'Somewhere close,' Steele murmured. 'You don't go through Stockbridge to get to anywhere else; not on a Saturday, at any rate.' Half a mile later, he was proved correct. Indicating at the last minute, the woman took a left turn off Comely Bank, and drew to a halt in a space no more than a hundred yards into the narrow street, beside a grey stone tenement building.

Skinner parked the Freelander twenty yards further along, pulling across to the opposite side of the road. Mrs Gopal seemed completely unaware of their attention as she stepped out of the Toyota, stepped up to a ground floor flat, opened its blue-painted door with a Yale key and stepped inside.

'And just look at what's parked there,' the DCC exclaimed, as the door closed behind the missing surgeon's mother. 'A silver Alfa 146 was it, Stevie? Registration T197 VSG?'

'That's the one, sir.'

Skinner beamed at his Spice-entranced son over his shoulder. 'What did I tell you, Wee Man? Every so often, you get lucky.'

'Maybe so, sir,' muttered Steele, following his glance, 'but what are we going to do about it? I mean, we can't—'

'That's true. I'll tell you what, you mind the baby, I'll go in and lift him.' The DCC laughed out loud at the sudden consternation which showed on Steele's face. 'It's okay, Stevie. I think I've got that covered.' He took his mobile phone from his pocket and began to punch in a number.

Less that ten minutes later the acting chief constable and the detective sergeant stood together at the blue door. Skinner rang the bell, leaning on it for a few extra seconds as he had at the Calton Road building.

Eventually the door creaked open. A tall young man stood in the murky hall of the flat, peering out at them. He was brown-skinned, and well-built, his muscles emphasised by his white tee-shirt.

'Dr Gopal?' asked Skinner. The man nodded.

'We're police officers. I think you'd better talk to us; don't you?'

45

'I don't believe it.' Sarah gasped. 'I know I said you could do what you liked, but . . . you took a toddler on a surveillance operation?'

'Sure,' Bob grunted. 'I've done it before. With this one here.' He nodded towards Alex, who stood beside the table, carrying her half-brother on her hip. Jazz was hungry; he was beginning to wriggle, restively.

'It's true,' his daughter confirmed. 'I was a bit older than James Andrew, maybe, but sometimes Pops would take me out with him if he was working on a stake-out at weekends. Of course he only ever did it if he was certain that there wouldn't be any action.'

'But today there was action,' said her step-mother.

'No, no,' said Bob, mollifying her. 'Not action. Stevie and I just decided we'd better talk to the guy, just in case he moved on. As luck would have it, we were just round the corner from Alex's temporary digs, so I raised her on the mobile and got her to come round and baby-sit.'

'In a car! In the middle of Stockbridge!' Sarah shook her head, and took the baby from Alex. 'You're a bigger kid than he is in some ways.' The three older children, sat on a row on the far side of the Bar Roma table, gazed at her, reassured by her gentle, reproving laughter.

Bob signalled to the waiters to set an extra place at their table; when it was ready he sat, between his wife and his daughter. Jazz sat in a high chair, next to his mother.

'So,' she asked, quietly, as Alex began to quiz the three youngsters about their morning at the pool. 'Are you going to tell me about my son's first day on the job? What the hell was it, anyway.'

'There could have been a connection with Gaynor Weston,' he answered. 'Some diamorphine vanished from one of the hospitals, just before her death. Stevie and I did a bit of extra-curricular work, trying to trace the doctor who was suspected of taking it.

'I didn't really think we would find him, but we did. We trailed his mother from his flat to another place in Comely Bank. We had to go in, Sarah, you must appreciate that.'

She grinned. 'I suppose I do. At least you didn't have Jazz watching the back door.'

Bob whistled. 'Hey, I never thought of that.'

She punched him on the shoulder, playfully. 'And was there a connection with Gaynor?' she asked.

He glanced at the children, to make sure that they were engrossed in their conversation with Alex. 'No. We found something we didn't expect at all.' Suddenly his expression changed; the cleft above his nose deepened, with his frown.

'What?'

'Dr Gopal's younger sister,' he said, his voice almost at a whisper. 'The kid went off the rails a while back, started mixing with altogether the wrong crowd, and got herself hooked on smack. When he found out, her father, who's a real old-timer, a disciplinarian, chucked her out, into the street – literally. He forbade the mother, and Surinder, to have anything to do with her.

'Mrs Gopal, poor woman, almost went crazy. Eventually, Surinder decided that for her sake, he would help, even if his father never spoke to him again; he would try to rescue the girl. So he rented the flat in Comely Bank, short term. Then he went round all her haunts until he found out where she was living. It was a squat, a real dive of a place, down in Muirhouse.

'One morning about ten days ago, he turned up there, out of the blue, battered her boyfriend – a real smackhead, by the way – and took her out of there. The bugger had got her hooked; he even had her on the game to fund his habit as well as hers. Gopal's had her under lock and key ever since, weaning her off her habit. That's why he needed the diamorphine.'

'Was she that bad?' asked Sarah.

'Apparently so. Surinder was afraid that if he cut her off cold, the shock might kill her. So he's been giving her decreasing doses, lengthening the intervals between each one.'

'How's she doing?'

Skinner grimaced. 'She wasn't too well when Stevie and I saw her, but her brother said that she was actually a hell of a lot better than she had been. He's almost ready to take her off altogether.'

He broke off as the waiter arrived with the menus, ordering soft drinks for the children, a glass of white wine for Alex, and mineral water for Sarah and for himself.

'So what are you going to do about it?' she whispered.

'Nothing at all. The girl was well enough to confirm her brother's story, and to say that she agreed with what he was doing.'

'But what about the stolen diamorphine?'

147

'Ah,' Bob countered. 'But was it stolen? Surinder's a doctor; he could say that he prescribed it in an emergency situation. Okay, he broke all the hospital regulations, but that's between him and his managers and they haven't reported anything to us.'

'Couldn't he have taken the kid to a rehab unit?'

'He considered that, but he was afraid she'd have been dead by the time they got round to treating her. No, Sarah, in the absence of a formal complaint from the hospital, I'm satisfied that the police have got no locus in this situation other than to find that boyfriend and put him out of business. Stevie'll start the ball rolling on that on Monday.'

She looked at him, doubtfully. 'I don't know—' she began.

He stopped her. 'Well, I do. I've seen the situation, and as far as I'm concerned that man is a hero. I'll make no trouble for him.'

She shrugged. 'It's your call, I suppose. So where does that leave you as far as the Weston investigation is concerned?'

'Up the creek, *sans* paddle,' he said, ruefully. 'It's a mystery, and that could well be how it stays.'

Sarah sighed. 'Maybe, like with your young doctor, no action could be the best outcome.'

Bob nodded. 'Could be. I'll think about that over the weekend.' He reached across the table and tapped Mark on the shoulder. 'So young man,' he asked. 'Did you go down that big slide after all?'

46

'This is nice, Andy.' Alex looked at her fiancé across the dinner table, as the waiter topped up their wine glasses. 'It makes me feel a bit special again. I like it.'

The candle-light shone on his green contact lenses as he met her gaze. 'You make me feel special all the time,' he said softly, once the girl was out of earshot. 'But if this is what it takes to make it work for you, I'll go along with it.'

He smiled, ruefully. 'You know, Brian Mackie, of all people, gave it to me straight between the eyes this week; he told me I was a selfish bastard where you were concerned. However I try to twist it around, I have to accept it. He's right.'

'I'm sorry if I've been suffocating you, honey. I'll give you room to breathe from now on. Promise.'

She shook her head. 'Let's not go over all that again,' she whispered across the table. 'Let's just enjoy ourselves now. It was a nice idea of yours, coming back to the place where we told Dad and Sarah we were engaged. It was an even better idea that we should come on our own this time.'

'You coming back to my place later?' he asked her, abruptly.

'Of course.'

'Good,' he grinned. 'That's the awkward bit out of the way. Now, what sort of a week have you had?'

'Work-wise, interesting as ever. Mr Laidlaw had a big instruction from an insurance company this week; they're fighting with a travel agent over who should compensate a man who was taken ill on holiday.'

'How's that?'

'The chap had a previous medical history; the insurers say they weren't told about it, and that such a material non-disclosure invalidates the policy.'

'And does it?'

'We say it does, and in the absence of proof from the travel agent that he did make the full circumstances known to our client, that's what the Court will say as well. The other party's case is that they made disclosure orally, to an employee of the insurer. No one's arguing about whether such a conversation took place, it did. The dispute is over what was said.'

'Meantime what happens to the guy?'

Alex shrugged. 'He waits, I'm afraid.'

'That's a bit rough.'

'Maybe, but it's not our fault.'

'Of course it is,' Andy insisted. 'It's your client who's refusing to pay the guy. Bloody insurance companies: they take the money then look for ways to weasel out of meeting their obligation, and firms like yours help them.'

'What should they do then?' she shot back at him.

'Pay the client then sue the travel agent over the alleged non-disclosure. It'd make no difference to you and Laidlaw. You'd still get your fees. I tell you this; if the victim in this case wants to make a fraud complaint against your client, I'll investigate it.'

'Keep your voice down!' she hissed. 'I tell *you* this, Andy; it's the last time I'll discuss my work with you. Christ, I thought you just resented my job. I was wrong; you've got a down on my whole bloody profession.'

'Change the subject; change the subject!' he said. 'I'm sorry; let's not ruin the evening.'

They finished their meal in virtual silence, Alex's outrage still simmering quietly. 'Okay,' Andy ventured gently, as their coffee cooled in front of them. 'Let's start again. Forget work. Tell me about your day.'

The start of a smile came back to her face. 'Well,' she began, 'this is the second restaurant I've been in today. I had a salad up at the West End with Pops and Sarah, my brothers and the McIlhenney children, after Pops recruited me as a baby-minder while he went off to sort someone out.'

She explained the events of Skinner's extra-curricular morning, and her own fleeting involvement in it.

Andy was frowning at her by the time she finished. 'That's incredible,' he said, the frown deepening into a glare.

'What? Taking Jazz with him? Old established practice as far as he's concerned. I remember when I was six, we sat outside a bookie's for three hours one weekend, just checking on who was going in there. Pops let me take the photographs.'

Martin shook his head. 'Not that. What's incredible is the fact that he just swanned into Brian's investigation. If anyone did that to him, he'd paper the walls with them.'

Alex stood up, abruptly and threw her napkin on the table. 'Right, that's it,' she snapped, no longer caring who heard her. 'This is obviously "Knock the Skinners" night. Well, not any more, it ain't. You can pay the bill; I'll get a taxi – back to my place.

'Give me a week or two to myself, Andy. I don't think I can handle this special treatment too often.' He was still staring as the double doors swung shut behind her with a bang which echoed round the restaurant.

47

'I didn't expect to see you here at St Leonard's, boss,' said Brian Mackie, as Skinner closed the door behind him. He glanced at the clock on the wall. 'Not first thing on a Monday morning, at any rate.'

The big DCC grinned, a touch sheepishly. 'Maybe not, but I didn't think it would be right for me to summon you to Fettes, just so I could give you an apology.'

'Eh?' Mackie looked puzzled.

'From me: for my excess of zeal on Saturday morning.'

'Ah,' said the superintendent, understanding him at once. 'Yes, I've heard about that; Stevie called me on Saturday evening and told me the whole story. Funnily enough, he apologised as well, for acting off his own bat.'

'It was excusable in his case,' said Skinner. 'He's young, he's enthusiastic and, though he wouldn't admit it, he's ambitious. There's no excuse for me though. Christ, Andy Martin made that clear enough: he called me yesterday after my daughter told him about it, and took it upon himself – rightly, I must say – to tear a strip off me.

'So I confess. I involved myself in your investigation without a by-your-leave, and that's no way for a commander to behave, whatever his motivation.'

'To tell you the truth, sir,' Mackie began, tentatively, 'I thought you might have come to give me a rollicking for not showing more initiative myself.'

'And why should I do that?' the DCC asked. 'As I keep on drumming into people, ours is a team operation. Anyone can feed ideas into the pot; the commander considers them all and decides on the lines of inquiry, but no one expects him to do all the original thinking.

'What isn't acceptable is an officer acting on his own without the commander's knowledge. It would have been no bother for Steele or me to have picked up the phone on Saturday and told you what we were doing. I was unprofessional and undisciplined and for that I'm sorry.'

And then he smiled. 'Mind you,' he chuckled. 'We picked a winner.'

The divisional commander nodded. 'You sure did. Appropriate or not, it was good work, and I wish I had thought of it myself. I think Maggie would have, if she wasn't out of action.'

'How is she, by the way?' asked Skinner.

'She's coming on. While you and Steele were chasing that woman all over Edinburgh, I was visiting her. She's giving Mario a hard time – poor bugger doesn't have a moment to sit down – but she is taking note of the surgeon's warning about keeping her arm immobilised until it's had a chance to heal properly.'

'That's good. Talking about hard times, I had one myself on Saturday after we were finished with Dr Gopal.'

Untypically, Mackie laughed. 'Did you really take the baby on surveillance, boss?'

'Sure I did; he loved it, too. A real bonding experience, it was. Just like Gopal and his sister, I hope.'

The superintendent's normal expression was restored at once. He swung round in his chair, frowning up at the DCC. 'Do you think he'll succeed?' he asked.

'In the short term, I'm sure he will. He's had the courage to take her this far, so I'd expect him to make it the rest of the way. Beyond that though, it'll be up to the girl.'

'What about the father? Will he take her back?'

'Not a chance, according to Surinder. He said that his mother will be out on the street too, if the old man ever learns what she's done. No, the girl – her name's Ayesha – will live with him once she's better; but given the hours he works . . .

'Well let's just say it could be touch and go for a while yet.'

Mackie nodded. 'I guess so. We'll help her in the only way we can. Steele's gone to find the boyfriend. I've told him to throw the fear of Christ Almighty into him, plus a few other deities as well. If we can keep him away from her for good, then her chances will be better.'

'I hope he gets the message,' said Skinner quietly. 'Because if there was a next time, I'm pretty sure Surinder would kill him, and he sure isn't worth that.'

'No.' The two detectives sat in silence for a while.

'So,' exclaimed the DCC, at last, 'back to basics: the Weston investigation.'

'Yes, boss. Not one of my great successes.'

'Not a failure either, Brian, by any measurement. You've taken it as far as anyone could.'

'But come up empty, apart from a DNA trace, and a possible print from an envelope, with no one to match either.'

'No one for now. Maybe for ever. Who knows? Time will tell, and that's how I want it left. I've spoken to Andy about this. Maybe, at first, his line on this was a bit harder than ours but now he agrees.'

The superintendent looked up. 'Close it, boss?'

Skinner shook his head. 'No; not formally. Leave it open, but just let it lie, until the Fatal Accident Inquiry. For now it's used up all the resources we can justify. Once the jury records its verdict, we'll see where we go from there.'

'They'll say unlawful killing, won't they?'

'Maybe. It depends on the evidence that the Fiscal chooses to lay before them. He may just present them with cause of death, without going into missing syringes and complications like that.'

'The family aren't pressing for full disclosure,' said Mackie. 'That's for bloody sure.'

'In that case, I'm more convinced than ever that we've fulfilled our public duty. There may be another lead out there, Brian, one that will lead us straight to the person who injected Mrs Weston. But there's no more we can do; if we find it, we'll have tripped over it rather than unearthed it through orthodox police work.

'So call this one a job well done, regardless of the outcome, and concentrate on the rest of your workload.' He turned towards the door. 'Now I must get on with mine. See you.'

'Hey boss,' Skinner stopped and looked round as the superintendent called after him. 'Did you enjoy yourself: back on the street on Saturday morning?'

He grinned. 'Did I ever!'

48

Neil McIlhenney was in the Chief Constable's outer office, casually conversing with Gerry Crossley, as Skinner stepped in from the Command Corridor, having called in on ACC Elder.

'Morning, Gaffer,' said the sergeant. The DCC nodded an acknowledgment. *The big chap's jacket's hanging on him a bit*, he thought.

'Go on in, Neil,' he said, following his assistant through the door.

'How goes it?' he asked, as he sat behind the big desk.

'Quiet weekend, sir,' McIlhenney answered, leaning across and laying a folder before Skinner. 'What there is of it is in there.'

'Ah, I didn't mean that. First things first, man. How's Olive? Sarah said that she was in bed when she brought kids home.'

The big sergeant leaned back in his chair, wearily. 'Yes, that's right. She was asleep in fact. She's a lot better this morning; in fact, she insisted on getting up to give Lauren and Spencer their breakfast. But the weekend was pretty rough. Ach, she was sick from the moment we got back on Friday evening right through till Sunday afternoon.

'We had a bit of help on Saturday, though. A woman from a medical charity came in to see us. A nice lady. Her outfit works with the hospital in supporting out-patients; not just cancer, all sorts. By the time she arrived, I was fair glad to see her.

'I tell you, boss, I can't thank you enough for looking after Lauren and Spencer. I would not have liked them to see that.'

Skinner winced, in spite of himself. 'We'll have them next weekend too, if you want.'

McIlhenney shook his head. 'Thanks; I appreciate that too. But our nurse said that she should be all right after the second treatment. It's only a top-up, and the drug they use is easier on the patient. On top of that, the visitor we had – Penelope Clark, she said her name was – reports back to the hospital, and that helps them judge the amount of anti-sickness medication they need to give.'

He sighed, heavily. 'Can I ask you, sir: how was Lauren over the weekend? Our Spence is on the young side to understand it all, but my wee lass was about twenty when she was born. I worry something hellish about the effect this could have on her.'

'And you know what, Neil? She's worried in just the same way about you.' The sergeant closed his eyes, and for just a second, his chin looked as if it might wobble, but then his whole jaw tightened in a resolute line.

'She had a wee moment over breakfast on Saturday,' Skinner went on, quickly, 'but she and Sarah went away and had a woman to woman talk, and she was fine after that. She's a great kid; they both are.'

'Aye,' said their father. 'They are that.'

He pulled himself up in his chair. 'Anyway, boss,' he said briskly, 'to business. If you look in that folder you'll see it's a succession of nil returns from all over the country.

'I spoke to Mario over the weekend . . .' he laughed, unexpectedly. 'The pair of us, bloody nurses, eh. Can you imagine that?

'He told me that Neville did have to check one bloke out last week, but that he was okay.' The big sergeant chuckled again. 'So much so that she went out with him.'

'Bloody hell!' Skinner gasped. 'She's what?'

'It's okay, boss; calm down, calm down. Mario said that he read her the Riot Act, or his version of it, about secrecy; about keeping her mouth shut on the job, so to speak. She was quite offended about that, apparently. He did also double check the guy himself, just to be sure: he's absolutely squeaky, no doubt.'

'Nonetheless,' Skinner growled, 'she shouldn't let her work cross over into her private life.'

'Maybe not, sir. But haven't we all done it, to an extent. And the guy was only really a suspect because she saw him limp.'

A smile flicked at the corners of the DCC's mouth. 'As long as that's the only way she saw him,' he muttered.

'For sure, I reckon,' his executive assistant retorted. 'According to Mario, he turned out to be gay.'

'Jesus,' laughed Skinner, 'it sounds as if no one's getting a return out of this business at all. First the mad Mr Impey has McGuire nearly shooting an Interpol agent, then Fettes's answer to Mata Hari pulls a poof.

'Fucking typical of this Hawkins investigation. I tell you, Neil, this guy better turn up somewhere soon, before this whole operation descends into farce.'

'I think it has already, boss. Mario said he was at the airport on Thursday checking some tips on the Amsterdam flight. All he got was a wee drunk Arab trying to smuggle six litres of Bell's into the country . . . imagine, smuggling whisky *into* Scotland . . . and a couple of Hari Krishnas.

'He's completely pissed off. And if the boy McGuire is, you can bet that all the other SB guys around the country are as well.'

'Don't I know it,' the DCC exclaimed. 'I tell you, if it was just down to me – and if the stakes weren't so high – I'd bin this bloody operation as well.'

49

The day was almost gone when the surprise visitor arrived.

Very few people, other than his personal staff, could walk into Bob Skinner's office unannounced; Sir James Proud, Jim Elder, Andy Martin, Sarah, Alex . . . and one other. The digital clock on the wall opposite the window showed forty minutes after five when Chief Constable Sir John Govan, security adviser to the Secretary of State for Scotland, peered round the door.

'Got a minute, Bob?'

Skinner smiled, and stood up. 'As many as you like, Jock,' he answered, walking round the desk to greet the newcomer. 'Would you like a coffee . . . or something else?' He pointed to his drinks cabinet.

'Well, since I've got a driver outside . . . if you've got a Macallan . . .'

Skinner nodded, opened the cupboard and poured some of the smooth malt into a heavy glass. Since he had no chauffeur, he poured himself a ginger ale, then sat facing his guest on one of the room's low, soft chairs.

The veteran Strathclyde Chief sipped his whisky and nodded approval. 'So,' he said. 'How's your poisoned chalice then?'

'Pure fucking hemlock, Jock. How's yours? And I'm not talking about that glass.'

'As if I thought so.' The older man smiled. 'Yes, I can understand why you turned Anderson down when he asked you to stay on in the security job. I have long experience of ignoring politicians at a local level. Reporting to one nationally is something new to me, and I can't say I like it.'

'I only learned one thing in that job, Jock, and that was never to trust any of the bastards. It doesn't matter what colour of rosette they wear, they're all the bloody same. Still, maybe it'll be easier when you retire from Glasgow and do the job full-time. How long have you left?'

'Six months. D'you fancy succeeding me?'

'Is that why you came here? To ask me that?'

'Partly.'

'Then the answer's no. I'm awaiting Jimmy's return with mounting excitement.'

'How's he coming along?'

'Very well, I'm glad to say.'

'That's good.' Govan produced a pipe and put it in his mouth, but made no attempt to reach for his matches. 'Sorry you don't fancy my chair, though. You being a Lanarkshire man and all, I hoped I could talk you into it; the Secretary of State asked me to try, as well.'

Skinner felt anger rising within him. 'That bastard's taken too great an interest in my career in the past; he can piss off now. Be sure you tell him that, Jock; those exact words mind.'

'My pleasure, Bob, my pleasure. But if you change your mind in the next couple of months, give me a call. Mr Committee Chair has told me privately that the Labour Group will support my nominee without question.'

'Thanks, Jock, but I won't. Go for Haggerty; that's my advice.'

'Ach, I can't do that. Willie's too much of a rough diamond; not politically aware. You know what I mean.'

'Aye, and that's exactly why you should appoint him.'

Sir John Govan sighed. 'In an ideal world, my young friend; in an ideal world. Now, about this hemlock of yours; I've got some good news for you.' Skinner looked up, intrigued at once.

'I was in London this morning,' the veteran Chief Constable continued, 'and I was asked to call in on our associates at M15, where I was received by the Director General, no less.

'He told me that he had just come from a joint briefing with M16, given by an envoy of sorts from the Central Intelligence Agency.'

'That sounds lethal,' the DCC interposed.

'You're right, in this case. The subject under discussion was our friend Michael Hawkins. At the beginning of last week, there was a fatal air accident in Poland; a light plane, came down in a field. The pilot, the only person on board, was a Kenyan passport holder, a white man named Matthew Reid.

'The trouble was that when the Poles tried to trace the next of kin, they discovered that, according to the Kenyan passport office, there was no such person. It took them a few days to think of a connection with Hawkins, but eventually, the possibility dawned on them. The body was badly burned so they had to send for dental records. When they arrived . . . guess what?'

'I don't believe it,' Skinner gasped.

'Neither did the CIA, at first, when the South Africans told them. Neither did our SIS people. They each sent their own people to confirm the identification, before they were convinced. Hawkins had a ruby set in one of his lower teeth and several gold fillings at the back; they all matched.

'There's no doubt it seems. Everybody's satisfied that Hawkins is dead.'

'In Poland, of all places. What the hell could he have been doing there?'

Govan smiled, grimly, without humour. 'There was a briefcase in the plane, and its contents survived the blaze. There was nothing in it but the phoney passport, plus a series of maps and scribbles: notes written over a period on the movements of a celebrated individual.

'Hawkins had been stalking Lech Walesa. God alone knows where the contract came from, but he seems to have been the target.'

The big DCC let out a whistle. 'So, for the past week, guys like us have been crawling all over Europe, looking for a target who, all that time has been a cinder in a freezer drawer in Warsaw?'

'You've got it, my son.' Govan paused. 'So now, the panic's over. The details of the global economic summit will be announced next week, and we can all relax . . . in your case, until it happens and you have to police the bloody thing.'

Skinner looked at him, steadily. 'And what about you, Jock?' he asked. 'Are you relaxed? Do you believe it?'

'I've been convinced,' the older man said. 'More important than that, I've had my orders from the top, and I'm passing them on to you as the man in charge of the operation in Scotland. The game is over: you can stand down your team.'

50

'That's the best news I've had in a long time, sir,' said Mario McGuire. 'That carry-on at the airport last week was just about the last straw for me.

'Those Dutch guys made no attempt to go through the landing cards at their end. If they had done that, and filtered out the obvious no-users, instead of just collecting the bloody things and handing them straight on, they'd have saved a hell of a lot of our time.'

'Blame the Poles first, inspector,' Skinner told him. 'They were included in the Hawkins alert, yet it took them the best part of a week to make the connection to the dead man with the phoney passport.'

'The identification was made from dental charts?' asked Andy Martin.

'That's right. Verified by a CIA agent from Berlin, or so Jock said after his third whisky, and by one of our own spooks.'

'So the body was a mess?'

'Flame grilled, Chief Superintendent, flame grilled.' He caught Martin's eye. 'I know what you're thinking, Andy, you're a suspicious bastard just like me. But the dental pattern was absolutely unmistakable, right down to the ruby and the bridge work on the left side of the lower jaw.

'On that basis, the Director of the CIA and the DG of MI6 have pronounced Hawkins dead. We humble beat-pounders have to accept it. So, like I said, you can stand down, Mario, and you, Neil, can forget about co-ordination and daily reporting.' McIlhenney smiled and nodded.

'Andy, Karen Neville will be back on your staff as of this morning.'

He looked back towards McGuire. 'By the way, what's this I hear about her pulling a suspect?' he asked, sharply.

'I think it was the other way round, boss, he pulled her,' McGuire answered, more than a little defensively.

'Come on, Mario, she didn't exactly batter him with her handbag, did she. Didn't the words "No thank you" occur to her?'

'She did what she thought was best at the time, sir. She saw this guy, he had no obvious reason to be at the conference, he fitted the

Hawkins profile and he had a limp. When he asked her to have dinner with him she accepted as a means of making contact rather than anything else.'

The DCC grinned, finally. 'Okay, I accept that.'

McGuire continued. 'The first thing she did after she made the date was to check him out; before she even told me about it. The guy is legit. He's who he says he is, beyond doubt. I know because I did a back-up check myself; even had the guy's photo faxed across from Australia.'

'That's fine, but once she'd checked him out, there was no need to keep the date, was there?'

'No,' the inspector conceded. 'Other than the obvious: she likes him.'

'But he turned out to be gay.'

'She told him the same thing.'

'She did?' Skinner laughed. 'And he believed her?'

'Ah, well,' McGuire murmured, hesitantly. 'I'm not so sure about that. Karen seemed very pleased with herself yesterday morning. I think those cover stories might have been blown.'

The DCC shook his head. 'Let's just draw a veil over the whole thing,' he said. 'Sounds like Neville was the only person who got anything out of this operation. If that's so, good luck to her.'

51

She raised herself up on her elbows, with a broad smile on her face. 'God,' she said, at last. 'You don't know how satisfying that was.' She felt the heat radiating from her body; glancing down she saw, silver in the moonlight which shone through the second-floor window, the sheen of sweat on her breasts, and clinging to it, a few light, curly hairs, shed from his downy chest.

'I've got a fair idea,' her young lover laughed. 'You told me often enough while we were doin' it.' As he looked up at her she seemed to see him in a new light. His face was gentler than she had appreciated before; his eyes softer, his hair more lustrous, his features more fragile. In some ways he looked as feminine as his cousin, in whose flat they lay.

'Ah, but you don't,' she assured him, 'nor why. Usually, when I have sex, however good it's been, I've always feel just a wee bit flat afterwards . . . and sometimes more than a wee bit. Not this time, though: this time I feel . . .' She searched for the word. '. . . triumphant.'

She chuckled at his expression. 'Don't flatter yourself, though, boy. It's got a lot more to do with me than with you: energetic though you surely were, for a beginner.' She patted his chest, approvingly.

'Look, we haven't known each other long, and I don't want this to get complicated. All I'll tell you is that for a while I've been in an enveloping relationship with someone . . . my fiancé, as it happens.

'I love him; there's no question of that. But he loves me too much. Lately it's become worse and worse, until; ach, I've just felt overwhelmed by the need to be myself again, to express myself . . . in all sorts of ways.'

She threw back the duvet and took his balls in her hand. 'Luckily, I moved in with Gina, and I found you, just in time to help me.' She grinned. 'Lucky for us both, maybe.' Rolling his testes gently in her fingers, she lowered her head down upon him, and took him in her mouth, sucking, licking, swirling her tongue around him, until, gently, yet firmly with his lean, youthful strength, he raised her up, eased her back as she yielded to him, and rolled on top of her once more.

'Yesss,' she hissed, still holding his sack as he slid into her, long and slender, delicately made in that part, too, just like the rest of him. 'We're all two people really.' She moved supply as she spoke, taking him deeper. 'There's the one everyone knows: and then there's the other one, with all those secret lustings and desires that we feel, but we're afraid to satisfy.

'Myra wasn't afraid though; she let the other person out. She lived her wicked dreams.'

'Who's Myra?' he whispered in her ear.

'My mother,' she answered.

He raised his head and looked at her. *Yes*, she thought. *He really is only a boy*.

'You said "wasn't". You used the past tense.'

'She was killed when I was very young. In a car: driving way too fast. She did everything too fast, did Myra, and paid for it in the end. I didn't have the chance to get to know her. Like I said I was only a child; I barely remember her. But when I became a woman, I discovered her, and how! I read her diaries. No one ever had, not even my father. I found out what she was like. I learned about her other self, and how she let it loose. It shocked me at first; then I was frightened, because I sensed the same thing in me, the same ... wantonness, if you like.' She smiled, bent her head down and bit the young man lightly on the nipple.

'But now I understand Myra completely, and I'm not scared of myself any more. I know why she was as she was. It was the power, you see. She loved having power, not over other people, but over herself, over her own life. The sort of power that most men take for granted, yet deny to their women.' She smiled, far away for a moment.

'She loved my dad, but she never surrendered herself to him, not completely. There was always that other person; that other Myra. The wild one; the free one, the one she kept from him.' She squeezed the youth's scrotum, quickly, teasingly: heard him gasp, felt him stiffen even more within her.

'Just as there's this other Alexis,' she whispered, 'the one that Andy almost smothered, the one who broke free just in time. Heredity reveals itself, always; you can't suppress it. I know that now. I've taken power over myself, and I'll use it in the way my mother did. I have the same hunger she had. Sure, I'll be a giver for Andy, as she was for my dad; but I have to be a taker, too, for me.'

'What do you want?' he asked her, his voice hoarse and cracking in her ear.

'What do I want to take from you?' Her eyes shone, fiercely. 'Nothing much. Only your body in all the ways that we can use it.

What do I want to give you? For tonight, the time of your young life. After that? Maybe a few more nights, then the memory, that's all.'

52

At the same time, on the other side of the city, Karen Neville propped herself up and looked at the bronzed, bearded man who lay beside her. His eyes were closed, but there was a satisfied smile on his face.

'You see,' she murmured. 'I told you there was more where that came from. And more . . .' she chuckled, 'and more . . .' She laid a hand on his chest.

'Are you sure you can't stay the night?' she asked. 'You have to admit, my bed's a damn sight more comfortable than that sofa contraption you sleep on.'

'You'll get no argument about that,' said Wayne, opening his eyes, 'but I really gotta get back to Dennis.'

'I thought you said he took a sleeping pill.'

'He does.'

'Well . . .?'

The Australian looked up at her. 'Well . . . if you set your alarm and run me home by seven-thirty . . .'

'It's a deal. That'll leave me plenty of time to get to work.'

'What have you got on tomorrow?' he asked. 'Is it that marketing seminar you talked about?'

She frowned, thought for a few moments, then reached a decision. 'No, it's not,' she said, then reached across and switched on the bedside light, so that he could see her eyes. 'Wayne, I've got a confession to make. I told you a lie.'

'What,' he laughed, 'you mean you really are gay after all?'

'Silly bugger. No, I'm not; and I'm not a freelance conference organiser either. I'm a copper, detective sergeant. I'm on the staff of the Head of CID in Police Headquarters in Fettes Avenue.'

He whistled. 'A bizzy, eh.' He leaned forward and nuzzled her breasts with his forehead. 'And what are these girls? Traffic Wardens.'

She pushed him away. 'Wayne, be serious for a minute. I'm not kidding.'

'You mean you really are a copper?'

'Yes, and if you say anything about working undercover—'

'So why the story about being a conference organiser?'

She giggled, in spite of herself. 'Because I really was working undercover. We had a big security crisis on. The heat's off now, though. The whole business was a false alarm, and I'm back in my normal job, so now I can be straight with you.'

'Appreciated.'

'You're not angry, are you?'

Wayne shook his head and grinned at her. 'Course not, girl. It's exciting; I've never been with a copper before. A couple of girl soldiers, yes, but never a plain-clothes police officer. Hey, maybe I should tell you about my real identity.'

'I know your real identity.' He frowned for a second. 'You're Wayne Ventnor, you work for Blaydon Oil on an installation off Western Australia, and you're recovering from a broken ankle. I can tell you that for sure.'

'You checked me out?'

She decided to economise with the truth. 'Mario, my boss, did. You're not alone though; it was a pretty wide sweep. But, like I said, the panic's over. Now we can have a normal relationship.'

'As far as that's possible when your partner's liable to run off chasing bank robbers at all hours of the night.'

'That won't happen. As I said, I'm on the Head of CID's staff; I hardly ever get involved in the active stuff. My job involves co-ordinating between operating divisions; I'm in the office nearly all the time.'

'Except when you're scrutinising economists.'

'That was a one-off, honest.'

'Great.' He laughed again. 'Wait till I tell smelly Dennis that he was a security risk for a while.'

'Wayne,' she said, her face serious, 'you mustn't mention this to anyone. Promise me.'

'Okay, sarge,' the Australian replied. 'I promise.' He reached back and switched off the light, then slid his arm around her naked waist. 'And now, come here. It's time for some more of that undercover investigation.'

53

It was not a Tuesday to which Bob Skinner looked forward with any great enthusiasm. Whenever he could, he would delegate meetings with the Police Board to Assistant Chief Constable Elder, but he realised that he could not ignore the Force's elected managers completely.

His smile was a little superficial as he swept into the small outer office. He had been late leaving home, and had been caught in the inevitable tailback at the Jewel and then through town, so it was well after nine a.m. when he arrived at Fettes.

'Morning, Gerry,' he said briskly to his secretary. 'Mail on the desk?'

'Yes sir,' the young man replied, 'and—'

Without breaking his stride, Skinner swept into the Chief Constable's office . . . and his tight smile widened into a beam, as he saw, comfortable in the old swivel chair, the Chief Constable.

'Jimmy!' he called out in his delight. 'My God, you look great sitting there.'

Sir James Proud chuckled at his friend's surprise. 'I don't feel too bad either,' he exclaimed. 'Don't get the wrong idea, though. I'm not here to stay: not yet, at any rate. I've got an appointment at ten this morning with the Force Medical Examiner, a cardiac consultant from the Royal nominated for the purpose of passing me fit for duty.

'Gerry arranged it for me a week ago, but I told him to keep it as a surprise.'

'You look fit enough to me,' said Skinner. 'It should be a formality.'

What he said was true. The Chief Constable looked a different person from the tired, ageing overweight man who had gone on holiday a few months earlier. Indeed, he looked like Proud Jimmy once more. He looked twenty pounds lighter, and five years younger as he swung round in his chair. His deputy, on the other hand, had put on five pounds and a few lines in his absence.

Skinner had visited his friend on the day after his return from Spain. He had been pleased then by what he saw, and it was obvious that progress to a full recovery was being maintained.

'So come on, Bob,' said Sir James, 'You've got time before the Police Board. Give me a run-down. What's been happening?' During their earlier meeting, the DCC had refused point blank to discuss work.

He smiled and nodded. 'Okay, I guess you're up to it.

'The truth is that for the last couple of weeks, Sweet FA just about covers it. We had a very awkward investigation last month, into the death of a woman out in East Lothian. Cancer victim: someone gave her significant help to kill herself. The team didn't get a sniff as to who it was though; a few false trails, that's all. I've chucked it at the Fiscal; he's decided to lead minimal evidence at the FAI and just bury it.'

'Has he indeed?' mused the Chief.

'Aye. Can't say I'm sorry. These things raise all sorts of moral questions.'

'Not for us, Bob. The law's the law.'

'. . . and we are merely its servants, I know. Imperfect servants in this instance, I'm not too unhappy to say.'

'Speaking of cancer patients—' On his visit to the Chief, Skinner had told him of Olive McIlhenney's illness.

'She's coming on,' he replied at once. 'We saw her at the weekend, in fact; Neil brought her and the kids out to Gullane on Sunday. She's finished her first course of chemotherapy, and come through it well. She's a bit grey-faced, but Sarah says her cough's a lot better. I tell you, Jimmy, she's a study in human courage.'

'How about Neil? How's he handling it?'

'As you'd expect,' said Skinner. 'I can sense a tremendous tension in him, but outwardly he's very calm and determined. I keep an eye on him, don't you worry.'

'D'you never think about sending him on compassionate leave?'

'Doesn't want it. And he's right. It's better for Olive's morale if she sees him going to work as usual. She has a cleaning woman in a couple of mornings a week, and her head teacher visits her quite often at lunch times, so she's not without company. She's doing some school work at home too; computer stuff.'

'What are her chances, though?' the Chief asked, quietly.

Skinner looked him in the eye. 'Slim.'

Proud Jimmy sighed. 'Ahh well, let's just hope, eh.

'So what about the rest of it. I read about this global economic conference: that's going to be a bugger for us, eh?'

'Jeez! Tell me about it. Jim Elder's been working on that for the last month, putting together a policing plan. We had a security scare too, with SB deployed all over the country looking for a guy who might have been out to target one of the guests of honour.' He paused. 'That's history, though. The man was reported killed a couple of weeks back.

'Our problems aren't over entirely though. We've been dropped deeper in it, just in the last twenty-four hours. I've scheduled a meeting with Andy and McGuire for three this afternoon, after the Board's finished and the councillors have been fed; that's when I'll break the bad news.'

Sir James sat up in his chair, attentively. 'Oh yes,' he said. 'What's this all about then?'

54

Skinner looked at Mario McGuire across the Head of CID's conference table. 'You seem pleased with yourself,' he said. 'Is Maggie taking her turn with the vacuum again?' His own spirits were high: the Police Board had been at its most docile, noting every report and agreeing every proposal without debate.

The inspector's smile widened. 'Not quite, boss; she's not up to that yet, but she's well on the mend. Her temper's healed up faster than her arm, thank the Lord.'

'When does she expect to be back at work?' Andy Martin asked: a shade brusquely, the DCC thought.

'All being well, the hospital said, she can go back on light duties – office only, no driving – in a couple of weeks. She'll start physio then and with that, in another month or so she'll be back to normal.'

'How the hell's she going to get to Haddington if she can't drive?'

'Couldn't she work in St Leonard's for a while, sir?' asked McGuire.

'Yeah, I suppose she could,' the Head of CID conceded. 'I'll speak to Brian about it. He'll be glad to have her back anywhere; his division's clear-up rate has gone down in her absence.'

'As long as you don't expect it to shoot up when she goes back, Andy,' said Skinner. 'Now, gentlemen, to the reason for this meeting.' He glanced at McIlhenney, who was seated on his right. 'Neil knows this story already, but I brought him along anyway because I want him involved.'

He gave a thin smile. 'I'll bet that ever since Michael Hawkins was taken off the active list, you boys have been laughing up your sleeves about the economic conference. What a Christmas present, eh? Something this size and no CID or SB involvement.' He gave a quick, wicked smile.

'Well, tough luck, colleagues. You might have known it was too good to be true.'

'Great,' McGuire muttered, as McIlhenney grinned at him. 'What's coming now?'

'You can guess, I'm sure,' the DCC retorted. 'Now that the South African's failed his pilot's test, the people in London have had a

171

rethink on security. They've decided that in the absence of a specific threat, they do not want Edinburgh to look like a fortress to the world's television viewers.

'So they have stood down the Ministry of Defence security team and have thrown the ball back to us.'

'What does that mean?' asked Martin.

'Frankly, Andy, it means a fucking nightmare. Under the original plan, the soldiers would have done the lot. Now, the intention is that each Head of State will be accompanied by his own normal protection people, under normal conditions. We will be responsible for liaising with them all, checking all booked accommodation before they arrive, accrediting them, and devising and issuing some form of discreetly visible identifying badge so that every officer in that hall knows who's meant to be armed and who isn't.'

'But that's crazy, sir,' McGuire protested. 'They're all going to be carrying?'

'That's how it will be. The Americans always insist that their Secret Service carry arms; they won't come otherwise. And if they do, the Russians must, and if they must, the Germans . . . and so on. So the decision is that everyone can bring their toys if they want, just as long as they're declared to us.

'We'll be responsible now for the whole vetting operation, including the journalist accreditation. The Foreign Office will pass us all the names of everyone who applies to cover the conference, and we'll have to run PNC checks on them all, before they're issued with their badges by the FO Press Office people.

'Oh aye, and, just in case that isn't enough for you, they've added a bit of extra spin . . . as they say.' He paused. 'With an eye to the elections to the Scottish Parliament, the Government has decided that the conference will be opened by an address from the potential First Minister, in other words, Dr Bruce Anderson, the Secretary of State for Scotland.

'Mario, you'll be responsible for looking after him, reporting both to me and to Sir John Govan.'

Martin frowned. 'Where the hell will we get the manpower?'

'From everywhere,' said Skinner. 'I want you to oversee the whole operation. You and your team will become an expanded Special Branch, if you want to look at it that way, merging with Mario and his people. Neil will work with you, too.

'If you find that you're struggling, let me know. Jock's said that he'll lend us people from Strathclyde if we need them, but I'm proud enough of our force to want to do without that.'

He paused. 'The word proud reminds me. The Chief had his official medical this afternoon. I'm enormously pleased to tell you that he'll be back at work as of next Monday morning.'

'Aw, that's great,' exclaimed McIlhenney, spontaneously, as Martin and McGuire both smiled with pleasure at the news.

'Now, like Maggie, he'll be on light duties only, initially. He's been told that it's mornings only for the first month, and I'll make damn sure he sticks to that. But still – he's looking great, and it'll be a relief to have him here even on that limited basis. It will also allow me to play a proper part in the conference policing . . . I'll be there most of the time, in overall command.'

Skinner pushed his chair back from the table. 'The Foreign Office is sending us, by close of play today, a full list of contacts in each country attending the shindig. I'll have Neil circulate it as soon as it arrives. Until then, Andy and Mario, you'd better call your troops together for an initial briefing.'

He stood, and the others followed. McGuire and McIlhenney headed for the door at once, but the DCC held back.

'Here Andy,' he asked, failing to sound casual, 'have you seen our kid lately?'

Martin nodded. 'We went to a movie on Saturday night, then for a meal.' He chose not to add that they had spent the night at his flat.

'How was she?'

'She was okay. In fact, she was better than that.' He paused, gnawing self-consciously at his bottom lip; a strange gesture for him, Skinner thought. 'Just lately Bob, it's got so that she and I couldn't sit down together without a fight starting. We had a big barney, oh, more than two weeks ago now, in a restaurant, and we sort of stayed away from each other for a while just to let it cool off.

'It seems to have worked, for when we met on Saturday, she was great. Back to her old self; bubbly, full of chat, and looking like two million dollars. Almost hyper, you'd have said. I guess she was right to move out; it seems to have done the trick for us.'

He glanced towards the window, smiling to himself at the memory of Saturday night and Sunday morning. Skinner looked at him, in turn, frowning slightly. 'That's good,' he said. 'That's good. I'm glad to hear it. I only asked about her because she hasn't been in touch for a bit. She was out when I called her at her temporary digs last night, and I don't like phoning the office.

'Listen, if you hear from her before I do, ask her to give me a ring. I've got something to tell her.' He paused. 'Sarah's expecting again.'

As Martin turned, Skinner realised that it was the first time he had seen him smile from the heart in all of three months. 'Bob, that's great. When did you find this out?'

'Just yesterday, for certain.'

'When's she due?'

'Months yet. Next May, she reckons.'

'A girl this time?'

'Sarah wants that, I know.' He let out a laugh that was half growl. 'As for me, I know how much bother daughters can be. Don't we just, pal.'

55

Bob Skinner enjoyed the drive back to Gullane. In the relatively short period during which he and Sarah had made their main home in Edinburgh, he had missed the wind-down time which it afforded him, the opportunity to return to his family freed from the tensions of an invariably fraught day at the office.

A Seal CD was playing in the car, as he turned off the roundabout at the foot of the Milton Link, and headed past the hypermarket, out towards East Lothian. A light rain was falling, but nothing to make the road conditions hazardous, or to lessen his pleasure as he reflected upon the success of the Police Board meeting, and most of all, anticipated the pending return of the Chief Constable to the office.

'It's the loneliness that's the killer,' the singer whispered.

'You're right there, pal,' the policeman said aloud. 'That's what gets to me most of all about doing Jimmy's job. While you're hauling yourself up the ladder, you hear them talk about the loneliness of command, and you think, "What a load of crap! How can you be lonely when there's a whole force at your disposal?" Then you get there, and the door shuts, and for the first time in your life, you've got no sounding board; no senior officer to look in on and ask, "Am I doing right here?", and if you do that with a subordinate you're seen to be unsure of yourself and as soon as that happens you lose their absolute trust and as soon as that happens you're no longer truly in command . . .'

Lit by the orange light of the dashboard, he laughed out loud. 'Welcome back, Jimmy. Welcome—'

He broke off as the car phone rang. Killing the CD sound, he pressed the receive button. 'Yes,' he said, anonymously, to the hands-free mike above his eyeline.

'Pops?' Alex's voice bubbled into the car. 'It's me.'

'Never,' he retorted.

'Don't be so smart,' she told him. 'Andy called. He said you needed to speak to me. I rang Fettes; and they said you had just left.'

'Yes,' Bob replied. 'I tried to get you at Gina's last night. Didn't she tell you?'

175

'I didn't see her. I got in late,' *From her cousin's place*, she thought, smiling wickedly at the other end of the line, 'and she left early this morning. What's the panic?'

'No panic. Far from it. Something I have to tell you, that's all. You're going to be a sister again.'

There was a silence in the car. 'Pops,' she exclaimed at last. 'That is great. Sarah told me you had another baby in mind. I'm really chuffed for you both.'

'Thanks kid. I hoped you would be.' Looking ahead, at the road, he imagined he could see her face. 'But just for a moment there, I thought—'

'Don't be daft. I couldn't be more pleased. I'll phone Sarah now.'

'Yes, you do that. She's dead keen to share it with another female.' He paused.

'How're you doing? I haven't seen you since yon time—'

'I'm doing fine, Pops. Never better.'

'You've no regrets then; about claiming your life back?'

'None. It was something I needed to do, for Andy's sake as well as mine. I think he realises that. Now I've done it, I've never been happier.'

'That's good. That's certainly how you sound. A lot more settled in yourself.' He felt himself frown. 'You know, Alex, I'm pretty sure that's what went wrong with your mother. She gave up too much of her youth too soon; that's why she went off the rails. I'm glad that you've spotted that danger, and done something about it before it was too late. You and Andy will be the better for it, I'm sure of that.'

'I'm sure we will, Pops.' He heard her laugh softly. 'We are already, believe me.'

'That's good.' In the dark, he sighed. 'You know, kid, I've never really thought about it before, but you sound like her. You sound just like Myra.'

56

'My God, Bob, you'd think there was a war on.' Sir James Proud looked around the headquarters gymnasium. Where normally there was a clear area, three rows of desks were arranged, each with its own telephone line.

'I'd rather there was,' Skinner muttered. 'Much less complicated. It's been like this since last Wednesday. I thought you should see it on your first day back.'

'It's Andy's show. He decided that it would be best run under one roof, and he's right. Until you get down to doing it, you couldn't imagine how complicated this exercise could be.

'We're having to make contact with bodyguards of all sorts from the thirty-plus countries that are going to be attending. For a start, that's run us into a significant sum for translators; that's why there are so many desks in here.'

The Chief Constable frowned. 'Not off our budget, I hope.'

'No, no. I've got that sorted. The Foreign Office will pick up that tab. They've actually supplied some of the people.

'Translation's only a minor problem by comparison though. We're having to gather in personal details for every protection officer nominated by every country. As we're doing that they all have to be vetted through the intelligence agencies.'

'Aren't their domestic vetting procedures sufficient?' asked Proud Jimmy, looking trim and neat in his uniform, which for the first time in many months, fitted him comfortably.

'Not for the American Secret Service. I thought the FBI were sticklers until I ran into these boys. I had a word with my pal Joe Doherty in Washington about them. He says they make their recommendations direct to the Chairman of the National Security Council, and he turns them directly into commands.'

'Who's the Chairman of the NSC?'

'The President, and it's his arse that's on the line; so he isn't usually open to persuasion when someone outside the Service thinks they're going too far. Their argument in this case is that since a number of the nations taking part in the conference are openly hostile to the US, it's not without the bounds of possibility that a fanatic might infiltrate one of the delegations. That's why they started this ball rolling by insisting on carrying their own weapons. They've vetoed one bloke from Pakistan already: they claimed he had links to the Taleban.'

'How long is all this going to take?'

'Almost until the opening of the conference at this rate, sir,' Andy Martin answered. 'Welcome back,' he said, shaking hands with Sir James.

'Thank you, Andrew,' said the Chief. 'I don't suppose that while all this is happening, the local criminals are showing consideration by taking time off.'

'Things have been quiet, actually. That probably means that they're all out casing the various hotels. That's another security problem; one for Mr Elder, fortunately.

'But you're right, sir. I do have to keep a foot in both camps. In fact, I've just been given a note to phone Dan Pringle about something, so if you'll excuse me . . .'

'Of course, of course. On you go.' Proud turned back to Skinner as the chief superintendent headed off.

'My goodness, Bob,' he said. 'Looking at this makes me sort of glad I'm going home at lunchtime.'

57

'Where are you, Dan?' asked Martin, having phoned the Edinburgh Central divisional CID commander on his mobile number.

'Up in Raymond Terrace, Andy, off the Western Corner,' Superintendent Pringle replied. 'I was just about to leave actually. I called you when I was on my way out here, but it's turned out to be a bit of a false alarm. It looked a bit colourful when my two detective constables turned up, but it's just a suicide. Sorry to have bothered you.'

The Head of CID chuckled. 'Don't mention it, mate. You got me out of the madhouse for a few minutes; I'm grateful for that. What was it made your people jumpy anyway?'

'Ach, it was just the way it looked. The stiff was a single bloke; the cleaning wumman came in this morning and found him sitting in his armchair, wearing his pyjamas and dressing gown, stone dead. She screamed, and all that, and phoned us in hysterics. "Help, Murder, Polis!" – you've heard it a million times. My boy and girl responded, along with a couple of uniforms.

'The thing that made them call me, and made me call you when I was told, was that the guy had a bag over his head. It looked a bit weird, I'll admit, but I saw when I got here that it was like wearing a belt and braces. The bloke had injected himself with something. The syringe was lying in his lap.

'The doctor's been,' he added. 'He certified death due to asphyxia, then left.'

Martin felt the hair on the back of his neck prickle. He leaned forward in his chair. 'The bag, Dan,' he asked, 'what was it like?'

'Just a clear poly bag. Nothing fancy.'

'How was it secured?'

'Round the neck, of course, wi' black tape.'

'And the roll that the tape came from. Was it there?'

'Aye. On the arm of the chair.'

'And the scissors?'

'There was a pair on the floor.'

Andy Martin's expression was growing more troubled by the

179

second. 'Have you called Arthur Dorward?' he asked.

'What?' said Pringle. 'The scene of crime team? No I haven't, because I don't see a crime here.'

'Well, you get them out there, Dan. Wait there for me, and don't let anyone touch a bloody thing. Are the press on to it?'

'Not as far as I know.'

'That's good. I want it kept that way. Be as discreet about this as you can.'

58

Detective Superintendent Pringle was surprised when Brian Mackie stepped through the front door behind the Head of CID. It was unusual for divisional commanders to venture on to each other's territory.

DCS Martin saw the raised eyebrows. 'I asked Brian to come along with me, Dan. There's something about the way you described this situation that's familiar to us both.

'Remember the Weston investigation a few weeks back, out in East Lothian?'

Pringle nodded. 'I remember you mentioning it at a commanders' briefing, and I remember reading about it in the papers. But that's all really; I don't know any of the detail. It sounded like no one was very clear what it was.'

Mackie shook his head. 'No, Dan, we all knew exactly what it was from the off. Someone injected the woman, then tried to make it look as if she had suffocated herself. It was a real amateur job, though. Whoever did it took the black tape and the scissors away with them.'

'Yes,' said Martin. 'When you described this scene to me I felt like I was back out at Oldbarns again, and I began to wonder. Could the same person be involved here, and could they have learned from the experience?'

'One thing you might not know, Dan,' Mackie added, 'or might not have remembered from that briefing. Gaynor Weston had a terminal illness.'

'So it was a mercy killing?'

'Use any term you like.' Andy Martin sounded grim. 'But I know what it was, and so do you. Let's have a look at him.' Pringle nodded and led them along the narrow hall of the Victorian terraced villa towards a sitting room at the rear. 'Dorward here yet?' asked the Head of CID.

'Not yet, Andy. But as you ordered, I haven't let anyone near the body since I called out his team.'

'Has anyone touched the syringe, the tape, or the scissors?'

'I think I saw the doctor pick up the syringe, then lay it back down.'

'Silly bugger. Make sure he's fingerprinted, then. We'll have to eliminate everyone who might have touched it.'

Pringle stood to one side to allow his colleagues to step into the small sitting room.

But for the plastic bag, the man in the chair would have looked as if he was enjoying a peaceful, dreamless sleep. He was sitting back in the big soft armchair, his head resting against the high back cushion. His eyes were closed. Martin stepped across to him, leaned down and looked into his face. At once he noted, contrasting with its overall waxy, yellowish colour, the small red blotches of the burst capillaries around his nose, and his mouth, which hung open slightly. The man was very thin. There seemed hardly anything of him in his cotton pyjamas and silk dressing gown.

He looked closely at the polythene bag. Black insulating tape had been wound several times round the dead man's neck, effecting an airtight seal, then cut off at the back, towards the left side.

'What's his name?' the Head of CID asked, quietly, almost as if he was afraid the sleeper might awake. He straightened up and stepped back from the chair, careful not to step on the scissors which still lay on the floor.

'Anthony Murray, according to the cleaning lady,' Pringle replied. 'He used to be a bank manager, but he took early retirement over a year ago. He was a widower; lost his wife, about five years back.'

'Has the cleaner worked for him for long?'

'Aye, since before the wife died.'

'Is she still here?'

'Naw, Andy. Poor woman was in a right state. I sent her home in a Panda car.'

'Fair enough, Dan. This is a very similar set-up, although it isn't as clear-cut as the Weston case. Just looking at him, you have to say it's possible that he did all this himself. Nevertheless . . . I want you to keep the body here until after Dorward's people have photographed it and the surrounding area. Then I want him sent to the mortuary up at the Royal. Leave the bag in place, though. Leave everything in place; send him just as he is.

'Dr Sarah Skinner did the postmortem on Gaynor Weston; I want her to take care of this one as well, and I want her to see the victim just as you found him.

'Was there a letter?'

Pringle nodded, and pointed to a small side-board beside the door. A single sheet of paper lay on it. Martin stepped across and looked at it. The suicide note was short and to the point. 'Three words, "Better this way",' the DCS read aloud. 'It's signed "Anthony Murray".'

He glanced back towards the chair, and the body in it. 'Maybe it

182

was better for you, Mr Murray: I hope so. It's left a right mess for us, though, and no mistake.'

59

'I'm sorry I had to insist on your coming to see me, Superintendent,' said the Assistant General Manager. Dan Pringle heard the words but picked up no hint of apology in his voice. 'I'm afraid it's our policy never to discuss the business of bank personnel over the telephone.'

'Even when they're dead?' The detective's thick moustache twitched slightly in a faint attempt at a smile.

'Even then, I'm afraid. Now, which employee do you wish to discuss? My secretary should really have asked you when you made the appointment.' Pringle looked at the neat, dark-suited, humourless little man and tried to imagine asking him for an overdraft. He shuddered at the thought, and resisted the temptation to tell Mr William Drysdale, in his own special way, that detective super-intendents did not necessarily need appointments.

'A man named Murray: Anthony Murray.'

'Ah yes. Mr Murray; Tony. Yes, I remember him. He was a manager in our Queen Street branch, until he ran out of steam around the middle of last year. It happens more and more these days, as banks transform themselves into properly run businesses instead of gentlemen's clubs.' Drysdale leaned back in his chair and puffed out his chest.

'There was a time, not so long ago either, when a chap would join a bank straight from school in the confident expectation that he had a job for life, with status in the community and a comfortable pension at the end of it. Not any more; in the current banking environment, if you don't perform consistently well and hit your targets, you're out. People pay the ultimate price these days for poor lending decisions.'

'What?' muttered Pringle, not quite under his breath. 'You mean you shoot them?'

'Pardon?'

'Nothing, sir, nothing; just thinking aloud. And Mr Murray, what about him? Was he drummed out of the Cubs?'

'What? Ah yes, I see, Hah, very funny, yes. I wouldn't say that exactly. Tony had thirty-eight years' service, so when he asked to retire early, the area general manager was pleased to accommodate him.'

'And if he hadn't asked?'

'Then yes, he probably would have been told to go.'

'Why was that?'

Drysdale shrugged. 'He just wasn't cutting the mustard any more; he knew it, too. The Chief Executive had asked a couple of questions about his performance review.'

'And that's all it takes to end a career these days, is it?'

Pringle's voice was loaded with irony, but the banker gave no sign of noticing. Instead he hooked his thumb into his waistcoat pocket and looked blandly across the desk. 'There is a time,' he pronounced, 'in every man's life, when he should just go and play golf.'

'So Mr Murray was a golfer, was he?'

Drysdale blinked and looked bemused. 'I've no idea. I was speaking figuratively.'

'Ahh. I'm sorry. Thick of me.' The superintendent glanced out of the window of the opulent office. On the skyline, he could see the top of the Scott Monument, surrounded by scaffolding as usual.

'When Mr Murray left,' he asked, 'did he strike you as being in a good state of mind? Did he seem depressed to have outlived his usefulness to you?'

'He was never a very cheerful sort, to be truthful. Morose, sometimes; when he spoke to me, at least.' *I'm not bloody surprised*, thought Pringle.

'Did he seem worse after his wife died?'

'Did she? I didn't know that. It's my policy, you see, not to become involved in the family situation. I mean if I did that all the time, I'd be a damned counsellor, rather than a businessman.'

'But isn't a happy employee an efficient employee?'

Drysdale frowned at this radical thinking. 'My job is to make the shareholders happy, Mr Pringle. I'm afraid in this day and age you can spend very little time treating the wounded, before – to borrow your word – you have to shoot them.'

'Oh aye,' said the detective, heavily. 'The ultimate price, eh.'

'That's right,' said Drysdale, rising to his feet to signal the end of the interview. 'Tell me, superintendent,' he asked, as he walked his visitor to the door. 'Do you bank with us?'

60

'Who do you bank with, Sarah?' Dan Pringle asked.

'The Bank of Scotland. But before I was married I was with the Royal. Why d'you ask?'

'I've decided to change mine. Are they okay?'

'Yes, both of them, as far as I'm concerned.'

'Thanks. I'll bear that in mind. Now, what have you got to tell me?'

'First of all, let me ask you something. How closely did your ME at the scene look at the body?'

'He just pronounced life extinct and gave me a probable cause. That was all I asked him to do. I saw no reason for anything more.'

'Mmm,' said Sarah. 'No harm done, but if he had looked a little closer, he'd have seen that the deceased was wearing a colostomy bag.'

'What does that mean?'

'In this case, Dan, it means that he had cancer of the bowel. He had most of it removed at some point. The survival rate from colonic cancer is better than some forms, but not for this man. Mr Murray had secondaries in his liver and bladder, plus a developing spinal tumour which must have been approaching the unbearable stage. I'm slightly surprised that a man in this condition was still at home.'

'I see,' murmured Pringle. 'Would he have been given drugs to control the pain?'

'Almost certainly. The drugs in his system didn't kill him though. In this case the injection rendered him unconscious and he suffocated. Your ME's probable cause was absolutely right. That's what's going to give you all a headache, I'm afraid.'

'Eh? How come, if it's as simple as that?'

'Two reasons. First of all, I don't think this man would have had the strength to tape the bag so that it was airtight. Second, he didn't inject himself; someone else did. The syringe went into the right thigh; I've traced the angle and there's no way that dying man could have administered that shot himself.'

Pringle whistled down the telephone. 'Is that right?' he paused for a moment or two. 'So how does that give us a headache? We've got a murder investigation on our hands. That's a bugger, I know, but routine.'

Sarah laughed, sharply, the unexpected sound making the divisional commander hold his phone away from his ear. 'Ah,' she exclaimed, 'but have you? I can't say for certain, not under oath, that Mr Murray didn't fix that bag on himself. And it was the bag that killed him, remember, not the injection. So was it a murder or was it a suicide? I don't see how you'll ever prove either way, until you find the person who gave him that shot, and persuade them to tell you what happened.'

61

Bob Skinner smiled at his wife as, lying sprawled on the sofa, he pressed the television remote. 'You're getting too sure of yourself, doctor.' BBC Scotland's trademark red balloon drifted across the big wide screen for a few seconds, before the portentous signature music of the Nine O'clock News boomed out into their living room.

'What do you mean?'

'I mean, my love, that postmortem evidence isn't the only sort. There is a way of proving whether the late Mr Murray topped himself with the poly bag, or had someone do it for him.'

'What's that, Mr Detective?'

'The scissors. The roll of tape. The poor chap wasn't wearing gloves was he?' Sarah shook her head, quickly. 'Right then. If his fingerprints don't show up on those scissors – or even better, if they're clean – most juries will accept that as proof that he didn't cut off the tape roll.'

'Wait a minute,' she argued. 'That doesn't prove that he didn't secure the bag himself, though. Conceivably, he could have wound the tape tight round his neck then the person who injected him could have cut it off. I can't rule that out.'

Bob grinned hugely, ignoring the latest political drama from America which was being played out on the television screen. 'That's fine,' he exclaimed, with a touch of delight in his voice. 'In that case, we'll still charge the accomplice with murder; he took part in the act of securing the bag, an act which killed Mr Murray, as you will state under oath. That's enough for me and it'll be enough for the Crown Office.'

'Will it be enough for a jury to convict on, though?'

'As long as we have other evidence that places the person in the house at the time, then it probably will be. Of course if he's left us a print on the end of the tape roll as well, and there are none of Mr Murray's, that'll be game, set and match.

'I doubt if we'll be that lucky though. Assuming that this is the same person who was with Gaynor Weston—'

'You are sure?' Sarah interrupted.

'Ach, of course I am; and so's Andy, and so are you. Look at the similarities; clear poly bag – it would be undignified to end your life in something with "Tesco" printed on it would it not – secured by black tape, victim injected; there's no doubt about it. As I was saying, on that assumption, the way I see it is that the helper assumed that the Weston death would simply be seen off as a suicide. When we started to make ambivalent noises after the body was found, he realised just how sloppy he'd been.

'That's why you've got a different pattern with Mr Murray's death. This time the tape, scissors and syringe have been left there. He's getting better, but there are still flaws in the set-up.'

Bob picked up the remote once more and snapped off the television picture, then swung himself into a sitting position. 'Actually,' he said, 'you and I can sit here having a detached, professional discussion about this thing, but I've got to remind myself at the same time just how serious this is.'

'How come?'

'How come?' he repeated. 'Listen, if someone walked into a bank, shot a teller and ran off with a pile of money, we, and every tabloid newspaper in the country would go bananas about it. But if the same person walked into another bank a few weeks later and did it again . . . Christ, love, just imagine the reaction!

'Yet that's what we're dealing with here. Forget the semantics, forget our clever technical debate about the whys and wherefores of Murray's death. We have a double murderer loose in our city, we made a porridge of catching him first time up and now he's done it again.'

Sarah frowned. 'Yes, I hear what you're saying. But what about the moral issues involved? In that respect, the two situations are completely different.'

'You say that to Andy Martin, who tends to be our collective conscience in situations like these, and he'll tell you that there is only one black and white moral issue involved – the taking of a human life by another person. Maybe in personal ethical terms you can argue that there might be shades of grey, but in legal terms you can't.

'It doesn't matter whether someone gets on their knees and begs you, "End my life, I can't stand it any more." If you do that you're breaking the law – and it's the oldest law that our society has. Now the fact is that when we didn't get a quick clear-up on the Weston case, some of us weren't too sorry. We saw it as a one-off, and maybe our private beliefs let us sympathise with Mrs Weston, and even with whoever helped her.

'But it isn't a one-off any more, Sarah. I'm . . . we're faced with clear evidence that same person has done it again, and our duty is just as clear. Catching him goes right to the top of our priority list. Consider this: Gaynor Weston and Anthony Murray were both terminally ill. They were going to die nasty, drawn-out deaths. But what if someone else asks for help; someone who does have a chance of survival?'

'No,' he said, emphatically. 'It has to be stopped here.'

She looked at him, soberly. 'Yeah,' she murmured. 'Looked at like that, you have to be right.'

He leaned back into the sofa and nodded. 'And there's more to be investigated.'

'What do you mean?' she asked him, for the second time that evening.

His eyes, narrowed, very slightly. 'What if Gaynor Weston wasn't the first? What if there's been a death in the past that has been written off as a suicide at divisional level? Or more than one, even? Christ, there could be a network operating here.'

'You're seeing the worst, aren't you,' said Sarah.

He shrugged, with a sad, resigned grin. 'Honey, that's my job. The trouble has been that from inside the Chief Constable's office, sometimes you just don't see it early enough.'

62

'I know the DCC isn't the best delegator in the world,' said Andy Martin, 'but normally he waits to be asked these days before offering advice on investigations. So when he does call me to raise something, especially when it's half-nine on a Monday evening, it emphasises how serious it is.

'I don't have to remind you two that he's back on the prowl, mornings at least.'

He looked at Detective Superintendents Mackie and Pringle. 'As of now, the investigation into the Weston death is re-opened, full strength. I've spoken to the Fiscal and had the FAI postponed indefinitely. It will run in conjunction with the Murray investigation, with you two in joint day-to-day control, reporting everything to me.

'I'd take full responsibility myself, but for my involvement with the preparations for the economic conference.'

The Head of CID hunched over his coffee. 'We don't need a big team on this, since there isn't any door to door work involved, but we do need integration so that we pick up any overlap between the two investigations. Brian, I want you to review the Weston papers, yet again, and see if there's anything we might have done that we didn't. Dan, Murray's death happened on your patch, so you're the leader on that one. In Maggie Rose's continued absence, since DS Steele was heavily involved with Weston, he's going to work with you directly on Murray, as the principal link between both inquiries.'

Pringle nodded. 'Fair enough,' he said. 'I like young Stevie. If we do come across any coincidences, he's not the boy to miss them.'

'Where are you going to begin, then?'

'I have already,' the superintendent replied. 'Remember? I saw the guy at the bank. He was worse than fuckin' useless, mind you. Today, we're looking for relatives. Mr Murray had no children apparently, but there's a younger sister. She's the next of kin; I've got a car taking her to the Royal this morning to make the formal identification. After that I'll go and have a chat with her, to see what she can tell me.'

'Where does she live?'

'Down in sunny Joppa by the sea.' He glanced at the window of the

Head of CID's office. Rain, driven on cold north-east wind, lashed against its panes. 'It'll be really nice down there today,' he added, mournfully.

'I'll envy you every minute of it,' said Martin, grinning as he stood. 'Okay, gentlemen, that's it. Remember, keep me informed all the way.'

He walked with the two divisional commanders to the end of the corridor, waving them off at the top of the stairs. Then, instead of returning to his office, he walked along the length of the Command Corridor and down the flight of stairs which led almost directly to the makeshift conference control centre.

Looking around he noted that all but two of the desks were manned. As usual, Mario McGuire was seated in the far corner, from where he could see everything that went on in the big room. He ambled across towards the Special Branch commander.

'Hi, Mario, how's it going?'

McGuire shot him a mock scowl. 'Exciting as ever,' he grumbled. 'I've rejected a journalist from the *Financial Times*; that's been the highlight of my day so far. No, scratch that; the highlight of my week.'

'Why did you bomb him out?'

'Her,' the inspector corrected him. 'She wouldn't put her date of birth on the application form; refused point blank. So we couldn't run a full computer check.'

'Couldn't you have done it through her National Insurance number?'

'Not this one. She's South African.'

'Her name wasn't Hawkins, was it?' Martin asked, with a faint smile.

McGuire shook his head. 'Naw, and she isn't dead, either.'

The Head of CID shrugged. 'Well, it's up to her, but if she doesn't have a ticket, she can't come to the party.' He paused. 'Listen Mario, can I ask you a favour?'

The dark eyebrows rose in surprise. 'Of course you can.'

'Right; it's like this. The Weston case, the one that Maggie was working on when she got cut, has gone pear-shaped again. There's been a second apparent suicide, with exactly the same pattern.

'The boss has ordered me to check the papers on every reported suicide in our area over the last three years, to see if any of them could possibly have been related. Trouble is, I'm stuffed for people-power, and I don't want to call in outside help any more than he does.

'I'm going to have to take Neville or Pye back from you, unless . . . Look, I know Mags isn't allowed back for a couple of weeks, but would you mind if I asked her if she could help on this one? It doesn't involve anything more strenuous than reading, and maybe the odd phone call, so she'd be able to do it at home. I wouldn't ask her behind your back though. So, what'd you say?'

'I say go ahead, sir. I don't have a problem with that.' McGuire grinned. 'Now if I said "No way", and she found out about it later: *that* would be a problem.'

63

Dan Pringle peered across Steele and out of the driver's side-window as the young sergeant drew to a halt outside the big stone terrace. The houses faced more or less due east, and on a fine day they would have enjoyed a clear view all the way down the coast to North Berwick and the Bass Rock beyond.

However, as the detective looked across the promenade and out to sea, all that faced him was the grey wall of drizzle which the howling wind drove onshore. 'My God,' he said. 'I hope their draught excluders are working.'

The two policemen jumped quickly out of the car and hurried up the steps towards the front door. Fortunately the woman at the tall bay window had seen them arrive, and opened it quickly.

'Mrs Paterson? I'm Detective Superintendent Pringle and this is Sergeant Steele.'

'Aye, aye,' the woman answered, quietly, 'Come in, quick, and let me get this door shut.' Steele looked at her as he stepped into the hall. Georgina Paterson was a thin, pinched woman, of indeterminate middle age. She wore a grey cardigan, pulled tight around her shoulders.

'In there.' She pointed to a door off the hall, to the left. To Pringle's great relief, a coal effect gas fire was blazing away. Ushering the detectives to a settee, the woman sat in the chair closest to it.

'I'm very sorry about your brother, Mrs Paterson,' Pringle began. He meant it; he was a kind man by nature. 'Were things, er, all right, at the hospital?'

She nodded. 'Yes, thank you. The staff there were very nice to me. They made Anthony look very peaceful; all things considered.'

The superintendent looked up at the high mantelpiece above the hearth. Various family photographs were set upon it, including one of a wedding group; bride, groom, best man and bridesmaid. He pointed to it. 'Is that yours?' he asked.

Georgina Paterson nodded. 'Aye, that's our wedding, mine and Bert's. Thirty years we'd have been married, but for . . .' Her voice faltered.

'I'm sorry,' said Pringle once more. 'Has your husband been . . . gone long?'

'Sixteen and a half years,' she answered, composing herself. 'He was a miner. He was killed in an accident underground, hit by a runaway truck.' She looked across at Stevie Steele, saw him glancing round the big room.

'I know what you're thinkin', son,' she said, not unkindly. 'A big house this for a miner's widow. But there was negligence, you see. My brother got me a good young lawyer, Mr Laidlaw, a customer of his at the bank, and he took up my case. The Coal Board settled out of court, and I got a great deal of money, plus a decent pension.

'It was Anthony who said I should buy this house. He and I used to like Joppa when we were bairns, and he thought it would be nice for me here. Also, since there are five bedrooms, he thought I could do bed and breakfasts in the summer, an' earn a bit more money.'

'And do you?' asked Pringle smiling.

'Yes indeed. I do very well too, especially in the summer, although I've got folk that come to me all year round – salesmen and the like. As usual, Anthony's advice was right; he's aye been very good to me. Rina – she was his wife – used to help me down here sometimes.' Mrs Paterson shook his head. 'My brother never got over her death, ye ken. After she went, I think that he was just waiting to go himself.'

The superintendent glanced up at another of the photographs above the fireplace. It showed a young man, in a University graduation gown. 'Is that your son?'

The woman beamed with instant pride. 'Aye, that's Francis, in his graduation gown. He's twenty-eight now. He's a doctor, you know,' she added, proudly. Pringle felt a tingling sensation in his stomach.

'Very good,' he said. 'Do you see much of him?'

'Not nearly as much as I'd like. He works in London, in Great Ormond Street, the hospital for sick kids, and he's still studyin', so he doesn't have much time off. He'll be up for his uncle's funeral though. I spoke to him just there at lunchtime.'

'Is he your only child?'

'No, no. Ah've a daughter, Andrina; named after her auntie. She's twenty-one. She's a nurse, up at the Western.'

'Ah, where her uncle was treated?' asked Pringle casually.

The woman looked up at him, her eyes suddenly sharp. 'How did you know he was there?'

'We know that he had been ill, Mrs Paterson. In Edinburgh, all of the cancer patients are treated there.'

'Oh, I see.' She hesitated, wringing her hands in her lap. 'Ah'm sorry to be so abrupt with you, Mr Pringle. The thing is, my brother was extremely embarrassed by his illness, and by the way it was. Anthony was a very fastidious man, so after the operation it was just mortifying for him to have to wear that bag. He never went out of the house afterwards, and he never saw anyone other than Andrina and me, or Francis, when he was up from London.'

'No one at all, Mrs Paterson?'

'Well, there was Mrs Leggat, the cleaning lady, she used to do his food shopping for him – no' that he ate much, poor man – and the out-patient visitors from the hospital and such, and Dr Lennie, his GP; but no one else, other than us.'

'No friends from the bank?'

'He didnae have many of those. His main friends were in the Rotary, and he cut himself off from them. But the bank? No none at all, really.'

'Did they know he was ill when they gave him early retirement?'

The bereaved sister shook her head. 'No. He knew, but he didn't tell them. He told me that if he had they wouldn't have let him retire, but put him on sick leave instead, so that if he had died they'd have had to pay out less to his estate than to him in his lump sum and pension. He was gey disillusioned towards the end of his career, Mr Pringle.'

'I can understand that,' said the policeman. 'He knew he was ill himself, though, before he went?'

'He knew for over a year, superintendent. He had symptoms all that time, but he kept them to himself. Eventually, just after he retired, he mentioned it to Francis, and he made him go to Dr Lennie. By that time . . .' She broke off for a few seconds.

'I went with him to the Western for his first appointment, jist tae hold his hand; you know how it is. His consultant, Mr Simmers, was a very nice man. He explained that the tumour was very large, but that there was still a chance, if it was removed, and if he had follow-up treatment. So they operated, and they gave him radiation treatment. He was all right for a few months, but towards the end of the summer he began to lose weight again, until he had trouble even walking about the house.'

'Did Andrina nurse her uncle at all, Mrs Paterson?' asked Pringle. 'When he was in hospital, I mean?'

'No,' Mrs Paterson replied. 'She works in the cancer place, right enough, but in the breast unit, in Ward One. Some of her friends looked after him though, and they let her know how he was doing.'

She sighed. 'I'm glad, you know, that Anthony went suddenly like that. He was a very dignified man, was my brother. It would have been awful to see him just wither away, totally helpless. I know that thought frightened Andrina. She really loved her uncle, you know, and he doted on her.

'In the last few weeks, she'd been visiting him just about every day. Her boyfriend used to go with her too, before he went off to University. Anthony was very fond of him too. He's a nice lad, is young Raymond.'

Sometimes, the best detectives find that the key questions ask themselves. 'Raymond who?'

Mrs Paterson looked across at Stevie Steele as he spoke. 'Raymond Weston, son. His father's a professor, up at the Western.'

64

'Andy, when was the last time you took a holiday?'

He looked at her, his elbow on the high round table which circled one of the pillars in the Standing Order bar. 'I seem to remember,' he replied, 'that you and I were in Spain this summer, at your Dad's place. I seem to remember that you and I were all over each other then.'

'And I'm sure we will be again, next year,' said Alex. 'But you're dodging the question. You know bloody well what I mean. When was the last time you took a few days to yourself, to play golf, or to go wind-surfing. That spare room of yours is full of sports gear, gathering dust, and here you are, looking unfit, dog-tired, and if I may say so, just a wee bit podgy.'

He smiled at her, sourly. 'Gee thanks. Go on, give us a quick chorus of "You fat bastard, you fat bastard, you ate all the pies!" so the whole pub knows I've put on a couple of pounds. For your information, girlie, I've started working out again in the Fettes weights room, and I'm back playing squash with your father twice a week, now that the Chief's back in semi-harness.'

'Good, but none of that gets you out of the office. What are you doing to relax and to help you get away from the stress? That's what I'm asking.'

He shrugged. 'This for a start. Having a relaxing stress-free pint with my fiancée, going for a tandoori afterwards and hoping that she'll come back to my place for B and B, or who knows, maybe even invite me to hers.'

'You can forget the latter,' she said quickly; too quickly, she feared for just a moment. 'I'm not having Gina ogling you over the corn-flakes. When I get my own place – and I looked at a really nice wee flat this lunchtime, down in Leith – it'll be different. As for the other possibility, if we can keep up our recent run of not falling out across the dinner table, you might just be on.

'Now, back to the point. When are you going to take some time off work?'

He capitulated. 'As soon as this summit conference thing is over,

198

and once we get a result on a major investigation that Brian and Dan are working on, I promise you I will book a holiday. Some January sunshine, in the Canaries, or Florida maybe . . . for two, though.'

She shook her head. 'Sorry, we've got a major proof scheduled for January. Anyway, I'm taking some time before then; next week in fact.'

'You're what? You never said.'

'Well I'm saying now. I'm going to Marbella on Saturday, with Gina. I'm not sure how hot it'll be, but we'll get some sun.'

'I see.' The two words seem hang in the air.

'Just as well you do,' said Alex firmly, batting them away. 'Then you won't go moody on me. Listen, I want to marry you, Andy. But as I've tried to explain, I've got to get a life first, or it could be a disaster. Once we are married, I won't be able to bugger off with a pal for some fun – nor will I want to – so if I choose to now, don't give me a hard time about it. Instead of that, go ahead and book your January holiday.'

'Maybe I'll just do that.' he murmured, taking a mouthful of draught Beck's. 'For two,' he added, into the glass, out of earshot.

'Good. Now let's talk about our respective working days, like we used to. What's with this conference?'

He looked around the busy bar. 'Sorry, love,' he said. 'I can't discuss that here.'

'What about your big investigation then?'

'That neither. That sort of chat was all right at home, when we were living together, but I can't talk to you about operational secrets in some damn pub. Your dad would tell you that. Look, you're the one who wanted change, girl; this has to be part of it.'

'Fair enough,' she said. 'Let's just go and eat then.'

'Nah,' he murmured wearily, finishing his beer and stepping off the high stool. 'You just go and catch your plane. It's no use, Alex, I can't share you . . . not even with you.'

65

Bob Skinner swivelled in his own familiar chair and gazed out of his office window. He smiled as he looked down the driveway which led to the main entrance of the headquarters building, watching the rush of the arriving staff, uniformed, CID and civilians, the third category having grown in numbers during the later years of Sir James Proud's reign.

As he watched the scene, the Chief Constable's Vauxhall Omega, driven by Lady Proud, rolled slowly up towards the doorway. Sir James emerged from the passenger side, with a brief nod to his wife. It would have been out of character for him to kiss her goodbye in front of his office, and completely unprecedented for him to do so while in uniform.

'Excuse me, sir.' He swung round in his chair at the sound of Ruth McConnell's voice. Even although she had been only a few feet away across the corridor, he had missed his long-haired, long-legged secretary while he had been filling the Chief's shoes.

'Sorry, Ruthie. Didn't hear you come in. I was admiring the view.'

She smiled back at him. 'Your morning meeting,' she said. 'The men are here, and Sarah's just arrived as well.'

'Christ,' Skinner muttered, rising to his feet. 'Don't keep my wife waiting. Is she looking okay?'

Ruth stared back at him, puzzled. He had told no one in the office, other than Andy Martin and the Chief, of Sarah's pregnancy. 'Morning sickness,' he explained briefly, watching her eyes widen, just as he stepped past her.

'Come away in, everyone,' he called into the corridor. One by one, they filed in and took seats around the low coffee table: Sarah, Brian Mackie, Dan Pringle and Stevie Steele, the young sergeant looking very slightly nervous to be in the vaulted heights of headquarters.

'It's nine o'clock,' he said. 'These days Sarah and I don't drink coffee this early, so you gentlemen can do without as well.

'I've called this meeting, and I'm running it, rather than Mr Martin, because he's asked me to give an overview of the investigation, and because he's snowed under with the security work for next month's conference. I've asked Sarah to come along since she's done the path. work in both cases, and since she was at the first murder scene.' He suppressed a smile; Skinner could never admit it to his men, but his wife's presence on an investigation team always gave him added confidence, such was his respect for her abilities.

'I've been reading the file on the Weston death. It seems to me that there are only two leads left: the mysterious Mr Deacey, and the DNA trace which Arthur Dorward turned up and which may or may not have been left by the person who helped Mrs Weston take her life. After the disappointment of the bogus Deacey, and the serious injury to Maggie Rose, both of those are stalled for the moment.' He looked at Pringle. 'Dan, give us an update on Murray.'

Bob Skinner never encouraged formality, but often there was something about him which simply inspired it. 'Very good, sir.' The thick-set superintendent nodded, and straightened in his seat as if coming to a form of attention. 'We've finished talking to the neighbours; none of them saw or heard anyone come and go. That's hardly surprising. Murray's house is in a cul-de-sac, and there's nobody directly across the road.

'I have a report from Inspector Dorward.' He glanced at Mackie, relaxing slightly. 'He hasna' been as helpful this time, Brian. There were no prints at all on the black tape. It was a brand new roll, of the sort you can buy in any DIY place. He even went over the tape that was taken from round Mr Murray's neck, after it was removed and sent to him. Not a trace. It was the same wi' the kitchen scissors. Arthur says that must mean they had been wiped, for there were bound to have been old traces on them.'

'And the syringe?' asked Skinner.

'Clean too, sir.'

'What about its packaging?' Sarah put the question quietly, but the two superintendents looked round as if it had been fired at them.

Pringle frowned. 'What packaging?'

'The sterile packaging from the syringe; the container for whatever drug was used.'

The superintendent shook his head. 'We never found any, Sarah.'

'No,' she said. 'Nor did I expect it. The assistant . . . let's call him that . . . was a bit more devious than at the first death, leaving the tape, scissors and syringe, but he couldn't have left the packaging. Those items would have had batch numbers on them that would have led you straight to him.'

'Do you have any other thoughts at this stage?' Skinner asked.

'Just this,' his wife responded. 'This person is a doctor, or some sort of paramedic. In each case the needle went straight into a vein in the thigh: upwards because that's the least awkward way, when you're injecting someone. A lay person might have been lucky once, but not twice, not nohow.

'Finding a vein for a needle is quite a skill. Some people are good at it, and some ain't. And it doesn't matter whether you're a doctor or a nurse. I've known middle-aged GPs spend five minutes prodding about with a needle trying to take a blood sample, and I've seen junior nurses who could slip a transfusion line into a vein inside five seconds, every time.

'Whoever administered these injections had that sort of skill. Gaynor Weston was a young, well-fleshed woman; her veins would not have been easy to bring up. Anthony Murray had been bombarded by drugs – so much so that the lab couldn't pinpoint what was used to help his death – and his were very fragile. Yet the injection in each case was done clean as a whistle. I'd have been proud of them.'

She looked at the two superintendents. 'I'd say that narrows down your search quite a bit.'

'More than you think,' said Pringle. 'It points to one person, in fact. Staff Nurse Andrina Paterson.'

'Who's she?' asked Sarah.

'Anthony Murray's niece . . . and Raymond Weston's girlfriend. We'd never have known of that connection had clever young Stevie here not asked the right question at the right time.'

Skinner nodded. 'Yes indeed. Well done, Stevie. Some day, son, you're going to make a mistake, but I'm not going to spend my life waiting for it.

'So what do we do about this? We could pull the girl in and sweat her, right away. But I think not; not at this stage, at least. Just let's keep an eye on her, and try to make sure that she's got no other friends or relatives who are terminally ill.

'We've had our lucky break at the start. Let's keep it on ice and do the rest of the proper police work. Dan, you and Steele complete the rest of the interviews; talk to the cleaner, talk to the out patient visitors, talk to the consultant. See what they can tell you about Mr Murray, see whether he told them anything about his niece which might corroborate her intention to help him do this.

'Meanwhile, Brian, you go back and check up on young Raymond Weston. I know his mother wrote him a letter, but that could be a smoke screen. Find out whether he really did go out on the piss with his pals on the night of his mother's death.'

'Can I say something, sir,' asked Stevie Steele, diffidently.

'Of course.'

The sergeant nodded. 'Thank you, sir. I just thought, this might be corroboration of a sort. The differences between the two scenes; the way the tape, scissors and syringe were left behind the second time, all over the body: I mean, that's pretty specific. The "assistant" surely didn't guess that from the little that was in the papers after Mrs Weston died. It says to me that they were pretty close to the investigation . . . that they might have had a whisper of what was going on.'

'Oh Jesus, yes,' Brian Mackie exclaimed. 'And Nolan Weston knew, didn't he, straight from us. What's the betting that he told his son . . . and he told his girlfriend?'

'At the moment, superintendent,' said Skinner, 'I'd say it's a shade of odds on. But let's make sure there are no other horses in the field before we place our bets.'

66

'Aw, he was such a nice man, sir, he really was,' Mrs Leggat moaned, pressing a handkerchief to her eyes. She looked at least seventy years old; Steele marvelled that she was still doing such a demanding manual job.

The late Anthony Murray's cleaning lady lived in a three-room flat in Clermiston which was as neat and tidy as that of her employer had been, before Arthur Dorward's team had torn it apart in their search for forensic evidence which might identify his visitor.

'So we've been hearing,' said Dan Pringle. 'We have to talk to people after every sudden death, for the Fiscal's report. You'll miss him, I'm sure. How long had you worked for him?'

'Nearly fifteen years, sir. Rina – that was Mrs Murray, God rest her – took me on tae help her in the hoose when she was still working. She had a wee dress shop down in Blackhall; did awfy nice things. She gied me a wee frock for ma Christmas yince, the year before she selt up. I thocht she would let me go then, but she never did. Och, it was terrible, when she took ill. She had cancer, same as him, only hers wis in the liver.'

She dabbed her eyes. 'It was awfy watchin' him tae, the poor man. And sich a shock when I came in and found him. I knew he didnae have long tae go like, but I never thocht it wid be that quick. Mind you, it shouldnae have come as a surprise. Jist the day afore he died, he smiled at me, sitting in his chair and he said "I'm ready for the off now, Mrs Leggat". Jist like that.

'Lookin' back, it wis as if he wis trying tae tell me somethin', the poor man. Ah thocht nae mair o' it at the time.'

'No reason why you should have,' said Steele, sympathetically.

'Maybe no. He'll be happy now, anyway. He missed Rina that much; he's had nothin' tae live for since she died.'

'Did he have many visitors?' Pringle asked.

The woman shook her little grey head. 'No' when ah wis there. A nice wumman frae the support services, she came yince; dinna ken whit her name wis though. His niece came in a few times too, at lunchtime mostly, in her nurse's uniform; wee Andrina. No' sae wee

204

now, mind, it's jist that I've kent her since she wis seven or eight year old.

'The day afore he went, in fact, he said that she was comin' tae see him that evenin'. Her and her boyfriend, he said. Whit was the laddie called again? That's right. Ray, Mr Murray said it wis. He said they were comin' tae help him wi' something.'

67

The office of Home Support was nowhere near the Western General Hospital, to the mild surprise of the two detectives, Instead it was in the city centre, just off Princes Street, in an attic above a pub in Frederick Street.

Dan Pringle was breathing hard by the time he and Steele reached the top floor of the building. 'A refreshment will be order after this, sergeant,' he gasped.

'Very good, sir,' said Steele, his breathing normal as he looked at the anonymous door with its grey-glass upper panel. He knocked lightly and stepped inside. The room was small, its space curtailed even further by the steep coomb ceiling beside the bay window. It was furnished by three grey metal filing cabinets, a chipped table, four chairs and two desks. One was unoccupied, but behind the other, near the window, sat an attractive ash-blonde woman.

'Hello,' the younger man began. 'I'm DS Steele from Edinburgh CID, and this is Detective Superintendent Pringle.'

The worker rose from her seat, extending a hand to the breathless Pringle. 'Penelope Clark,' she said. 'My colleague Faye told me that you had phoned and asked if you could come to see us. What can I do for you?'

Pringle nodded to Steele as he shook the woman's hand and gratefully took the seat she offered.

'You could begin by telling us a bit about your organisation,' the sergeant answered.

Penelope Clark nodded. 'Certainly.' At that moment Stevie Steele fell in love with her voice. Then she smiled and his capture was complete. 'We're a registered charity and we work as an extension of the National Health Service. We're an additional resource, helping patients in a variety of different situations once they've been discharged from hospital.

'There are three of us: Faye Reynolds, me and a chap called John Goody. The people we see might be geriatrics who've had fractures, amputees after surgery, those with hip replacements, and others. Our main service has to do with mobility; we help our clients get back on their feet, sometimes figuratively, but usually literally.'

'But you visit cancer patients too, is that right?' Dan Pringle was recovering. His breathing was only slightly heavy.

'In certain circumstances, yes,' the woman agreed. 'Our definition of mobility is a fairly broad one. Sometimes the problem can be a psychological one; in those circumstances our job is to help the patient regain the confidence to face the world again.'

'How about Anthony Murray? Was that why you were sent to visit him?'

Penelope Clark frowned. 'I can't discuss a client, superintendent. We're bound by the normal rules of confidentiality. We couldn't work otherwise.'

'I think you can talk about Mr Murray,' said Pringle, gently. 'He's dead.'

The woman's hand flew to her mouth, and a shocked expression swept across her face. 'Oh dear,' she murmured. 'I knew he was terminal, but it still comes as a shock. He must have deteriorated quickly. I saw him on Monday of last week and he still seemed to have some vitality in him.'

'You can't have had much hope of getting him mobile again, I wouldn't have thought.'

'His was an attitude problem. We were sent to counsel him about his colostomy bag. He could move around well enough, but that damn thing was like a ball and chain to him. It happens with some people, men usually. We had no success with Anthony, I'm afraid. Latterly, I came to realise that he simply didn't want to go out again. He was happy to sit in his own house; waiting for God, as they say.'

She frowned. 'But tell me,' she said. 'Why are you asking these questions?'

'Frankly, Ms Clark,' said Stevie Steele, 'we think that someone may have made the introduction.'

68

'You know what I'd love to do, Mario?' Maggie asked, wistfully.

'Scratch your bum with your right hand?' her husband suggested.

She smiled at him. 'That's true, but it's not what I was thinking. No, I was thinking that I'd love to start all over again, chuck the police and become a social worker.'

'What the hell brought that on?' he retorted.

She nodded towards the pile of folders on their small dining table. 'Can't you guess? It's this job that I'm doing for Andy Martin. When I said I'd take it on, I didn't appreciate what it would be like. I've spent the day reading my way through a whole succession of private hells that have passed for people's lives.

'Those Fiscal's Reports over there, they've got stories in them that would tear your heart out. With the odd exception – like a father who hanged himself after he was caught abusing his daughters – every person in there is a victim of one sort or another. There are people who were hounded to death by bad neighbours, people who were allowed to run up ridiculous amounts of debt by shops and credit card companies, people who over-reached themselves in business simply trying to fulfil the promises they had made to their families, people who were driven to it by loneliness, and people who were just plain depressed.

'Suicide is a significant cause of death among people of all ages, and as far as I can see every one of them is preventable.'

Mario frowned. 'I don't know if I'd have wanted to prevent that father you mentioned from topping himself.'

'Of course you would, if you could have done it by preventing the abuse through better family support. All these people needed someone who just wasn't there when it mattered the most. It just made me feel that I'm in the wrong job. Far more people want to be police officers than social workers, and the effect of that's showing over there on our table.'

He reached out a thick hand, and rubbed the back of her neck, gently, kneading the muscles, soothing the tension that he felt there. 'Listen, darlin',' he said. 'You are a social worker; so am I. We're both of us doing jobs that benefit society. Okay, on some days the benefit might be more apparent than others, but you've got to take the long view.

'Look at me today: I spent it stuck in a converted bloody gym, vetting security men and journalists. Yet because of what my team did, the world's leaders are going to feel a bit safer when they're in our care next month. Look at you, and that arm; your injury wasn't for nothing. Through it you've rid society of a wicked, vicious man who'd killed one woman and was living off another in the worst possible way.

'Sure, there are more boys and girls who want to join the polis and strut up and down in the paramilitary uniform than there are those who want to be social workers and work with the poor and needy. But it's a bloody sight harder to recruit a really good copper than it is to recruit for a profession which is far more of a vocation, and where just about everyone comes through the door with stars in their eyes and bursting to do good.'

He turned her face towards him. 'You'd be a good social worker, Mags; there's no doubt about that. But you're an outstanding copper, and for my money that makes you even more valuable to society.'

Blushing slightly, she grinned at him. 'You're not so bad yourself.'

'I know that. I'm a good officer, but I'm not as good as you. Better in a rough-house maybe, but you're brighter than me; you see things that I don't.'

'I'll tell you one thing, McGuire,' she said. 'I can see that within that hard-man exterior—'

'There lies a sensitive soul?' he laughed.

'You? You're as sensitive as a wrecking ball. Your hard man pal, Neil, now he's sensitive, but you . . . What I was going to say was that you're the most sensible man I know. You never get flustered, you're always controlled, and you always do the right thing. You've still got a lot to do in this force.'

'There are people in the queue ahead of me. There's you for a start, and there's Brian.'

'Count me out. My next billet will be something specialist like drugs; plus, we are going to have kids sometime in the next five years. As for Brian, he's good but he's peaked. You've still got the potential to wear a lot of silver on your uniform.'

'Have I told you lately that I love you?' he murmured, oddly embarrassed for a moment. 'Okay,' he said, 'that's Neil, Mackie and me assessed: sensitive, peaked and sensible. How about the Big Man? I know how hard he is; I've seen him in action. How would you describe his inner man?'

'The boss? He's different. He's got an amazing mind for a start; he's a brilliant analyst, volatile, unpredictable. But inside? I don't know. Other than Sarah, I doubt if anyone knows what he's really like deep down. I'll tell you this though; there's something about him that frightens me.'

He looked at her, his expression sombre. 'Me too,' he said.

Shifting his position beside her he looked back towards the table. 'What about that lot?' he asked. 'Any possible matches for these other two deaths?'

Maggie shook her head. 'Not yet. But I have to look at every detail of every folder very carefully – and there are about three hundred of them. I've got a way to go yet.'

69

'I'm glad I have this chance to talk to both of you before you go across to the ward for your treatment, Olive,' said Derek Simmers. 'It's early days yet, and I am not one to raise expectations unrealistically. Nevertheless, when I see a positive indicator I can't keep it to myself; that's just not in my nature.'

Neil McIlhenney felt his wife's grip on his hand tighten suddenly, to the point of pain. Excitement rose within him, but he fought to keep it from showing on his face.

'I've had the result of the X-ray which was taken when you were in last week. It shows a small but significant shrinkage in the area of the principal tumour. After only a month of chemo, that's pretty good going. It tells me that the tumour is especially sensitive to the type of treatment which we're giving you, and encourages me to proceed with the rest of the course. The small downside is that your blood is sensitive too; that shows in the various counts, especially platelets, but there are things that we can do to manage that.

'On the basis of that I've scheduled another scan for two weeks' time. If that shows further progress,' he smiled, 'I think we can give you a week off to take that holiday we talked about at the start.'

Neil felt his hand tremble, but realised that it was being transmitted by his wife's grip. 'Thanks for telling us that, Deacey,' she said, her voice steady as always, and matter-of-fact. 'As a teacher, I've always liked Fridays: I won't forget this one in a hurry.'

'Me neither,' said her husband, sincerely.

The consultant smiled at her, straight into her eyes. 'Breaking news like this makes my day too,' he said. 'On you go now. They're for you waiting across the road.' He showed them to the door. As he held it open he glanced at Neil. 'There are two people waiting for me too, upstairs in my office. Colleagues of yours, in fact; I have no idea what they might want.'

Simmers waved his patients goodbye at the entrance to the clinic, then turned the corner and sprinted up the stairs.

His visitors were seated in his tiny room when he arrived there. He looked at them one by one with his physician's eye as they introduced themselves: Superintendent Pringle, middle-aged, heavily built, florid, probably drank too much, arguably in the coronary at-risk category; Detective Sergeant Steele, tall, strong-looking, around thirty, physically at his peak.

'Good morning, gentlemen,' he said moving behind his desk as he spoke. 'In what way can I help you?'

Pringle, in his turn, looked at the consultant, seeing a big, sturdy man, yet struck at once by the softness of his eyes, which seemed to betray a vulnerability in him. 'We'd like to talk to you about a patient of yours, now unfortunately deceased; Mr Anthony Murray.'

Simmers frowned. 'Ah yes, poor old Tony. I heard that he had died. A blessing really; he was being very difficult about going to the Hospice, but that was the only place for him. In a very short time, he'd have been in great need of the sort of pain control that they're used to providing.'

'Did you expect him to die?'

The consultant stared at the policeman, wondering if he might be mad. 'Of course I did, superintendent. He had advanced, metastasised cancer which was beyond all treatment. Of course I expected him to die.'

'No, sir, I mean did you expect him to die so soon?'

'Ah, I see. To be frank I didn't. I visited him at home fairly recently – not something I do as a rule, but he was a neighbour and he was so sensitive about his bag that he simply would not leave his house – and he seemed frail, but still with us. He was away short of turning his face to the wall, as cancer victims can do on occasion.

'However, that said, someone in his condition can deteriorate very rapidly, so while I didn't expect it, when I heard he had gone, I was not overly surprised. I'll miss him though: a good, gentle man. I liked him very much.'

Stevie Steele spoke softly. 'You must miss more than a few people, sir. I don't envy you your job, although I admire you for doing it.'

Derek Simmers looked at the young detective with a mixture of surprise and gratitude. 'Thank you, sergeant,' he murmured, 'but the fact is, I'm rotten at it.'

'We've been told the opposite, sir.'

'Ah, maybe you have, maybe you have. Speaking clinically, I suppose that whoever told you that has a point. But they don't know about my failings, though. I so admire colleagues like Nolan Weston. I admire them their detachment, in the face of the most awful personal tragedies. Christ, Nolan even operated on his first wife, poor Gay, to find that she had a ferociously malignant tumour. I know how fond he was of her, and yet he held himself together, he kept his detachment.

212

'I find that almost impossible sometimes, and yet that's what my job, as you put it, sergeant, is about. Inspiring and maintaining hope, even on those occasions when there is none. You are, for your patients and their nearest and dearest, a bridge across an abyss. Sometimes you see them across, to recovered health, but all too often your treatment is hopeless, and they fall in.

'It's worst of all when you know from the start what the outcome will be.' As the policemen looked at him, they saw tears mist the gentle blue eyes. 'Only this morning, I saw a patient, a couple in fact, for I regard both partners as being in my care. I gave them what was for them good news, and they thanked me with all their hearts.

'Yet I know that my patient will die, gentlemen. In all probability within a year, for the very factor which is positive at the moment will turn negative, and very soon. These are remarkable people, yet all I can do for them is help them make the most of the very limited time they have left together, knowing all the while, as I knew in Tony Murray's case, what the end will be like.

'I hate situations like these, even more that I hate those when my patients collapse into inconsolable fear. I tell you, the Oath we doctors take has a lot to answer for.'

Simmers drew a deep breath and pulled himself up in his chair, blinking to clear his eyes. 'I'm sorry for that outburst, gentlemen. Please do me the favour of forgetting that I said any of it. All of us have safety valves of a sort – although God alone knows where Nolan Weston's must be!

'Now. Is there anymore I can tell you?'

Pringle shook his head. 'No sir, I don't think so.' He and Steele rose, and eased themselves out of the tiny office.

As they turned to leave, Steele asked, casually, 'Out of interest sir, did you know that Mr Murray had a niece in this department?'

Simmers nodded, vigorously, and smiled. 'Andrina, you mean? Yes I did know that. She's a very talented young nurse. They tell me that she's a wizard with a needle – a great gift in this place, I'll tell you.'

70

'I'm pleased your boss could spare you for this job, Sergeant Garland,' said Brian Mackie, as the car pulled away from the station in the sleety afternoon rain which soaked the drab street.

'It's a pleasure, sir. I don't know what your force is like, but up here in Grampian when you're asked to be the Head of CID's exec, you don't turn it down. For all that, you know that you'll be tied to a desk for the duration. That doesn't mean you have to enjoy that side of it.

'Whenever a request for assistance comes in, I always grab it for myself, and just tell the DCS I'm doing it. Usually it's okay with him.'

Mackie looked idly out of the window as Garland drove. He had always had a soft spot for Aberdeen, despite its winter chills. There was something about the orderliness of the grey granite city which appealed to him.

The Aberdonian detective turned off Union Street into Broad Street, then turned left past Marischal College. 'I did my asking around yesterday just as you asked. I found this room-mate of his, the lad Beano; his real name's Brian Litster.'

The superintendent grunted. 'Funny, that. I was called Beano at school too.'

'Is that right sir?' said the sergeant, politely. 'As luck would have it, we've got something on this one, an official caution for possession of cannabis, just two weeks ago. The University doesn't know about it, and he wants to keep it that way, so I'm pretty confident that he won't have said anything to the boy Weston about your visit.'

'I've arranged to meet him in the Union at Robert Gordon's, rather than at the College back there. That's where young Weston has most of his classes.'

'Why not down your nick?' asked Mackie.

'I didn't want to scare him that much, sir; just make him a wee bit nervous.'

'Fair enough. You've met him. I haven't.'

As he spoke, Garland reached Robert Gordon's, Aberdeen's second, technologically-based University. He parked in a space marked

'Official Visitors Only,' flashing his warrant card at a curious janitor as he and the Edinburgh superintendent stepped out.

As they stepped through the main entrance a tall, gangling youth stepped out of the shadows beside the door. 'Sergeant Garland . . .' he began, anxiously.

'Hello Beano.'

'I've booked a tutorial room,' said the student, half whispering even though the hallway was empty, save for them. 'I thought it would be better, rather than being out in public in the reading room.'

'Fine,' the sergeant replied. 'This is Detective Superintendent Mackie, by the way, from Edinburgh.' Mackie nodded a solemn acknowledgement, but did not offer a handshake.

The boy led the way up a single flight of stairs, into a corridor and along to the third door on the right. As they stepped inside Garland flipped a brass catch, changing the word 'Vacant' to 'Engaged'.

'Second Wednesday in October,' Mackie barked, even as they were taking their seats around the old wooden table, its varnished top scarred with graffiti. 'Where were you, in the evening?'

'I can't remember,' Beano protested.

'Of course you can. It was the night before your room-mate was told his mother was dead. Concentrate on that.'

The young man gulped, then burped. The hoppy smell of beer filled the room. 'Pardon,' he mumbled and, for the first time, the detectives realised that he was a little drunk. He screwed up his eyes to emphasise that he was thinking.

'There was a party for First Years. The Drama Club staged it, so we all went. We reckoned that there would be plenty of birds at it,' he added with a gawky grin.

'Did Ray Weston go?'

'I suppose so.'

Mackie glared at the young man, forcing him to look back. It was a skill which he had tried to learn from Bob Skinner. 'Your suppositions aren't good enough, son. Now use that sodden brain of yours. You share a room with Raymond Weston. Did he go to the Drama Club do or did he not? I'm not here to piss about with you. Out with it.'

Beano gulped again; for a moment the detectives thought that he was going to be sick, but he steadied himself. 'No,' he said, almost fearfully. 'No, Ray didn't go.'

'So where did he go?'

'He told me that he was driving down to Edinburgh. He has this girlfriend down there.' He broke off for a quick leer. 'A cracker, he says. She's a nurse; she lives in a flat with some other nurses but she's got a room of her own, so they're all right for . . . you know what I mean.'

Mackie nodded. 'I think I remember,' he said, dryly. 'But try harder. Are we just supposing again or did he actually say that he was driving home for a quickie with the girlfriend?'

As the policemen looked at him Beano began to shiver. 'You won't tell anyone about this will you?' he begged. 'Especially not Ray.'

'Why not?' asked Garland, more gently than the superintendent. 'Are you scared of Ray, Beano?'

The student nodded, briefly.

'He didn't look very tough to me,' said Mackie.

'Well he's tougher than me!' the boy exclaimed, suddenly, almost shouting at the policeman. 'He scares me. And he knows people.'

The Aberdonian looked at the boy. 'Was it Ray who gave you that grass, Beano?' he asked, his gentleness gone.

'I bought it in a pub.'

'Don't bullshit me now,' the sergeant snapped, 'or I'm going straight to your Principal. Then it'll be suspension, and your parents will know why. Was it Ray?'

Brian Litster stared at the floor. 'Yes,' he whispered. 'He can get other stuff too.'

'What kind of stuff?' asked Mackie, quietly.

'Pills; diazepam tablets, he says they are. He sells them.'

'And does he take them himself?'

'He smokes a wee bit of grass. He doesn't do anything else, though. He just sells them; cheap, too. A pint for a pill.'

The boy looked up at Garland. 'Can I go now?'

It was Mackie who nodded. 'Yes, you can go, although I may want to speak to you again, in Edinburgh. Thanks for your co-operation; I mean that.

'Bear this in mind, though; if you were to decide that it might be safer to tell your room-mate about our chat, and warn him, then you'd be guilty of attempting to pervert the course of justice. I'm sure my boss would want to interview you himself about that. I tell you, son, if Ray Weston scares you, then no way do you want to meet DCC Skinner.'

Abruptly, Beano stood and bolted for the door, leaving the two policemen staring at each other across the table. 'Bingo,' said Garland. 'Do you want Weston lifted?' he asked.

'Christ no,' said the superintendent. 'I want him watched, though, every step of the way, as long as he's in town, and I want to know whenever he heads back to Edinburgh. This boy's a very hot property, all of a sudden.'

71

'Sarah?'

She looked up from changing Jazz's Pampers. The infant, his strong legs getting straighter by the day, kicked and struggled as she fastened the pad and slid him into his sleep suit. 'Yes?'

'Can I borrow that brain of yours?'

She picked up her son and held him out at arms' length. 'Sure, if you'll take charge of this fellow for a bit. I know it's Lads' Night, and you have to go in half an hour, but see if you can tire him out first.'

Bob accepted the burden, and without a word, hefted his chortling son on to his shoulder, fireman style. 'I'll bet you'd fancy coming along with me, wouldn't you, pal.' For many years, he had been one of a small select band who gathered in North Berwick every Thursday to practise their limited footballing skills in the Sports Centre games hall.

He stood Jazz on his feet on the nursery floor and rolled a soft rubber ball over to him. 'Let's see what you can do.' The toddler swung his left foot at the ball, missed it completely and fell on his padded bottom.

'Just like your dad,' said Sarah.

'Try the other peg,' said Bob. 'Puskas did okay, and one of his legs was only for standing on.' He retrieved the ball and passed it again, to his son's right. Jazz kicked out again, and made contact. 'There you are. Know what, kid? I think I'll buy a set of goal posts for the back garden, for you and Mark.'

'And for you, as well you know. Now, why do you need my brain?'

He smiled at his wife as he passed the ball back. 'It's to do with the Weston and Murray investigations.'

'You're really getting your teeth into those, aren't you. I wonder if Andy knows what a favour he did you by asking you to take them over from him?'

'He didn't go that far. Like I said, he asked me to "give an overview". I quote.'

'Listen, he knows you even better than you do, in some ways. What he gave you was an open invitation to take over those investigations, and just looking at you, I can tell you're doing just that. Now, what do you want from me?'

Bob rolled the ball into the corner of the nursery, sending Jazz chasing after it. 'I've been thinking about that heroin,' he began. 'The stuff that was used to see Gaynor Weston on her way. We ran out of leads from the hospital pharmacies, and officially, we're satisfied that it didn't come from any of them. Given the priority that has been attached to the investigation up to now, we didn't look at the possibility that it might have come from other than a hospital pharmacy.

'I was thinking about asking other forces for assistance, asking them to check pharmacies in their areas, until we came up with this link between Weston's daughter and Murray's niece. Then Brian Mackie called me this afternoon to say that the boy Raymond's been selling pills up in Furryboots city. That's made me wonder: is there another way that the diamorphine could have been obtained?

'Would you like to think about that while I'm out tonight, and see if you can come up with any theories?'

'Sure,' she said, bending to sweep Jazz up from the floor. 'I've been pondering on that for a while, as a matter of fact. I can give you a workable theory right now. Take someone with a steady hand who's good with a hypo; then give that person access to phials of diamorphine. If you use the finest needle you could puncture the rubber top of the bottle and draw the heroin into a syringe; it's a clear liquid, so you could leave the needle in place, attach another syringe and simply replace it with water.

'That done, you return the phial to the drugs trolley. No one's going to notice the microdot, for that's all that would show, on the rubber seal. The only person who'll be any the wiser will be the poor patient who's injected with water.'

Bob frowned, as he stroked his son's head gently with his big hand. 'How many phials would it take to kill?'

'Half a dozen and you'd go out like a light.'

'Yet there was only one puncture mark on Gaynor Weston's thigh, wasn't there?'

'So what?' Jazz was dropping off to sleep, so Sarah's voice was a whisper. 'If you were a doctor, or a nurse, you'd just put a line in and administer them through that, one after another.'

'What about Murray?' he asked her. 'You said you couldn't pin down the drug that was used on him.'

'I couldn't for the purposes of evidence. The lab report showed a whole cocktail of substances in his bloodstream; there were steroids, morphine, ibuferon, and two sedatives, lorazepam and temazepam. All of those could have been administered orally, and would have been normally prescribed to someone in Mr Murray's condition.'

'Was the morphine the same as the other stuff?'

'No. This was oramorph; it comes in ampoules usually. You break off the top and the patient swallows it.'

'Could you extract that from the container without anyone knowing?'

'No way. Anyhow, you'd need too much of it. I'll tell you what I did find unusual though; the use of two different sedatives from the same family. One or the other, but not both.'

'Does that tell you anything specific?'

'No, but I'll take a guess. I would say that whoever did this took a look at Mr Murray, made a judgement on his condition, then took some morphine tablets and temazepam, ground them down with a mortar, formed a solution with boiling water, then later on, injected it. You would do that for speed of absorption, rather than feed them it in solid form.

'The shot didn't kill him, but it rendered him unconscious and allowed him to asphyxiate without distress.' She shrugged one shoulder, since Jazz was weighing down the other.

'Those are my theories, for what they're worth. They're all you're getting out of me tonight; professionally at least. Now, if you've got some time to spare before you go to kick the crap out of your pals, go and check Mark's homework, while I put this one to bed.'

219

72

'Alex, Mitch Laidlaw gave you a raise last week, you had confirmation this afternoon that you've bought a flat, you're getting plenty of jollies from your toyboy – even if he is a bit of a dweeb – and we're off on holiday the day after tomorrow: so why the hell is your face tripping you?'

'He is not a dweeb,' she shot back at her friend and temporary landlady. 'He has the body of a young Greek god, I'll have you know.'

'Well he'll have to give it back sooner or later. He's my cousin, I can say what I like about him. Anyway, he's a minor issue. Think of all the fun you're going to have in Marbella, now that you're free and more or less single. Lighten up, girl. Brighten up.'

She glowered at Gina. 'I don't feel very bright, okay. I'm still pissed off at Andy, okay. He sat there on that bloody bar stool the other night and came right out with it. "I can't share you, Alex. Even with you," she mimicked. He hasn't been listening to a bloody word I've said.'

'Sure he's been listening,' Gina countered. 'He's just having a hard time understanding it, that's all. So would I in his shoes. One minute you and he are a perfect *ménage à deux*, the next you're kicking over the traces and asserting your right to fuck anything in long trousers if you so choose.'

'I didn't assert any such thing.' A brief smile flickered across Alex's face. 'Well, maybe I did. That wasn't in my mind when I moved out, but when your cocky – and I use the word advisedly – young cousin came on to me, a whole lot of things fell into place. I felt like someone again.

'I thought that I was succeeding in improving my relationship with Andy. After a difficult beginning, he seemed to be accepting my independence, but then on Tuesday, he started behaving like a possessive old fart all over again.'

'Then switch on the Xpelair, my dear,' said Gina, 'and blow him away; break off your engagement.'

'But I don't want to do that. He's my old fart . . . don't grin like that, you know what I mean . . . it's the possessive bit that gets to me.

220

I want to marry him, but in my own good time.'

'Then give him back his ring and tell him to offer it to you again in five years or so.'

'I can't do that. If I break it off it'll be the end of it; I have to stay engaged to him.'

'If you do, are you going to tell him about—'

Alex's look cut her off short. It would have done her father proud. 'Are you kidding?'

'But don't you think you owe it to him?'

'No, I do not. It's my body, Gina. He has no ownership rights, none at all. Now let's drop the subject. I'm sorry; I'll cheer up I promise.' She grinned. 'As of now, in fact. Come on, we've got no gentlemen callers tonight, either of us. Let's us girlies go an have a bevvy.'

73

Brian Mackie was in his office, in the early afternoon, dictating a sanitised note for the record of his interview with Beano Litster in Aberdeen, when the phone rang. He picked it up and heard, to his private delight, Maggie Rose's voice at the other end. He had just been thinking of how much he missed his deputy.

'Good afternoon, Brian,' she said. 'This is a left-handed phone call just to keep you in touch with my trawl through the suicide files. God, if I'd known that I was taking on—'

'I can imagine. Depressing is it?'

'You don't imagine; that's the trick. You switch your imagination off for the duration. Poor old Mario, he's come home to serious grief every night since I started doing this job. Did you know that there were over a hundred suicides in our force area last year alone? And I've got three years' worth to go through.'

'Do I get the impression that you're not calling to tell me that you've made a big breakthrough?'

Maggie laughed, shortly. 'You do indeed, superintendent. I'm just calling to let you know that I am now one third of the way through, without finding the slightest hint of anything that reminds me of the Weston or Murray deaths. I am also calling simply to blow off steam. After all, why should my innocent husband catch all the flak?'

'Why indeed?' Mackie answered. 'How's the arm, by the way?'

'Itching like what I'm too much of a lady to say. I've got a light cast on it at the moment, to immobilise it. That comes off on Monday; then the rehab work should start.'

'That's good. You'll be glad to hear that the maggot who did it has been charged with murder in Birmingham, remanded in custody, and sent back up here. There's a pleading diet at the Sheriff Court on Tuesday, at which, I am reliably informed, he will admit to serious assault and be sent to the High Court for sentence.'

'He's pleading, is he? I'm surprised at that; I didn't think he was the type.'

Mackie grunted. 'David Pettigrew gave him a straight choice; plead to the assault or be tried for attempt to murder. He thinks he's got a deal, but Big Bob told me that he's had a word with the Lord Advocate. When the case comes up for sentence the Crown will lay it on thick, say that this was a hair's breadth away from murder and ask for fifteen years. They doubt if he'll get that, but they reckon that the judge, whoever he is, will be scared to give him less than twelve, in case the Crown appeals against it. The Bench doesn't like being accused of leniency; especially in cases like this.'

'He'll do his stretch down south though, won't he?' asked Rose.

'It'll take at least a year to bring him to trial for the other offence . . . if they ever do, because one of the key witnesses is dead, they've discovered. Whatever happens he's got at least one winter in Peterhead to look forward to.'

'You've made my day,' said the Chief Inspector. 'I'm glad I phoned. I feel better now.'

'That's good,' laughed Mackie. 'See you soon.'

The phone was hardly back in its cradle before it rang again. 'Yes?' the superintendent said curtly.

'Hello sir,' said a voice at the other end. 'It's Craig Garland, here, from Aberdeen. I'm just phoning to let you know that Raymond Weston just left the city, heading south. I've been following him ever since, at a discreet distance. He's just stopped and gone into a pub in Stonehaven.'

'Let's hope he doesn't get nicked for drunk driving.'

'Do you want me to follow him all the way, sir? My boss has given me clearance to do so.'

'No, sergeant, you don't need to leave your patch. What's he driving?'

'A red Polo: registration mark F213 TJL.'

'That's fine. I'll make arrangements at this end; we know where he's going. I'll drop a formal note to your boss, but meantime, thanks Craig, for all your help.' Mackie hung up, then dialled Superintendent Pringle's direct number on his hands-free. 'Dan,' he announced, as soon as the call was answered, 'Brian here. The boy Raymond's coming home for the weekend.'

'Right,' Pringle grunted. 'He needs tae be met, then. What do you think?'

'As I see it, we just keep Weston's house and the girlfriend's flat under observation. Do we know where she lives?'

'Aye, Stevie sweet-talked her address out of the hospital personnel department.'

'Let's just watch them both until he shows. We don't need CID for that job, just a couple of uniforms in unmarked cars, with their collars turned up and their hats off. Wherever and whenever he shows up, they can call us then.'

'Fair enough. I think we should wait till they get together before we lift them. And wherever they are we should have a legal excuse to search.'

'That's no problem,' said Mackie, at once. 'I have information from Aberdeen that Ray Weston's been using and supplying prohibited and controlled drugs. I'll go and see the Sheriff this afternoon and get a warrant to search the girl's flat and Professor Weston's place, both of them if necessary.'

'Ah don't think the Prof'll like that.'

'Then it'll be tough on him, won't it, mate. This is a double murder investigation. Mind you,' he added, after a moment's thought, 'I think I'll run it past the DCC, just to cover our tails.'

'Aye,' Pringle agreed, 'just as well if you do. Mine's getting too near retiring age for it to be left exposed.'

74

'Hi Dennis,' Karen called out as she stepped into the apartment. As her relationship with Wayne had developed, so the hemiplegic had become more friendly towards her.

'Evenin', Missy,' he greeted her, in broad Aussie tones. As always, when his attendant was going out for the latter part of the evening, he was in pyjamas and dressing gown.

'How's your research work going?' she asked him.

'It's everything I hoped it would be. I will leave Scotland a wiser man, and I'll bet you not too many people can make that claim.'

'Don't you be so cheeky,' she chided him. 'We've been exporting knowledge for a long time now. Come to think of it, that's all we've got left to export.'

'Hi.' Wayne's voice came from the bathroom door, at the far corner of the living area. She looked at him, with his newly trimmed beard and his bright shining eyes, and felt her stomach roll over with anticipation. As he walked towards her she noticed that his limp was almost gone.

'Ready for the off?' he asked.

She nodded. 'I've booked two seats for the ten o'clock screening out at the UCI. You quite sure you want to see *Saving Private Ryan*? I've heard that the opening is one of the bloodiest things ever filmed.'

'We can close our eyes at the bad bits,' he suggested. 'Remember in *Jaws*, when they're looking over this wrecked boat and a head comes rolling out? God, I almost wet myself when I saw that; nothing can be any worse.'

'How are we going to know which are the bad bits until we've seen them?' Karen asked.

'Roll me through next door, mate,' said Dennis Crombie from his wheelchair, 'then you can go and find out.'

The cinema complex was thronged, as it was every Friday evening, making Karen pleased that she had booked the seats. And the beginning of the film was as realistic as every critic had described it: for the first twenty minutes and more, she felt as if she was half a century back in time, and on those Normandy beaches. In fact, neither closed their eyes, but watched fascinated, hand squeezing hand involuntarily with each explosion, each awful on-screen death.

Eventually, Private Ryan saved, they emerged from the UCI complex impressed and emotionally sodden. 'It makes you feel lucky you didn't live in those times, doesn't it?' said Karen.

'Yeah,' the Australian replied, then smiled. 'Your place or yours?'

An hour later, they lay in the dark listening to the rain assaulting the bedroom window. 'Nice night, huh?' he whispered.

'In here, it is.' She slid even closer to him, drawing on his heat. 'Wayne,' she asked suddenly, 'where are we going with this thing?'

'Where would you like to go with it?'

'That's just it. I'm not exactly sure; I've never been in a relationship when I've thought further ahead than what I was going to give him for Christmas. Hell, I don't even know whether you'll be here for Christmas, but I find that I want you to be. On top of that I sort of think that I want you to be here next summer too. How long are you staying? When does Dennis's research end, and when do you have to take him back to Australia?'

She looked up, and saw him smile. 'It's just about over,' he said. 'But that doesn't mean we're going home yet. You've read about the world economic summit?'

'Read about it? I spend every day planning for it, vetting journos and the like.'

'All's smooth I trust?'

'Yes. There will be so many security guys in that hall – all of them vetted, carrying guns and wearing their wee eagle badges – it should be the world's safest place for the duration.'

'Well I'm pleased to hear that,' he said, emphatically. 'The reason being that Dennis has been asked to join the Iranian delegation to the summit, as an adviser. As usual, I'll be rolling him in there.'

'That's quite an honour for him.'

'Too damn right. It also means that the Iranians are paying our expenses from now to the end of the conference, not to mention a fat fee.'

'That's great . . . but once it's over?'

He settled down into the bed. 'Afterwards? Well, neither of us have any close ties back in Oz, so . . . hell, it would be a shame to pass up a chance to live through a Scottish Hogmanay.'

She hugged him, tight. 'After that, mind,' he added, holding her off for a moment, 'I have to go back to the rig. But since all my work is offshore, I have decent leave intervals, fares paid to wherever I want to go. There's no reason why I can't spend my time off here.

'Why don't we plan next year on that basis, and see how it goes?'

She wrapped herself around him once more. 'Why don't we just do that,' she murmured. 'You know, Wayne, you really are a lovely man.'

75

Brian Mackie stared out of his bedroom window into the night; it was raining hard in Musselburgh too. He looked across at Sheila, still and asleep on her side, facing the opposite wall, then crept softly out of the room and downstairs to the hall.

He picked up the telephone, dialled Dan Pringle's divisional office number and asked to be put through to the CID office. A sleepy voice answered. 'DC Regan.'

'Hello,' he said, 'it's Detective Superintendent Mackie here. What the hell's happening with the Weston and Paterson stake-outs?'

'Nothing, sir,' replied the detective constable, awake all of a sudden. 'Mr Pringle phoned twenty minutes ago, and I checked then with both cars. The girl's in her flat, but the boy hasn't shown up yet at either place. I've checked with Grampian, Tayside and Fife; he hasn't been in a traffic accident, and he hasn't been lifted for anything. He seems to have vanished, sir.

'Er, there's one of these rave events on at Ingliston all night tonight. Maybe he's gone in there.'

'That's a possibility, I suppose,' Mackie conceded. 'We'll have officers there; get Control to raise one of them on the radio and have the car park checked. Oh aye, and have the Pandas in the city centre keep an eye out for his motor in the streets near to the nightclubs. Long shots, both, but better than sitting all night doing bugger all.'

He hung up the phone and walked into the kitchen. Wide awake, he made himself a coffee and settled down to read, in front of the gas fire. Gradually the warmth got to him: the pages of his book became more and more fuzzy until . . .

He sprang back to consciousness with the ringing of the phone, jumped out of his chair and dived into the hall. Sheila was there before him, at the foot of the stairs, picking up the receiver. He heard her answer.

'Hello Dan. Yes he's here. He doesn't look too sure what time it is, but he's here. Hold on.'

Brian checked his watch; it was eight twenty-three. He took the phone from his partner and grunted into the mouthpiece.

'The boy's turned up,' said Pringle, gruffly. 'He showed up in his motor at his dad's house ten minutes ago. The girl still hasn't stirred. I've told the uniforms to stay on station and let us know whenever either of them makes another move.'

'The girl could be on duty today, Dan.'

'Naw. I checked yesterday; the breast unit doesn't work at weekends.'

'Let's wait and see then.'

'Aye. I hear you phoned during the night.'

'Mmm. Couldn't sleep.'

'Me neither. It's a bastard, this job Brian, is it no'?'

'Tell me about it. Speak to you later.'

He had just stepped out of the shower when Pringle called back. Sheila, well-groomed even in her dressing gown, appeared in the doorway of the en suite bathroom. 'Dan says,' she announced, 'that, and I quote, "The wee bastard is on the move already, heading towards the girlfriend's flat in Saughton." '

'He says he's told the watchers to do nothing other than follow them if they move on from there. Failing that, he says he'll meet you there at ten o'clock.'

He made a face. 'Sorry. I really feel guilty about working on Saturdays.'

'That's all right,' she said. 'You can do the ASDA run on your way home.'

He smiled. Domesticity was still a new experience for Brian Mackie: he rather liked it.

76

'They're still inside,' Dan Pringle growled as Mackie slid into the back of the Vectra, behind Stevie Steele, in the driver's seat. 'Watching *Live and* fuckin' *Kickin'* likely. Ah don't know: chasing kids on a Saturday morning!'

The rain had eased but the day was still grey and damp. They were sitting in a street made up of blocks of three-storey flats, with flat roofs, and steel framed windows which and seen better days. Ray Weston's car sat outside the second block along.

'Potential double murderers,' said the younger superintendent. 'And the girl's a bit more than a kid. I wonder where young master Raymond disappeared off to last night. Probably a disco right enough, if he didn't take the girlfriend.'

'Let's go and lift them and find out. Have you got the warrant?'

Mackie nodded, took a folded sheet of paper from his jacket, and handed it across. 'There you are. Remember now, this warrant relates to specific offences, so we've got to treat this as a drugs raid; at first. Maybe technically we should have called in the Drugs Squad, but it's okay. I've cleared that with the boss too.'

'Stuff the Drugs Squad anyway,' Pringle muttered. 'Let's just get them.'

'Fine. Which floor?'

'Top, sir, on the left,' Steele replied.

'Do we know how many people are in there?'

'The watchers counted three women in last night: Andrina Paterson and her flatmates; also one male, unknown, a boyfriend probably. He and one of the women left together, just after nine-fifteen. So that leaves Paterson, Weston and one other girl.'

'Right,' said Mackie. 'Dan, it's your patch. Lead on, sir.'

Pringle nodded, with a grim smile, and stepped out of the car into the soft drizzle. As the other two detectives followed, he waved to a car behind. Two uniformed officers emerged, donning their caps.

The burly superintendent strode briskly along the street, his colleagues in his wake, and turned into Andrina Paterson's block. Saving his breath this time, he climbed steadily to the top floor, finding a door with a paper pinned to it, bearing three names, 'Paterson, Gallagher, Smith'.

He nodded a signal to the others, and knocked, firmly.

After only a short wait, the door was opened by a woman in her early twenties, wearing a long T-shirt which reached down to her knees. Her impatient frown turned to one of alarm as she saw Pringle's grim expression, and the paper which he brandished in her face.

'I have a warrant to search these premises for controlled substances,' he barked. 'Stand aside please.' The girl had no option but to obey as he barged past her.

'Ray Weston. Where is he?' asked Mackie, evenly. She pointed to a door at the end of the hall. Pringle stepped up to it thrust it open.

The naked couple on the bed leapt apart. Ray Weston started at the intruder, white-faced and open-mouthed with surprise. Andrina Paterson clutched the cover to her chest, and screamed at Pringle. 'What the bloody hell is this? Who the bloody hell are you?'

Brian Mackie put a hand on his colleague's shoulder and stepped past him. 'Ray,' he began, 'we've met before on a couple of occasions. I'm sorry for the embarrassment, Miss Paterson, but we can't give advance warning of this sort of visit.

'Mr Weston, I have information that you have been in possession of and dealing in prohibited and controlled substances. The Sheriff has given us a warrant to search this flat, and your father's house. We'll do all that if we have to, but personally, I'd rather not. So tell me if you're holding anything right now, and spare everyone the bother.'

The pale-faced boy stared at him for a while, then pointed to a black leather jacket which was slung over a chair beside the window. It was the only garment in the room which was hung up. The rest, jeans, a nurse's tunic, shoes, socks, male and female underwear, were spread on the floor. 'There,' he whispered.

Mackie stepped across and picked it up. He felt his way into the right-hand pocket, and produced a tin of tobacco, a packet of cigarette papers, a lighter, and a roughly wrapped package, laying each in turn on the window-sill. Then he reached into the left-hand pocket and produced a small white, round, plastic bottle. He shook it, and heard it rattle.

'What are these?' he asked.

'Diazepam,' Ray Weston replied.

'For which you do not have a prescription, I take it.' The boy shook his head.

'And in the package?'

'Marijuana.'

Andrina Paterson was no longer looking at the detectives. She was staring instead at her boyfriend, with fury in her eyes. 'You stupid—' she began.

'Later, lass, later,' said Pringle. He took a dressing gown from a hook behind the door and tossed it to her. 'Away somewhere else and get yourself dressed. We need you to come with us. You, son, you get your kit on right here.'

'What about me?' The woman in the T-shirt was standing in the doorway. As Andrina Paterson slipped into the dressing gown and opened a dressing table drawer, the policemen turned.

Mackie held up the package and the pill bottle. 'Did you supply him with these?'

She drew in an indignant breath. 'I'd have chucked him out of that window if I'd known he had those.'

'Before this morning's over,' Pringle growled, with an ominous glance back at the bed, 'the boy might wish you had.'

77

'I'm glad you could come in to sit in on this, Karen; I need a woman for this interrogation. Normally it would have been DCI Rose, but—'

'That's all right sir. I was sitting on my hands today anyway. Wayne's taking Dennis for a drive up to Perthshire.'

'What?' said Mackie. 'On a miserable day like this?'

'He'd promised; whatever the weather was like, he said. Dennis has to get himself worked up for trips like that. I just hope his wheelchair doesn't rust.

'Where is the Paterson girl?' Neville asked.

'In the bathroom. We whipped the pair of them out of there pretty sharpish, so I said that since we were waiting for you, she could go and freshen up.'

As he spoke, the door opened, and Andrina Paterson came into the room, a uniformed woman constable behind her. Karen eyed her appraisingly; she was a short girl, with a trim waist, neatly built but with strong, well-muscled arms, a trait that she had noticed before in nurses.

'Join us, please,' said Mackie, standing and showing her to a chair across the table from where he and the sergeant were seated. 'I repeat my offer to you. You can have a solicitor if you wish. I'll delay this interview for that purpose.'

Staff Nurse Paterson shook her head. 'No, like I said before, let me hear what this is about, then I'll decide. I haven't got the money to splash out on lawyers.'

'If that's how you want it. We can stop the interview at any time if you wish.' He reached across and switched on the black box tape recorder, identifying himself and Neville formally, stating the time, place and subject of the interrogation.

'Miss Paterson, I want to ask you a few questions about the death of your boyfriend's mother, Mrs Gaynor Weston.'

The nurse stared at him, in apparent astonishment. 'But what about Ray's drugs?'

'They've got nothing to do with you, as we both know. Anyway, that's a relatively minor matter. Now: Gay Weston. You recall the circumstances of her death?'

'Yes. She killed herself. She had cancer and decided to opt out.'

'So you approve of that?' asked Mackie quietly.

Andrina frowned. 'I approve of people having the right. A lot of nurses do. At the end of the day, it's often the drugs rather than the tumour that take people out anyway.'

'When did you learn that Mrs Weston had cancer?'

'Ray told me.'

'Before she died?'

The girl thought for a few seconds. 'No. Afterwards; he definitely told me afterwards.'

'Did he say anything about the circumstances?'

'He told me that his dad had discovered it. He told me that she had taken an overdose.'

'Did he say how?'

'By injection.'

Mackie frowned. 'Didn't it strike you as unusual for someone to kill themself with a syringe?'

'Why should it? People kill themselves with syringes often enough in this city. Druggies and such.'

'Don't be flip with me Andrina, this is too serious. Come on, now. You're a bright person, I can see that. Haven't you worked this out yet?'

She looked at him, silently.

'Okay,' he said. 'I'll spell it out for you. I'm looking at a situation where I have two apparent suicides. I've got Ray's mother, and I've got your Uncle Tony. A big coincidence, for sure. You've been having a bad run of luck in the relative stakes of late.' Andrina Paterson's eyes narrowed and her mouth tightened. The superintendent continued, regardless.

'This is where you really get unlucky though. Our pathologist has determined that neither Gay Weston or your uncle were alone when they died. They both had help; and that help came from the person who injected them both, someone who was skilful to professional standards with a hypodermic.

'I hear you're damn good with a needle, Andrina.'

The girl gulped; her hands began to tremble, but only very slightly. 'I think I'd better have a solicitor now, don't you?'

'I think that would be a good idea,' said Mackie, switching off the tape.

78

'I'll bet you wish you were next door, Raymond,' barked Dan Pringle, looking round the drab, windowless room. 'Next door with your nice girlfriend and that nice Mr Mackie.'

He glared across the table at the boy. 'Well you're no',' he snapped. 'You're in here with me, and you're not getting out until you tell me what I want to know.'

'That remains to be seen, superintendent,' said the solicitor. The man was frowning. *More than a bit pissed off to be hauled away from the golf club, even on a wet day*, the policeman surmised.

'Listen, Mr Lesser,' he rumbled. 'You've got a right to be here, but don't you think that you're running this interview. Don't you think that for one fucking minute. We're in charge here, Sergeant Steele and I.' He glanced to his left.

'Now, let's cut out all the crap, Ray, son. Where did you get the grass?'

The tall youth lifted his eyes from the table. 'You don't need to admit anything,' the solicitor whispered, but his client waved him away with a long slim hand.

'From a guy I was at school with. I bought it from him.'

'Are you going to tell us his name.'

'No. He's a friend.'

Pringle shrugged. 'Fair enough; you posh school lads stick together. Where did you get the pills?'

Raymond Weston looked back at him across the table. There was something about the lad, Pringle admitted to himself. A sort of wild, rangy presence, not physically threatening to a grown man perhaps, but he could understand how he was able to dominate his room-mate Beano, and to attract a tasty wee girl like that Andrina, even though she was a few years older than him.

'I took them from my dad's study.'

'Did you sell them?'

'Not exactly. I swapped them for beer.'

The superintendent nodded. 'Right. You can regard this as an official caution. Don't do it again, understood, or you'll be banged up in Aberdeen, rather than studying there. You'd hate that, son; inside a week your arsehole would feel as if it had been cored like an apple.'

The solicitor stared at him across the table, not knowing whether to be relieved, astonished, or to be flattered that his mere presence had made the formidable detective crumble. 'Well, if that's it.' He began to stand. 'Come on Raymond. I'll take you home.'

'Sit down, man,' Pringle growled. 'Don't you know when the decks are being cleared. I'm going on to the real business now. Can you guess what that might be?'

The tall youth leaned back in his chair. 'I could try,' he said. 'I'm bright enough to know that you don't send two superintendents out on a Saturday over a wee bit of smoke and a couple of junior aspirins. I'd say this has something to do with my mum and Andrina's uncle.'

'Why would you say that?'

'Because I can't think of anything else.'

'As it happens, you're right. We've got evidence that both of them were helped to kill themselves. Wrap that any way you like, it means murder. Now wipe that smug look off your face and get serious, because there's only two people in the frame for it; you and Andrina.'

'Now wait a minute—' Raymond exclaimed.

'I'm telling you son. Someone gave your mother the jab that killed her, someone did the same for Uncle Anthony. Your girl's a nurse with access to drugs. Where else would we look?'

'But you're . . . That's crap!' The boy was rattled, at last, Stevie Steele saw.

'Convince us, Ray,' he said quietly. 'Where were you when your mum died. We know you weren't in Aberdeen.'

'I was with Andrina. I spent the night with her in Edinburgh.'

'So why didn't you tell us that right away?'

'Because my dad thinks I see too much of her. I didn't want to start another row.'

'And what about the night Mr Murray died? You saw him then, didn't you?'

Ray Weston nodded. 'Andie and I went to see him in the evening. He'd phoned her and asked us to come round.'

'So?'

'So we had a coffee with him, Andie fixed him a gin and tonic and we left. With him alive!'

'When was this?'

'We were gone by about half past eight.'

'And afterwards?'

'I took her home.'

'And after that, what did you do? How do we know that you didn't

236

go back on your own later and help the old man on his way.'

The boy shook his head. 'I can't tell you that.'

'You'd better, son.'

Ray's lips set into a tight line. 'No way.'

'Do you want to be charged with murder?'

'Now just a minute—' the lawyer began.

'Shut up,' snapped Steele. 'Do you, Ray?'

'No.' The youth looked desperate. 'But I can't tell you. I was with someone else.'

'Another girl?'

He nodded.

'You must give us her name.'

'You don't understand. I can't.'

'You've got no choice.'

'I have.' He pointed to the tape recorder, its red light on. 'I will not say her name into that thing.'

Pringle shoved a notebook and pen across the table. 'Write it down then,' he said, darkly, 'or you are locked up. Name and address.'

Raymond Weston sat in silence for over a minute, fidgeting, staring at the table top and at the book. Eventually, at last, he pulled it towards him, picked up the pen and scribbled two lines on the blank page.

Pringle reached across and picked it up. As he read the words, his thick black eyebrows came together.

'Oh shit,' he said, heavily, passing the note to Steele.

'Oh shit,' said the sergeant.

79

'You took your time,' said Pringle as Mackie stepped into his office.

'I'd to stop to get the girl a lawyer.'

'Aye, I thought that might be it. What did she have to say for herself in the end?'

'She said that when Gaynor died, she and the boy were spending the night at her flat. But the flatmates were on nights, so there were no witnesses to that. She says that they went to see her uncle early on last Sunday evening and that afterwards Raymond took her home and went back to Aberdeen.

'What about you?'

The burly Pringle's moustache drooped mournfully. 'The first part of that agrees with his story. We've got that DNA trace, haven't we?' Mackie nodded. 'Then we should take samples off the kids in that case, just to see if either of them matches up. If they're lying about that—'

'I don't think the DNA will help us much even if it does turn out to be a match for one of them. We couldn't actually prove when it was left on the glass, and the kids could argue that they had been there on another day. Anyway, Andrina seemed like a pretty straight girl to me. I didn't think she was lying.'

'You'll better hope she was, chum. The boy's version of last Sunday varies from hers. He says that after he left her, when the old man died, he was with another girl. Young Raymond's got something, or so it seems; I just hope he turns out to be a lying wee bastard.'

'Why?'

'Because this is who he says he was with.' He handed the notebook to Mackie.

The younger man ran a hand over his domed head as he looked at the page.

'Oh shit. Who's going to break this news?'

'Toss you for it.'

'No, Dan,' he said, 'we'd better do it together; first thing Monday morning. Meanwhile, I suggest that we take saliva swabs from these two for the DNA comparison, then let them go ... to await developments.'

238

80

'What's wrong, Pops?' asked Alex as she stood in the doorway of the Deputy Chief Constable's office. 'You've got me worried sick. Have you got bad news for me? Has something happened to Sarah? Has she miscarried? Or is it one of the boys?'

Skinner sat at his desk, gazing at his daughter, unsmiling. 'Sarah's fine, and so are the kids. Grab yourself a coffee, sit down, and calm down.'

'Calm down!' she exclaimed. 'I'm no sooner off the plane from my holiday and through the door than you phone me and tell me to meet you in the office – on a Saturday afternoon – and you won't tell me why.' She looked tanned, but tired, as she filled a mug from the filter machine on the side table.

'Early start?' he asked.

'Yes we'd to be at the airport for eight; that meant getting up at half six.' She moved across to the group of low chairs in the corner of the big room.

'No, don't sit there,' said Skinner. He pointed to a chair which faced his across the desk. She shrugged, and did as he said.

'Did you have a good holiday?' he asked. Alex looked at him. There was an edge to the question, something behind it. She sensed a bomb waiting to explode.

'Yes,' she replied, looking him straight in the eye, 'we did. Now what the hell is this? Why are you sitting there like a smoking volcano?'

There was something about his daughter's anger which made him back off slightly. 'Sorry,' he said. 'I promised myself I'd keep my cool. It's just that I've been sitting on this for the best part of a week. I thought about dealing with it right away. I thought about hauling you back from Marbella, in fact.'

She glared at him, astonished, but still on the front foot. 'And why would you have done that? What right would you have had?'

'In the circumstances I'd have had every right. My reasons for not doing it were personal, not professional.'

'Ah, I'm your daughter so I got to finish my holiday. This mystery gets deeper and deeper.'

'Actually,' said Skinner, 'I wasn't thinking about you at all. I was sparing someone else's feelings.' He leaned forward, elbows on the desk, and engaged her aggressive stare with one of his own. 'I don't like it when my daughter's name is given to me as an alibi witness by someone who's under suspicion in a double murder investigation. I find it really, bloody, embarrassing – as did the officers involved, especially when the man in charge of the inquiry, their direct line commander, is her fiancé.

'Like I said, I've been sitting on this for a week, waiting for you to get back from Marbella, so we could have this conversation. I'm actually way out of order here, you know. By rights it's Dan Pringle and Brian Mackie who should be interviewing you, in a smelly wee room at St Leonard's, or Torphichen Place. But I'm bending the rules again, just for you. So please, love, do one thing for me before we go any further: get off your high horse.'

But her anger had vanished already, to be replaced by a look of concern. 'Okay, Pops, I'm sorry. Now tell me what this is about.'

Skinner picked up his mug from its coaster, held it up to his mouth in both hands, and sighed. He took a sip then, deliberately, put it back down. 'Last week,' he said, 'Dan and Brian were on a joint investigation into the deaths of two people, in very similar circumstances. We were treating it as murder.

'They identified two suspects, one male, one female; there was a very strong circumstantial case against them. Their defence in the first case was pretty poor; they said they were together at the time, miles away from the scene. That was all; no independent witness to corroborate their story.

'But when it came to the second death, the boy produced an alibi. He said that around midnight, when it happened, he was in bed with someone other than his girlfriend . . . with you, as it happens. The lad's name's Raymond Weston. Let's see, it was the Sunday before you went to Marbella.

'So? Is that true?'

Suddenly, Alex could feel her heart hammering, her pulse racing. She gasped, then took a deep breath, to steady herself, then another, and a third. He was gazing at her across the desk, not angrily now, for he had his answer. The detective, the man she had never looked in the eye before, was gone. Her anxious father sat in his place.

'Yes,' she sighed. 'It's true.'

'Okay,' said Bob. 'The boy's off the hook. There was a DNA sample left at the other scene anyway. It didn't match either of them.'

It was his turn to sigh. 'What is this, Alex, with this lad?' he asked, wearily. 'I know you and Andy were having a bad time, but I thought you were still committed to each other.'

'We still are; I still am. It's just that he was being so, so . . . stifling at the time. He was choking me emotionally, and part of me was so angry, and Ray was there, an attractive, interesting boy who fancied himself, and me. There were no ties with him, it was all under my control and so I said to myself, "Girl, you're only young once. Don't let anyone rob you of that," and I had a fling with him. It's over now: the night before I left for Marbella I told him that his time was up.' She paused, and frowned. 'I didn't know about the girlfriend, though.'

'Serves you right then, kid. He went straight to her, more or less, after he left you last Saturday morning.'

'Hah!' Her quick laugh took him by surprise, and strangely, lightened him. 'So we were using each other really. Fair enough. I've got no complaints about that.' She looked at him. 'Pops, when you were my age, didn't you ever feel like that? Didn't you ever fancy being with someone else? Didn't you feel oppressed?'

'Alexis, when I was your age, or a bit older maybe, I was the oppressor for most of the time. However, since we're shaking out the skeletons here, just after my twenty-first, I had a short but intense fling with an emerging young actress. I won't tell you her name, but she's quite a star now. It ended as easily as it began, no recriminations, no regrets on either side, except . . .' He paused and grinned, scratching his chin.

'Afterwards the guilt got to me, and I confessed all to your mother; she and I were engaged at the time. She forgave me; there were a couple of tears but she forgave me, just like that, after I'd promised not to do it again. She didn't write about that in her diary though: it must have been too big a blow to her ego, I guess, to be committed to paper.

'Aye, she was some ticket, your mother. And now I look at you, and I see history, struggling to repeat itself.'

'Don't bring Mum into this, Pops.'

'Of course I will,' he exclaimed. 'She's what this is about, isn't she?'

'You hardly knew her! As you found out fairly recently, to your cost.'

Bob shook his head, and laughed, softly. 'Alexis, my lovely daughter, I knew your mother from when we were kids until the day she died. You knew her for four years, and for most of that time you were too wee to wipe your own bum. You can't even remember her, girl, so don't presume to lecture me about her.'

'But you didn't know *all* of her. You didn't know what was in the diaries.'

241

'No,' he admitted, 'but I'm not stupid, and I wasn't blind. I knew what a devious and manipulative little bitch she could be. I worked out way back that Myra always got what Myra wanted . . . even me, I came under that description. But I didn't mind any of it, you see, because I loved her and I *wanted* her to have everything she wanted.

'So if I had known about the tart in the diaries – and I still try to kid myself sometimes, that at least some of those stories might have been fantasies – maybe I would have put up with that too. Or maybe not. Maybe I'd have broken her neck, literally. But no, your being there would have stopped me from doing that.

'Alex, you may be imagining that you are your mother reincarnated; you may even have enjoyed the notion during your escapade with this boy. But you can take it from me, you are not Myra. I'm the linking factor between you. I know, knew, you both, I love you both . . . Oh yes, I still love her inside,' He tapped his chest. 'and I always will.

'I promise you, there are fundamental differences between you and her. She was bright, for sure, but you're brilliant. She had limited professional horizons, yours are boundless. But the most important thing of all is this. Essentially, let's face it, she was bad. You? Through and through, you're good. I'll show you proof: your reaction when I told you about young Weston's steady girlfriend. If you'd known about her you'd have patted him on the head and sent him home. Am I right?'

Reluctantly, she nodded. 'Yes,' he continued, at once, 'because that's your morality. When we were engaged and on holiday, your mother screwed my best pal, another woman's husband. Why? Because she didn't have any morals, she didn't have any control inside her to tell her what was right and what was wrong. When that's missing from someone, there's no telling what they might do.

'I've spent my life dealing with people like that, Alex. The fact that I loved your mother with all my heart, doesn't prevent me from recognising now that she was of that sort. If she was alive now, and we were man and wife, then that knowledge wouldn't prevent me from loving her still. That's in me, though I keep it to myself.'

He stood up, came round the desk and sat on its edge, taking his daughter's hand. 'Now, as for you . . . you can play the bad girl as hard as you like but you can't change what's at the heart of you: goodness. That's how it is; pretending doesn't make you what you're not.'

He reached under her chin and drew her eyes back to his. 'Look, kid, given my recent track record, I'm not the guy to lecture you on how to run your sex life. I won't presume to advise you about you and Andy either, about what you should do. I think I know well enough, but you've got to work it out between you.

'There is this though. You've put me in the most difficult professional position I've ever encountered. Locked in my desk is an almost complete report by Mackie and Pringle on their investigation, and you feature in it, as Ray Weston's alibi on the night of Anthony Murray's murder. Now you've dropped in the last piece of the jigsaw.

'Andy's my Head of CID. He's been preoccupied for the last week, but he'll expect automatically to see that report, and he's entitled. He's asked me about it a couple of times already, and I fobbed him off by telling him it wasn't finished. Now that it is, there is no way I can keep it from him, however much it might hurt him. If I even try, he'll smell a rat.

'So,' he said, 'on Monday . . .'

Alex nodded. 'I know, I know. But you'll let me talk to him first, Pops, won't you?'

'Sure; that would be best. Do it tonight or tomorrow though.'

'Yes. But when I do, there's something else that I know now I have to tell him. It's something you should know too.'

81

Andy looked at her across the kitchen. 'Let me sum up what you've just told me,' he said. He was wearing glasses, rather than his tinted contacts, but still she could see the hurt in his eyes.

'You've been having it off behind my back, with some kid who's just about young enough to be my son. Now, through some sort of Murphy's Law, that fact has become an important piece of evidence in a criminal investigation, and three detectives under my command know all about it.

'That's what you're saying, is it?'

Alex nodded, watching the ice cubes swirl round in her gin and tonic. 'I'd say that was a fair summary of it. Andy, I'm sorry it had to come out this way, I really am. As I said, I may have done it because of you in a way, but I never meant to hurt you by it. Ray didn't mean anything to me.'

'Maybe not, but he sure means something to me. Most men would feel very serious about someone fucking their fiancée, you know. You're not saying that he didn't know you were engaged, are you?'

'No. I told him I was.'

'Jesus! The boy must think I'm a right inadequate prat; he must be laughing all over his face. I'll be the talk of the Aberdeen University Union bar right now, and so will you.'

'He's not that sort of guy,' she protested.

'Crap! He's eighteen, and he's a little toerag. Listen, you go on about not wanting to hurt me. Did you ever think about how badly I could hurt him?'

'Andy, you wouldn't! You could break him in two.'

His laugh was cruel; a sound she had never heard before. 'I wouldn't need to lay a finger on him. Dan Pringle told me, just before he forgot to mention Weston's horizontal alibi, that he and the Thin Man caught the kid with a parcel of cannabis and a bottle of pills that he'd nicked from his old man. Your Ray smokes grass and barters stolen drugs for beer with his student pals; bet you didn't know that.

'Dan's getting soft; he let him off the possession thing with an informal caution. I have the power to overrule that decision and have

244

the boy prosecuted for theft and dealing. Minor stuff, I'll grant you, but enough to end his University career and give him a record that he'd carry for the rest of his life.'

Alex's Marbella tan paled as he spoke. 'Oh Andy,' she moaned, 'you wouldn't do that to him.'

'Tell me why not,' he barked. 'If he was some punk from Pilton and you were a tart off a street corner Pringle would have sent him down the road without a second thought. Why should I give him preferential treatment? It's as if I was rewarding him for letting you work off your frustrations on his dick.'

She winced at his expression; then her eyes narrowed. 'And what if he stood up in the dock, or went to the papers, and said that he was only being prosecuted because of me?'

He stared back at her. 'People stand in the dock and slag off the police all the time, love. Does the thought worry you because it might hurt me, embarrass you, or damage your career prospects?'

She nodded, more to herself than him. 'This discussion's run its course, I think.' As she spoke she pulled the engagement ring from her finger and laid it on the kitchen work-surface. 'Better luck next time,' she said. 'Sorry to have spoiled your Sunday.'

She started for the door, but he caught her arm. 'Alex, no,' he said. 'I went too far; I'm sorry.' For a moment she tried to pull free, then stopped and let him turn her to face him. 'I'm sorry,' he repeated. 'I went over the top there. I am not going to overrule Pringle or do anything else to the boy. You just gave me a serious kick in the ego, that was all.

'Look, you told me often enough, but I guess I wasn't listening. I had no idea that I was being as possessive and as constricting as that, but I suppose I have to take some of the blame for what's happened. Remember that daft thing I said ten days ago in the pub, about not sharing you with you? Well forget it, please. Of course you've got to have your own space – up to a point. By that I mean that you can sleep anywhere you like as long as I'm the only person you sleep with. Can you handle that small restriction?'

She looked up at him with a curious, soft smile. 'Are you saying that you'll forgive me, if I promise not to do it again?'

He drew a deep breath, let it out in a sigh, and grinned. 'I suppose I am.'

Well,' she said, 'since you're in a forgiving mood, let me try you with something else.

'Over the last few months, I've had a hard time sorting out my ambitions. You made your agenda perfectly clear, and that meant that I had to think about mine, before I was anything like ready to do so.

245

For a very little while, earlier on this year, I thought "Yes, let's put the career on hold. Let's have our family and get it over with." So for a month I stopped taking my pill.

'After a very short time, I realised that that was not what I wanted. However, it only takes a second as they say. I fell pregnant, Andy. At the very time when you were going on about wanting kids now, while you were still young enough to play hide and seek with them, and I was just working out what I felt about the whole thing, I was stupid enough to get myself knocked up.

'I thought long and hard about it. Should I tell you, should I keep the baby, should I talk to Sarah, should I . . .' As she paused for a second or two, he felt the tension build up within him once more.

'Are you going to tell me . . .' he began.

'In the end I decided not to talk to anyone, since I knew quite well what I had to do. I had a termination, Andy. On the day after I moved out of here, I went into the Eastern General and had it done.'

He felt the rage well up within him; far different in intensity to the anger he had felt when she had confessed her indiscretion a quarter of an hour earlier. His eyes were blurred as he looked at her; he felt his muscles tense. He wanted to hit her, not just once, but many times; he wanted to beat her insensible, then go on beating her until his strength was gone. His mouth opened, then closed, trying to form words.

He turned away from her, and held on to the work surface, tight, struggling with his wrath, until he had it under control.

'You are telling me,' he whispered, when he could, 'that you were pregnant with our child, and you had it killed.'

'I had conceived and I had a termination,' she murmured in reply.

'Don't bandy words with me, girl. You were carrying my baby and you had it snuffed.' He turned back towards her. 'You didn't even tell me about it. You didn't involve me in the decision. Why in God's name not?'

'Because I knew what would happen. I knew the argument we would have. I knew that your beliefs wouldn't let you listen to me, and that you would forbid it, or try to. I guessed that if I had told you about it, then made my own decision, we'd be finished. So I went ahead, with the intention that you would never find out.

'But yesterday afternoon, when I was speaking to Pops, I realised that I had to tell you about it. I saw that if we were going to have a life together . . . and I really did want that . . . then everything had to be out in the open.'

'But you didn't tell me when it mattered,' he repeated, desperately. 'You kept our kid a secret because you knew that what you wanted to do ran contrary to my upbringing and to my belief.'

246

'It's my body we're talking about here, Andy,' she countered. 'I am sorry, truly, but no one, be he husband, lover or anyone else has the right to tell me what I will do with it. I will only ever have a child when I want, and with whom I want. I always wanted to have a family with you, my love: but . . . not . . . yet.

'When I had my termination, it was with us in mind, long-term.'

'Don't give me that,' he spat back at her, bitterly. 'You had my baby killed because it was in your way.

'That investigation that Brian and Dan are working on: they're looking for someone who's been helping people to kill themselves. When they find him, he'll be charged with murder, and found guilty; quite right too, because that's what it is. From where I stand, I can't see much difference between you and him.

'I could forgive your fling with the boy: that's easy. But not this, no way.'

Alex picked up the ring from the worktop, and slipped it into the breast pocket of his shirt. 'I came here for confession, my dear, not forgiveness. It's the fact that you think you have the right to forgive that's persuaded me, finally, that we have no future together.'

82

'I hope this temporary office is okay for you, Chief Inspector. Our uniformed colleagues aren't too pleased with me for pulling rank to have two of their inspectors moved in together for a while.'

Brian Mackie grinned round the door at his deputy. Her right arm was in a protective plastic casing, but she was using it nonetheless, arranging folders into piles on the room's small table.

'I hope you didn't carry those in here,' he said.

'No chance,' Maggie Rose replied, putting the last small group of files in place on the table. 'Mario carried them up for me.'

'How's he doing these days?'

'He'll be happier once next week's conference is behind him. It's the sort of routine vetting and accreditation work that bores him silly.'

The superintendent shrugged. 'Not all paths to glory run across easy ground,' he laughed, pointing at the bundles on the table. 'I can guess what those things are. Your homework for the last couple of weeks, yes?'

'Yes indeed: three hundred and more sad stories. I finished my trawl through them on Saturday.'

'And have you come up with anything?'

She wrinkled her nose in a typical gesture. 'There's no single case here there that leapt out at me. I was going to give you a report this morning, but if you've got time now...'

'Sure,' said Mackie. 'Why not?' He closed the door behind him and sat down, as she picked up the small bundle of folders and took her place behind her desk.

'How's the main investigation going?' she asked, casually.

A pained expression crossed his face. 'Dead in the bloody water again, thanks to a phone call I had from the boss at the weekend.'

'What, from Andy?'

'No. From the Big Boss; he's been overseeing the investigation for the last ten days or so, which is just as well. Dan and I happened upon a strong suspect for both deaths, Gaynor Weston's son, no less. We thought we had him until he came out with an alibi for number two, a story which Big Bob's call on Saturday evening confirmed.

'While Anthony Murray was breathing his last, Raymond Weston was under the duvet with the Head of CID's fiancée.'

Rose looked at him, momentarily stunned. 'Alex? He was with Alex Skinner?'

Mackie nodded. 'She confirmed it when she got back from holiday. And that, Mags, is now one of the deepest darkest secrets of this department. Apart from Bob, Alex and now, I guess, Andy, only Dan, Stevie Steele, you and I know about this, and that's the way it will stay. The report will be going into the DCC's safe and it will stay there.'

'Weston knows,' murmured Maggie. 'Ray Weston knows. What if he brags about it?'

'After the chat Dan and Stevie had with him, he won't be breathing a word, believe me. All that aside, though, it looks as if the kid's in the clear – apart from having made himself just about the worst enemy you could imagine – and we've got a stalled investigation: unless you can kick-start it, that is.'

'I wish I could help you, Brian,' she said. 'But I don't think so. I've been through every one of these over the last few weeks. There's not a single case in here where self-suffocation was the cause of death. I began by sorting them into categories as I was going through, by the method used in each case. I tell you, people come up with some awful ways to top themselves.

'That didn't take me any further really, other than to confirm that there wasn't a single case of overdose linked with asphyxia among the files I was checking. So I went through them all again, looking at the background circumstances of each victim. Most of them were related to depression or hopelessness, arising from a range of causes: mental illness, debt, marriage break-up were the most common. However I did find some where serious or terminal illness had been the reason for the suicide, and I separated them out.' She lifted up the pile of folders. Mackie guessed that there were around thirty of them.

'Once I had done that,' Rose continued. 'I looked at the methods used. Some hanged themselves, one woman jumped off Salisbury Crags; predominantly though, the victims overdosed. They used a variety of drugs, in pill or liquid form, and the overwhelming majority combined these with large quantities of alcohol. With one single exception, in fact, the fatal substances were taken by mouth.'

She picked up the file which lay on top of the heap on her desk. 'Out of all of these reports, this is the only one where the person injected herself. I don't think it's a winner, though. The victim was a woman from Bathgate named Nicola Marston. She had inoperable cancer of the liver, with secondaries in most of her other major organs.

249

In addition to that, she was an insulin-dependent diabetic. She killed herself by injecting four times the normal dose.'

'Let's have a look,' said Mackie, taking the folder from his deputy. He laid it on the desk and leaned over it, shoulders hunched, reading carefully. It took him over five minutes to read statements which were stacked together in the thick report, and finally, the investigating officer's summary report to the Procurator Fiscal. When he had finished, he scanned through the documents once more.

'I guess you're right, Mags,' he grunted as he closed the file. 'The only common factor linking the three cases is that all the victims are single people, living alone and suffering from terminal illness. The consultant in this case, Derek Simmers, is the same man who looked after Anthony Murray, but that isn't relevant since all cancer patients in our area are referred to the same small group of consultants.' He picked up the papers as he stood.

'I'm going up to Fettes this morning for the divisional CID heads' meeting. The DCC's taking it himself today, so I'll let him see it. I don't think it'll make his morning though.'

83

'Looks like that's it then, gentlemen,' sighed Skinner. He was as frustrated as the two superintendents. 'I agree with Maggie's view that the Bathgate case doesn't fit with the other two, so there's no sense in upsetting the family involved by raking the whole thing up again.'

'It'd be difficult anyway, sir,' said Mackie. 'There's a note on the file saying that the body had been released for cremation.'

'Doesn't make any difference.' The DCC held up the folder for a moment. 'There's nothing here which would have given us grounds to ask for an exhumation order. No, I'm afraid that for all your sterling efforts, we're back to square one. All the bloody aggravation has been for nothing.'

He glanced across the desk, and to his left at Neil McIlhenney. 'Since you two know the facts of the case, and since you have to work with him, I'll tell you this. Neil, you haven't been involved in this inquiry – in fact you know bugger all about it – but you're my right-hand man so you should hear this too.

'Andy Martin and my daughter have decided to end their engagement. I would tread carefully around the Head of CID for a bit; he's feeling very sore about it. Fortunately he's got the conference preparations to keep him distracted.'

'He's not feeling sore at us, is he, sir?' asked Pringle, a touch anxiously.

'Of course not. Nor is there any reason why he should. You guys did a very professional job.'

'We could have buried it, boss,' said Mackie. 'When the Weston lad gave us Alex's name in his alibi . . . I mean, the evidence against them was all pretty tenuous by that time . . . we could simply have sent him and the girl home and forgotten all about it.'

'No you couldn't.' Skinner jabbed the folder with a finger, emphasising his words. 'It was there; it had to be followed through and confirmed. If the boy had been lying he'd have been firmly in the frame. He wasn't though, so it looks like we've run into the buffers again. With the two kids eliminated as suspects, aside from the coincidence of the consultant Simmers having treated both Murray

251

and the Bathgate woman, as far as I can see we're stuffed.'

Mackie nodded. 'Short of finding this mystery man Deacey, I'd say we are boss. And even if he walked off the street right now and gave himself up—'

'Wait a minute!' The urgency of McIlhenney's interruption cut him off in mid-sentence. 'Who did you say?'

The other three men looked at him, Mackie's surprise tinged with annoyance at the outburst. 'Gaynor Weston had a male friend that we haven't been able to trace,' the superintendent said. 'He was mentioned in her computer diary, but no one knows who he is; not her son, not anyone. We had one lead, but that went badly wrong on us. When Maggie got cut, it was him they were after.'

The sergeant looked at him. 'But that guy's name was Joseph; or so Mario told me.'

'That was his real name. He'd been living under an alias for a while. He was our only possibility. So now we're left with this odd name, Deacey, and we haven't a clue who it fits. But anyway, as I was saying, even if we did find him, he doesn't link into the Murray investigation.'

McIlhenney leaned back in his chair and stared at the ceiling for a while, in silence, as if he was thinking something over, very carefully. Eventually, he pulled himself forward and looked at Skinner. 'I'm afraid he does, sir, and to the Bathgate case. But no way is he the man you're after.

'I can tell you who Deacey is; he's Derek Simmers, the consultant. It's his nickname, you see. He rarely goes by his Christian name; since his schooldays that's what all his friends have called him.'

'Then we'd better talk to him again, Brian,' said Pringle, emphatically. 'Two could be coincidence, three looks like conspiracy. I think we should try to have this guy suspended while we check back through his time at the hospital.'

'Just hold on there,' McIlhenney exploded. 'This man's in charge of my wife's treatment. She has confidence in him, and she's making good progress; take him out of it and God knows what could happen.'

'If he's killing people,' the gruff superintendent countered, 'he needs to be taken out.'

'Killing them! He's doing his fucking best to save their lives, you fucking idiot!' Neil was on his feet, looming over Pringle. The divisional CID head was a formidable man in his own right, but wisely he stayed glued to his seat and looked across the desk in an appeal for help.

'Easy, sergeant, easy,' said Skinner, gently. He stood and took his assistant by the arm, pulling him gently towards the door. 'Come on, let's you and I step into the corridor for a bit.' McIlhenney was still shaking with rage and tension, but he nodded and followed him outside.

'Just calm down now; get a hold of yourself,' said the DCC, when they were alone. 'Superintendent Pringle doesn't exactly wear jackboots, but he's old school nonetheless. You know that. Christ, you should; you're a younger version of him. If you weren't so involved in this personally, you'd probably have agreed with him.'

McIlhenney leaned back against the wall, his eyes closed, breathing slowly to steady himself. 'Maybe before, boss,' he said hoarsely, 'but not now. Not now.' As he finished speaking, his voice cracked, his chin dropped on to his chest, and he started to sob, helplessly. As Skinner looked at him, he thought that it was one of the most shocking things he had ever seen, and one of the saddest.

'Neil, let's go along to your office.' He took the burly, thickset man by the elbow and led him the short distance along the corridor to his small room. 'Just sit in here by yourself, for as long as you need.'

'I'm sorry, boss, for losing it,' the sergeant whispered, beginning to recover himself. 'It's just so fucking hard to handle, that's all.'

'I know, pal. I know. Listen, don't worry about what Dan said back there. That's not going to happen. We're going to have to look into this, you know that, but it'll be done very carefully, and no one will rush into anything. I promise you that. You just stay here for a bit, now.'

McIlhenney nodded. 'Yes, sir. Give my apologies to Mr Pringle, will you.'

'Like hell I will,' the DCC retorted. 'He *was* being a fucking idiot.'

He closed the door on his assistant and returned to his own office. He looked at Pringle as he resumed his seat beside the window. 'Brain first, mouth second, Dan.'

'Aye, sir, I'm sorry, I wasnae thinking at all.'

'Okay, let me do some of that for you. Brian, when you saw Nolan Weston, you mentioned the name Deacey, didn't you?'

'Yes, sir, we did. He didn't react at all.' He pursed his lips for a second, then added, slowly. 'And they're pretty close colleagues, so—'

'Exactly: the name must have meant something to him. Before you do anything else, I want you to re-interview him, and find out what he can tell you about Deacey Simmers.' He glanced at Pringle again, with a faint smile. 'But gently, Dan, okay?'

'Don't worry, sir,' the superintendent replied. 'I'll kiss his you know what, if I have to.' He paused.

'Going on from what Brian was saying, there's another thing someone didn't say that might be significant. When the boy Steele and I interviewed Simmers, up at the hospital, he never once asked us what we were on about. A detective superintendent and a sergeant turn up to ask him about the death of one of his patients, yet he didn't ask us why. In the light of everything, boss, does that no' strike you as odd?'

Skinner frowned. 'I wish I could say no, for Olive and Neil's sakes, but I have to agree with you; it certainly does.'

84

'Of course I know who Deacey is, Superintendent Mackie. When you asked for this meeting at my home rather than in my office at the Western, I guessed that you'd worked it out too.'

Nolan Weston smiled softly across the conservatory at the two detectives. The last of autumn had gone from the garden outside, save for a few wet, brown leaves which clung on to the skeletal branches of the trees.

'So why didn't you save us the trouble of finding out?' asked Pringle. He was about to add, 'After all, this is a fucking murder inquiry!' until, just in time he remembered his promise to Skinner.

The surgeon's expression changed in an instant to one of contrition. *How controlled he is*, thought Mackie. *How much tougher than Simmers.*

'I can only say I'm sorry about that. I'm afraid that at the time I decided that the tragedy of Gaynor's death had touched enough of us, and that I would keep it away from Deacey's door.'

'Did it occur to you that Mr Simmers might be that "third arrow" your wife mentioned?' the younger detective asked.

'Not for a moment, or I doubt if I'd have brought it up. We go back a long way, Deacey, Gaynor and I. We were at university together, a typical triumvirate of friends. Gay and I got engaged when we graduated, and married shortly afterwards; Deacey went off to England to do his internship, then he did some post-grad study in an oncology centre in Canada.

'We didn't have any contact, apart from Christmas cards, until he was appointed a consultant at the Western General.'

'Were you surprised by the idea that your former wife and Mr Simmers might be having a relationship?'

'You still haven't shown me that they were, superintendent. If that was the case then yes, I'd be mildly surprised. Yes, they were great friends as students, but their relationship was always on that level. Deacey and I weren't rivals for her hand, or anything like that.

'However I suppose they might have been having an affair; if they were it'd have been entirely their own business, since they were both

255

single. But if you were to ask me, I'd say that it was more likely that Deacey would be someone she'd turn to in time of need.'

'To help her end her life?' Pringle asked, in a voice which was for him, surprisingly soft.

Professor Weston frowned and rubbed the top of his bald head, anxiously. 'No, no, no: that wasn't what I was implying at all. Deacey Simmers is a very special man; he's a great friend in time of crisis. He is also a very gifted physician. She may well have gone to him for a second opinion, before deciding on her course of action.'

'Wouldn't he have needed your case notes if she had done that?'

'If Gay had described the situation as I explained it to her, and considering that I was involved, he wouldn't have needed them. There was no alternative prognosis.'

'In your opinion,' asked Mackie, 'once Mrs Weston had decided on her course of action, as you put it, might Mr Simmers have been so good a friend that he decided to help her through with it?'

Nolan Weston looked him in the eye. 'Ever heard of the Hippocratic Oath, superintendent?'

'Yes, but that's not an answer.'

'It's the only one I could possibly give you. I can only examine my own conscience, no one else's. I've already told you what I believe I would have done if she had come to me.'

'When we saw Raymond at your house, he denied any knowledge of the name Deacey. Was he lying to us?'

'No. I doubt if they've ever met.' He frowned at Mackie. 'Look, go easy on my son, gentlemen, please. He told me about his interview with you, about the cannabis and the sedatives which he took from my personal supply. I hold myself responsible for that to an extent. While Avril's been pregnant I've been taking them to help me sleep. I mentioned that to Ray, and he did something very stupid as a result. I assure you that will not happen again.'

He smiled. 'I hope I don't have the same problems with my new son. Avril had a boy, three days ago.'

'Congratulations,' said Pringle.

'Thank you. Raymond told me about Andrina's uncle also,' Weston continued. 'I can understand why you made the connection between his suicide and Gay's death.'

'Not suicide. There might be a legal grey area in Mr Murray's case, but as far as we're concerned they're the same, and the same person was involved in both. Did your boy tell you anything else about the chat he and I had?'

'He told me about the other young lady, if that's what you mean. I didn't approve of his treating Andrina that way, but then, I'm not really in a position to throw stones, am I? He didn't tell me who the other girl was, only that she was a friend of Gina, my niece.'

'Professor.' Mackie's tone was sharper than before. 'Have you ever discussed the substance of our first conversation with Mr Simmers?'

Weston nodded. 'I told him about it.'

'And did you tell him about the hypo and the roll of tape being removed from the scene?'

'Yes. I believe I did.'

'Well do us all a favour,' said the superintendent, heavily, 'yourself in particular. Don't talk to him about this one. Okay?'

85

'What's the betting Weston's called him?'

'Not a chance, Dan,' Mackie exclaimed. 'The boy didn't mention Alex's name, even to his father, after your talk with him. The Prof got the same sort of message: he'll have understood it all right.'

This time, Deacey Simmers was waiting for the two policemen in his little office. 'Two superintendents this time,' he exclaimed as he greeted them. 'Your investigation must be in trouble.'

'It was, Mr Simmers,' said Pringle, easing himself into a tight-fitting chair, 'until we got lucky. We were looking for this bloke Deacey, see; then we found that we had interviewed him and didn't even know it. See the surprises this job throws up from time to time!

'So, Deacey, tell us about Gaynor Weston. Were you and she having an affair?'

Simmers leaned back in his seat, and looked back at the super-intendent. Neither man was smiling. 'I should have asked you this at out first meeting, Mr Pringle. What is all this about?'

Fuck that, thought Pringle. *Me Tarzan, you Jane. I ask, you answer.* Then, as it had earlier, Bob Skinner's face appeared before his mind's eye. 'In due course, sir,' he said, politely. 'But first, we have to ask you about your relationship with the late Mrs Weston. You did know her, sir, didn't you? You are the Deacey she referred to in her social diary, aren't you?'

'Yes, superintendent, I am.'

'So I ask again, were you and she having an affair?'

'Really, Mr Pringle, is that relevant?'

'Possibly, sir. Answer, please.'

'The word "affair" in the context in which you are using it implies something illicit. That was not the case as far as Gay and I were concerned. We had known each other for many years, from our schooldays in fact: I was at Daniel Stewart's and she was at Mary Erskine. Then we went up to University together. I found myself on the same course as Nolan Weston; he and Gay met and fell in love.'

'Did this upset you?'

'Frankly, it did, for a while at least. Gay and I had had a little fling by that time, but when Nolan came on the scene that was that. I got over it though, and the three of us stayed pals. After we all qualified, I went off to extend my studies. Gay and Nolan got married and had a son, so that tied them to Edinburgh. It didn't hold him back though. His career developed very well indeed. When I was appointed to my present post eight years or so ago, I found that he and I were colleagues.'

'Did you meet up with Mrs Weston again at that time?'

'I saw her at a couple of parties. About a year after I arrived here, she and Nolan split up.'

'That had nothing to do with you, had it?'

Simmers glared at Pringle, bridling. 'Certainly not,' he snapped.

'So when was your relationship with Mrs Weston renewed?' asked Mackie.

'Not that long ago, actually. After the divorce, she and I would speak occasionally by telephone, me calling her mostly to make sure she was all right. I think we probably met about three times in six years, once accidentally in the street, and the other occasions by arrangement for a drink. During most of that period I was in a relationship myself, so there was no question of us dating as such.

'Then maybe around nine months ago, Gay called me and invited me to Oldbarns for dinner. I went out there expecting a party, but it was just the two of us. We talked for longer than we had since our student days. In fact, we hadn't spent that length of time alone together in over twenty years.'

'Did she say why she'd called you like that, out of the blue?'

Simmers shook his head. 'No, she didn't, but I suspected that there was some sort of crisis in her life. She talked about Nolan and their continuing relationship, which I didn't really want to hear, to tell you the truth, since I know Avril very well and like her very much. And she spoke of this ad-man Futcher, which I didn't approve of either for similar reasons.'

'Because he was married?'

'Exactly. For all that though, and although she denied it, I sensed that she was troubled. At the end of the evening . . . to answer your original question, Mr Pringle . . . she said, "Come on Deacey, let's go to bed. Maybe you're the one after all." So we slept together, for the first time since the end of our schooldays.

'After that, we saw each other, oh, maybe once a month. On occasion we'd go to the opera, or the theatre, but usually, I'd go out to Oldbarns, we'd have dinner, and I'd stay the night. Always, though, there was this thing that I felt hovering over us. At the time, I hoped that it meant she was thinking about putting an end to her other relationships. Now, of course, I'm convinced that she was worried about the developing growth on her leg.'

'Didn't you ever notice it?'

'No. She always wore jeans when we were together.'

'Not always,' said Mackie, quietly.

'She would only ever get undressed in the dark, superintendent. Surprisingly for such a strong personality, she was slightly shy. I remember that about her from when we were youngsters.' He sighed. 'Yes, even then.

'The last time we had breakfast together, I asked her to marry me. She said that I should ask her again in three months.'

'And that was the last time you saw her?'

'Yes,' he said, firmly.

'And when was the last time you saw Anthony Murray?' asked Pringle.

The consultant frowned at him. 'Two days before he died.'

'And Nicola Marston?'

'Nicola . . .'

'A patient of yours from three years ago.'

'Yes, I remember her. When you have people's lives in your hands, man, you never forget them. The last time I saw her would be at our last consultation in DCO, when I had to tell her that her condition was terminal.'

Simmers looked back at Mackie. 'Look, please tell me what this is about. Otherwise, this interview is at an end.'

'Two patients and a lover, sir, all apparent suicides, with injection involved. The only three such suicides in this part of Scotland in the last three years. And you are the only common factor.'

'Are you accusing me?'

'No, sir, we are not. Not yet, at any rate. If you would give us a sample of your saliva, it might help to eliminate you altogether.'

'In that case,' said Deacey Simmers, 'hold on, while I find a swab.'

'We'll have to be present when you take the sample, sir,' said Pringle.

'Why?'

The detective's diplomacy reserve was totally depleted. 'Because however nice and chummy my colleague here might seem, we're both suspicious bastards. We have to make sure it's yours.'

86

Andy Martin looked around the converted gymnasium. All but one of the desks stood empty; the long table against the wall was heavy with row upon row of processed forms.

'Is that it, then, sergeant?' he asked.

'It is indeed, sir,' said Karen Neville. 'The last Parisian policeman; the last Japanese journalist, all thoroughly checked out and cleared for action. The supply of eagle badges for the armed officers is upstairs, ready for issue at the security briefing on Monday, although I've no idea how we ensure that everybody wears them.'

'We don't. It's up to the head of each security team to ensure that his people comply once they're issued. However the boss or I will tell them at the briefing that anyone found with a gun and without a badge will be arrested and locked up for the duration. Hopefully that'll get their attention.'

'What's left to do, now that the paperwork's cracked?'

'We have to check everybody's hotel accommodation, just to make sure that there's nothing ticking behind a bath panel, or in a toilet cistern, anywhere. Special Branch will co-ordinate that, but it'll be done by Major Legge's army team.

'The first delegations, or at least their advance guards, start to arrive on Saturday, so that leaves tomorrow and Friday to get it all done, and the accommodation sealed off.'

He glanced round the gym again. 'Everyone else has gone home, I take it.'

'Yes, sir, Mario left to pick up his wife around fifteen minutes ago. I've been waiting for clearance on a Dutch journo; it's just come though, so I'm off too.'

'Fancy a drink?' asked Martin. 'Or have you got a date?'

Karen was taken by surprise. 'I'm washing my hair tonight, sir – as we ladies say – so I'm okay for a quick drink. Yes, that would be nice. Where do you want to go?'

'How about O'Neill's on the South Bridge? That's not far from where you live.'

'Fine. I can leave my car in Chambers Street overnight. It's close enough to home.'

They drove in convoy across town, Karen leading the way. As she had guessed, parking was easy in the wide street so late in the day, and they found adjoining bays. For once, the skies were clear, and the night was cold and crisp as they walked the short distance to the bar, one of several with an Irish theme to have sprung up in the capital.

As the burly, red-haired barman poured a pint of lager and a gin and tonic, Karen found a table in the corner. Martin set the drinks down and sat facing her.

'So,' he began, awkwardly. 'How have you liked Special Branch?'

'Very much.' She looked at him as he picked up his beer. She had heard from colleagues that the Head of CID had been a legendary ladies' man in the days before his engagement; but as he sipped his pint she found it hard to believe. He seemed shy, diffident and strangely insecure, by comparison with the powerful, assertive figure which he cut in the office.

'D'you want to stay there?'

His question took her by surprise, and worried her for a moment or two. 'Only if you're kicking me out of your office,' she answered, cautiously. 'I prefer it there.'

He smiled at her: a quick, dazzling, engaging smile, backed up by a sudden sparkle in his green eyes, and in that moment she understood how the legend had come about. 'That's good,' he said, sombre once more. 'I hoped you'd say that, but I thought I should ask. Mario would have you in a minute.'

'It's nice to be popular. Mind you,' she added, 'I thought I was in everyone's bad books a few weeks back.'

'When you dated your Australian suspect, you mean? Yeah, at first, you probably were, but when I heard the full story from Mario, I saw that you were right. It was a means of keeping contact so you took it. You made a professional judgement, and I'll always back that.' He took another mouthful.

'Things still okay on that front?' he asked.

She grinned back at him. 'Down Under, you mean, sport? Yes thanks, we're getting along. It's not the most orthodox relationship I've ever had, with him nurse-maiding a wheelchair case, but it has its moments.'

'What happens when he has to go home?'

'He goes back to his oil rig. It's off Western Australia, but that's just another piece of ocean as far as Wayne's concerned. He says he'll give up his flat in Perth, and register my place as his home address.

262

That way the company will pick up the cost of his travel back here every time he has home leave.'

'Good thinking, Ms Neville. What does he do on his rig?'

'He's the drill-master. An important guy: makes a bloody fortune so he tells me.'

'That's even better. You've landed on your feet in every respect; I'm happy for you.'

She nodded. 'Thanks. I just wish I could say the same to you. I'm sorry about your break-up.'

He winced. 'So am I,' he said, hesitating before adding, 'but better here than down the road a piece, as they say.'

'You'll still be friends, though, won't you?'

'We'll never be enemies,' he answered. 'Let's put it that way. But we can't go back to how it was before, when she was just my best friend's daughter. Some cuts go too deep.'

'And is he still your best friend?' she asked, quietly.

'Bob's been great. After I told him about it, he invited me down to Gullane and the pair of us went to the pub and had a few beers . . . no, a right few beers. It was his way of telling me that some things will never change.'

87

Neil McIlhenney's in-tray was empty; he had worked his way through the papers which the DCC had referred to him for action or comment. He had finished an analysis of the relative clear-up rates, category by category, by each of the CID divisions. As he waited for Skinner's Monday morning summons he sat hunched over the desk in his small office, staring out of the window.

He had done a lot of staring, out of many windows, over the last couple of months, he realised. Almost invariably he thought of sunny days to come, of he and Olive, Lauren and Spence, enjoying a normal lifestyle once again. No decisions were being forced upon them by the education authority, but Olive knew that even if she won complete remission from her illness, her classroom days were over.

They had discussed the respective merits of her accepting an offer to switch to the expanding quality control side of education, or of her resigning and setting up in business as a designer of computer-based teaching packages. Whichever option they chose, Neil understood that in reality it was another target to be pursued, another piece of the scaffolding which underpinned his wife's tremendous determination to beat her enemy.

Deacey Simmers was the most important part of that support structure. And Neil knew exactly why Bob Skinner had excluded him from his meeting that morning with Brian Mackie and that tactless bampot Dan Pringle: it was because Simmers was the only item on the agenda. As he stared out into the crisp winter morning, he could picture the three of them grouped around the DCC's desk, the big man doing his trick of watching the driveway, seemingly far away, while absorbing every word that was being said to him.

He was expecting it, but when the phone on his desk buzzed twice, he jumped nonetheless. He knew the signal, so he let it lie unanswered, rising instead and walking out into the corridor, past Ruthie McConnell's rabbit-hutch, as she called it, to Skinner's office. The red light outside was shining, but he opened the door and stepped in. Pringle and Mackie had gone.

'Sit on the comfy ones,' his boss said, pointing to the informal seating in the corner as he filled two coffee mugs. 'I know, I know,' he muttered as he poured, 'must cut down on his tar, but what's the alternative. Tea? A right poofter's drink that.'

McIlhenney slumped into one of the low chairs, took two coasters from a container and tossed them onto the rosewood table to protect it from the heat. 'Meeting go all right, sir?' He tried to sound casual, but failed.

'You won't think so, I'm afraid,' Skinner replied, quietly, as he set down the two coffees. 'Dan and Brian brought their lab results with them. Simmers' saliva swab matches the trace that Arthur Dorward's lot found on a glass at the scene of Gaynor Weston's death. Also, his prints were on the envelope of the letter Gaynor sent to her son.

'When the lads interviewed him last week, he admitted to them that he and she had been on intimate terms, let's say. But he said that the last time he saw her was more than two weeks before her death. On top of that, it turns out that he was a near neighbour of the man Murray, and called in on him quite regularly.

'I can't take that lightly, Neil. It looks bad for your friend.'

'Shit!' McIlhenney hissed, his mouth tight set. 'Still, boss, if he twigged the position he might be in, we can allow him one wee lie, can't we?'

'He still has to be asked about it, though. Mackie and Pringle have asked me to allow them to pick him up for a formal interview,' Skinner continued. 'They also want a warrant to search his house and his office for traces of diamorphine, and any other incriminating material. Inevitably the hospital will have to know that he's under investigation in connection with the deaths of two patients – there's no evidence left in the Bathgate case.

'You know what that will mean.'

'Sure. Even if we don't charge him straight away, he'll be suspended.'

'Right. But I have to tell you this; on the basis of the evidence I have before me, his loving relationship with the dead woman, his presence in her house that night, his ready access to Anthony Murray; with all that allied to his professional skills, all my training and experience makes me believe, objectively, that he's guilty.'

The DCC looked at his assistant, almost helplessly. 'Neil,' he asked. 'In my place, faced with all this what would you do?'

McIlhenney smiled. 'Boss, you were right about me. I'm out of the same mould as Superintendent Pringle. If this was just an ordinary case and I was on it, the suspect would be sitting in St Leonard's right now, with a tape running and me shouting in his fucking ear.

'But it isn't an ordinary case. And my wife's life is at stake here, so don't ask me for objectivity.'

The big sergeant looked his boss in the eye. 'I've been thinking about this for the last week, boss, since Deacey's name came up in this thing, and I can tell you it's bloody complex. It seems to me that you're telling me that you see him as a man who believes that he can exercise power over life and death, and square it with his conscience.'

Skinner frowned, then nodded. 'I suppose I am,' he agreed.

'Well I have to tell you . . . and I have hellish difficulty saying it, because it makes me face up to something I'd rather avoid . . . but Deacey Simmers' greatest pain comes from the knowledge that he doesn't have that power.

'People in his care, people like Olive and me, we sit in his room and we listen to his words. They come in perfect order; words like inoperable, incurable, palliative and so on. We're literate; *objectively* we know what they mean. But *subjectively*, that's another matter. They're very precise those words, yet no way do they apply to Olive.

'Even now as I sit here, I will not admit to you or anyone else . . . and most of all I will not admit to me . . . that she's going to die. Deacey Simmers, though; from the outset he's told us that her disease indicates that she is. He's laid those words out for us. Then he's said; "Okay, now these are the treatments I have to offer. You will have them; then what happens is up to you and up to fate."

'Deacey is a caring person, an inspiring person, and he's totally helpless in the face of many of the cases that are sent to him. Everyone who goes into his room gets the plain unvarnished truth, and yet he manages to send people out of there with feelings of determination, and flowing from that, hope against hope. He will never slam the door on anyone.

'If you're saying that this man imagines that he has life-determining power and that he interprets that as allowing him to put people to sleep, then with the greatest respect, boss, and for the first and last time in my life, I have to tell you that you're talking bollocks.

'Deacey knows better that anyone that for my Olive, and all the others like her, his treatments have the same chance of success as a snowball has of putting out a furnace. Yet even in the absence of that power which you say he's perverting, he gives us something; a sense of purpose which makes our situation bearable. He helps us to focus on that one chance in twenty.

'No way did he kill Gay Weston or anyone else. I'll tell you this too. Behind that calm façade of his he's lonely and fragile, and I get the feeling that sometimes he's overcome by what he does; yet he carries on, and that's what makes him what he is: a great man.

'You let those two arrest him, boss, let the Fiscal charge him, and I'll promise you this. When he comes to trial I'll go into the witness box and give evidence in his support, even it I have to leave the force to do it.'

Skinner reached out and put a hand on his assistant's shoulder. 'Neil, if it comes to it, you can speak for him with my public blessing. But let's see if we can avoid that.

'It seems as if all of my best people have had a finger in this investigation at some time or another . . . except for you. The papers in these two cases are on my desk; take them away with you and see if you can come up with another suspect. I've told Dan and Brian to sit on their hands for another week. That's how long you've got.

'Maybe you'll turn out to be as important to Mr Simmers as he is to you.'

88

There are those who believe that the Edinburgh International Conference Centre is one of the finest pieces of late twentieth century architecture in Scotland. There are others who believe that the great drum-shaped building is a blight on the skyline of the capital city. Andy Martin did not regard himself as a philistine, yet he was a confirmed subscriber to the latter view.

A constable in uniform checked the Head of CID's warrant card as he pulled up at the car park entrance, looking at it studiously before waving him on. He knew the chief superintendent well enough, but ACC Elder was on the prowl and he had no wish to start the week badly.

Martin strode out of the car park and into the Centre. In the foyer area twin lines had formed as the delegates queued to have their briefcases searched and to pass through the metal detector gateways. The policeman walked past the lines and round the barrier. He was not carrying a firearm, but nevertheless he wore a gold eagle badge as a short-cut into the hall, since everyone without one was subject to the security check.

Mario McGuire stood at the wide doorway of the main auditorium, looking across its expanse. 'Morning sir,' he called out. 'Come for a look at the sardine tin, have you? God alone knows how they managed it, but they did. We've got thirty-six delegations crammed in here.'

'What's today's programme?' asked Martin.

'Officials only; finalising the agenda and order of speakers for when the big boys get here.'

'Are the delegations limited in size?'

'Yes, the class two nations, judged by GDP, can have four delegates in the hall at any one time; class one nations are allowed eight.'

'Has the seating plan worked out all right?'

The inspector flashed a smile. 'They managed to do it alphabetically, just,' he said. 'I wouldn't fancy being one of the Irish delegation though. They're the meat in the sandwich between Iran and Israel.'

'That's okay,' Martin grunted. 'My granny's Irish. Once that lot start talking the rest won't get a word in. Any other awkward neighbours?'

'I don't know how the Russians and the Saudis are going to get on.'

'No problem, the Russians will be on their best behaviour ... otherwise the Saudis might not buy them lunch.'

'Then there's the UK and the US.'

'We're still on buddy terms, I believe. Cigars aren't allowed in the hall, are they?'

McGuire looked at him. 'You're in a chirpy mood today, sir.'

The Head of CID grinned. 'I had a drink with Karen Neville the other night. It did me good; it made me realise that if I go around being a miserable bastard all the time the only person who'll be the worse for it will be me. So I'm trying to find the old Andy again. He's around somewhere; I spent the weekend going through my address book looking for him.'

'D'you not fancy the boss's secretary?'

'Ruthie McConnell? Don't we all? She's living with someone, though.'

The Special Branch commander shook his head. 'Not any more. Karen says she's chucked him. She's plugged into all the gossip, is that one.'

'I'll bear that in mind. About Karen, I mean; I must be careful what I say around her. As for Ruthie, she's a bit too close to the Big Man for me ... in spite of those legs.'

McGuire shot him a sideways look. 'Listen, sir, take some man-to-man advice, will you: don't rebound too far in the other direction. The old Andy was always a bit of a myth, wasn't he?'

'A legend in his own bedtime, you mean? Aye, he was ...' He laughed. '... to an extent. Thanks Mario, I'll bear that in mind too.'

He glanced into the hall once more, and pointed to a wheelchair-bound figure to the left of centre of the seated area. 'I take it that's Karen's boyfriend's pal.'

'Dennis Crombie? Aye, that's him; a dour bugger he is too.'

'So would you be if you had to be lifted on and off the crapper all the time. Is the Wayne fellow around?'

'He was here earlier, when he brought Dennis in. He's probably gone for a coffee. It's about that time.'

'Not with Neville, I hope. Not here.'

'I doubt it. She's on duty frisking the female delegates.'

Andy Martin's grin seemed to McGuire like a throwback. 'I think I'll go and help her,' he said.

89

'What have you got there?' asked Olive.

Neil, hunched over the dining table, looked over his shoulder at her. 'Work. I shouldn't have brought it home. Sorry.'

'What is it?'

'Och, it's just the files on an investigation that the boss has asked me to take a look at. It's stalled, and he wants a different perspective on it.'

'Let me see,' she said, pushing herself slowly from her chair and coming over to him. He watched her as she walked. She was pale, and her movements betrayed her weakness, but there was a vitality in her eyes which seemed unquenchable.

'No,' he answered, closing the folder. 'You don't let me look at your school stuff.'

'No, because you're not qualified, and because children's futures might be affected if I allowed myself to be swayed by something you said.'

'Same here,' he countered, rising from the table, turning her . . . how much more easily he could do that now . . . and taking her back to the comfortable chairs in front of the television. 'This is a murder investigation – three actually – and someone could go to the slammer for life if I let you see those files, then was influenced by your half-arsed analysis.'

'Thank you very much. Since you've been the DCC's exec, you're getting too big for your trainers, McIlhenney.' *But not as big as he used to be. He must have lost over ten pounds since this thing started,* she thought. 'I'll tell you what, let's just discuss it hypothetically, no names involved; you just describe the situation and I'll tell you what I think.'

'Okay, Miss Marple; anything for a quiet life. As long as you go to bed afterwards. You look tired.'

'Must be these platelets that Suzanne's been going on about. She says that they're going to put some more into me tomorrow, once I've had my scan. You still all right to drop me off?'

'Of course. And pick you up afterwards.'

270

'Good. Now tell me about your problem.'

He sighed. 'Wouldn't you rather watch *Taggart*?'

'What? That rubbish. No way; the real stuff's much more interesting. Go on.'

'Okay; hypothetical though. Three deaths, the first three years ago, never investigated at the time, the second and third fairly recent. There's one thread that ties them all together: an individual, who's a strong suspect for the second, and who lives in the vicinity of the third.'

'What about the first?'

'That's a fairly tenuous link. That death may well have been straightforward misadventure, with no one else involved. That's how it was treated at the time.'

'Misadventure? What do you mean by that?'

'I mean suicide.'

'Well don't mislead me. Now why is this person such a strong suspect for the second murder?'

'Because he had a physical relationship with the victim, was at the scene, on the night, and he kept quiet about the fact when he was interviewed by Pringle and Mackie.'

'Two superintendents,' Olive murmured. 'Serious stuff this. What about the third case? What's the connection there?'

'The guy lived near the victim.'

'So did thousands of other people, I assume. There has to be more than that. What is the link between all three cases? Was the man related to all three victims?'

'No.'

'Then what is it? Were they all Masons, or something?'

'No. The link was professional.'

'He was their lawyer?'

'No.'

'Doctor?'

Neil felt the water growing deeper by the minute. 'Yes. He treated all three people.'

She seemed to withdraw from him for a few moments, as she thought. It was a trait he knew well. 'Did he benefit from the deaths?' she asked him.

'No. They did, in fact.'

'These people were dying, Neil, weren't they.'

'Yes. Look, can we stop the Twenty Questions now.'

'Like hell. They all had cancer, hadn't they.'

'Okay, Yes they had. They were all terminally ill, and they all appeared to commit suicide, but in at least two of the cases the second and third, we know they had help. Someone else was there, and played a part.'

Olive fixed her husband with that Look. 'There's nothing hypothetical about this, Neil. You're not describing a stalled investigation. You're talking about one that's bloody well solved, aren't you. You're not casting a fresh eye over this, you're looking for an alternative.'

'Don't be daft. I'm a bloody DS: it's not for me to walk all over an investigation that's been signed off by two superintendents.'

'Exactly,' she snapped. 'so why are you looking over these papers, and why are you quite clearly, so bloody anxious about it? This doctor: it's someone we know, isn't it.'

He leaned back, beaten, and gazed at her. He should have known better than to give her the opening, than to let that mind of hers loose on the problem. 'Aye,' he said. 'It's Deacey Simmers. The guys want to lift him, and I've got a week to show them why they shouldn't.

'Oh Christ, love; I wish I'd never brought those papers home.'

'Suppose you hadn't; I'd still have known that something was bothering you, and I'd have had it out of you.' She paused. 'Listen, understand this, and maybe it'll help. One thing I've learned from that man: in fighting this thing, the most important people to me are me, you, Lauren and Spencer. Deacey's a doctor, Neil, not a faith healer. He's shown me the road to remission and started me on it, but he isn't leading me. I'm finding my own way, with long life, you and the kids waiting for me at the end.

'That said, I don't believe he's a Doctor Goodnight any more than you do. He didn't help these people to die: so who did? Could it be an organisation?'

He shook his head. 'No. There aren't any of those; not any more. This is an individual, and it's someone that Gay Weston and Anthony Murray knew and trusted. The problem is that everyone else has been eliminated: we're only left with Deacey, and he's done nothing to help himself.

'They've placed him at the Weston house on the night, and they've found a book at Murray's place, signed "Best wishes, Deacey", a book which was only in the shops in the two weeks before he died. He doesn't know any of this yet; it'll all be put to him next Monday, when he's re-interviewed.

'He can say what he likes, but unless he can prove categorically that he was somewhere else at the moment of Mrs Weston's death, he's done for that one. Murray, maybe not; but what's in that file will convince any jury that he helped his girlfriend on her way.

'The only thing that will help him is me finding the person who did.'

272

'Is there another link between Weston and Murray?'

'There was, but not any more. That's been eliminated.'

'Then what about the third case, the one three years ago?'

'No. there's nothing else connecting all three. I've been through the Fiscal's report on Nicola Marston; there's sod all in it.'

'Okay, but suppose there was something else linking her to either one of the other two people. Would that help?'

He gazed at the fireplace, pondering her question. 'Maybe yes, maybe no: it'd be a place to start, though, I'll give you that. But where will I find it? There's no evidence other than that suicide report over there, and it takes me nowhere.'

'What about her case notes?'

'What d'you mean?'

'If she was a patient at the Western General as you say, then there must be a fair chance that they'll still have a file on her.'

Neil smiled. 'Maybe you should come to work for us once you leave teaching,' he said. 'I'll see what I can find. I don't hold out much hope, mind, but at least it's somewhere else to look.

'Now, climb your weary way to bed. Big day tomorrow, for us both . . . and who knows, maybe for Deacey too.'

90

'I'm on reasonably good terms with the Chief Executive of the hospital NHS Trust, Neil. I suppose he's got the authority to let you look at the notes on Nicola Marston, although you might have to go along to the Western to do it. I'll call him when I get back from the EICC, I promise.'

'Thanks, sir,' said McIlhenney, sincerely. 'I doubt very much whether there'll be anything in it, but it's something to do, truth be told; easier than going out and re-interviewing all of Gay Weston's neighbours.'

'Mmm. I don't think I want you to do that, unless you've got something specific in mind. I'm not going to tie your hands, but I want you to tell me before you talk to witnesses.'

'Fair enough, boss.'

'Right; I'll speak to you later, but now I'd better put in an appearance up at the EICC.' Skinner glanced out of his office window. 'That looks like my driver.' He pushed himself from his chair and headed for the door.

The city centre morning traffic was minimal, most drivers having been directed to temporary Park and Ride areas under ACC Jim Elder's policing plan, and so a fifteen-minute journey took five.

Andy Martin was in the foyer area which was brightly lit by the high glass front of the building, when he arrived just before ten o'clock. 'All well?' the DCC asked.

'If you fancy the Tower of Babel as a working environment,' his friend chuckled, 'it's fine. All the security people are happy with our arrangements: that's the main thing as far as I'm concerned.'

'This is the last preliminary session, yes?'

'That's right: all the procedural stuff should be agreed this morning. The Heads of Government and finance ministers start to check into their accommodation this afternoon, ready for the formal opening by the Prime Minister and Bruce Anderson tomorrow at nine sharp. You want to see the set-up?'

'Yes, let's take a look at it.'

As they walked past the barrier one of the private sector security guards stepped forward to intercept the DCC, but Martin stopped him in his tracks with a quick shake of his head. 'Have all these blokes been vetted?' Skinner asked.

'Thoroughly. Twice in fact; by their employer before they were hired, then again by us.'

'That's good. I remember once turning up at a function in Glasgow and finding on the door a guy in uniform that I'd lifted for assault and robbery a few years before.'

The two police officers stepped out into the auditorium. The staging was complete, state-of-the art and impressive; the Union, UN and Council of Europe flags were set, vertically on a background of very pale blue, with, to their right, a giant video screen, on which was displayed the delegate who at that moment, occupied the speaker's rostrum. It, and a small Chairman's table, were the only furnishings on the stage.

'So the presidents and the prime ministers won't be up there,' the DCC murmured.

'No. There are too many. Our PM's in the chair for the main sessions, but the others will be seated with their delegations, unless they're performing.'

'Who'll get to speak?'

'All the big guns, in the course of the conference. The Russian and Chinese Presidents are the main speakers tomorrow, on Thursday the new German Chancellor and the head of the European Commission are the headliners, and on Friday, it's the US president and our guy. He's winding it up.'

Skinner looked around the hall. 'Let's hope they achieve something, otherwise the cost of this would have been better spent feeding the poor. Look at it all, the bloody window-dressing, our cost, the travel and hotel bills. Bloody frightening when you add it up.'

'Hello sergeant,' he said suddenly as Karen Neville stepped past him, escorting a woman delegate into the hall.

'Good morning, sir,' she replied, carrying on down the centre aisle and directing her charge to the seating area allocated to New Zealand.

'Everything okay?' Skinner asked, amiably, as she returned.

'No problems at all, sir.'

The DCC grinned. 'Is the boyfriend here then?'

'That's him there, sir.' She pointed to a tall, brown-haired bearded man who was walking back towards the main doorway from the direction of the left hand aisle. 'I'm not supposed to talk to him on duty, though.'

'I'll make an exception. Introduce us, why don't you.'

'Okay.' She waved at the Australian, beckoning him across. 'Wayne, come here. Someone wants to meet you. DCC Skinner,' she said as he approached, 'this is Wayne Ventnor.'

'How do you do, sir,' said the newcomer as the two shook hands. 'I've heard a lot about you just lately.'

'About this man too,' Karen added. 'This is my immediate boss, DCS Martin.'

'Hi Wayne,' exclaimed the Head of CID. 'Good to put a face to the name at last. Maybe we'll see you at the office Christmas piss-up if you're still here.'

'It's a deal, mate,' Ventnor replied, enthusiastically. 'I'm a real national stereotype; piss-ups are my speciality.'

'You're going to love it here, then. Have you been dropping off your friend?'

'Yeah. That's me free till lunchtime. I think I'll spend the time taking a look at this new museum of yours. Karen's turning me into a real Scotophile.' He nodded. 'So long, gentlemen; nice to meet you both. So long, gal, I'll see you tonight, yeah?'

'All things being equal,' she answered. 'About nine, as usual, once SB's turned in.'

Skinner frowned as the Australian walked away. 'SB, Karen?' he said, sternly. 'We don't talk about that to outsiders.'

'No, sir,' she replied, hurriedly. 'I didn't mean Special Branch. SB's short for Sleeping Beauty. It's what we call Dennis. Wayne helps him to bed around nine, and then we go out.'

The DCC smiled. 'Ah, I see. For a minute there I thought you were turning into a security risk. On you go, then.'

She looked at him, relief written on her face, and headed back towards the foyer. Skinner's smile vanished as quickly as it had arrived.

'What's up with you?' asked Martin.

'I'm not sure she might not be a security risk after all,' he growled. 'There's something about that Aussie that's giving me a niggle. Maybe it's just the voice, maybe it's just that all these surf bums tend to look the same.

'It's probably nothing at all, and yet . . . I can't help feeling that I've seen that one somewhere before.'

91

'Here you are, sergeant, this is the one you're looking for.' Neil McIlhenney murmured his thanks to the hospital records clerk, a cheery little woman, and took the thick file from her.

Seating himself at a desk in the corner of the small office he looked at the green folder. Alongside 'Patient's Name', he saw 'Nicola Marston', and in the space marked 'Consultant', 'Mr Simmers'. The word 'Deceased' in heavy red lettering was stamped across the cover. Staring at it, he shivered for a moment, before he opened the history and began to read.

He saw at once that the file was in reverse date order, for the first document was a note which read, 'Patient's death reported by police. Postmortem shows death due to overdose of insulin.' The scrawled signature was only just legible. McIlhenney read it aloud: 'D Simmers'.

The detective had not intended to read the history page by page, yet he was unable to stop himself. He pored over each entry from the top down with an eye which was no longer that of a total layman, making his way backwards through the course of Nicola Marston's illness, studying the notes in each stage of her treatment.

Although the regime was far from identical to that which Olive was undergoing, there were some similarities, most notably the concern of Deacey Simmers and his Registrar for the side effects of their therapy on the patient's blood. Before he was half-way though the file he found himself identifying with Nicola Marston, sitting by her side at each consultation, feeling her pain and distress as she struggled through the inevitable, violent sickness which followed each chemical transfusion, imagining her pleasure as he happened upon positive indicators from her scans and X-rays.

All the while that he read, he recognised the danger to himself of exposure to such a story, but he forced that consideration to one side. This was not Olive, this was not Olive, he told himself. This was a woman who had given up.

Very few pages remained unread when he found the name. One that he had read in the police report on Anthony Murray: one that he knew.

He raced through the rest of the folder, closed it, then sat at the desk, his head in his hands, thinking hard. At last he nodded, a decision made: he took out his mobile phone and dialled Skinner's direct number.

'Yes,' came the snapped reply. The impatience in the normally steady voice took the sergeant by surprise. 'Boss?'

'Sorry, Neil,' said Skinner, at once. 'I've got something on my mind.'

'I won't keep you then, sir; but so have I. There's something in this report and I'd like to follow it up. To do that, I need to make one call, and I need to go and talk to someone.' He chuckled softly into the phone.

'I think I must have been working with you for too long, gaffer. I'm starting to get hunches!'

92

Sarah grinned. 'Of course we're pleased to see you Alex. It doesn't matter that there's European football on television tonight, does it Bob?'

'What? Oh sorry girls, I was miles away there. No, no, sod the football.'

His daughter laughed. 'You know what they say about the secret of life, Pops. It's sincerity: once you learn to fake that, you've cracked it. You still need to do some work in that area.'

'Seriously, I mean it. Anyway, it's only an English team. So what did bring you out here?'

Alex shook her head, rearranging her long dark curls on her shoulders, and fixed her big blue eyes on her father. 'A bonding trip, Pops. With my brothers and with you two.'

'I don't suppose for a minute that you wanted to ask me how Andy was getting along,' he said, idly. 'No, that would have nothing to do with it. Bonding, sure, that's it.'

'You, you . . .' she spluttered, then smiled, '. . . always could read me, couldn't you.'

'He's doing fine, kid. He had a couple of days of moping and chewing people out, but he seems to have pulled himself out of it. In fact, I didn't realise how much he'd changed in the time you two were engaged. The truth of the matter is, I reckon, that you were suffocating each other.'

'Do you think there's a chance,' Sarah began, tentatively, 'that once the two of you have had a chance to readjust, and to get your own personalities back, that you might get together again?'

'Not as much as a flicker, step-mother. Andy's very easy-going in some ways, but completely unbending in others.'

'So are you, kid,' Bob murmured.

'Maybe so, but my principles are consistent. Andy has a selective conscience, you know. He squares it with contraception, no problem, but as soon as one of his tadpoles goes astray, that's it, he might as well be wearing a pointy white hat and carrying a shepherd's crook. You should have seen him when I told him about my termination . . .'

'You still can't say abortion, can you.'

'Okay,' she shot back at him, her voice raised, 'have it your way; my abortion. He went berserk all because I'd exercised my rights over my body. Yet that same guy would put a bullet in someone's head tomorrow, if the need arose, then go out for a pint with the lads.'

'No,' said Sarah, intervening to calm her, 'I guess it doesn't look like there's a chance, does it. What about this boy Ray? Do you think you might see him again?'

Alex's smile returned in a flash. 'God no! He's got a brain the size of a pea; I was only ever after his body. No, I'm footloose again. Just like my ex. Seriously though, I'm glad to hear he's getting over it. He's not sniffing around that Neville woman, is he?'

Bob shook his head. 'No, he'll keep her at arms' length.'

'He'd have to with that chest of hers.'

'Yeah, it's as well I got her out of uniform; the tailors were having trouble. But really, Karen's not a factor. She's spoken for. And that's why I was preoccupied earlier, to tell you the truth. I still feel I should be able to place the guy.'

93

The woman took a while to open the door: it was understandable, McIlhenney realised, as soon as he saw her twisted, claw-like hands.

'Miss Ball,' he said. 'Good evening to you. I'm Sergeant McIlhenney: I phoned you earlier.'

'Yes, of course,' she replied. 'Come away through, I've been expecting you.' He followed her through an open doorway and found himself not in her sitting room as he had expected but in the kitchen.

'Before we begin, sergeant, can I ask you something I ask all my visitors? Would you please make us a nice pot of tea. I can manage a bag in a mug these days, but I do so much prefer it properly made.'

'So do I,' said the detective. 'Show me where the tea is and I'm your man.'

Five minutes later, he poured perfectly brewed Darjeeling into two china cups and placed them on a side table between his hostess's chair and his own. 'Well done,' she exclaimed. 'Now, I'm at your disposal. This is still about Gaynor, isn't it. I haven't read anything in the papers lately, so I suppose the mystery remains.'

'It does, Miss Ball. Now I've been asked to see if I can solve it.'

'So, how can I help?'

McIlhenney settled into his seat. 'When you were interviewed by DCI Rose, you mentioned that you have support from a disabled charity. Can you tell me which one it is?'

The woman nodded. 'Yes, of course, it's called Home Support. It's more than a disabled charity really; it looks after the continuing needs of people who've been through the hospital system.' McIlhenney felt the first small pulse of excitement run through him.

'When you have a visit, is it the same person who comes all the time?'

'It is, yes. We all have case officers.'

'Who looks after you?'

'A very nice lady called Penelope Clark.'

The sergeant managed to keep his expression unchanged. 'Can you remember if Gaynor ever met her?'

Joan Ball's eyes seemed to take on a knowing look, but her voice

281

remained even as she replied. 'Oh yes, of course she did. They were great pals. One of the first times Penelope visited me, Gaynor called in for something, and I introduced them. They hit it off and after that, whenever she visited me in the evening or at weekends, she'd go next door to say hello.'

'When was the last time you saw her?'

'Last week. Before that, a couple of months ago.'

'Would that have been during the time when Mrs Weston was at home? In the two weeks before she died?'

Joan Ball thought for a moment. 'Yes, it was.'

'Did she call on her?'

'Yes, she did. That time she came during the day, which was unusual for her – she normally does her rural visits out of hours, as it were. She noticed that Gaynor was in and popped in to see her.'

Both cups of tea were untouched and cooling. McIlhenney took them into the kitchen poured them down the sink, and poured a slightly stewed refill for Miss Ball. 'That's been very helpful,' he said, as he replaced the cup on the side table. 'I have to go now, but I may need to talk to you again. If I do, I'll call you.'

'No,' she said, sipping awkwardly. 'Come to see me. You make damn good tea.'

McIlhenney grinned. 'I'll try,' he promised. 'I'll let myself out.'

'If you would.' He had almost left the room when she spoke again.

'Very able woman, Penelope. Well qualified for her job too. She's a doctor, you know.'

94

'Hey look at this,' Brian Mackie called down from the bar, nodding towards the door. 'The Bomber is back.' Mario McGuire, Maggie Rose, Karen Neville and Stevie Steele all sitting looked round together to see the Head of CID heading towards them, dressed in a black leather jerkin and black denim jeans.

Neville and Steele looked at each other, puzzled. 'That used to be Andy's standard uniform for a night out in the pub,' Maggie explained. 'Bomber jacket and jeans. Until he went respectable, that is.'

'Mine's lager if you're on the bell, Thin Man,' Martin shouted to Mackie, over the noise of a dozen conversations, as he took one of the two vacant seats at one of the Abbotsford's big, rectangular tables.

'Glad you could all make it,' he said, as he looked around the booth. 'I thought about having a formal team briefing this afternoon, then I said to myself, "Shit, we all know what we've got to do anyway. We might as well get together in the pub." Thanks, Brian.' He drew his chair over a little to allow the superintendent more room for his long legs.

'You do all know, I take it,' he added quietly. 'Brian, you're top gun with the Secretary of State, along with Stevie. You're on station at the official residence in Charlotte Square at eight-thirty sharp, ready to escort him up to the Centre. The PM's leaving from there as well, by the way.

'Mario, Karen, you're with me in the auditorium as discussed, checking people in then watching the action. The boss will be floating about all over the place, keeping an eye on everything.' He smiled at Rose. 'Maggie, you're lucky. You're out of it.'

He leaned across the table, even though there was no one in earshot. 'I'm not expecting any bother tomorrow, not with all the firepower that's going to be in the hall, but I'm not having us go in naked either, so we'll all be wearing our wee gold eagle badges and carrying a friend inside our jackets.' He looked at Neville and Steele. 'Brian, Mario and I are all experienced cowboys. Are you two all right with that?' Both sergeants nodded, solemnly.

'That's fine, then.' He took a long pull at his pint. 'So if everyone's happy, we can enjoy a night out.' He grinned in Karen's direction. 'For those of you who haven't been near something this big before, let me tell you that the nerves, the tension you're feeling inside, they come with the territory. It doesn't matter how often the three of us have been to the well, we all feel just like you do. This wee get-together is to help us all chill out a bit.

'This is my favourite kind of team building, anyway; we say far more to each other here, when we can all put our ranks to one side, than we do when we're sat in our collars and ties round an office table. We haven't been doing nearly enough of it lately.'

'True,' Brian Mackie agreed. 'We haven't had a decent party for a while either. Tell you what, Sheila and I plan to have a house-warming, round about New Year time. Make a mental note for now and I'll give you all a date later.'

'Ahh,' said Andy, 'you may be gazumped on that one. I happen to know that a certain grey-templed Deputy Chief Constable and his wife are plotting a similar event at their newish pad out east, round about the same time.'

McGuire whistled. 'We'll need to watch ourselves out there,' he murmured.

'You kidding? Bob could bevvy for Scotland.'

'Naw, I didn't mean that. What I meant was that if you get comatose in their house, then given her new line of work Sarah might have your insides out on the kitchen table.'

'She'd put yours back again very quickly, McGuire,' Maggie murmured.

The inspector, glass in hand, pointed towards the main area of the bar. 'Don't know if you've noticed, guys and gals, but this place is suddenly filling up with journos. I recognise at last half-a-dozen of them from today's session.'

Martin shrugged. 'We can go somewhere else. This is maybe a bit touristy; they won't know about Number Thirty-seven, though.'

'I like it here,' Karen protested.

'Is the Aussie picking you up from here, or what?' asked McGuire.

'No. I'm not seeing him tonight. He has to help Dennis get ready for his big day tomorrow, he said.'

'Hey,' said Andy, softly. 'It's a big day for us all tomorrow. I'll get another round in here, then we can think about moving on for the last one. I want everybody checked in tomorrow at Fettes by quarter to eight, to sign out firearms, so we'd better have a ten o'clock curfew. Yes?' As his five colleagues nodded agreement, he rose to his feet and stepped up to the counter. On impulse, he called back over his shoulder, 'Final word on the party stakes; Friday night, my

284

place, to celebrate this crap being over.'

'Will it be a good party?' a small, dark-haired girl asked him, as he raised an eyebrow to catch the barman's attention. She was leaning on the bar, nursing a pint of Guinness.

He grinned down at her. 'They usually are.'

'You involved with the conference?' She had a clipped accent; southern hemisphere, he thought, but he had difficulty in placing it.

'Catering,' he said, in a voice loud enough to carry to his table. 'You?'

'Indirectly. I'm a journalist but I can't get into the Hall.'

'Why not?'

She wrinkled her nose; not an unattractive nose, he noticed. 'Because some bastard of a copper wouldn't give me accreditation, all because I refused, on principle, to tell him how old I was. As if that bloody mattered. Even though I had a commission from the *FT*, I wouldn't give in. So now I'm just hanging around the fringes, doing colour pieces for my newspaper in Jo'burg, and hoping for some sort of a scoop.'

The barman turned his attention to Andy, who shouted his order over the hubbub. 'And a pint of Guinness, on top of that,' he added, then gave the little reporter his most dazzling smile. 'What's your name?' he asked.

'Estelle. Estelle Lawrence.'

'I'm Andy. You stick with me, Estelle,' he murmured, 'and you never know what you might come up with.'

95

Bob Skinner worked hard, played hard and exercised hard. He liked to go to bed tired and ready for a sound, peaceful sleep, for he was wary of dreams; there had been too many bad ones in the past.

There had been the weeks after Myra's death, when he had wakened every night after an hour or so, lathered in sweat from a nightmare of vague darkness and corruption. There had been the hours after his life-threatening stabbing when he had drifted in a fog of recalled glimpses of days so awful that his mind had taken refuge in amnesia. There had been other moments too, secret times in his career, from which people would still return on occasion to visit him.

Then there was her. He was almost certain that he would never see her again, and he did his best not to think of her during his waking hours, yet at night, even with Sarah by his side, she had crept through his defences once or twice into his dreams. And in those dreams he was afraid of her; for he knew that she had the advantage of him in the pure implacable hatred that she felt for him.

Now, as he lay in the early hours of the morning, a watcher would have seen him toss and turn, yet it was none of his old foes who troubled his sleep. Instead he saw repeated flashes of the face of Wayne Ventnor: visions of him lifting his friend Crombie into bed, with Karen Neville, suffocating in her unfeasibly large breasts, swinging from a ladder, oily and perspiring, on his off-shore rig, standing in a jungle clearing holding in each hand, by the hair, a severed human head . . .

He sat bolt upright in bed in the same instant that he awoke, eyes wide, cold sweat on his forehead. *Hawkins?* he thought. But no, Hawkins was dead; and anyway, when he had seen the Australian in the auditorium, there had been no trace left of the limp which had caught Karen Neville's eye at the outset of their relationship.

Calming himself, he put himself back into his dream, a form of self-hypnosis which he had learned from an expert, and he realised at once what it had shown him. No, it was unfeasible, he told himself at once. He liked Karen Neville; his mind was probably projecting subliminal jealousy of the Australian. But then he looked at his sleeping wife and dismissed that notion. In times of crisis, Bob Skinner lived by his instincts: indeed they had saved his life. This was something that had to be checked.

In the dark, he glanced at the luminous clock by his side. It showed five minutes before seven, too early to call McIlhenney. Silently he slipped out of bed, careful not to wake Sarah, and stepped into the bathroom. He shaved and showered slowly and deliberately, remembering the pressure under which he, Andy and the rest of the team were operating, looking after the world's leaders, with their rival phalanxes of armed guards, telling himself that such circumstances play tricks with the mind, but failing utterly to drive away his concern.

Sarah was awake when he came out of the bathroom. 'You're early,' she mumbled, hazily, tousled hair hanging over her left eye, reminding him of . . . no, she was Sarah, God's gift to him, no one else. 'Couldn't you sleep? Were you worrying about the conference today?'

'No,' he laughed, trying to make himself sound light-hearted. 'I slept like a log. Too well, that's the problem.'

'That's good, that's good,' she said, nodding to herself as he began to dress, and swinging quickly out of bed. 'Be a love, will you, when you're dressed, and make me some brown bread toast and piccalilli.'

'You what?'

'I fancy it, that's all,' she answered, matter-of-fact. 'But first, since it's morning, I think I might as well be sick.' She headed quickly for the bathroom door.

He was used to the ritual, and although the sudden craving had him mildly surprised, he did as she asked. Just as he replaced the piccalilli jar in the fridge, she came into the kitchen, carrying a bleary-eyed Jazz. She looked at what was waiting for her on the plate. 'Oahh!' she moaned. 'I don't think I fancy that now. But thanks anyway.'

Bob looked at the kitchen clock; it was twenty to eight. He picked up the phone and dialled his assistant. McIlhenney sounded weary as he answered. 'Neil, hello. 'S'me. Sorry to dig you up so early, but how are you placed to go into the office? There's something needs handling, quick.'

The sergeant hesitated. 'The thing is, boss, Olive's not too well this morning. She's had a bit of a reaction to those platelets they gave her.'

'No problem,' said Skinner at once. 'I'll just leave a bit earlier, and do it myself, before I go up to the EICC. If I put the foot down I could probably be there as fast as you anyway. You look after Olive. I'll swear Ruthie in as a deputy; she can hold the fort in everyone's absence.'

'Thanks,' the sergeant grunted. 'Listen, boss, there's something else. Last night, I got a result. But I want to play it out myself. Is that okay?'

'Right now, Neil,' the DCC replied, 'anything would be okay. Do what you think best. If you need any help, just let me know.'

He hung up, finished his coffee, kissed Sarah and Jazz goodbye, then rushed towards the door, ruffling Mark's hair on the way as his older son put in his first appearance of the morning.

Normally, he drove sedately in to Fettes, but when he had to, he could make the BMW fly. He overtook at least a dozen cars on the single carriageway between Gullane and Longniddry, tore down the A1 at close on a hundred miles per hour, then took every short-cut and rat-run across town that he could think of, until he arrived at headquarters. 'Eight twenty-five,' he muttered, glancing at the car clock just before he switched off. 'Not bad.' He strode purposefully into the building, nodding only briefly to the men on the door, then ran upstairs.

In the corner of his office behind his chair, bolted to the floor, there stood a small safe. The combination was his mother's birthday. He spun the dial three times, listening for the clicks, then opened it, and took out a slim folder, with one word written on the outside. 'Hawkins.'

Impatiently he flicked through the photographs and photofits, until he found the awful image of Hencke Van Roost with his trophies, one in each hand. He had been right; Wayne Ventnor looked nothing like the South African assassin. He breathed a sigh of relief.

But there were other men in the shot, behind their leader. There were six of them, in fact. Two were black, one stood no more than five feet three, two were balding; but the sixth was tall, and dark-haired. He was clean-shaven, and looked to be around the same age as Van Roost. Only the central figure in the photograph was fully in focus; all of the figures were blurred. The sixth man could have been Ventnor, but even with his sharp eyesight, Skinner was uncertain.

He took a magnifying glass from his drawer, held it over the scene and studied the figure as closely as he could. 'Look at the eyes,' he whispered to himself. 'It's the eyes that give them away.' As he said the words he thought of Hawkins burned to a crisp in tangled wreckage in a Polish field. 'No it's not,' he corrected himself. 'It's the teeth.'

Suddenly a kaleidoscope of images and possibilities whirled in his brain. He picked up the secure telephone on his desk, and dialled a number. The duty telephonist at the offices of MI5 answered circumspectly, with a voice which the policeman did not recognise.

'This is Skinner in Scotland,' he said. 'I need to speak to the Director General, urgently.'

'Oh,' the man's soothing tone was that of a professional deflector. 'I'm not sure if I can raise him at this time. Can I put you through to the duty officer?'

'No, thank you. Now listen to me carefully. I am on a secure line and I need to speak to the DG, now; don't try to fob me off with anyone else, and don't put someone on the line pretending to be him either, for I know him. He can be reached at all times, as you and I are both aware, so connect me now.'

The 'or else' seemed to hang in the air, unspoken but understood. 'I'll try his car, sir. Hold on for a moment, please.'

The moment seemed like an hour, but eventually there was a click. 'Yes?' said a calm plummy voice, one that he recognised. 'What can I do for you, Bob?' In the background, Skinner heard the noise of traffic.

'You can pull out all the stops, sir. Burn the line to your opposite number in South Africa and find out all you can about the other members of Hencke van Roost's platoon. In particular, I need to know about a man, tall, dark-haired, who may have had an Australian connection and whose name may have been Wayne Ventnor, although, like Hawkins, he could have been called something else then.' He recited his mobile number. 'Call me back on that as soon as you have anything. I'll be on the move.'

'But what about security?'

'Bugger security,' Skinner snapped. He glanced at his watch. 'You've got twenty-one minutes. After that, I'm either going to embarrass myself before the whole fucking world, or something very bad is going to happen!'

96

Stevie Steele stood at the doorway of Number Six Charlotte Square, looking out into the street. Since the last round of games which the city's traffic managers had played with a confused motoring public it had always been quiet outside the official residence of the Secretary of State for Scotland, but on this momentous morning in the city it was almost ghostly. The usual fleet of maroon-coloured buses were operating; Steele saw two of them dropping off passengers on the far side of the square. But there were no cars, no delivery vans, no crash-helmeted cycle couriers, and very few pedestrians.

Other than the public transport the only vehicles in the Square were two black Jaguars parked outside the magnificent grey-sandstone terrace, two police cars front and rear, and four motorcycles. They stood on the other side of the street, three of their riders waiting beside them, their crash helmets in their hands.

The young sergeant flexed his shoulders, trying to work his firearm into a more comfortable position beneath his jacket, feeling its weight in the holster strapped to his ribcage, feeling his heart thumping slightly, his pulse raised by the tension of his onerous duty. He had done close protection work before for visiting VIPs, but this was different; this was big time; the biggest. He looked down at his dark jacket, at the sun glinting on the small gold eagle badge in his lapel. He checked his watch: sixteen minutes to nine, one minute to go.

The radio in his hand gave a small bleep; and a voice spoke from it. Steele recognised ACC Elder, even although he sounded strained. 'Charlotte Square acknowledge.'

The sergeant pressed a button. 'Sir.'

'Delay departure by two minutes, sergeant,' said Elder. 'The Russians are late leaving the Caley. Tell the outriders not to get too close if you come up behind them in Lothian Road.'

'Understood, sir.' He looked at the senior outrider, a sergeant, who was standing beside him. 'Did you get that?'

'Aye,' the man replied. 'No sweat. I'll get ma cowboys saddled up.' He headed down the steps and across the street, black boots shining as his signalled to his men to mount their cycles. Steele counted off the minutes, then the seconds. At exactly thirteen minutes to nine on his synchronised watch he pressed the bell on the door-jamb of Number Six, then stood aside and waited. A few seconds later the heavy door swung open and the Prime Minister stepped out, flanked by his two permanent bodyguards. He gave the young sergeant a watered down version of his world-famous smile, and jogged down the steps.

Dr Bruce Anderson, the Secretary of State for Scotland, followed in his wake, Brian Mackie by his side and his Civil Service private secretary, briefcase in hand bringing up the rear. 'Okay, Stevie,' said the Superintendent as they headed for the second Jaguar. 'Everything seems peaceful. Let's deliver our client.'

97

A small crowd of people stood on the pavement in Morrison Street, opposite the entrance to the Edinburgh International Conference Centre. Apart from the Scottish Office minders, and two uniformed police officers, they were all journalists, not accredited to enter the conference itself, but given secondary passes to allow them limited access to the arrival.

They stood in professional, dispassionate silence as the President of the United States stepped out of his armour-plated car under the Centre's decorative canopy, watching as he was greeted by the Lord Provost of Edinburgh, gold chain glinting, by Chief Constable Sir James Proud, silver braid shining, and by the American Consul General, in a dark lounge suit.

Andy Martin was waiting in the foyer as the group moved inside: the world's most powerful man shook his hand as the Consul General introduced him, gave him a drawled, 'Good morning and thank you,' and moved on.

The chief superintendent had never seen the President in the flesh before. On the basis of the documentaries he had watched on television and the studies he had read of his ascent to power, he had always wondered how the man had reached the world's most powerful office. Close to he began to understand: there was a presence about him, an aura which was almost visible, and which had been lacking in all of the other world figures who had walked past him previously that morning, even the formidable Chinese and French leaders.

As he gazed after him, the President walked through the security archway – the metal detector having been turned off for that moment, to ensure that his belt buckle did not set it off – smiled and waved briefly over his shoulder to the police and officials gathered in the entrance.

'Two more to go, sir,' said Mario McGuire as he stepped alongside Martin. 'The Russian and our PM.'

'Don't forget the Secretary of State.'

'Easily done,' the inspector grunted, as they stepped closer to the entrance. 'D'you remember the saying about that old Prime Minister.

What was it? "An empty car drew up outside Number Ten and Mr Attlee got out." That could have been told about Anderson.'

The Head of CID laughed. 'You've been spending too much time with the Deputy Chief Constable. That's how he feels about all politicians these days. If someone told him there was a bomb in here, I reckon he'd clear out the civilians and lock the leaders in.'

As he spoke, McGuire nudged his elbow, and gestured towards the group across the street. 'There's a friend of yours over there.'

Martin's eye followed his pointing finger. Estelle Lawrence stood among the group of journalists, waving at them with a slightly uncertain smile. He grinned and gave her a brief wave in return.

'Here, sir,' the inspector muttered, 'you dropped us right in it last night, bringing that one back to the table and having us all pretend we were catering contractors. Christ, when Maggie said she was in charge of dishwashing . . .' He shook his head, laughing softly to himself.

'After we all left, did you manage to stick to your ten o'clock curfew?'

'Oh aye, no problem. I might have trouble tonight, though. I'm picking Estelle up at nine from her hotel.'

McGuire pointed across the street once more. 'I'm not so sure about that. See who she's talking to?'

The Head of CID looked back at the journalists and saw Estelle deep in conversation with John Tough, a local news reporter whom they both knew well. Suddenly her expression changed; she shot them both a venomous glare.

'Know what?' said the Special Branch commander. 'I think us two catering contractors have just been dropped right in the soup.'

98

Skinner thumped the steering wheel in frustration, and swore loudly as the stolid, uniformed sergeant held up a big, gloved hand. He had already been stopped by two other officers, either ignoring, or ignorant of the call from Control that the DCC's car was to be waved through all barriers.

He sounded his horn, but the man simply turned his back on him. The DCC jumped out to rend him limb from limb, but as he approached the main entrance of the Caledonian Hotel came into his line of vision. The Russian convoy was just pulling out, a black Rolls Royce limousine with full escort.

'Sergeant,' he barked, 'clear out of the way once they've gone.' The man turned, gulped as he recognised the angry figure behind him, and stepped aside.

Sliding back behind the wheel of the BMW, Skinner moved off heading for Lothian Road, only to see the Prime Minister's convoy swing out of Charlotte Square at speed, cutting across in front of him. He swore again, but knew that patience was now his only option, and so he pulled in behind the rear outriders as they swept past the great hotel, heading for the EICC. One of the bikers dropped back, and took up position alongside his window, peering into the car from under the visor of his crash hat, recognising and acknowledging him with the wave of a gauntlet.

He was snarling with frustration as the cars in front slowed almost to walking pace, marking time, he realised, to allow the elderly Russian President to make his ponderous entrance first, but at last, they turned right into Lothian Road, the one-way system irrelevant under Jim Elder's movement plan. He looked at the car clock: six minutes to nine.

He swung violently into the car park, narrowly missing the young constable who moved momentarily to block his path, but sensibly stepped backwards, out of the way, drew to a halt in the first available space, jumped out of the car and moved quickly to catch up with the Prime Minister's party. He was twenty yards short of the great glass entrance when the phone in his pocket sounded its urgent signal.

Stopping in his tracks and snatching it from his pocket, he pressed the green button and held it to his ear. 'Yes,' he snapped.

The DG's calm plummy tone was gone. 'Your man Ventnor,' he said tersely. 'Is he on your patch?'

'Right in the middle of it.'

'In that case you have a major problem. You were right, he was in van Roost's jungle group. He was his second in command, in fact, and it was he who saved his life when he took his leg wound. He's half-Australian, half-Afrikaner, and he's an explosives expert. D'you remember the Asian Head of State who was blown out of the sky in one of Hawkins' jobs?'

'Yes.'

'Well, the intelligence community suspected that he had help in making the bomb, but they never worked out who. You may have come up with the answer. My hypothesis is that when Hawkins was killed Ventnor was brought in as a replacement.'

'That's a contradiction. It would mean that Hawkins wasn't after Walesa, he was on this job all along. Therefore he wasn't in Poland and he isn't fucking dead. He's here, and he's posing as an adviser to the Iranian delegation.'

'But he was identified,' the DG protested.

'By his teeth alone! Somehow they've faked that. My guess is that his paymaster for this job came up with a body, and put a dentist to work on the lower jaw; who knows, maybe they used Hawkins' own teeth. When they found the stiff in the plane the top of his head was gone, so the dental identification was only partial.'

Even against the background street noise, the detective heard the gasp from the other end of the line. 'You have to stop the conference, Skinner,' the DG shouted. 'You have to clear the hall before there's a massacre.'

'It's probably too late for that. The Prime Minister's just gone inside; the plan is that he goes straight into the hall, up on to the stage with our Secretary of State, and at that point the event is declared open. As far as I know, Hawkins and Ventnor are in there now.

'Look, if you're right and we're dealing with a bomb, they ain't going to blow themselves up. The whole place was checked by sniffer dogs first thing this morning. If there is a device in there, the clever bastards have taken it in with them, and I think I know how.'

'What do you mean?'

'I think Hawkins is sitting on it. The best chance we've got is if we can arrest them right now, and take them by surprise in the process so they don't have a chance to trigger the thing and take us all out with them.'

'Do you have to arrest them?'

Skinner knew exactly what the man was saying. 'Don't be daft,' he retorted. 'This event's being broadcast live. I can't shoot two guys on world-wide television.' He cut off the call, slipped the phone back into his pocket, and began to run.

The uniformed inspector in charge of the detail at the entrance saw him approach, and saw the look on his face. 'Where's Andy Martin?' the DCC called out.

'In the foyer last I saw, sir.'

The DCC sped into the auditorium. As he dived through the metal detector archway it buzzed loudly. The two civilian security guards who were manning did not recognise him and together, they moved to stop him. There was no time for explanations; first one, then the other, went down, winded by short disabling blows. He left them gasping and ran into the wide passageway which encircled the main auditorium.

To his relief, Martin and McGuire were standing in the main doorway. They had their backs to him and were looking into the hall. Beyond them stood the Prime Minister and the Secretary of State. *If I can stop them*, he thought. He moved towards them, but too late. As he reached the door, the two politicians set off down the shallow sloping centre aisle, and as they did, the assembly rose to its feet in spontaneous acclamation.

Skinner grabbed Martin by the arm and hauled him out into the passageway. 'Andy,' he gasped, breathing hard, as he looked at his astonished friend. 'Problem. Big-time problem.' McGuire spun round also at the sound and stared anxiously at the DCC.

'Wayne Ventnor, Karen's Australian; he was the sapper in Michael Hawkins' squad of jungle killers. Find him and arrest him, now. Get all the help you can, split up and search the whole place. But don't involve Neville!

'Before you go. The man in the wheelchair, Crombie. Is he in the hall?'

'He should be, sir,' the inspector answered. 'He's with the Iranians in Karen's sector, far side of the left aisle. But why—'

'He's Hawkins: it's some disguise, right down to the false teeth maybe, but I'm sure of it. If he's not Michael Hawkins, then my name's Camilla Parker Bowles . . . and I've never been on a horse in my life.

'Now go on.'

As his two colleagues ran off, Skinner stepped across to the doorway and looked into the hall, down and to his left, but his view was obscured by the assembled politicians and delegates, who were still on their feet clapping the Prime Minister and the Secretary of State onto the stage. Turning, he ran round the passageway, to the next doorway, at the top of the next aisle.

Karen Neville was standing there, unperturbed, looking into the hall. *Could she have known*? he wondered for an instant. But no, his ego refused to let him believe that his judgement of a woman could have been so badly wrong once again.

'Dennis Crombie,' he said, ignoring her surprise at his sudden appearance. 'Where is he sitting?'

'About half-way down the aisle, sir, on the left; that's the Iranian position. Israel nearest the gangway, then Ireland, then them, last in the row.'

'Is he there?'

'Yes. I was looking down at him just as everyone got to their feet.'

Skinner felt a trickle of sweat run down his spine. 'What's the betting . . .' he murmured under his breath. He stood on tip-toe, trying to catch a glimpse of the Iranians; among the many tops of heads, he picked out several wound in white cloth, standing in the area Neville had described.

'How many should there be in the delegation?' he asked.

'Eight, sir. Seven Iranians and Dennis.'

As she spoke the Prime Minister came to the centre of the stage, beaming, nodding and gesturing to the gathering to be seated. Skinner stared down their ranks as they complied, counting the Iranians aloud. 'One, two, three, four, five, six . . .' Then an empty place; and finally, an empty wheel-chair, on the outside of the row. Neville looked where he looked, saw what he saw. Her hand went to her mouth.

'Oh my G—'

'Exactly lass.' Skinner murmured. 'Either there's a faith healer in the house, or your man Crombie's a wrong 'un.

'Now where the hell's he gone? Because he hasn't passed us by.' He looked down into the auditorium. On either side of the stage there were two sets of double exit doors. Those on the left seemed to be swinging very slightly. Beside it were two hard-looking men, both of them wearing little gold badges.

He looked at the woman beside him, and saw shock on her face. 'No time for discussion,' he snapped. 'How did Crombie and Ventnor get here?'

'By car,' she answered, her voice cracking for an instant. 'Dennis got a disabled permit for the Centre car park.'

'You know what their car looks like?'

'Yes.'

'Okay I want you to grab Andy or Mario; the first armed colleague you see, then go and find it. Meanwhile, I'm going to get that wheelchair out of the hall.'

'But why, sir?'

'Because it's a bomb, Karen. Your boyfriend and his pal have been planning all along to blow this place to Kingdom Come. Now go!'

As she turned and sprinted along the passageway, feeling her holstered side-arm banging against her hip, Skinner stepped briskly down towards the Israeli delegation. Reaching them, he turned in and made his way along to the Iranian position. He recognised the Prime Minister at once from television footage. The man glanced up at him with fleeting curiosity, but then looked back towards the stage, where the British Prime Minister was standing at the lectern, surveying his audience.

'Good morning, my fellow Heads of Government, and good morning, Heads of State,' he began, his voice ringing round the auditorium. 'Good morning Excellencies, and welcome to you all.' Crombie, or Hawkins *né* van Roost, had chosen his moment perfectly. While everyone in the hall was gazing at the PM, he had simply risen from his chair and quietly slipped away. Only the two or three men behind him could have seen his departure and they had clearly been too preoccupied to have been surprised or alarmed, had they even noticed it.

Skinner stopped by the empty wheelchair, took it by the arms and tested its weight. He could barely lift it. 'Christ, how much explosive has he got packed in here?' he whispered. He crouched down and looked under the seat, between the wheels. Bolted to the steel chassis, he saw a heavy box, one that had not been put there by the chair's maker.

Skinner took his phone from his pocket and was about to dial Martin's number when he paused. He had no idea, he realised, how the bomb might be triggered. For all he knew the microwaves from a cellphone might be enough. For all he knew an arming device might have been activated, causing the device to explode at the slightest movement. For all he knew, Wayne Ventnor might be sitting in the car park at that very moment, his finger on the button of a transmitter which could atomise him and everyone else for yards around.

He bet his life on the third possibility.

Grabbing the wheelchair he kicked off the brake, then pulled it backwards, out into the furthest aisle, and began to roll it down towards the exit beside the stage. The two guards looked at him in surprise as he approached. 'Open the door', he mouthed as he wrestled with the impossibly heavy device, steering an erratic course down the aisle, hoping that they were Americans and would understand him, rather than trigger-happy Russians who might do anything. Uncertain for a moment, the guards looked at each other, then finally, as he was almost upon them, threw the exit open and allowed him to propel the chair through into the corridor, and out of the auditorium.

Behind him, he was dimly aware of the Prime Minister's inspirational tones, as he continued to mesmerise his nation's guests.

He was sweating heavily as he looked ahead, to see another pair of doors twenty yards away, their paintwork heavily scuffed and marked. Dropping his centre of gravity, Skinner pushed as hard as he could, his legs pumping until he had worked himself up to a run once more. His mind was a blank as he drove the lethal object at the second doors, sending them flying wide apart as it hit them at speed, and bursting out into a concrete loading bay beyond. Hoping against hope, he looked around and saw only cardboard boxes in which some of the technical equipment had been delivered. Mercifully the area was empty of people.

Giving the chair one last push, he turned and crashed back through the doors, running back along the corridor as fast as his powerful but tiring legs would allow. He had made it half-way to the auditorium doorway when he heard the blast and when the shockwave caught up with him, lifting him bodily then slamming him, senseless, to the ground.

99

Karen was racked by sobs as she burst out into the foyer. As she fought them back, and wiped the tears from her eyes, she saw Inspector Jack Good, the officer on duty at the door, staring across at her. The two security men sat on the ground beside him, but she had no time to think anything of it.

'Has anyone gone out of here?' she demanded.

'I don't know,' Good replied. 'I've been looking after these people. What's up anyway? Mr Skinner came tearing in here a few minutes back, these two tried to stop him and he just laid them out.'

She ignored him and called across to the two constables who were flanking the door. 'You two, have you seen anyone leave?'

The taller of the men, on the right of the entrance door, looked over his shoulder. 'Three guys went out of here a couple o' minutes back,' he said. 'A well-dressed bloke with a beard, another fella, scruffy like; both of them big chaps, and an Arab guy wi' a turban thing on his heid. Ah asked them if they'd had enough; the scruffy bloke said "Just about". They went along there.' He pointed to his left.

Neville turned back to the Inspector. 'Find Mr Martin, or DI McGuire,' she ordered. 'Tell them the targets have gone to the car park, and that I'm off in pursuit.' He looked after her, bewildered, as she ran through the doorway, and out into the street.

The Centre car park was by no means full, but it was busy nonetheless, most of the spaces taken up by suppliers' vans and staff cars. She looked over the low wall as she approached the gateway, but saw no sign of Ventnor or Hawkins. The constable whom Skinner had almost run over was still at his post. 'Three men, recently?' she gasped.

He understood. 'Away over there, at the back,' he said, pointing to the furthest corner of the park, tucked behind the east wing of the Centre.

She nodded and ran down the roadway, scanning the rows of vehicles, realising how difficult it is to spot a single car among dozens of production-line clones. At last she caught a glimpse of a metallic green roof, and a flash of white material. A second later the soft 'clunk' of a closing door reached her ears.

Drawing her pistol, she stepped into the rank of parked cars; holding it in both hands, arms outstretched. As she approached the green vehicle she saw that the bays on either side were vacant. 'Wayne,' she shouted, almost a scream, as she reached it. 'All of you! Get out of that fucking car!'

Hawkins was behind the wheel, Ventnor was in the front passenger seat, while the third man sat in the back. She stood directly in front of the vehicle, her pistol levelled at a point between them so that she could react to any sudden movement. 'Out!' she called again. 'This is loaded, the safety's off, and I will fire.'

Her lover grinned at her, as he opened his door, calmly and stepped out. On the other side, Hawkins did the same. He no longer wore his heavy glasses, and for the first time she caught a resemblance to the man in the photographs she had been shown weeks before.

'You're not going to shoot me, Karen, love,' Wayne drawled. She saw that he was holding a small box in his right hand.

'Don't bet your life on it, you bastard. Right in the balls if I have to. The other man: I want him out too.'

'Shapoor's harmless, love. Don't you worry about him. Old Hencke and me, we're the dangerous ones. Now just you stand aside and let us drive on out of here.'

'No way.'

He held up the box in his right hand, and pressed downwards with his thumb. She frowned for a moment, then gasped in horror as a compressed, booming, rolling sound came from within the Conference Centre. 'You're too late, Karen,' he said, still smiling as he dropped the box. 'The rest of the Iranian delegation is cosmic fucking dust by now, the Paddies, the Israelis and every one else for yards around them have all bought it. Within an hour there will be a new Government in Iran and a whole new Middle Eastern power structure.

'That's if there's any Middle East left. Sometime in the next thirty minutes CNN will have a call from a so-called Iraqi source claiming responsibility. There's a fair chance they'll take Baghdad right out in response.'

His smile disappeared, and a look which might have been a plea came into his eyes. 'Now, come on, stand aside and let us drive out of here. You've been a great help to us, so far. Don't screw it up now, otherwise Hencke might have to break his promise to me.' She realised that the man she had known as Crombie was holding a gun, and in the fraction of a second which it took her to register the fact, Wayne's right hand came into view and she saw that he had one also.

301

'Please, Karen,' he said, 'do the sensible thing. Like I said, we both know you can't shoot me.'

'No, but I can.' The voice calm and deadly.

Twenty yards away, Andy Martin stood, barely in their line of sight, his pistol drawn and aimed. Instinctively the two bombers looked towards him. Wayne's right arm moved: and that was it.

Martin fired twice, inside a second, both shots hitting Ventnor in the middle of the forehead. In the same moment, Karen swung her pistol on to Hawkins and pulled the trigger. Only once, but it was enough; her bullet took out his right eye and exited through the back of his head.

The Iranian inside the car screamed and raised his hands. 'Out, out, out!' she yelled at him.

As the man opened the back door and threw himself on to the ground, the chief superintendent was aware of another cry. Softer, terrified, female. He turned towards its source as she stared at the figures on the ground, at the spreading pools of blood.

'What the hell are you doing here, Estelle?' he shouted.

'I slipped our escorts,' the little journalist whispered. 'I wanted to find out who you really were.'

He frowned, grimly, as he re-holstered his pistol. 'Well, now you know. I told you to stick with me if you wanted a scoop . . . if they let you tell the story, that is.'

100

'How is Mr Skinner?' Karen asked. 'I heard they took him away in an ambulance, but nothing after that.'

'He's fine,' Martin replied. 'He was knocked out for a few seconds when his head hit the deck, that's all. Bob's had tougher scrapes than that and walked away from them. Sure, someone called for an ambulance, but the big fella sent it back empty.

'More to the point,' he continued, 'how are you? How was your interview with the Fiscal this afternoon? Did it go all right?'

'Yes. Mr Pettigrew was very kind. I've always imagined that when you ... when something like that happened, the officer involved would be really heavily questioned.'

'Sometimes. Depends who's doing the questioning. Davie's a good guy; plus the boss had a word with him before he saw either of us. He was fine with me as well.'

'What worries me, sir—'

He raised a hand and glanced around their surroundings. He had brought her to the Roseburn Bar because it was sufficiently far from the West End to be journalist-free. 'Listen, up the road, discipline says it has to be "sir", but in here, it's Andy.'

She smiled. 'Okay. What worries me, Andy, is that I didn't prevent that bastard from triggering the bomb.'

'How could you have done that?'

'I could have shot him as soon as he stepped out of the car.'

'Sure you could. Suppose you had done just that, and he'd been unarmed, the box had turned out to be Smarties, and Estelle, a foreign journalist desperate for a story, had happened on the scene – to find you with a smoking gun in your hand, standing over the body of the guy who'd let you down.

'Not even Bob would have been able to keep the Fiscal off your neck then.'

She shuddered at the thought. 'What about Estelle?' she asked. 'I thought you were seeing her tonight.'

'Not tonight, or any other,' he chuckled. 'She's gone running off to talk to an agent about syndicating her story. It'll be worth a million to her.'

'She doesn't know about Wayne and me, does she?'

'No way does she know about that; nor will anyone outside our force, ever, not even Pettigrew. Estelle knows what she saw and what I told her . . .' He paused.

' . . that the two dead men were international terrorists hired by an Iranian dissident group angered by their government's softening line towards the West. That Shapoor Bahwazi, the third man in the car, an attaché with the Iranian delegation, was one of its ringleaders. That their first objective was to kill the Iranian Prime Minister, but that the way the seating plan worked out they extended it to include taking out the Israelis.'

'What's happened to Bahwazi?'

Martin smiled, coldly. 'The Prime Minister, no less, ordered him expelled from the UK this afternoon and flown back to Teheran. That way, there'll be no fuss, and no high security trial on our patch. He'll be up against a wall within a week, after they've got the other names in his group out of him. You'll probably catch the execution on CNN. They had their telephoned communiqué, by the way, but by that time the CIA had warned them off broadcasting it.

'By then of course, they'd already run the story, as had everyone else, of the explosion in the Conference Centre, made safe by the boss.'

She sighed, heavily. 'I still blame myself for that; in spite of what you said.'

'And I'll say it again, until you accept it. You've got nothing to blame yourself for, except maybe for charging out there to tackle two dangerous guys on your own. Look, Wayne didn't give you any warning, he just triggered the bomb . . . which by that time was in a safe area, thanks to Bob. No, Karen, you did great.'

'But I couldn't shoot him, Andy,' she protested. 'It was my duty, and I couldn't do it. If you hadn't turned up—'

'No, it wasn't your duty at all; there were no civilians about. It was your life alone that was at risk, and you had three options open to you . . . if you had been on your own.'

She frowned as she sipped her lager. 'What were they?'

'One, you could have let Hawkins kill you. Unacceptable. Two, you could have stood aside and let them go. Understandable. Three, you could have shot Hawkins in the hope that Wayne couldn't bring himself to kill you either. As it turned out that's what you did.

'Better that way,' he murmured. 'Better in the long term that you didn't put him down yourself; believe me.'

'You've had to shoot someone before, haven't you.'

He nodded. 'Twice. The first time was the night Mario was hit.

Afterwards we never knew who actually killed the guy, whether it was Brian or me. We both hit him, more than once. The second time . . . I'd rather not talk about.'

'Does the experience still affect you?'

'There's the odd bad dream. If it gets to you too badly, you'll never carry a firearm again. At my rank, I suppose in theory I don't have to. But if I'd made that choice . . .' in spite of himself, he shuddered.

'We wouldn't be sitting here right now,' she said.

'Nah! I've got faith in you. You'd have popped Hawkins and Ventnor would have put his hands up and we'd have walked away.'

'Yeah,' she muttered, suddenly bitter. 'And I'd have had to go into the witness box and give evidence with him in the dock, and his brief digging up all sorts of stuff about my sex life. Better the bastard's dead. Except that . . .' Her voice cracked and she looked away.

He took her hand, enfolding it in his. 'When you really mean that,' he said softly, 'you really will be all right.

'You know, we're wounded soldiers, you and me, with a terrible thing in common. We've just got to make the best of it.'

'I suppose so.' She looked up at him again, and gave his hand a quick squeeze. 'Andy,' she asked, hesitantly. 'I don't fancy being alone tonight. Would it be bad for discipline if I came home with you? Just this once, of course.'

He looked at her, and he knew that he would never really be the old Andy Martin again, however hard he tried. His disappearance had had nothing to do with his engagement to Alex, either. That man had died on a black night in another place.

'Just this once,' he replied, 'I think it would be for the best.'

305

101

Olive McIlhenney was watching the television in the corner of the living room, but with little interest. She knew that upstairs in her daughter's bedroom, Spencer and Lauren would be glued to the small portable set, expanding their encyclopaedic knowledge of Coronation Street, but since the onset of her illness the characters had seemed flat and the storylines boring, in comparison with her own real-life drama.

Still she watched it, though, for something to do while she waited, hoping all the while that her visitor would be on time, since she felt ill-equipped for the mounting tension which she was experiencing. When Neil had wanted to call the visit off, her insistence that she had got over her earlier setback was a little short of the truth.

She looked at the clock as the doorbell rang, and saw that her visitor was in fact a minute early. Carefully, in the slow steady way which had been forced upon her, she rose and walked out to open the door. 'Ms Clark,' she said. 'Good to see you; good of you to come.'

'Call me Penelope, please,' said the woman, as she stepped inside. 'It's no problem at all. I'm free every night for the rest of this week.'

'Come on through, then.' Olive ushered her through into the lounge, pointing her at the comfortable sofa. There was a coffee table between it and her chair, and on it sat a bottle of red wine and two glasses.

'Have a glass with me,' she insisted. 'My list of pleasures is a bit curtailed, but I'm still okay for sex and drink. I insist on quality in both respects, so this is pretty decent stuff.' She smiled as she filled both glasses most of the way to the top.

'Cheers,' said Penelope Clark, taking a sip. 'I'm glad to hear that you're trying to live as normal a life as you can. That's very important. Now, what exactly did you want to talk to me about; woman to woman, as you said?'

Olive took a breath, stopping short of the point of pain. 'I need some lifestyle advice, Penelope,' she began, cautiously. 'I have every confidence in Deacey and in my treatment, but I'm under no illusions that Neil and I will ever walk up another Munro together.

'When this thing,' she tapped her chest. 'is battered into remission,

306

what will I be able to do? What plans can I make? Can I go back to the classroom, can I have another baby if I want? How physically fit am I going to be?'

The other woman looked at her, running her hand over her ash-blonde hair, playing for time as she considered her answer. 'My dear,' she began, 'I don't think you should be under any illusions here. If you get some degree of remission, for a period of years even, you will never be fit enough to teach again. As for having a child, if you ever fell pregnant, you'd be advised to terminate.

'You'll have a life, oh yes. But in all honesty I can't say that you're likely to be able to do much more than you can now.'

Olive threw back her head. 'Jesus,' she whispered. 'This is it?'

'I'm afraid so.'

'But I find this hard to take as it is.' Her fists clenched. 'I tell you this, Penelope,' she exclaimed, as if she had been goaded beyond endurance, at last, by her fate. 'If it got any worse, I could not stand it. The idea of a slow steady decline, with Neil and the kids having to watch, with him having to do the most personal things for me . . . the thought of that appals me.

'I will do anything to avoid that. I tell you, if it happened, I'd climb into a nice hot bath and cut my wrists.' Her voice rose, until she broke off in a paroxysm of coughing.

'Ssh, ssh,' said her visitor, soothingly. 'Don't even think such a thing. That would be awful for them. Imagine Neil coming in and finding you: worse still, imagine if it were Spencer or Lauren. If they saw something like that it would mark them for life.'

'What else can I do?' Olive shot back, her breathing restored. 'The hospital never gives you enough drugs to off yourself. I've noticed; they're damn careful about that. But if it comes to it I'll find a way, suppose I have to shuffle down to the Waverley Station and chuck myself in front of a train.'

Penelope Clark picked up her glass and took another sip. 'There is a way,' she said, quietly, 'that would be less painful for Neil and the children; and most of all for you.'

'What's that? Neil has so much crap in the garage that I couldn't get the car in to do a hosepipe job.'

The woman on the settee shook her head. 'That's not what I meant. Listen; I'm a doctor, Olive. If it did come to it, and you were really sure, I'd be prepared to help you.'

'How?' The word was slow and feather-soft.

'I'm about the hospital a lot. I have access to drugs; I could prescribe, or procure, something sufficiently powerful, painless and virtually instantaneous. If you could arrange for the children to stay

307

with someone, as you've done before, and for your husband to be out one night, I could visit you.'

'But you'd get into trouble afterwards. You could go to jail, Penelope.'

'No, I'd arrange it so that it looked like you had committed suicide . . . which is, of course, exactly what you would have done.'

'Still,' Olive murmured. 'I don't know if I could let you do that.'

'That would be my ethical decision, not yours. All I would be doing would be offering you a better way to achieve something upon which you were already determined.

'You can spare Neil and your children from the thing you dread; you can do it humanely. I can offer you that choice, Olive. Whether you take it is up to you, but I think it's right that you should have it.'

'The trouble is, Dr Clark,' said Neil McIlhenney, as the kitchen door swung fully open, 'the law doesn't agree with you.' He stepped into the room, with Bob Skinner following behind. There was a dark bruise on the Deputy Chief Constable's forehead.

'I shouldn't apologise for setting you up like this, but I will,' the sergeant said. 'The truth is it was Olive's idea; when she heard what was at stake she insisted on doing this.'

Penelope Clark looked at him, apprehensively. 'What do you mean, "at stake"?'

'Deacey Simmers' reputation, and freedom. He was right in the frame for killing Gaynor Weston and Anthony Murray.'

She put her hand to her mouth. 'But I never meant that,' she gasped.

'I'm sure you didn't; and maybe when he was arrested you'd have come forward. But it would have been too late by then. The damage would have been done. You know how sensitive Mr Simmers is. The faintest whiff of something like this could have finished him.'

She nodded. 'You're right. He might have been your next suicide.

'How did you know I was involved in those deaths?' she asked.

'I found your name in Nicola Marston's notes. I knew you'd been to see Mr Murray too. So I went to see Joan Ball; she told me about your connection to Mrs Weston.'

'Did you help the Marston woman?'

She turned to look at Skinner as he spoke. 'Nicola asked me, hypothetically, how much insulin it would take for a fast-acting lethal overdose. Hypothetically, I told her. I wasn't there when she died though. I didn't know about it until Deacey told me.

'I felt terribly guilty about it, at first, but over the next couple of years, I thought about it more and more. Eventually, having been an opponent, I swung right round and became a member of the pro-euthanasia camp.

'That was as far as it went though, till Gay told me about her illness and asked me to help her end it. She was a strong woman, she had made a firm decision, and in my view a correct one; so I agreed. I went out to Oldbarns late at night, injected her, made sure she was dead, and went away. I didn't realise how many silly mistakes I'd made until Nolan Weston let something slip in conversation at the hospital one day.'

'So you were more careful with Mr Murray,' Skinner interposed.

'Yes, although not careful enough, it seems.'

'No. not quite.' The DCC smiled, faintly. 'Tell me this. When you helped Gay Weston to die, was Mr Simmers there?'

'No. He had been there earlier in the evening, for supper. Gay told me, in fact, that he'd been a bit disappointed when she asked him to go. He thought that he'd be staying the night as usual.'

Neil and Olive McIlhenney sighed with relief, in unison.

'What about Mr Murray?' Skinner continued. 'Did he ask you to help him?'

Penelope Clark looked up at him. 'No,' she said. 'I made the offer. Anthony was such a lovely man, and he was struggling so hard to hold on to what was left of his dignity, that I couldn't stop myself. He jumped at the chance. When I put the bag over his head, the last thing he said to me was "Thank you".'

'And what did Gaynor Weston say? It wasn't "Thank you Mrs Futcher", was it?'

Neil McIlhenney's jaw dropped, as he stared at Skinner.

'That's the one big problem I have, you see, doctor,' said the DCC, 'the fact that Gaynor Weston was your husband's girlfriend. When Neil asked me to witness this, and told me about you, I made some inquiries through a contact at the BMA. He checked the files and told me that although Clark's your maiden name, the one you qualified under and the one you've always used professionally, you're also Mrs Terry Futcher.'

The woman jumped to her feet. 'Look,' she protested. 'You have to understand about Terry and me; we're happily married in our own way, but I have my life and he has his. I don't enjoy his attentions over much; never have. That's why we don't have a family, and that's why I don't mind his screwing around, although we keep up the pretence that I don't know about it.

'I love him though, and he loves me, and we agreed a long time ago that we'd stick together, come what may.

'I knew about Gaynor almost as soon as it started; Terry's careless with his diary and I knew who she was through her work for the firm. But I'd never met her until that day that Joan introduced us. I liked her at once, all the more because I realised that she was no threat to my marriage. She was a hell of a sight more independent than Terry ever was, and I knew early on that he wasn't her only boyfriend.'

'I know it looks bad, but Gay and I were friends.'

'Did she know who you were?'

'I never told her, and if she knew she never let anything slip. I have no idea if Terry ever showed her a photograph of me. But her relationship with my husband had no bearing on my decision to help her end her life. You have to believe that.'

'It doesn't matter whether I do or not,' said Skinner. 'If a judge saw malice there, though, that would matter, big-time.' As he looked at her, Penelope Clark Futcher sat slowly back down on the settee.

'However,' the big DCC continued, fingering the bruise on his forehead and wincing as he did, 'it isn't going to come to that. Because, more by your luck than your judgement, we have no hard evidence against you, Dr Clark, nor the prospect of ever finding any . . . and under Scots law a person cannot be convicted on the basis of an uncorroborated confession.

'All that I can do is have a quiet word with Home Support, and make sure that you are never again put in a position where you might be tempted to offer your special help to a terminally ill patient. Make no mistake, I will do that, unless you promise to resign. I'll do the same with the BMA too, unless you promise never to practise medicine again. Will you give me those undertakings?'

'Yes,' the woman whispered, after a moment's hesitation.

'In that case, you're free to go. And take this both as a request and a warning: don't ever be tempted to do such a thing, ever again.'

She had almost reached the door when Olive spoke. 'No, Penelope,' she said, 'please don't. Because you're not God, you're not the Pope, you're not infallible. With what you've been doing, you only have to be wrong once . . . and my dear, you were wrong about me, about us.

'You probably don't understand this, given what you've said about your own marriage, but my family's the driving force behind everything I do. I don't have a choice at all. I don't have the luxury of opting out. I have to go on, for Neil and the kids' sakes as much as my own, because I will not entertain the idea of our being parted before our rightful time.

'For them, I have to fight this thing: to my last breath, if it comes to that. And believe me, lady, I will.'

102

'Where have you been?' Sarah looked at him appraisingly as he stepped carefully across the threshold. At the same time she noted the police car's tail lights, which were disappearing down their driveway.

'And why did you have a driver?' she asked, suspicious of his deliberate gait. 'Have you been celebrating your victory over the Forces of Darkness by hob-nobbing with the great and the good?'

'Leaving aside my concussive injury,' he said, with equal care, tapping his forehead but feeling nothing, 'I have to tell you that the real Forces of Darkness are bastards and cannot be swept aside by a few rounds from a Browning.

'That said, I have indeed been hob-nobbing with the great and the good. Drinking many toasts to them, in fact . . . to two of the finest and best people I have ever met.'